Jean Barois

By Roger Martin du Gard

THE WORLD
OF THE THIBAULTS

The Thibaults

Summer 1914

Jean Barois

ROGER MARTIN DU GARD

Translated by Stuart Gilbert

New York: The Viking Press

1949

PRINTED IN THE U.S.A. BY AMERICAN BOOK–STRATFORD PRESS, INC.

To M. Marcel Hébert

Your religious feelings can but be wounded by some of the tendencies of this book. Aware of this, I am all the more grateful to you for permitting me to dedicate it to you.

The presence of your name in the forefront of these pages is more than a token of a respectful and unfailing affection that began twenty years ago. I feel sure that it will win for me—from all who know the rare nobility of your mind and the inestimable contributions you have made in the field of criticism—a closer attention and, as it were, an afterglow of the esteem which sheds its brightness on the eloquent self-abnegation of your life.

October 1913.   R. M. G.

CONTENTS

PART

I

I. THE WILL TO LIVE

I

THE RESIDENCE of Mme Barois at Buis-la-Dame, a small French country town some fifty miles north of Paris. The year is 1878.

In Mme Barois' bedroom the curtains are drawn, and behind them the slats of the venetian blinds glimmer black and silver in the moonlight. The room is in darkness but for a pale sheen that floods the parquet, lighting up the hem of a woman's dress and a man's boot softly tapping the floor. There is the sound of two people breathing, two people watching, waiting . . .

Now and again an iron bedstead creaks in the adjoining room, and a child can be heard muttering rambling phrases; one cannot tell if he is delirious or talking in his sleep. The door between the two bedrooms is ajar, and the faint glow of a night light ribbons the slit.

A long silence.

THE DOCTOR, in a low voice: "The bromide's working. He'll have a calmer night."

Mme Barois rises with an effort and tiptoes to the door. Her face is set and haggard as, narrowing her eyes, she peers into the lighted bedroom, her cheek pressed to the doorjamb.

Mme Barois is a tall old woman of an ungainly build and heavy gait. The light from the unshaded night light ruthlessly probes the furrows on her face, the sallow, distended skin; strongly marked shadows emphasize the pouches under her eyes, the sagging cheeks and swollen lips, a double chin. The face suggests an austere, rather grudging kindliness, gentle obstinacy, rigid self-control.

MME BAROIS, in a whisper: "He's sleeping."

She closes the door softly, then lights a lamp and returns to her chair.

THE DOCTOR, placing his hand on his mother's; then, by force of habit, sliding his fingers up to her wrist and half unconsciously feeling her pulse: "You too, Mother, need rest. That long journey was too much for you."

MME BAROIS, shaking her head: "I can feel you're vexed with me, Philippe, for having taken Jean to—to that place."

Dr Barois is a small wiry man of fifty-six, deft and prompt in his gestures. He has grey hair, a shrewd face, all in acute angles, the nose-bridge like a knife-blade, a moustache tapering to neatly waxed points, a small peaked beard. Sometimes a smile of gentle irony narrows his lips. His keen, restless eyes glitter now and then behind the pince-nez.

MME BAROIS, after a short silence: "Still everybody here agreed it was the best thing to do. And Jean was always pestering me to put his name down; he felt so certain he'd come back cured from Lourdes. All the way in the train he made me keep on telling him the story of Bernadette."

The doctor takes off his pince-nez and blinks at his mother with affectionate, shortsighted eyes. She stops speaking. Their thoughts meet and clash; the years have made a rift between them. After a few moments she continues. "No, it's no use hoping you'll understand. You and I, my son and I, don't understand each other any longer. That's what they've done to you at Paris, to the boy you used to be!"

THE DOCTOR: "Mother dear, I'd rather we didn't talk about that journey to Lourdes. Not that I blame you in the least. Except for having told me of your intention only when it was too late for me to intervene. You see, Jean wasn't fit to undertake a long journey like that, in a slow train, third class."

MME BAROIS: "Aren't you taking too gloomy a view of his condition, my dear? You've seen him as he is tonight, feverish and inclined to be delirious. But you didn't see him as he was this winter."

THE DOCTOR, uncomfortably: "That's so. I didn't see him once this winter."

MME BAROIS, more boldly: "Since he had that attack of bronchitis he's never looked quite himself, that's sure. He was always complaining of a pain—here. But, I can assure you, he didn't look a bit like a sick child. Often in the evening he was in high spirits, almost too high spirits."

THE DOCTOR, putting his eyeglasses on, bending towards his mother, and clasping her hand: "In too high spirits in the evenings, was he? Ah!" He shakes his head. "You forget the past too quickly, Mother."

MME BAROIS, obstinately: "You know my views on the subject, Philippe. Nothing will convince me that your poor dear wife had— what you think. No, it was Paris that killed her, poor thing, as it's killed so many others."

The doctor is hardly listening. The lamplight falls on his mother's hand; he fondles it absent-mindedly. A thick, soft hand, mottled with little brown spots; gnarled fingers. In a sudden throw-back to a trick of childhood he strokes the wedding ring, thinned almost to breaking point, which the swollen joints will keep imprisoned there until the end. And impulsively, perhaps for the first time in his life, seized by a craven desire to weep, to escape, to shut his eyes to the inevitable, he raises to his lips that old hand, changed out of recognition by the years, which none the less he could never confuse with any other. Mme Barois, somewhat embarrassed, draws her hand away.

MME BAROIS, almost roughly: "Don't forget, for one thing, that Jean takes after *our* family in every way. Why, he's the very image of you, Philippe! Everybody says so. That child has nothing of his mother, nothing!"

A short silence.

THE DOCTOR, moodily, to himself: "I've been so terribly busy all this winter." He realizes that he hasn't answered his mother and turns to her affectionately. "Doctoring is a hard profession, Mother, in cases like mine. Knowing one's son is ill, only a few hours' journey from Paris. And letting all one's days be taken up, hour after hour, by others. And every time one books another appointment,

being reminded that it's impossible to keep the page blank even for
an afternoon; never having a moment's freedom! Ah, if only I
could throw up everything and come to live here with you two!"
Peremptorily. "No, of course I couldn't do that. Out of the question." He takes off his eyeglasses, wipes them, ponders for some
moments, then replaces them briskly. His voice becomes curt, incisive, professional. "We must keep him under closer observation
than ever, night and day, and fight back the disease inch by inch."

Mme Barois makes an incredulous gesture. The doctor stops
speaking and throws a quick searching glance at his mother. A
momentary indecision—as when, in the course of an operation, he
has abruptly to change his tactics. Then his gaze steadies, sharpens;
he has fixed on a new plan of campaign.

A long silence.

2

A week later. Sunday morning.

THE DOCTOR, entering Jean's bedroom: "Good morning, Jean. And
how are we this morning? But why's that window shut when it's
such a lovely day?" He takes the boy's hands and has him stand
facing the light. "Let's see your tongue. Good. Have you been
sleeping well this week? Not too well? You're always changing your
position in bed, are you? And you wake up because you feel too hot?
I see . . ." He pats Jean's cheek. "Now off with your clothes! I want
to listen to your chest."

Jean is a pale-faced lad of twelve, with clean-cut but characterless
features. His gaze is more distinctive—affectionate, pensive, without gaiety. He has a poor physique; the ribs show as bluish streaks
under the thin, pale skin.

THE DOCTOR: "Now let's have a look. Put your back to the wall as
you did last time, and let your arms hang loose. Raise your chin,
open your mouth. Right." He takes off his glasses. "Now breathe
deeply. Again."

As he listens to Jean's chest he puckers up his face and blinks his eyes. The father's keen anxiety, cut off as he is from the world by his short sight and his intense absorption in the sounds he hears, contrasts with the indifference of the boy, who is yawning, gazing listlessly out at the sky. The examination lasts a long time.

THE DOCTOR, quietly: "Thanks, my dear. Put your clothes on again." With an affectionate smile. "Now I'll tell you what we're going to do, old chap. We'll go to the garden, just the two of us, and have a little chat in the sunshine until your grandmother comes back from Mass. What do you say to that?"

JEAN: "Grandma can't have gone yet." Timidly. "It's Whit-Sunday, Papa. I'd have liked—"

THE DOCTOR, gently: "No, Jean, that wouldn't be at all wise. You'd get hot walking, and it must be quite chilly in the church."

JEAN: "But it's so near—"

THE DOCTOR: "And then—I must catch the three o'clock train; I've a consultation this evening, in Paris. And naturally I want to see a bit of you while I am here." In a different tone. "I've some things to say to you, Jean, important things." A short silence. "So, come along!"

The old house owned by the Barois family for many generations stands at the highest point of the town. The main building seems to shore up the church, on whose tower it abuts. Two low wings, roofed with tiles, project towards the street from each end of the main building; they are linked together by a prison-like wall, in which is a spacious gateway. The space thus enclosed is partly courtyard, partly garden. Several times each day the sound of bells plunges down into this echoing sound-trap, making even the walls vibrate.

The doctor leads Jean to a trellised arbour covered with Virginia creeper.

THE DOCTOR, in a tone of forced joviality: "Sit down, old chap. Make yourself comfy. It's nice here, isn't it?"

JEAN, on the brink of tears, though why he doesn't know: "Yes, Papa."

The doctor has his "hospital face," as Jean calls it; the nose-wings wrinkled, eyes probing and intent.

THE DOCTOR, resolutely: "This is what I have to tell you, Jean. Just three words. You are ill." Silence. Jean keeps very still, gazing at the ground. "Yes, you're ill, and more so than you think." Another silence. The doctor keeps his eyes fixed on the boy. "I wish you to realize this, because if you don't make a really big effort to get well, it may become—extremely serious."

JEAN, forcing back his tears: "Then—then I'm not getting better?" The doctor shakes his head. "But I thought, after what happened at Lourdes . . ." He ponders for some moments. "Perhaps it hasn't begun to show yet?"

THE DOCTOR: "I know nothing about what happened at Lourdes. But I do know this: as things stand, as I find you today, you are very, very far from well."

JEAN, with a weak smile: "But—what have I got?"

THE DOCTOR, frowning: "You have—" He hesitates before continuing. "I'd better try to explain, Jean. And listen well to what I'm going to tell you. Your mother—" He takes off his glasses and starts wiping them, fixing his eyes on Jean. "Can you remember your mother at all?" Jean looks uncomfortable and shakes his head. "Your mother used to live here, in the country, before our marriage. She was never very strong, but her health was satisfactory. After our marriage she had to come to live in Paris, because of me. Your birth was a great strain on her constitution." The doctor takes a deep breath. "It was then she started being ill." He emphasizes the words. "An attack of acute bronchitis, to begin with. Do you know what that is?"

JEAN: "The same as I had?"

THE DOCTOR: "She made a bad recovery. Every night she had fever; she couldn't sleep well and kept tossing about in bed." The boy gives a slight start. "She often had a pain"—deliberately he leans forward and touches Jean's chest—"just here."

JEAN, nervously: "Like me?"

THE DOCTOR: "I did my best to make her look after herself. I told her much the same things as I'm telling you today. But, unfortunately, she wouldn't listen." A short silence. He has to fumble for his words, but his voice never falters. "Your mother, let me tell you, was a good, gentle, saintly woman—and I loved her most dearly. But she was many years younger than I and—very, very religious." Sadly. "I never managed to have the least influence over her. Every day she could see me giving my patients medical advice, and often curing them; and yet she hadn't confidence. And then, of course, she didn't feel really ill. What made things still harder was that I'd just got my post at the hospital, and this took up so much of my time that I couldn't look after her as well as I'd have liked. I wanted her to come and stay here, for the country air, but she refused. She started a cough. There were consultations. But it was too late." A short silence. "Things went very quickly. A summer, an autumn, a winter—by the spring she was no longer with us."

Jean bursts into tears. The doctor observes him with a cool, observant gaze—as when at a patient's bedside he is waiting for an injection to make its effect. Some minutes pass.

THE DOCTOR: "You mustn't take it so hard, Jean. I don't want to make you sad, you know. I'm only trying to talk to you as I would to one of my grown-up patients, because, well—it has to be done. You've inherited from your mother a tendency to have the same illness as she had. A *tendency,* you understand? No more than that. Which means that if you're exposed to certain unfavourable conditions, you may get the same disease. That, my dear boy, is exactly how you stand today. Since last autumn your health has been very poor, and it's high time, yes, high time to—"

In a sudden access of fear Jean slips off the bench and presses himself to his father, who gives him a rather clumsy hug.

THE DOCTOR: "There, there, Jean! There's no need to be frightened. I'm here to look after you."

JEAN, through his tears: "Oh, I'm not frightened really. I've thought of that already—that I was in heaven."

The doctor thrusts him away almost roughly, then makes the boy stand facing him.

THE DOCTOR, vehemently: "There's no question of dying, Jean. What you've got to do is to *live*. You can save yourself if you choose; well, do so!"

Taken aback, the boy stops sobbing and stares at his father. He'd have liked to be drawn up on his father's knees, petted and consoled. But he comes up against the cold gleam of the pince-nez. A new emotion is stirring in him, of fear and vague resentment; but also —such is the ascendancy of intelligence and strength—of perfect trust, of faith.

THE DOCTOR: "You wouldn't know, of course. The human body seems such a beautifully fitted and adjusted mechanism, doesn't it? Well, it's nothing but a vast battlefield, with millions of cells at war, devouring each other all the time. I'll explain it a bit more clearly. Hosts of tiny, harmful germs are attacking us every moment, and amongst them, naturally, are the germs of T.B. You know what T.B. means, don't you?" Jean nods. "Well, these germs always make a dead set at somebody like you, who has a tendency that way. What happens then is simple. If the body's strong, it drives them off; if it's not, they force their way in." He grips Jean's arm and emphasizes every word. "So there's only one way of defeating them: to build up your strength as quickly as possible, so as to get the whip hand again. You can cure yourself, never fear; all you need is to set your heart on being cured. It's a hard task, but you can and *must* see it through. Really it's only a matter of energy and perseverance. *Now* do you understand? All existence is a struggle; life is simply winning through. And you'll soon find you can win through, provided you really and truly make up your mind to do so." Impulsively Jean has come nearer, and is nestling against his father. The doctor puts his arm round the boy's shoulders. "If I could drop my practice for a while, close my surgery, and give all my time to you, I'd pull you through; that I guarantee." Vehemently. "Well, what I cannot do, what I have not the right to do, you can do by yourself, if you'll be guided by me." He looks him in the eyes. "Well, Jean? Will you promise to do as I tell you?"

JEAN, in a rush of emotion: "Yes, yes, Papa. I promise you. I'll start at once. I'll do everything you say." He is silent for some moments, obviously thinking hard. Then, almost as if he were talking to himself, he adds: "And Abbé Joziers will say Masses for me as well. I'll ask him."

THE DOCTOR, gently: "By all means. But that wouldn't be enough. First, there's a lot of spadework to be done, you know, and only you can do it." Jean moves a little away from his father, who goes on speaking in a gravely affectionate tone. "I ask you, my dear boy, to *believe* what I'm telling you. That's the most important thing, really. It was because she lacked confidence that your poor mother died." The boy comes back to him. "You know quite well that I wouldn't for the world cause you pain by what I'm saying; in fact I'm greatly counting on your religious faith to help see you through. But there's a saying which you know: Heaven helps those who help themselves. Pray with all your might, Jean, but never forget that the course of treatment I'm going to prescribe comes first; everything else—yes, even prayer—is of secondary importance." With a fervour that carries conviction. "Yes, my dear boy, if you want to get well you must follow the treatment I'm going to prescribe, I won't say merely with perseverance and good will . . ." In a great peal all the bells of Pentecost acclaim the Elevation. The doctor has to raise his voice, almost to shout, to make himself heard through their throbbing clangor. "I won't say merely with energy; but with enthusiasm, an almost fanatical determination. With a steadfast purpose to regain all the lost ground, to build up new strength, to fight the disease back inch by inch, and to conquer death through your passionate will to live. To live, Jean! Ah, if only you had learnt what that really means: to live! Not merely to stay alive, but to go on loving what you love, seeing that sunlight playing on the walls of your old home, and for many and many a year hearing those bells pour their music down, flooding your ears. Just look around.

Look at those trees, that golden light, that blue sky, the church tower. Look!" He clasps the boy's shoulders and shakes him. "To *live,* Jean!"

Quivering with excitement, swept off his feet by an uprush of emotion such as he has never known before, the boy gazes rapturously at his father; his cheeks are flushed, his eyes sparkling.

After observing him gravely for a while, the doctor draws Jean towards him. The bells have fallen silent, but for some moments their vibration lingers in the sunlit courtyard before dispersing into the upper air. A long silence follows.

THE DOCTOR, weighing his words: "Three things: food, fresh air, rest. Now, try to fix in your memory what I'm going to say."

3

The residence of Mme Pasquelin, Jean's godmother, at Buis. A dimly lit sitting-room. Outside the window, snowy winter twilight. Round the fireplace, lit by the firelight, a silent group. Mme Pasquelin is standing, her arm round Jean, who is weeping on her shoulder. Little Cécile is pressing herself to her mother's skirt, unnerved by the sight of Jean's distress, and crushing her handkerchief to her mouth to stifle her sobs.

On the tablecloth lie two crumpled telegrams:

Pasquelin, Buis-la-Dame, Oise. Mother much shaken by journey to Paris. Operation delayed by unforeseen complications. Very anxious. Barois.

Pasquelin, Buis-la-Dame, Oise. Mother died eleven this morning at nursing home without regaining consciousness. Operation impracticable. Break news to Jean very prudently, avoiding any shock.

Barois.

4

Three years later. A small tiled room behind the sacristy, dimly lighted by a window facing a high wall. There are two chairs, two praying desks. A crucifix hangs on the wall in front of them.

Abbé Joziers has a young face, with a high, domed forehead from which the fair, close-cropped, curly hair is already beginning to recede. Frank, cheerful eyes tell of sunny, active faith. The impression of severity given by the thin upper lip is corrected by the lower, which is rather plump and often ripples in a somewhat ironic but good-natured smile. Smile and gaze have the genial, if almost aggressive, assurance of those for whom all the problems of this world and the next have definitely been solved, and who feel serenely confident of being the sole and sure repositories of the truth.

After carefully shutting the door, Abbé Joziers turns and stretches both hands towards Jean.

THE ABBÉ: "Well, Jean, old chap, what is it?" He clasps one of Jean's hands. "Do sit down."

Jean Barois is a tall, lithe boy of fifteen with a well-knit body, a broad chest, a long but sturdy neck. He has an energetic face; a square forehead crowned with thick, stiff brown hair. Slotted between the curved, slightly puckered eyelids, which convey his keen attention, the eyes are keen and forthright; he has his father's piercing gaze. But the lower portion of the face is still quite childish; the mouth especially is hardly formed and seems to change its shape at every moment. The heaviness of the under-jaw is mitigated by the fullness of the chin.

The young face wears a look of dogged resolution, the outcome of a long uphill struggle towards health; three years of stern self-discipline, of alternating hopes and setbacks—with his life at stake. But the battle has been won.

THE ABBÉ: "Well?"

JEAN: "I did a lot of hard thinking, sir, before deciding to take this step. I've wanted to consult you for quite a while, but kept on putting it off. But now . . ." He is silent for some moments. "There are some things troubling me today, questions to which I don't know the answer. About religion, I mean. All sorts of ideas that never entered my head before. Especially since I started going to Beauvais for those lessons." Hesitantly. "I need someone to discuss them with, someone to explain . . ."

THE ABBÉ, gazing serenely at Jean: "But there's nothing simpler. I'm entirely at your disposal, my dear boy. So there are certain matters which are troubling you? Well, let's hear what they are."

A look of earnestness beyond his years settles on Jean's face. He raises his head a little. The tension of the muscles draws down the corners of his lips, which are shadowed by a faint growth of down. His eyes are fever-bright.

THE ABBÉ, smiling encouragement: "Come along, Jean; out with it!"

JEAN: "Well, sir, to begin with—what exactly are free-thinkers?"

The priest squares his shoulders and replies briskly, without a moment's hesitation. A faint, pleased smile hovers on his lips. The restrained emotion in his voice is characteristic of the man; his teeth are almost clenched, and he stresses certain words out of all proportion to their context or significance.

THE ABBÉ: "You ask what free-thinkers are? Simpletons, for the most part, who imagine that it's possible for us to think freely. To think freely! But only lunatics think freely." He laughs cheerfully. "Am I free to think that five and five make eleven? Or that I can use a verb in the plural after a subject in the singular? Surely it's obvious there are rules which every sane person abides by—of grammar, of mathematics, and of every activity of the mind. The free-thinker fancies he can dispense with rules. But nobody can achieve anything unless he has something solid to build on. To walk you must have solid ground under your feet. And to think coherently you need solid, well-tested principles—which religion, and religion only, can supply."

JEAN, gloomily: "I rather fear, sir, that I've tendencies towards becoming a free-thinker."

THE ABBÉ, with a laugh: "You don't say so!" Affectionately. "No, my dear child, you need have no fears on that score; I'll answer for it. But how could you even dream of such a thing?"

JEAN: "I've changed. Until quite lately I never had any religious difficulties; I'd never have thought of questioning anything, I took it all for granted. But now—now I have strange moods when I try to clear things up in my mind, and then I get into a hopeless fog! It worries me horribly."

THE ABBÉ: "But, my boy, that's perfectly normal." Jean looks surprised. "It's a sort of growing pains. Yes, you're at the age when a youngster really begins his conscious existence, when daily he discovers hosts of things of which he'd had no notion hitherto. You see, he tries to bring to adult life the simple faith of childhood; and, well, they simply don't tally." The shadow is gradually lifting from Jean's face. "It's nothing, really. All that's needed is to get over this difficult phase as quickly as you can, to buttress your faith with solid arguments, and adapt it to your changed conditions. That's where I can help you."

JEAN, smiling: "Only to hear you speak, sir, does me a world of good." More briskly. "But I've another question. Let's take the case of a sin, a sin which has become almost a habit, with which one's quite familiar, but which one's quite determined to stamp out. Well, one prays, one vows to stop it, and all seems for the best. And then, fight as one may, habit proves stronger than the Will of God."

THE ABBÉ: "That, my boy, is why nothing can be more dangerous to faith than a sin that's committed frequently, even a venial sin. It's just these repeated shocks to the religious sentiment that must be avoided at all costs."

JEAN: "I know that. But why should it be impossible not to give way?" The priest smiles indulgently; Jean, absorbed in his thoughts, fails to notice. "I can't understand the reason for these temptations, all these trials of our faith. When one's a child, one finds it quite natural that there should be happy people and unhappy people, healthy people and invalids. That's how the world is, and you take it for granted. But later on, when you begin to think, you're shocked at all the injustice and evil that exist. If only one could say that unhappiness is always a punishment that's deserved, it would be ever so much simpler—but one can't! I know God must have had his reasons for making the world as it is, but really—"

THE ABBÉ: "Ah, but don't forget that God did not create the world as it is now. It is man who by his first disobedience of the order given by his Creator is responsible for all our woe."

JEAN, obstinately: "But if Adam had been perfect, he would never have disobeyed. And, after all, at the beginning of the world, wasn't it God himself who created the serpent?"

No longer smiling, the priest raises a monitory hand. He gazes hard at Jean and, though affectionate, his gaze unconsciously betrays his awareness of his superior position.

THE ABBÉ: "As you can well imagine, Jean, you're not the first to be puzzled by these seeming contradictions. It's our old friend—or, rather, enemy—the Argument from Evil. It has been refuted time and again, and in all sorts of ways. You have done well to tell me of this difficulty of yours. And as you're troubled by the problem, I'll lend you some books on the subject which will set your mind at rest, definitely." Jean says nothing, but he seems a shade disappointed. "But, mind you, I'm not blind to the good side of your indignation. It's only by realizing the suffering that exists on earth that we can strengthen the instinct of charity within ourselves —and none of us can go too far in that direction." He clasps Jean's hand. "You, Jean, are at an age when the heart is opening to new experience and brimming over with compassion. I realize that the first shock of these discoveries may well be very painful; that's why a word of warning cannot come amiss. Beware, my boy, of letting

your emotions run away with you; there's much less Evil in the
world than, at first sight, you might suppose. Bear this in mind: if
the sum of Evil were greater, or even equal to the sum of Good—
why, chaos would reign everywhere! But when we look around us,
what do we see? A wonderful order prevailing throughout the
universe, and making us feel how pitiably small we are. Every day
scientific pioneers are making new discoveries, which enable us to
appreciate still better the glorious perfection of God's scheme. As
compared with that abounding goodness, how trivial, relatively, are
the *individual* penalties of sin! Then, again, human sufferings—and I
don't deny they exist, alas; how could I, considering that my mission
is to treat and, if possible, heal them?—yes, human sufferings, even
if they seem unjust, have their value, as one day you'll find out
for yourself. It's through them, and through them only, that man
can develop the goodness that is in him and make progress on the
way of his salvation. And which is it that really matters: this life on
earth or the life to come?"

JEAN: "But there aren't only men on earth. The animals—"

THE ABBÉ: "The suffering of every creature is willed by God, my
dear Jean; He made it a condition, indeed the prime condition, of
life. That thought should be enough to curb your rebellious instincts, whose origin is in poor, human pride. Yes, the existence of
that Perfect Being, infinitely good, all-powerful, who created heaven
and earth out of nothing, who every day gives us a thousand proofs
of his fatherly love for us—his existence is our best assurance of the
necessity for evil in this world, which He made as it had to be for
our betterment. And even if his purposes seem dark to our imperfect vision, our duty is to bow to his Will—nay more, to will as He
does these sufferings we do not understand but which He has thought
best for us. *Fiat voluntas tua* . . ."

Jean says nothing; he frowns slightly, trying to take in what the
priest has been saying. In the near-by vestry shrill young voices are
singing to the accompaniment of a wheezy harmonium.

THE ABBÉ: "To speak quite frankly, Jean, I see in you a slightly, oh, very slightly, exaggerated tendency to introspection." He smiles. "Far be it from me to speak ill of the noble activities of the mind. But, all the same, the longer I live the more I feel that intelligence serves its true purpose only when it is directed to an end outside itself, when it aims at some practical result. Intelligence should inspire and quicken action; indeed, without it, activity is sterile. But, if it does not lead to action, intelligence is futile, like a lamp lit beside a lighthouse, burning itself out in vain!" With deep feeling. "You've come to me, Jean, to ask for guidance. Well, I'll always urge you to act rather than to meditate. By all means cultivate your mind; it's not only permissible to do so, but your duty. But cultivate it with a human end in view. If our Lord has entrusted you with something rather precious, an intelligence above the ordinary, make it bear fruit—but see that the great family to which we all belong profits by it. Don't be like the unprofitable servant who hid his talent in the earth. By all means increase your store, but only so as to share it with others. Try to be one of the givers.

"I have been through the same phase myself. I started dabbling with these so-called 'advanced' theories, but, God be thanked, I very soon saw my mistake. It's through action, through self-devotion and in self-forgetting, that a man can get the best life has to offer, can achieve mental and spiritual health—the one true and never-failing happiness. Believe me, Jean, this happiness, which we sometimes seek so far afield, is really within easy reach; it springs from such natural feelings as love for our fellow men. And all the rest is vanity!

"Drop in at the Church Club one evening; I'll give you the books I spoke of, and then if you'll stay with us for half an hour or so, you will see for yourself"—his eyes light up with pride and happy enthusiasm—"what noble hearts some of our young folk have, and how rewarding it can be to do our very utmost for them." He rises to his feet. "Yes, Jean, that's the one real joy in life: to feel one's doing a little good for one's fellow men and"—he presses his hand to his chest—"imparting to them some of that warmth of heart that God has placed in us—here."

5

The Pasquelins' morning-room; a long narrow room on the ground floor, crowded with old-fashioned furniture. Cécile is by herself, tidying up the disorder her mother left on going out. A dark October evening is closing in. At a sound of footsteps on the pavement outside she runs to the window and waves her hand. A satchel under his arm, Jean is crossing the street. She hastens to the front door to meet him.

Cécile Pasquelin is a tall, slim girl of sixteen; though not pretty, she has the grace of youth, an exceptionally charming carriage of her supple neck and rather narrow shoulders, which now are wrapped in a white woollen shawl. Her head is small and round as an apple; her black, slightly prominent eyes also are very round, and an almost imperceptible squint gives her gaze a strangely tantalizing charm. Her brown hair falls in a fringe over her forehead. She has a well-shaped mouth, with moist, full, mobile lips and short, sharp teeth that flash brilliantly when she smiles. The smile is light-hearted, superficial. Sometimes she drops into a slight lisp.

CÉCILE: "Hurry up, Jean. I'm afraid the milk's nearly cold."

Jean's meal is set ready on a tray. As he takes large bites of his bread and butter, Cécile's eyes are sparkling. She has drawn her stool in front of him and, when their eyes meet, both young people laugh—for no reason, out of mere gaiety of heart.

JEAN: "And now, to work!" He tips out the books in his satchel onto the table. Cécile lights the lamp, draws the curtains, puts a log on the fire, and moves her chair nearer to the lamp.

CÉCILE: "What is it this evening?"

JEAN: "Greek verse." The room is pleasantly warm. A low droning sound comes from the lamp and the fire. There is an occasional rustle of Cécile's dress, or when Jean turns a page. At one moment, when he is doing this and Cécile is examining a stitch at the tip of her knitting needle, Jean looks towards her. There is something in his voice that puzzles her. "Do you know, Cécile, I found something rather—rather striking this morning, in a bit of Aeschylus I was construing. He's talking about Helen, and he says, 'A soul serene as a calm, windless sea.' Fine, isn't it? 'Serene as a calm, wind-less sea.'"

He gazes at her. She lowers her eyes but says nothing. She is holding her breath—as when in a game of hide-and-seek you see the one who's "seeking" come quite near, almost brush against you, and then go on, without having noticed. Jean is poring over his Greek text again.

Half an hour later a woman's footsteps clatter on the tiled floor of the hall, and Mme Pasquelin bustles in. She is a small, dark woman, with a sallow complexion and jet-black hair frizzed over the forehead. She has fine eyes, with a suggestion of a squint like Cécile's; a bright, yet gentle gaze; a smiling, slightly pursed mouth. She has once been quite a beauty, and remembers it. Active, loquacious, she is always on the move, chattering away in a shrill voice, with a rather pronounced Picardy accent. Always bursting with energy, she never spares herself; she is always ready to take a hand in any local activity, in organizing or reorganizing the charitable societies of the parish and similar good works.

MME PASQUELIN: "Hard at it, my dears?" Without waiting for an answer she continues. "Do get a proper chair, Cécile; I hate to see you all doubled up on that silly little stool." She goes to the box containing logs. "It's lucky I came; you're letting the fire go out, you two, as usual."

JEAN, getting up to help her: "Don't trouble. I'll put some logs on."

MME PASQUELIN: "No, you'd take too long over it, Jean. It's nearly out." Deftly she flings two logs into the fireplace and draws the metal curtain half-way down, to make the fire draw. Then, straightening up, she unhooks her cape, goes to the window, and pulls the curtains tighter, talking all the time. "Oh, my dears, I thought I'd never get back home. It's been an awful day, I'm quite worn out. Everything was in such a muddle, I had to lose my temper half a dozen times. That Abbé Joziers is really most exasperating. He talked the Vicar into having the boys' catechism class at half-past nine on Thursday—just the time we'd fixed for the committee meeting of the sewing-bee. I told the Vicar what I thought about it. 'How do you expect me to be at both ends of the town at the same time?' I asked him.—Jean, will you lift the shutter now? The logs have caught. But it's quarter to six, you know. If you want to go with us to Communion tomorrow, you've only just time to make your confession. The Abbé leaves the church at half past, so you'd better hurry up." Jean rises. "Wrap yourself up well. There's a cold wind tonight."

Next day. The seven o'clock Communion is being administered. Mme Pasquelin rises and moves towards the altar, followed by Jean and Cécile. Side by side, with eyes downcast, they slowly walk towards the Holy Table. Abbé Joziers, who is officiating, raises on high the consecrated Host.

ABBÉ JOZIERS, in a contrite voice: *"Domine, non sum dignus.* Lord, I am not worthy . . ."

Cécile and Jean are kneeling, their elbows touching, their ice-cold hands close together under the white cloth. The same faintly morbid yet delicious thrill of awe, a yearning towards the infinite. The priest draws near. In turn, they slowly raise their heads, tremblingly part their lips, then let their eyelids close upon the ecstasy of joy welling up from their hearts.

At this moment they are utterly united; freed from the trammels of their earthly bodies, two young souls rise effortlessly to the supreme pinnacle of love and mingle there, at one with God.

II. THE SYMBOLIST COMPROMISE

When I was a child, I spake as a child, I understood as a child: but when I became a man, I put away childish things.

I Corinthians: 13:11

I

Abbé Joziers
   The Presbytery
      Buis-la-Dame, Oise   Paris, January 11

Dear Abbé Joziers: I wish I could send an answer worthier of the trust you place in me. Unfortunately I am unable to give you the reassurance as to my moral welfare that I know you expect. This first term has been unsatisfactory in several ways, and I still feel terribly "lost" in Paris, where everything is so new to me.

However, I have now mapped out my days on lines I mean to keep to. In addition to the preparatory courses at the School of Medicine, I have entered my name at the Sorbonne as candidate for a Natural Science degree, with the result that for some weeks past I have been spending even more of my time in the Latin Quarter. (I hope, dear Abbé Joziers, that what I have written above will not cause you any uneasiness—I may mention, in this connexion, that I was greatly touched by the affectionate advice you gave me in your last letter. No, you need have no fears in that respect; thank God, I have enough strength of will, enough idealism, to resist the temptations you had in mind, and in any case—why, surely you have not forgotten the deep and pure emotion that came to me at Buis and is with me still, and the project, so near to my heart, that is at once the great hope of my life, and my safeguard?)

These science courses take up a great deal of my time, but they are a useful complement to my medical studies, and I can't tell you

22

how absorbing I find them. Anyhow, what could I do with leisure, if I had it? As you may know, my father has been appointed to a professorship, and his lecture courses make still more demands on a life that was already crowded and in which, frankly, I have little place.

You will, I am sure, be glad to hear that I have struck up acquaintance with a young Swiss priest, Schertz by name, who has come to get a Paris degree with a view to teaching natural history in his own country. He is very keen on biology; we work in the same laboratory, and I greatly benefit by his assistance and companionship. These studies are absolutely fascinating; I can't quite analyse my reactions as yet, but some of the lecture courses literally "go to my head." Indeed, I think these first contacts with science bring on a sort of dizziness—when one begins, even in a dim way, to glimpse some of those stupendous laws of nature that govern the vast complexity of the universe.

As you advised me to do, I am constantly trying to gain a deeper insight into this universal order, and to confirm still more my veneration of its divine Creator. But you cannot imagine how much I miss your infectious optimism, and I can only hope that Abbé Schertz's friendship may compensate to some extent. His natural high spirits and his zest for work vouch for a robust faith which may very well help me to recover my moral balance. For I need help of that kind; in the last few weeks especially, I have been through moments of most harrowing depression.

Forgive me once again for distressing you with "confessions" of this order, and please believe me, always your affectionate and loyal pupil,

Jean Barois

2

Dr Barois' dining-room. Dinner has just ended, and the doctor rises from his seat.

THE DOCTOR: "You will excuse me, Monsieur Schertz, I hope."

Jean and the Abbé, too, have risen to their feet. "I have to be at Passy at nine, for a consultation. It has been a great pleasure to me, making your acquaintance, and I'm sorry the time has been so short. So good night, Jean. And I hope, Monsieur Schertz, that you will come again." He smiles. "Believe me, I set great store on that paradoxical theory of mine: that one should act first, and reflect at leisure! Young people nowadays think too much, and, as they've no experience of action, don't think straight."

Jean's bedroom. His friend the Abbé is seated in a low armchair, his legs crossed, his elbows resting on the arms of the chair and his hands clasped under his chin.

Abbé Schertz is a man of thirty-one, with a long, flat body whose angularity is emphasized by his tight-fitting cassock. He has big, sinewy arms, sedately measured gestures. His face is broad and bony, his complexion pale, and the slope of his forehead is accentuated by the way he has of brushing his black hair straight back from his brows. The scantiness of the eyebrows makes the clean-shaven face look still more glabrous. The massive bony structure of the brows juts out over pale, keen eyes with greenish pupils, slotted between jet-black eyelashes. Schertz has a long nose, with a deep, mobile furrow extending to the cheek-bone on each side; thin lips that sometimes set in a hard line and turn quite white. His manner is earnest, almost prim, but pleasant. He is inclined to indulge in long phrases and expressions not in current use; in fact he gives the impression of thinking in a foreign language and translating his thoughts.

Jean is sitting on his desk, swinging his legs.

JEAN: "I'm glad you got on with my father. I'm extremely fond of him." He smiles. "Do you know, I once used to be scared of him!"

SCHERTZ: "You cannot mean it!"

JEAN: "Yes, he overawed me. But, really, I knew him so little—until these last few months, when I've been living with him. Ah, how a profession like his ennobles a man!"

SCHERTZ: "Ah, yes, indeed he has a noble character, you feel that at once; but, mind you, it isn't owing only to his profession. Otherwise every doctor—"

JEAN: "Naturally. I grant you that, in my father's case, there must have been a natural predisposition. What I meant was that he hasn't the support of religion."

SCHERTZ, with sudden interest: "Ah? As a matter of fact I'd suspected as much."

JEAN: "My father came of a fervently devout family and was given an education on purely Catholic lines. All the same, for many years I believe, he has never put his foot inside a church."

SCHERTZ: "And given up believing too?"

JEAN: "I think so. As a matter of fact he has never discussed these things with me. Only—well, one can read between the lines, of course. And naturally . . ."

SCHERTZ: " 'And naturally . . .' What were you going to say?"

JEAN, after a brief hesitation: "I wanted to say that Father's profession, when you think of it, is almost bound to weaken faith." Schertz makes a gesture of surprise. "Because of the hospital work, for one thing. Try to imagine what it must mean to a thoughtful man whose sole duty every day from morn to eve is to minister to human suffering. What opinion must he have of God?" Schertz is silent. "Do I shock you?"

SCHERTZ: "Not in the least. You interest me. Of course it's simply the old Argument from Evil."

JEAN: "A very cogent argument."

SCHERTZ: "As you say, very cogent."

JEAN: "And one which, so far, even our greatest theologians have never seriously refuted."

SCHERTZ: "Never."

JEAN: "What! You agree to that?"

SCHERTZ, smiling: "But how could I do otherwise?"

Jean puffs at his cigarette without speaking. Then abruptly he throws it into the fireplace and looks the Abbé in the eyes.

JEAN: "Well, you're the first priest I've ever heard say a thing like that."

SCHERTZ: "Have you ever put the question bluntly to another priest?"

JEAN: "Oh, often."

SCHERTZ: "Well?"

JEAN: "I was given every conceivable answer. That I was too sensitive, too squeamish. That I had a rebellious spirit. That Evil is a necessary condition of Good. That trial and temptation are needed for the betterment of man. That, beginning with man's first disobedience, God willed that Evil should exist, and we must will it with him."

SCHERTZ, smiling again: "Yes? Anything else?"

JEAN, shrugging his shoulders scornfully: "Words! Just words! Arguments that were hardly even specious." Schertz throws a quick glance at Jean; then his face clouds over and he refrains from looking up. "If we go to the heart of the matter we come up against a fallacy. I'm asked to believe in the power and the goodness of God on the strength of the order reigning in the universe. The moment I point out the many imperfections in this order, I am forbidden to criticize it because it is the work of God. A flagrant begging of the question!" He takes some steps before continuing, in a louder tone: "The result is that I've never been able to reconcile those two affirmations— that God is the sum of all perfection, and that this world of ours, with all its imperfections, was created by him."

He halts in front of the Abbé, fixing his eyes on him, but Schertz looks away. There is a short silence. At last their eyes meet; Jean's are dark with an unspoken question, and the Abbé cannot altogether evade their appeal.

SCHERTZ, with an uncertain smile: "So you too, Jean, are troubled by these tremendous problems? I'm sorry to learn that."

JEAN, fretfully: "How can I help it? I assure you I'd far rather not be obsessed by them like this. But . . ." He paces around the room, his hands in his pockets, sometimes shaking his head, as if continuing the discussion in his mind. He is wearing an even stubborner look than usual; his brows are puckered by the stresses of a pent-up emotion that sets his lips in a hard, tormented line. "Listen, Schertz! Just now you were speaking of my father. Well, there's something that always rather shocked me, even when I was a small boy. It was that anyone could dare to condemn a man like him, on religious grounds, just because he never set foot inside a church or partook of the Sacrament at Easter. At home, at Buis I mean, they take a very severe view of his conduct."

SCHERTZ: "Because they don't understand him, obviously."

JEAN, with an air of surprise: "But surely as a priest you too should condemn him?" Schertz makes a non-committal gesture. "Personally, I've always, *always* refused to do so; all my instincts rebelled against it. Why, a life like Father's is—is one long aspiration towards everything that's noble and sublime. How could anyone find fault with it, on religious grounds? No, it's preposterous! A life like his, you know, is something apart from all that; it's above—" He breaks off abruptly, takes a few steps, then halts and faces the Abbé with a look of acute distress. And his voice too betrays profound despondency. "And then, old chap—oh, what a dreadful thing it is to think that a man like my father is an agnostic! That others like him are agnostics! And yet they aren't savages, are they? They were brought up in our religion, have once been practising—some of them devout—Catholics. And yet one day, deliberately, they discarded the religion of their youth. It makes you think, doesn't it? One tells oneself, 'I believe, and they do not believe. Which is right?' And then one can't escape an insidious afterthought: 'That remains to be seen.' Once that stage is reached one's peace of mind is wrecked. 'That remains to be seen.' That thought is the first accursed step on the path that leads to atheism."

SCHERTZ, earnestly: "Ah, but wait a bit! You've stated the case wrongly, and you're falling into a very grave error. It's true that men of your father's stamp may repudiate the tenets of the Church as we find them today. But be assured that the power within them that makes for goodness and nobility is exactly the same as what we find in the best of priests, the very best."

JEAN: "So there are two ways of being a Christian?"

SCHERTZ, who has let the discussion take him further than he intended: "Well—er—that's not impossible."

JEAN: "And yet, when all is said and done, there *should* be only one way."

SCHERTZ: "Certainly. But don't forget that, underlying all these differences of opinion—which are mostly on the surface and mean far less than you suppose—yes, underlying these, there's always the same thing, the same aspiration towards infinite goodness, perfect justice."

Jean gazes at him without speaking. A long silence. Schertz seems ill at ease. "Do you know, I rather like the smell of that tobacco? I'll make an exception and have a cigarette, if you . . . Thanks, old chap." He is determined to give a new turn to the conversation. "I've brought those lecture notes you asked for—the preliminary course."

Jean takes the notebooks and flutters the pages absent-mindedly.

Some days later. The Abbé's bedroom in a quiet boarding-house giving on the Saint Sulpice square.

SCHERTZ, springing up from his chair: "Ah, a pleasant surprise!"

JEAN: "I thought I'd drop in for a chat before we go to the Sorbonne."

The Abbé moves the books off the solitary armchair. Smiling, Jean wanders round the room. There is a small desk, a large deal table for experiments, with an array of bottles, jars, a microscope. On the walls hang anatomical plates, a portrait of Pasteur, a panoramic photograph of Berne, a crucifix.

JEAN, laughing: "Really, it beats me how you can live in this atmosphere!"

SCHERTZ: "Sorry! It's my sulphuric acid, I expect."

JEAN: "No, I didn't mean it literally. But I often wonder how a priest can live in this scientific atmosphere."

SCHERTZ, coming nearer to Jean: "Why shouldn't he?"

JEAN: "Well, even I—and remember I'm not a priest—find it hard to breathe in, terribly hard." Behind his smile lurks an unvoiced sadness. "Ah, one day I really must have a good long talk with you, make a clean breast of my troubles."

SCHERTZ, pensively: "Yes, why not?" He glances round the room, then fixes his gaze on Jean's eyes, as if to probe their secrets. After a while he lowers his eyes; he is thinking deeply. "You really want to do that?" They gaze at each other in silence, conscious of a tension in the air. It is impending, and they know it: one of those memorable hours when two young men, in the protective warmth of friendship, unburden their hearts to each other, mingling their thoughts without reserve, in perfect trust. Schertz's voice is very gentle as he asks: "What exactly is wrong, Jean?"

JEAN, emotionally: "Everything! I'm up against a—a most damnable moral crisis!"

SCHERTZ: "Moral?"

JEAN: "Well, let's say religious."

SCHERTZ: "How long have you been feeling like this?"

JEAN: "Oh, ever so long. Long before I was aware of it. Why, for several years, I should say, I've had to struggle—yes, fight really hard—not to lose my faith."

SCHERTZ, promptly: "No, not your faith. Only the unthinking, credulous faith of a child—which is a very different thing."

JEAN, following up his thoughts: "I didn't fully realize this until a few months ago. It's Paris, perhaps; the atmosphere of Paris. And especially the atmosphere of the Sorbonne, of those lecture rooms where all the great laws of the universe are analysed—without once mentioning the name of God."

SCHERTZ: "His name isn't mentioned, yes; but they're talking of Him all the time."

JEAN, bitterly: "I used to talk of Him more openly, not just by—by implication."

SCHERTZ, with a smile of encouragement: "The first thing is, obviously, for us to understand each other—to get the background clear."

Shyly. "I might be able to help you, old chap, only really I know so little of your religious life. How exactly do you stand at present?"

JEAN, despondently: "I wish I knew! Really, I'm all at sea. All I know is that things are as bad as they can be, with me." The Abbé has settled into a chair, crossed his legs, and is leaning forward, his chin propped on his locked fingers. "I'm torn between conflicting tendencies, and my mind's in a fiendish turmoil, all the more exasperating because *once* I had the peace of mind—that sort of comfortable warmth—which comes of believing simply, trustingly. I assure you I haven't done anything to bring myself to this pass. Quite the contrary; I always forbade my rational self to meddle with such questions. But I can't keep it under control any longer. Objections, doubts, are piling up around me; almost daily I run up against a new one. And I've been forced to recognize that there's not a single article of Catholic doctrine that isn't riddled with contradictions, in the light of our present knowledge." He takes a magazine from his pocket. "Look! Have you come across this? An essay by Brunois, 'The Issues between Faith and Reason'?" Schertz shakes his head. "This came into my hands by chance not very long ago. Until then I'd never had an inkling of what was being done nowadays in the field of biblical research, or of the attacks that were being launched by competent historians. It came as a shock—and a revelation!—when I read that article. I learnt all sorts of facts that were quite new to me. For instance, that the Gospels were written between the years sixty-five and one hundred; which means that the Church was founded, and could carry on, without them. Think of it! Over sixty years after Christ's birth! It's much as if, in our day, someone wanted to write down Napoleon's words and deeds, without a single written document to go on, only vague memories and anecdotes. And that's the sort of book it is, the Book of Books, whose absolute accuracy no Catholic must call in question." He turns some pages of the magazine.

"The writer goes on to say that Jesus never believed himself to be a God, or the founder of a religion, or even a prophet, until quite near the end of his life, when he was infected by the credulity of his disciples.

"That a very long time elapsed before the doctrine of the Trinity took shape, and several Councils had to be convened before Christ's dual nature was established and the distinction drawn between his human and his divine personalities. It comes to this: years of intense controversy were needed to establish this vital article of Christian faith and to link it up, more or less satisfactorily, with Christ's teachings. You'd never guess this from the catechism; that doctrine of the Trinity is one of the first things we are told to believe in, and we're asked to regard it as an elementary, quite simple truth, directly revealed by Christ himself, and so self-evident that it has never been called in question by anyone." He turns some more pages.

"Here's another passage, about the Immaculate Conception. The writer tells us this is an almost modern notion, which took its rise as late as the twelfth century. Two mystically minded English monks were responsible for it. It was not discussed or formulated until the thirteenth century. And its starting point was an absurd mistake made by some Greek translator who used the Greek word παρθένος, a maiden, when translating an ancient Hebrew word which simply described Mary as 'a young woman.'

"Ah, I see you're smiling! Then you knew about it already?" Crestfallen. "So of course you can't really understand the effect that information of this sort produced on me—it was like a bolt from the blue. Mind you, I'm still wondering if it's trustworthy." Schertz nods. "But the really amazing thing is that an article like that should appear, with all its details, over the signature of so well-known and cautious-minded a scholar as Brunois. In fact what startled me most was the tone of the article. The points I've mentioned come in quite incidentally, in support of Brunois' main argument. They are introduced without a word of comment, as if they were matters of common knowledge, facts of history that have been cleared up once for all. The writer does no more than give a few references so as to let ignoramuses like myself know where to find the authorities for the points he takes for granted. I mention this particular article because it's just come to my notice. But, on all sides, in every field of knowledge, I keep running up against anti-Christian arguments of this kind. Am I to believe that all modern knowledge is in flat contradiction to our faith?"

SCHERTZ, affectionately: "But, my dear Jean, I thought you were in contact with an abbé at Buis—a very learned priest, I gathered?"

JEAN: "Learned? I wonder! He's a man of action, a saint who's never had a qualm of doubt and, if he were to have one, would quickly overcome it by plunging into some activity." With a rather bitter smile. "He lent me some books on theology."

SCHERTZ: "Yes? Did they help?"

JEAN, shrugging his shoulders: "I found in them a lot of specious, purely verbal arguments, put forward as if they were unassailable, which a moment's serious thought exploded like so many toy balloons. They'd convince only those who were convinced already. Am I shocking you?"

SCHERTZ: "Not a bit. On the contrary, I understand your difficulties quite well."

JEAN: "But—"

SCHERTZ: "Better than you can possibly imagine." Jean begins to make a gesture of amazement, which Schertz checks with a wave of his hand. "But that can wait. Please go on with what you have to tell me."

JEAN: "Well—really that's all. Whenever I try to argue it out with myself, in the hope of strengthening my faith—indeed, every time I lay a finger on what's troubling me—I find I deal another blow to all that I believed in. Yes, it's just by trying to prove one's faith that one undermines it, as I've learnt to my cost. No, there's nothing to be done about it; my faith is crumbling away, bit by bit."

SCHERTZ, quickly: "No, no! I'm certain that's untrue."

JEAN: "Oh, I assure you I'd do anything to keep my faith." In a tone of utter hopelessness. "There may be people who can do without religion. I'm not one of them. I need it, yes, I *need* it, just to live

—as I need food and sleep. Without religion I'd be—oh, I don't know how to describe it!—like a tree whose roots had no earth to feed on, starved. I'd lose everything that counts in life. You see, old chap, I know myself for a Catholic, in every fibre of my being. And now that I have to struggle so fiercely to keep my faith, I feel this even more strongly. All I think, all I desire, and all I do is conditioned by the religious instinct; it's ingrained in my nature, and if I were to lose it my whole life would founder in a sort of quicksand of—of incoherency."

SCHERTZ: "But surely this religious crisis you're living through has periods of respite? Surely there still are days when you can draw near to God?"

JEAN, uncertainly: "I don't quite know how to put it. At bottom, I don't actually feel that I'm drifting away from God, even when my faith is at its lowest ebb." He smiles. "No, I can't explain it, I'm afraid." The Abbé makes a gesture that seems to indicate he understands it very well. Jean ponders for some moments before continuing: "Really, what makes it all so terribly difficult is this: in the Catholic religion everything hangs together—faith, doctrines, morality, our contacts with God through prayer; they're an indivisible whole, you see." Schertz shakes his head, but Jean fails to notice this. "And so, if one rejects even the smallest part, one loses all."

The Abbé rises and takes some steps, his hands locked behind his back. When he speaks, emotion makes him stumble over his words, as if he were translating laboriously.

SCHERTZ: "Ah, old chap, but what a tragic age is this in the religious life of mankind!" He halts in front of Jean and gazes at him earnestly. His tone grows steadier as he continues: "Now, shall we try to put it in a nutshell? On one side you have your intellect, which boggles at certain points of dogma or frankly rejects them. On the other side, you have your religious sensibility—it's very active in your case, I think—which, if I may put it so, has tasted God and cannot do without him."

JEAN: "Exactly. Not to mention an instinctive fear, which has its origins in my childhood and, most likely, in heredity as well—the dread of losing my faith."

SCHERTZ: "Yes . . . Do you know, it's much like a phase I went through myself?"

JEAN: "You too! When was that?"

SCHERTZ: "Just after I'd left the Training College."

JEAN, eagerly: "Yes? And now?"

SCHERTZ, smiling and pointing to his cassock: "You can see for yourself." Jean seems about to put a question, but Schertz waves it aside. "Mind if I tell you of my own experience?" Jean gives him a grateful smile, and the Abbé settles down in his armchair, resting his chin on his locked hands, knitting his brows, a far-away look in his eyes. "Until I was ordained I'd never studied science seriously, though I always had leanings towards it. So, once I'd taken Orders, I took it up as my special study. Looking back, I can see exactly what happened to me; and many others, I know, have had the same experience. How exciting it is, one's first contact with the scientific method! It comes like a revelation and breaks on you like a great wave, sweeping you off your feet. You feel as if your brain had been scoured clean, made ready for anything! And then a day comes when you look back on the past—and everything's changed. All those familiar things you took for granted—it's as if you were seeing them now for the first time. You analyse them, test them. And from that day there's no escape; you can't stop analysing. Isn't that so? Well, that's what the discovery of the scientific method does for you."

JEAN: "Yes, it sweeps one off one's feet."

SCHERTZ: "Mind you, I never suspected it was as definite as that. I thought I could always beat a retreat, if needed. So I put my books back on the shelves and betook myself to the monastery at Bürgen. For—for—" He cannot find the word.

JEAN: "A retreat?"

SCHERTZ: "Yes, a retreat. I spent five winter months there. At first I sought help from the Fathers, some of whom were highly educated men. But they merely made categorical statements, whereas I wanted to—to discuss. In fact we were at cross-purposes. They always ended up by smiling serenely and reminding me that nothing was impossible to God. And, of course, there was no answering that! I remember one of them saying to me, 'The amazing thing is that, with ideas like yours, you haven't lost your faith.' That set me thinking. It was so; my faith hadn't wavered once. Just as you were saying about yourself a moment ago, I had a conviction, a positive conviction, that nothing essential had changed in me. So I couldn't feel remorse. All I knew was that I was in the grip of something stronger than my will, and, moreover, something of a very lofty order and worthy of respect. So what was I to do? I tried to compromise—"

JEAN, shaking his head: "A dangerous way out."

SCHERTZ: "I was forced to recognize that it was no use struggling; the case for science was too strong. And I refused to resort, as some intellectual priests resort, to half-hearted concessions that don't go far enough. No, I preferred to give ground boldly, to be honest with my-self—with the feeling deep down in my consciousness that God would not have me do otherwise." He is silent for some moments. "So I left Bürgen, returned to Berne, and tried, with the help of books and meditation, to solve my problems." He smiles. "Ah, old chap, when you come to think of it, those two opposing forces—how unevenly matched they are! On one side you have the enemies of the Church—I'm thinking only of men of real learning, who have made their mark—and, on the other, our defenders of the faith, who do nothing but declaim, parade hoary old arguments, and wind up by threatening to excommunicate you. Try as one may, there's no doubt which group inspires more confidence. Really, the standpoint of the Holy See passes one's understanding. They inveigh against science without knowing the first thing about it. And they're ignorant of even the most elementary rules of thinking; all rational discussion is ruled out. They make the most extravagant assertions, with the result that they cut the ground under their own feet. It took me two years to arrive at this conclusion, but they weren't wasted. Thanks to those two years' strenuous thinking I've regained my peace of mind—for good."

JEAN: "Your peace of mind!"

SCHERTZ, leaning forward, obviously wishing Jean to pay particular attention to what he is going to say: "I discovered, my dear Jean, that in the matter of religion we have to draw a clean-cut line between two totally distinct elements. One of these is our religious sentiment, pure and unsophisticated, which amounts to what I'd call a pact with the Divine Being; it includes, too, the personal, direct relations existing between God and all whose souls are drawn to Him. The second element is what I'd call dogmatic; it includes hypotheses made by theologians about God and all the relations—not personal, but ritual—between man and God. Do you follow?"

JEAN: "Yes."

SCHERTZ: "Well, only one of these elements is appropriate to our modern religious sensibility, and it's the first—one's personal relationship with God."

JEAN: "How can you speak of *modern* religious sensibility? Surely religion isn't something that follows the fashion like—like women's dresses?"

SCHERTZ: "Ah, that's only a manner of speaking. Religion may not follow fashion, but it keeps step with the moral progress of mankind. Here's an example. Don't you agree that the men of the Middle Ages owed much of the robustness of their faith to an absolutely literal interpretation of the dogmas of the Church? Well, that's not the case today. Far from it; you've only to look at the Catholics of our generation, those who are really devout. Many of them don't know the first thing about religious theory; they give the dogmas second place—and they're no worse Catholics for that.

"Let me sum up what I've been saying. With you, with myself, with a great many fellow Christians, that first element, personal faith, is intact. It's the belief in dogma that is tottering, and we can't do anything about it. The Roman Catholic religion, as at present formulated, has features that can hardly be accepted by many enlightened minds; and not at all by those who have studied deeply as well as widely. The God it sets up is too narrowly human; that belief in a personal God, rather like an earthly king, or a celestial artisan who put the universe together—no, it's asking too much! That sort of religion doesn't meet our needs, it doesn't satisfy our—how shall I put it?—craving for perfection.

"Human beliefs, like everything else, are subject to the laws of evolution; they steadily progress from the less good to the better. So obviously it's essential that religion should adjust itself to the modern mind. And Rome is making a mistake in opposing this adjustment."

JEAN, excitedly: "Yes! But when you blame the Church today, as you've just been doing, how can you feel sure it's you who are right? Mightn't it simply be that you—"

SCHERTZ, cutting in: "Wait! Don't forget that in every man's belief, even if we grant its divine origin, there is bound to be a subjective element. People are only just beginning to allow for this. It's only quite recently that orthodox believers have admitted that some of the stories in the Old and New Testaments are to be taken in a figurative sense. Here are some examples. Christ's descent into the nether regions, his being led by Satan to a mountain-top. No serious-minded theologian would dare to say, 'That mountain had a physical existence; that descent took place in the literal sense.' No, what he'd say today is, 'Those passages have a figurative meaning.'

"Well, that sort of mental honesty—which calls what is obviously symbolic by its proper name: a symbol—that's what is needed by people like you and me. But we must not apply the principle reluctantly and half-heartedly, like those orthodox theologians who apply it only to biblical legends which are quite plainly mythical. No, we must apply it to each and every statement of fact, when the modern mind cannot admit its credibility. And there, Jean, you have the solution of all your difficulties."

There is a long silence. Jean is lost in thought but does not shift his gaze from the Abbé's forceful face.

SCHERTZ: "And don't forget, old chap, that before many years are out all theologians of any intellectual standing will have reached these conclusions; in fact they'll be amazed that nineteenth-century Catholics managed to believe so long in the literal truth of those poetic legends. 'They are splendid visions,' I can hear them saying; 'stories full of messages for us—but their content is ideal. The evangelists accepted them uncritically, and the early Christians could do the same, owing to their lack of mental training, and their credulity.'"

JEAN: "But you can't have it both ways, surely? Either the dogmas of the Church are true or else they're—worthless!"

SCHERTZ: "Ah, no indeed! Truth and reality, they're different. Many people, I know, share your difficulty. But when you say 'truth' you're thinking of 'authenticity,' which isn't the same thing. We should concentrate on the truth, not of the literal facts, but of their moral significance. We can admit the eternal verities that underlie the mysteries of the Incarnation and the Resurrection without admitting that these were concrete events, authentic in the historical sense, like the defeat at Sedan or the founding of the French Republic." The Abbé rises, walks round the table, and takes his stand facing the chair in which Jean is seated, pondering deeply. The young priest is deeply moved; the look of rather formalistic gravity has left his face, his eyes glow with a compelling fervour of which Jean had not believed him to be capable. Schertz points to the crucifix. "When I'm kneeling there, in front of the cross, and I feel my love for Jesus surge up from the depths of my being like a great wave, and I hear myself say 'My Redeemer . . . !'—oh, I can assure you it's not because I'm meditating on the doctrine of the Redemption like a boy learning his catechism. No, but I'm thinking—and, *ach,* how *wundervoll* it is!—of all that our Lord did for mankind. I remind myself how all that's best in man today, and all the splendid hopes we place in the man of tomorrow, come from Him alone. And then my doubts are stilled and I bow down before our Redeemer, the divine symbol of self-sacrifice and perfect goodness; of the suffering, willingly accepted, that washes away guilt. And every morning, when I kneel at the altar to partake in the Eucharist, my emotion is so intense that I seem to feel the Real Presence, and throughout the day that sense of strength and uplift never leaves me. Yes, what is the Eucharist but a symbol of the divine grace acting on my soul? But my soul calls for it, craves for it, with an almost physical hunger!"

Jean is still thinking hard; the extreme emotion behind his friend's words has raised in him the spirit of contradiction; his voice is even calmer than before.

JEAN: "I see what you mean. Still, surely an ordinary Catholic who is firmly convinced of the literal truth of the Incarnation and the Real Presence puts far more fervour into his prayers and his attendance at the Holy Table than you can ever put, with your—your reservations."

SCHERTZ, vehemently: "I don't agree! The one thing that matters is to extract for ourselves the truth that best suits our needs, and to cling to it. Let me make myself clearer. Our intellect rebels against certain points of dogma; that's a fact we must accept. But the symbol we extract from it is clear, self-evident; it satisfies our reason and furthers our spiritual well-being. So how can we hesitate?"

JEAN: "But surely if you strip Christian doctrine of its traditional forms it loses much of its efficacy? Christianity is, and has always been, a doctrine. 'Go ye, therefore, and teach all nations . . .' It's the acceptance of this doctrine in its entirety that makes the Christian."

SCHERTZ: "And that's the very reason why it's so needful today to modify the form—not the substance, mind you!—of Christian doctrine. History teaches us that through the centuries the dogmas have been constantly changing, expanding, keeping step, in short, with the evolution of mankind. That, indeed, was the condition of their vitality. Why, then, keep them hidebound, swathed like mummies in the trappings of tradition? It's obvious that traditional religion doesn't meet the requirements of modern thought, so why shouldn't we exercise the same rights as the theologians of the Early Church and adjust the dogmas to contemporary needs?" The Saint Sulpice clock strikes four. The Abbé rises and lightly taps Jean's shoulder. "But we must have another talk about these problems."

JEAN, who has been gazing into the middle distance, seems to come out of a dream: "Really, it's all very difficult. I'd got so used, you see, to regarding the traditional forms of our religion as—as absolute values. And, frankly, there's a lack of coherence in the religion you've been describing that goes against the grain, so far as I'm concerned."

SCHERTZ, buttoning his overcoat: "It takes all sorts to make a world, you know. And, considering how different men are from each other, isn't it only to be expected that they should worship the same God in different ways?" He smiles. "Well, we'd better make a move, hadn't we? My advice, old chap, is to let these problems settle themselves. And remember St Paul's admission: 'Now we see in a glass darkly. . . .' "

They go downstairs and walk in silence for some minutes towards the Sorbonne.

JEAN, abruptly: "But really one must be logical. Why do you persist in observing the rites of the Church when, on your own showing, they have only a symbolic value?"

Schertz stops walking, jerks his chin out of his upturned coat-collar, and fixes his eyes inquiringly on Jean's face, as if he doubts whether his friend is speaking seriously. Then a look of sadness comes over his face.

SCHERTZ: "Ah, I see! You haven't understood me." He reflects for some moments; then, weighing his words, continues: "My answer's this: because it would be sheer folly to cut oneself off from that fountain of living water, religious practice. It's far better to act as if religion were true in every detail; because it *is* true—in depth. Take prayer, for instance; how marvellous is the spiritual uplift it can give us!"

JEAN: "So, on your view, there's no need for set phrases or a ritual?"

SCHERTZ: "No need? Quite the contrary. Those set phrases and the rites of the Church are the best vehicles for the divine message, and none of us, even the most independent-minded, can afford to dispense with them. But each of us should interpret them for himself, according to his spiritual state, and use them according to his need."

JEAN: "In fact, we might as well turn Protestant!"

SCHERTZ: "Certainly not! An individualist, not to say anarchist, religion like Protestantism leaves us unsatisfied; whereas an organized, social, and—how shall I put it?—communalized religion like ours—that's just what human nature needs."

JEAN: "In other words, free-thinking, pure and simple?"

SCHERTZ: "No, my friend. We Catholics will never have the right to make that break with our religion."

JEAN: "The 'right'?"

SCHERTZ, gravely: "We have no right to sever ourselves from the body of our fellow Christians. How did religion build up its undeniable social virtues? By the combined efforts of all believers. Well, to stand aloof is to act like an individualist."

JEAN: "But surely your whole attitude is individualistic!"

SCHERTZ, frankly horrified: "Oh, no indeed! You're quite mistaken. I say that a man can choose his symbols according to his personal stage of development, but never forgetting that every symbol he adopts has its counterpart amongst the symbols adopted by the masses. That's how we keep in touch with our fellow men—the right kind of individualism." Jean says nothing. There is a short silence before Schertz continues: "Think, Jean, of all it means, the Catholic religion. Remember that for countless human beings it is the only window opening on the spiritual world, and that so many, perhaps the majority, cannot see further than the simple picture they have formed of it. Don't you understand how wrong it would be for you to cut yourself off from them? The truth is that all varieties of religious experience have a common source; a sort of impassioned appeal or a yearning of the soul towards the infinite. And in God's eyes we are all alike.

"Do as I do. I don't shut my eyes to the difficulties inherent in religious faith today; but I don't dwell on them either. 'Pray to thy Father which is in secret . . .' I know that all human organizations have defects. But I think that, for the majority, Catholicism is vastly superior to other persuasions, because it is literally, in the fullest meaning of the word, an association. And I accept the observances it enjoins because, for one thing, I find in them a source of spiritual strength that I could find in no other persuasion, and also because without them Catholicism would lose that religious solidarity which is necessary to so many souls."

The Abbé falls silent. They now are in the Sorbonne, threading their way along a corridor crowded with students.

Jean is trying to set his thoughts in order: One thing's certain; I must think this matter out. Until now I've tried to keep myself from thinking; I believed there was nothing to be gained by brooding on these problems. There I was mistaken. One can't put the clock back and return to the simple faith of one's childhood. So the only thing to do is to go forward; and there must be a way of straightening out the tangle; Schertz, anyhow, seems to have done so. Only I realize I don't know the first thing about all this—and without *knowing* I'll never make any headway. Yes, I must get down to essentials. The dogmas especially. So far I've concentrated on externals only: the rites and so forth. But Schertz always insists on what underlies these, the solid core. And hitherto the outer husk of forms has hidden from me the solid core. So it's for me now to dig down to the level at which the claims of human reason and religious dogma are reconcilable; that's obvious. There lies my only chance of regaining my peace of mind.

3

Abbé Schertz
  Professor of Biological Chemistry
    The Catholic Institute
      Berne   Paris, Easter Monday

My dear Hermann: I needn't say how much I appreciate your concern about my father's health. Happily it is improving. But he has had to give up his consulting days and lecture courses, and he confines himself to his hospital work in the mornings. Even that, really, is too much for him. However, his colleagues say that if he takes great care of himself there is no reason to fear a relapse, anyhow for several years.

This letter is shockingly belated, but I hope you will forgive me; I have been so busy all this winter. Your letters are an unfailing pleasure; they bring back those happy evenings of two years ago, our endless confabulations, our readings aloud. Only it saddens me to feel them so remote. Not that the good effects of your influence have worn off. Have no fear, old chap; I feel assured that you have laid the spectres of my doubt for ever, and I shall owe you gratitude all my life long for the comprehensive, tranquil faith I now possess; the solidly based yet tolerant faith a man can depend on, come what may. But once one is caught up as I am in the study of medicine, there's no escaping its grip; I hardly ever open a book that isn't a medical textbook.

I have even less time available, as I have made a point of keeping to my study of natural science as well. It's a field of research that has always fascinated me—vastly more than medicine—and I shan't be satisfied with a mere pass degree! My chief is pressing me to take the Senior Medical exam. next year; but I would rather concentrate on the Teachers' Final. Of course a medical career seems indicated in my case; but a professorship in science would be more to my taste—only I recognize that, as a career, it's somewhat chancy. So I hardly know what to decide. As you are aware, I have not only myself to think about, and my decision will affect another's life. But all this indecision is very trying and, for obvious reasons, I can't discuss my perplexities with anyone else.

I was most pleased to learn that you have now been given a post after your own heart. My one regret is that you get so few vacations and the prospects of seeing much of you in the future seem more than slender. Indeed, I can't repress a selfish grievance against this new appointment which separates us so effectively.

However, let me say *au revoir,* old chap, and hope that somehow, somewhen, we may meet again. Please send me one of your long, ever-welcome letters in reply.

Ever yours,
Jean Barois

III. THE RING

THE CLOSE of a May afternoon. As Jean enters the small flat where he has been living since his father moved from Paris to Buis, he picks up a letter pushed under his door. It is from Mme Pasquelin.

> Buis-la-Dame,
> Sunday, May 15
>
> My dear Jean: I have no idea what your father says in his letters about his health, but, personally, I am definitely worried; in my opinion he is in a bad way.—

Jean's shoulders sag. He almost wishes now that he had left the letter unopened.

> —He has changed greatly since last spring, and especially since he had that attack, slight though it was, last month, and he is continuing to lose weight. The cheerfulness he showed all through the winter has left him, and he has practically given up following his treatment. He says he's "done for," there's no hope of his recovering. It is heart-rending to see a man who used to be so active doing nothing all day, mewed up by himself with a man-servant in that big house which has so many memories for us all. We wanted him to come to live with us—the garden would have been a godsend to him—but he refused to budge.
>
> All this is very sad, my dear Jean; but I felt I should speak to you frankly.

Jean's hands are beginning to tremble, his eyes are misted.

> I fear we must now face the fact that your father may not recover; that is why I am writing. I know how deeply you and your family

44

felt his indifference to religion and, as we are his oldest friends and neighbours, I consider it our duty to try to remedy this sad state of affairs. So whenever I am with your father, I make a point of bringing the conversation round to this subject—for him so all-important. You, dear Jean, must help us by referring to it—discreetly, of course —in your letters.

His arms droop wearily; a vague resentment simmers in his mind. He skips a page, and his eyes fall on the words, "Cécile is quite well . . ." He glances towards the mantelpiece. Her photograph is gone! Then he remembers: Ah, yes, I put it away when Huguette started coming . . . It's six. She'll be here any moment now.

An acute discomfort seizes him; Cécile and Huguette mingle in his thoughts, their faces blurred together. He pulls himself up sharply. No, it can't go on like this. And suddenly, in a flash of intuition, he realizes that "it" is finished. The only reason for its lasting so long was that he'd never given it serious thought.

Cécile is quite well, though she has filled out a little lately, and this has tired her, I think. Several afternoons a week she takes her sewing over to your father's and stays quite a long while with him. She too does her best to direct the conversation to . . .

Jeans frowns again. A picture has risen before him of the doctor lying on the sofa in front of the fireplace. Dusk is falling. Cécile is seated at the window, the small, slightly prominent forehead bent above her needlework, while she weaves into her chatter phrases she and her mother have thought up in advance. An odious picture!

He mutters, "Why should Cécile be dragged into it?" Rising, he walks to his desk and, unlocking a drawer, takes out Cécile's photograph, then studies it in the lamplight. An old, slightly faded photograph, it shows her seated in a high-backed chair, her hands folded in her lap, her head inclined a little to one side. Her eyes are smiling, and her hair is dressed as in her early girlhood with a big bow behind her neck. As he gazes, Jean feels his emotion rising: No, nothing's changed. There's only Cécile—nothing else, nobody else matters.

Poor little Huguette! Still he can smile when he thinks how little she will feel it when he breaks the news: It's over. Let's take up our lives again as they were before we met. I'm returning to the girl who has never lost her place in my heart.

Half an hour later. The ferrule of a parasol taps the door. Huguette is wearing a flimsy dress, a lavishly beflowered picture hat.

HUGUETTE: "Sorry, darling, if I'm late. Well? Aren't you going to kiss me? Oh! Mind my hat!" He seems to be seeing her, for the first time, in perspective, and feels hardly a trace of emotion. She has dropped her parasol on the bed and is slowly peeling off her gloves. "I'm dreadfully sorry, dear, but I can't dine with you tonight. I've just seen Simone at Vachette's, with her new boy—you know who I mean. He's got three stalls for the show at the Cluny and we're dining together first. Not too vexed, darling?"

JEAN: "Not a bit."

She comes towards him. The light from a lamp on a low table plays on the silken ripples of her skirt. Her bare hands and slightly parted lips glimmer an invitation, and in a sudden uprush of desire he pictures her body, satin-smooth, accessible. Taking her in his arms, he buries his face in her hair and thinks: No, it can't end like this—just one night more, and tomorrow, tomorrow . . .

HUGUETTE, wriggling free, laughing: "Just a moment, dear. I must wash my hands."

He watches her run to the wash-stand, carefully roll up her sleeves, and, with a familiar gesture, slip off her rings and drop them tinkling into an ash tray. Suddenly his passion changes to antipathy. How she seems at home here! No, it can't go on. I've got to make a break with her, escape. At once. Tonight. Now that his resolve is made, he feels relieved, clear-headed, and can observe her critically. At this moment, scrutinizing her nails, her forehead puckered, she is almost ugly. Yes, all is over, irrevocably; something has snapped, beyond repair.

HUGUETTE: "You'll see me to my bus, won't you?"

They go out together. The Rue de Rennes, at seven, is crowded with people from the suburbs hurrying to catch their trains at the Montparnasse station. Jean walks in front, to force a way through the crowd.

HUGUETTE: "There's my bus. So that's fixed up? If you don't meet me after the show, I'll go straight home. Bye-bye, darling. Oh, damn! It's starting!"

She dashes forward, elbowing her way to the forefront. He follows the slim black form with his eyes, sees her spring onto the moving step and scooped up by the fatherly conductor's arm. The bus recedes into the darkness, spangled with lights.

Jean shivers slightly and remains standing at the bus-stop, beside a café terrace. A sour smell of absinthe fills the air, people are streaming past, paper-boys crying the evening news.

2

Cécile is standing at the window of the doctor's house at Buis, gazing out into the courtyard. Jean and Mme Pasquelin have just appeared in the gateway. On catching sight of them, Cécile steps back hastily, in a sudden access of shyness; they mustn't guess her eagerness. But she continues watching, at a little distance from the window. "He hasn't changed," she murmurs to herself as she sees Jean walking briskly up to the front door. He roves the house-front with his gaze, which comes to a sudden halt when it falls on the closed shutters of his father's bedroom.

Cécile runs out into the hall. Leaning against the banister, she listens in frozen stillness to the sound of hurried footfalls on the steps. Then Jean flings the door open and stops short. His face is very pale, there is no joy in the look he gives her, only intense anxiety.

CÉCILE: "He's upstairs—sleeping."

JEAN: "Ah, he's sleeping." The strained look leaves his face, and

, now he gazes fondly at Cécile, holding out his hand. Full of tender-ness, his eyes respond to the girl's timid smile of welcome.

MME PASQUELIN, opening the drawing-room door: "We'd better stay here for a bit since he's sleeping." Suddenly Jean thinks: The way they say "he"! Not "your father" or "the doctor." Remoteness. Yes, my father's dying. "Sit down, Jean. I've had the drawing-room opened again, and we always sit here so as not to disturb him when we talk. These last few nights I've slept in your poor grandmother's bedroom so as to be nearer, in case . . ." She has remained stand-ing. Now she casts an affectionate glance at the two young people. "Stay here, my dears, I'm going upstairs. I'll come and tell you, Jean, when your father wakes up." In the doorway she looks round and says to Jean, almost shyly: "Cécile's very pleased to see you again, I know."

Jean and Cécile are alone. There are some moments of silence and constraint. Cécile is gazing at the carpet, one hand resting on a low table, the other on her blouse, nervously toying with a needle she stuck in it without thinking, when she was at her sewing. Jean goes up to her and clasps her hand.

JEAN: "Ah, Cécile, it's a cruel price we're paying for the joy of being together again today."

Raising tear-dimmed eyes, she presses a finger to her lips. He mustn't speak; no words can express . . . Their shyness overrules emotion; each is wondering if this joy in their reunion doesn't fall short of their expectation. Jean leads her to the sofa. She sits there very straight, breathing rather quickly. He still holds her hand. Nei-ther moves. There is a long silence, tense with unspoken thoughts.

Jean hears footsteps overhead. I wonder how I'll find him. Greatly changed, no doubt. And he conjures up his father's face: the shrewd, incisive gaze, the lips imperious even when they kissed, the smile, self-confident and sometimes ironical, but how full of secret kindli-ness!

He looks at the drawing-room furniture, and everything evokes a memory of his childhood. That was the chair in which Grandma sat, the evening when . . . And now she's dead. Soon I'll be saying, "My father *used* to live here, *used* to sit in that chair." And some day others will be saying, "Jean Barois lived here; he *used* to . . ." He shivers.

In his musings he has forgotten the warm, vital presence beside him. Now, suddenly, the thought of her trust in him strikes through his sombre mood, quickening his pulses. He raises the moist, yielding hand he has been clasping to his lips, several times—almost reverently at first, pensively; then with growing ardour, and a surge of joyful emotion sweeps him off his balance.

Cécile raises her head, then gently lets it sink upon Jean's shoulder, her eyes closed in a happy daydream. Tenderly he seals the soft eyelids with a long kiss.

Footsteps; a door creaks. Cécile opens her eyes and moves away from Jean.

MME PASQUELIN: "Jean, your father's awake now."

The doctor's bedroom. Mme Pasquelin opens the door softly, then draws back. Jean pauses on the threshold for a moment, a moment of lacerating apprehension. Then, as he enters the room alone, an easing of the tension comes with the sight of his father's smile.

The sick man is propped on pillows, his arms stretched out; he has not changed greatly, though his breathing is terribly laboured. Still smiling, he watches Jean approach.

THE DOCTOR, in a hoarse whisper: "I'm in a bad way, as you see. In a very bad way, I fear." He moves his arm, and Jean, bending to kiss him, extends his hand. The doctor grasps it; then a shadow like a presage of death falls on his face, and passionately he draws his son's hand, his arm, his body, down towards the bed. "My son!" His voice breaks on a sob. Pressing the young man's head between his palms, he sees only the face of long ago, a child's. He strokes it feverishly, presses it with this side and that against his stubbly cheeks. "Ah!" With a short sigh he sinks back upon the pillows. He signs to Jean to wait, not to call for help; it will pass . . . Then, his eyes closed, his lips half parted, his fists clenched on his heart to quell its turmoil, he remains quite still.

Jean gazes intently at his father. With his grief mingles a curious perplexity. Why is it he looks so different? Because he's got so thin? No, it's something more. But what?

A little colour comes back to the sick man's cheeks; he opens his eyes. When he sees Jean his brows grow furrowed, his lips tighten. Then his features relax, and tears well up in his eyes.

THE DOCTOR: "My dear boy! My own dear son!"

The sight of his father's tears, the forlorn affection of his voice, make Jean strangely ill at ease. Is nothing left of the man his father was? Some minutes pass, and with them Jean's grief recedes; for life is stronger than death. Unsummoned, thoughts of Cécile have crossed his mind, a memory of the way she looked at him just now. And he feels an uprush of desire, no less compelling for its immateriality; the yearning for some ecstatic mingling of their souls, an interpenetration of their thoughts and dreams. And he still can feel on his lips that silken softness of her eyelids. A sudden zest for life courses through him, and with it a fretful impulse to escape this stagnant, thwarting atmosphere of death. But abruptly his mood changes, he feels his face reddening with shame.

The doctor wipes the tears off his cheeks, and his eyes settle on his son.

THE DOCTOR: "Tell me, Jean. They asked you to come, didn't they? ... Yes, yes, I know. .... Who was it? The doctor? No? ... Your godmother then?" Jean shakes his head evasively. The doctor's voice hardens; all sentiment has left it. "They were quite right. I haven't far to go. In fact I was expecting you." Overcome by emotion or, perhaps, to keep himself in countenance, Jean bends over the hand lying limply on the counterpane and presses his lips to it. The doctor withdraws his hand and uses it to raise himself onto his elbows; his look is earnest, he has something to say that cannot be postponed. "Yes, I was expecting you to come. Now, listen, my dear boy. I haven't much to leave you." Jean does not take his meaning

for a moment. Then he makes a protesting gesture. The sick man
slowly raises his head to show that he is getting tired, has more to
say, and must not be interrupted. He speaks in short phrases, his eyes
closed, as if reciting something learnt by rote. "I might have left you
more, but I somehow muddled things. Anyhow, you'll have enough
to live on. And an untarnished name, I hope; that's something."

"Now listen carefully. Cécile and you—you have—an understanding, haven't you?" Jean gives a slight start. The doctor smiles affectionately. "Yes, she told me about it. She's a dear girl and will make
you happy. I'm very glad. . . . And it's up to you, Jean, to make her
happy—so far as you can. It's not so easy. You'll see. We may try to
understand women, but it's beyond us, really. We must accept the
fact that they're different. Quite different from us. And that alone
makes it hard enough. Your mother—I feel I was much to blame."
A long silence. "Next—about your health, Jean. You know how it is
with you. And, of course, you didn't do your military service. That
was just to be on the safe side. Anyhow, you're completely cured;
you can take that from me. I assured your godmother there was
nothing to be feared now—and I meant it. Still, my dear boy, you'd
do well to think about your health now and again, and take care not
to overwork, especially later on when you are in your forties. That'll
always be your weak point. You'll promise me, won't you? Good."
He smiles contentedly. "Don't forget what I've been saying. That's
all." He lowers his head to the pillows and straightens out his
arms with a sigh of relief. But a moment later another thought
comes to him, and he opens his eyes again. "Your godmother has
been most kind to me, you know. She has done much, I can't tell
you how much, for me. She'll let you know, of course." However, he
cannot resist the temptation of announcing it himself. A smile comes
to his face; first a mere ghost of a smile that glimmers through the
veil of suffering; then gradually it develops, lighting up his eyes, his
forehead, the whole face—and there is something almost childish in
its happy plenitude. He beckons to Jean to come nearer, and Jean
bends over the bed. Putting his arm round Jean's neck, the doctor

draws Jean's head down near his lips. "Jean, hasn't your godmother told you anything? No? The Abbé came here yesterday." With the air of imparting a momentous secret. "I made my confession." He moves Jean's head a little back so as to savour the effect of this announcement on his face. Then again draws Jean's face near his. "I'd intended to receive the Sacrament today, but when I learnt that you were coming I postponed it. So tomorrow you and I, all of us together . . ." Jean straightens up; he tries to conjure up a look of pleased surprise, but has to turn away. A vague but poignant feeling of disappointment has come over him. The doctor is gazing straight in front of him, with a hint of fear in his eyes. "You know, my dear boy, people may say what they like, but"—he shakes his head—"that unknown quantity—it's a terrible thing to face."

Next day. The doctor's bedroom; a bleak, austere room on the second floor. The Communion service is over. Not wishing to betray her emotions, Mme Pasquelin is busy setting in order the chest of drawers, which has served as an altar. The sick man is sitting up, propped by pillows. The morning light streaming in through the window obliterates his features but harshly emphasizes the whites of his eyes. His head is drooping, his hair tousled, his beard unkempt; his cheeks are cadaverously sunken. Without the pince-nez his gaze is vacillating, but lit with a dim, almost childish rapture.

Cécile and Jean stand at the bedside. This morning their love oppresses them no longer; it has the tranquillity of something solid and perdurable. Each has the certitude of loving for the first—and the last—time.

There has been a remarkable change in the invalid's condition overnight. The strained look has left him and given place to one of infinite repose—which, welcome though it is, alarms them. The dying man's wandering gaze strays over them, lingers, and moves again, but they do not feel its impact. It glides indifferently by, as if it were focused across walls and window on the blue beyond. Then a forced smile—affectionate, yet what worlds away!—forms on the wasted face.

THE DOCTOR, in a toneless but quite clear voice: "So you're there, both of you, my dears. I'm glad, very glad. Give me your hands." The smile grows rigid, conventional. He seems to be playing a part, and in haste to get it over. Gathering their hands in his, he fondles them. Mme Pasquelin has halted at the foot of the bed, a new look on her face. The doctor gazes at her. "Don't you agree? Nothing could be better. Our two dear young people . . ."

Cécile bursts into tears and moves to her mother, who takes Jean's hand and draws him, too, beside her. Unmoving, linked together, they call to mind a statuary group.

The doctor's gaze hovers for a moment on Cécile and on her mother; then abruptly he fixes his eyes on Jean, with a look of unconcealed aversion, a keen flash of rancour, which quickly softens to one of harrowing entreaty; that too dies out almost at once. Jean has guessed the thought behind that look: You will go on living, while I . . .

A boundless compassion fills his heart; if only it were in his power to confer that new lease of life! Impulsively he moves away from the two women and bends over the livid face. But the dying man makes no movement. That mask of unperturbable aloofness has returned to his face, and some moments pass before he is conscious of Jean's kiss. Then with an effort he conjures up a fleeting smile, but his eyes betray no human feeling.

Jean turns and walks towards Cécile, his arms outstretched.

3

M. Jean Barois
Buis-la-Dame, Oise   Berne, June 25
Dear old chap: The sympathy I so naturally expressed in your be-reavement certainly did not deserve so kind and affectionate a letter

as the one that has just reached me. I thank you for it, dear Jean, from the bottom of my heart. I was particularly touched by the trust you show in me, when you ask my advice about the serious problem you mention in your letter, and I am glad to be able to give you an unequivocal answer.

Quite definitely I do not think that on religious grounds there is any obstacle whatever to your marriage with Mlle Pasquelin. I can see that the rather primitive nature of her faith and the excessive importance she attaches to religious observances have given you pause. But, frankly, I cannot understand you. Fundamentally religious emotion is always one and the same; there's little point in analysing the different forms it may assume. At a certain level, the highest, all aspirations towards God meet and are united, however different their starting points may be.

You say that if she knew your present feelings about religion, she would break off the engagement. That may well be so. But it would be owing to a mere error of judgment on her part.

So, in my opinion, it would be a great mistake to broach this subject with her. She would certainly fail to grasp the distinction you draw between conventional faith and the moral and human basis of the religious feeling. And, like the simple soul she is, she would be deeply shocked. You would merely be inviting catastrophe by any such ill-timed sincerity—quite uncalled-for as things stand. Thanks to your education and your logical mind, you have risen above the purely instinctive type of faith, and it's for you alone to make, in full awareness, this decision which concerns her happiness and yours, and to shoulder full responsibility.

And, really, there is so little for you to fear. You seem to forget how much she and you have in common: the same heredity, the same upbringing—fundamentals, these! Moreover, your own temperament is so intrinsically religious that you should never have any difficulty in keeping in harmony, indeed in sympathy, with the state of mind of your wife-to-be. She too will evolve, and thus the rift between you will gradually close, not widen.

I felt thoroughly convinced of this on reading your description of the Communion service at the death-bed of that noble man, your father. When you two were kneeling, side by side, each believed in something different; she in the Real Presence of Christ's body, you in the symbol of his superhuman love. Yet suddenly, in the same thrill of emotion, these different conceptions were lifted onto a higher plane in which they fused, became one, and your two souls were no longer separated. And thus it will be in your future life together.

Forgive me, my dear Jean, for the seeming presumption of giving you advice on so delicate a matter. But for so many years I have had the honour of being your confidant that I am in a position to gauge the depth of your feelings for Mlle Pasquelin, and their loyalty. It would be a grievous mistake if, in deference to any exaggerated scruple, you frustrated the happiness which both of you deserve.

With much affection and in all sincerity,

Yours,

H. S.

IV. THE CHAIN

▪▪

*Marriage is a danger only to the man
who has ideas.*

Herzog

I

Abbé Schertz
  Professor of Biological Chemistry
    The Catholic Institute
      Berne

My dear Hermann: You were quite right to reproach me with my long silence. But, happily, your letter shows that your affection has not been impaired by my remissness—and that, for me, is the chief thing.

First of all, I must thank you for the concern you show for my wife's health. I have been most anxious about it throughout the last two years; her accident had more serious consequences than I could have believed possible when I wrote to tell you of it. It led to all sorts of complications, and even after eighteen months' treatment she is still in very poor health; so much so that we may have to abandon any hope of ever having a child.

It has been a terrible ordeal for her and has badly shaken her morale.

But don't imagine I am trying to excuse the rarity of my letters on the strength of my domestic anxieties. Often and often I have settled down to write to you and abandoned the idea when I realized how far afield I had travelled from the religious convictions we used to share, and how difficult and distasteful would be the task of explaining this to you. Still, I feel I must bring myself to it, and we are both of us capable—don't you agree?—of keeping our friendship intact, whatever our differences of opinion.

My religious life falls into three distinct phases.

The first ended when I was seventeen and it dawned on me that there were anomalies in "revealed" religion; when I learnt that doubt was not the outcome of a perverted imagination, nor something one can dispel with a brisk shake of the head, but an obsession as compelling as truth itself. It is like a surgical syringe thrust deep into the heart of faith, draining its lifeblood away, drop by drop.

Then, when at twenty I made your acquaintance, I clung desperately to your broad-minded interpretation of Catholicism. You remember, my dear Hermann, how eagerly I grasped at the solutions you proposed to me? To you I owe some years of real peace of mind. And my marriage, to begin with, consolidated your work; those daily contacts with my wife's whole-hearted faith deepened my respect for religion under all its aspects. Your symbolistic interpretation provided exactly the compromise needed, and enabled me to live in close communion with an orthodoxy at whose cast-iron dogmas my intellect persistently balked.

But this peace was only superficial. Beneath the surface a ferment of resistance was developing. Still, even now I cannot see clearly what it was that made the old doubts surge up again.

Of course the position we took up could not be durable. Those symbolistic interpretations are based on far from solid ground and provide only a temporary halting place. By dint of stripping Catholic tradition of all that is no longer acceptable to the modern mind, we soon reduce it to nothingness. Once you admit that the literal meaning of the articles of faith can be discarded—and can a really thoughtful mind do otherwise than discard it?—you open the door to every variety of mental independence: free inquiry and, in the long run, free-thinking.

Surely you too have realized this? I can't conceive that you can still be satisfied, morally or intellectually, by a compromise so arbitrary and so vulnerable. It's a mere playing on the natural meanings of words; a subterfuge. Your link between the present and the past was too precarious; how can a man stop half-way on the road to freedom? To seek to retain the Catholic religion for the sake of its sentimental appeal and the time-proved social values it stands for is the conduct not of a believer but of a dilettante with a taste for folklore! Far be it from me to deny the historical importance of Christianity; but, if we are to be honest with ourselves, we must own that nothing vital can any longer be extracted from its doctrines—by those, anyhow, who refuse to allow their intellect to be befogged.

Thus I soon discovered that the faith of my childhood—a faith "bred in the bone" in my case—which I had so long regarded as the mainstay of my life, had gradually receded from me. And it is one of the many blessings I owe to your influence on the course of my mental development that, thanks to you, my transition to absolute denial was not so painful as it might have been. Yes, it is to you I owe it that now at last I can analyse so dispassionately those extinct dogmas which meant so much to me in my early life.

But I must allow also for the influence that my present duties at Wenceslas College have had, if indirectly, on the readjustment of my belief. This may seem paradoxical, considering that the College is under clerical control. However, the professors are selected by the University, the teaching is, on the whole, remarkably free, and the lecture courses I give are not subjected to any sort of censorship.

When I put in for this professorial post I had only the vaguest notion of the difficulties ahead. For one thing, I had little or no experience of public speaking. But from the very first lecture I felt a ripple of attention—you must know what I mean; it's unmistakable—pass through the group of students attending my course.

This is the second year, and their interest shows no sign of flagging. I give them all my time and—I can honestly say it—the best of myself. Whatever my daily research work and my private meditations bring me goes into my lectures. I want all the young people who attend them to get from their brief contact with myself something more than a mere smattering of scientific fact. My great hope is to raise their moral level, to uplift their personalities, and to leave a permanent imprint on these young minds that are so malleable.

And I really believe that I am getting results not unworthy of the tremendous effort I am putting forth.

So you see my post isn't quite what you seem to think, when you ask me if my duties leave me time to work on my own account. For me it's not in the least a "job" to be done; it is the greatest joy of my life and a consolation for my troubles. (I prefer to say little of the rift that my emancipation has created in my married life, but you can easily guess that I am not spared afflictions of this order.)

So there, my dear Hermann, you have my present existence. And yours—how goes it with you? I greatly hope that I have not distressed you by unburdening myself so frankly in this letter. After all, I have only given practical application to a passage in St Luke that you know well: "And no man putteth new wine into old bottles; else the new wine will burst the bottles. . . . But new wine must be put into new bottles; and both are preserved."

With very affectionate greetings,

Yours as ever,

Jean Barois

M. Jean Barois
  Professor of Natural Science
  Wenceslas College, Paris

My very dear Jean: I can hardly tell you how amazed I was by your letter, and how profoundly distressed. What suffering you must have gone through before coming to your present state!

But I have not lost faith in your discernment and I believe that some day or other you will come back to a less extremist view. I grant that for men like us, who have no longer the simple faith of earlier days, only two ways lie open: either that of a moral anarchy, unguided by any rules or restrictions whatsoever; or that of a symbolistic interpretation, which reconciles tradition and the modern mind and enables them to abide by and in that noble institution, the Catholic Church. Our religion is the only organization which offers the ideals you and I stand for their full scope, and the only one to

confer objective validity on the moral law in which we both believe.
No branch of science, no philosophy, can provide any satisfactory
argument enforcing the idea, for instance, of duty. But religion *does*
provide such arguments.

Why, then, kick against the pricks and try to break loose from any
form of authority?

Like you, I refuse to believe blindly—but is that any reason to reject Catholicism altogether? Was it not Renan himself who advised
us "to retain all that part of Christianity which a man can endorse
without believing in the supernatural?"

Reading your letter, I much regretted that your friend Abbé Joziers
is now abroad on missionary work. This is, I feel, a great loss for
you. I know how narrowly orthodox his views are, but he would
have realized the critical phase you are going through, and affection
would have prompted him to come to your aid in an effective way.

I too, my very dear friend, would like to come to your aid, as I
did once before, and I hope you will not spurn my helping hand. In
this hope, and with unchanged affection, I am,

As ever yours,

Hermann Schertz

P.S. Your quotation from the Gospel of St Luke was incomplete;
you omitted the last and all-important verse: "No man also having
drunk old wine straightway drinketh new: for he saith, The old is
better."

Abbé Schertz
　　Professor of Biological Chemistry
　　　　The Catholic Institute
　　　　　　Berne

My dear Hermann: You liken my emancipation to the conduct of a
small boy in revolt against an irksome disciplinarian. But, though I
admit that since my marriage I have come into more direct and frequent contact with the exigencies of strict Catholicism, I can honestly assure you that I was not swayed by any personal emotion

when I resolved to discard for good such remnants of Catholicism as lingered on in my mentality.

You are hoodwinking yourself, I fear, when you interpret on lines that make it palatable to you personally a religion which has given clean-cut definitions of its tenets, and expressly condemns any interpretation such as you propose. For, nothing if not logical, and shrewdly strict in its prohibitions, the Church has never failed to banish from the fold in which you claim a place such lukewarm believers as we were, you and I—and you still are.

The assured tone of your letter justifies me in reminding you of some phrases in the *Dei Filius* ordinance of the 1870 Vatican Council, which seem to me to fit your case. They run thus:

"If any man does not accept as sacred and canonical in their entirety and in all their parts the Books of the Scriptures (as enumerated by the Council of Trent), or denies that they were divinely inspired: let him be anathema.

"If any man declare that miracles cannot take place and therefore all accounts of miracles, even those in the Holy Scriptures, should be accounted myths or fables; or that miracles can never be positively verified and the origin of the Christian religion is not validly demonstrated by them: let him be anathema.

"If any man say that circumstances may arise under which, in view of the progress of science, he may be led to assign to the dogmas of the Church a meaning other than that which the Church has assigned and now assigns to them: let him be anathema."

And, lastly, this passage, which is clear as crystal:

"For the doctrine of the true faith revealed by God was not bestowed as a philosophical instrument for the betterment of the human intellect, but has been committed, as a divine endowment, to the Bride of Christ, that the Church may be faithfully guarded and taught infallibly. Wherefore it behooves us ever to conserve the meanings which our Holy Mother Church has assigned, once for all, to the sacred dogmas, and never to deviate from them at the behest of an intelligence claiming to be superior to them."

Thus inexorably, my dear Hermann, the Church excludes us from her pen. Why, then, prompted by some sentimental affection (un-reciprocated, to all intents and purposes), cling to that aged foster-mother, who has no further use for us and regards the efforts we make to stand by her as so many crimes! You'll find out one day that you have made only half your progress towards the light, and boldly, swiftly, you will take the few remaining steps.

Then you will find me waiting for you, outside the pen, in the clear light of day.

Your ever affectionate friend,

J. B.

2

A bedroom. The dawn is rising. Opening his eyes, Jean blinks at the strip of light between the curtains.

JEAN, sleepily: "What's the time?"

CÉCILE, in a clear, composed voice: "Half-past six."

JEAN: "Only half-past six! Did you sleep badly?"

CÉCILE: "No, darling." He smiles vaguely by way of answer and settles down into the bed. "It's Saturday. You've no lecture this morning, have you?"

JEAN: "No."

CÉCILE, affectionately: "Darling, there's something I want to ask you."

JEAN: "Yes? Ask away."

A short silence. She nestles up to him, as in the past, presses her face against his shoulder, and remains thus, without moving.

CÉCILE: "Listen . . ."

JEAN: "Well . . . ?"

CÉCILE: "Please promise not to be angry. Don't get in one of your cruel moods."

Jean props himself on his elbow and gazes at her fretfully. Only too well he knows that obstinate look in her eyes, masked though it is by tenderness.

JEAN: "Well, what is it now?"

CÉCILE: "Oh, if that's how you feel—"

JEAN: "What do you know about how I feel? Tell me what you want. Out with it!"

CÉCILE: "You can't refuse me this."

JEAN: "But what is it?"

CÉCILE: "Well—I'm doing a novena. You know that, don't you?"

JEAN, gloomily: "No."

CÉCILE, taken aback: "What? You didn't know it?"

JEAN: "You never told me."

CÉCILE: "But you must have noticed, surely?"

JEAN, icily: "A novena. I see. What's it for? Ah, yes, I understand. To have a baby. So you've come to that!"

CÉCILE, with sudden passion, bringing her face close to his: "Oh, please, darling, don't say anything more, don't try to stop me. You see, I'm positive my prayers will be heard. Only, I'd like you too . . . Really, I'm not asking very much of you; only to come with me this evening to Notre Dame des Victoires. It's the last day, the ninth, of my special intercession, and . . ." She moves away a little and looks at Jean, who shakes his head sadly.

JEAN, gently: "You know quite well—"

CÉCILE, putting her fever-hot hand on his lips: "No, no! Don't say any more."

JEAN: "—that it's out of the question."

CÉCILE, losing self-control: "Can't you keep quiet? Don't say anything yet." She presses herself to him. "Surely you can't refuse me *that?* I'm asking so little, and think what it would mean to us, to you and me, to have a child. All I ask is for you to come to church with me; you needn't say a word, or do anything at all. So there's no need to answer. Of course you'll come."

JEAN, frigidly: "No. I can't do that." A short silence. Cécile is weeping. Jean turns on her irritably. "Oh, for goodness' sake, stop crying; tears won't help." She tries to restrain her tears. Jean holds her wrists. "But can't you understand what you want to make me do? Are you so blind that you can't see the—the *ugliness* of what you're proposing?"

CÉCILE, in a choked voice: "But what can it matter to you? Oh, Jean, won't you—just to please me?"

JEAN: "Do try to think seriously for just a moment. You must know quite well that I don't believe those prayers and candles and all the rest of it are the slightest use. Do you want to coerce me into acting a part, playing the hypocrite?"

CÉCILE, sobbing: "But what harm can it do you? You'd only be doing it to please me."

JEAN: "How could you suppose that I'd agree? Surely you can realize that, in asking me to do a thing like this—after all the painful discussions we've had on these subjects—you're—you're simply lowering us, both of us, by the mere suggestion?"

CÉCILE, whimpering: "Just to please me, darling."

JEAN, roughly: "No!" Cécile gazes at him with distraught eyes. Neither speaks for some moments. "I've explained it to you dozens of times. What's best, what's cleanest, in me is precisely this honest doubt of mine. It's just because I attach so much importance to all professions of faith that I can't make a dishonest show of one to please you. But of course it's no good; you'll never understand the first thing about my feelings on the matter."

CÉCILE, impulsively: "But, Jean, at that time there won't be a soul in church who knows you."

For a moment Jean fails to grasp her meaning and stares at her in bewilderment. Then a look of keen distress crosses his face.

JEAN: "So you, of all people, think an argument like that can weigh with me!" They remain lying side by side, feeling the warmth of each other's nearness, yet utterly remote in thought, estranged. "Do, please, try to understand. This nine days' devotion of yours is your affair; I'm not trying to prevent it, I only refuse to take part in it. Surely I have a right to do that."

CÉCILE, obstinately: "You're always talking about your rights; why not talk about your duties for a change? You have a duty towards me. No, it's no good my trying to explain; nothing would make you understand. But you absolutely *must* come to church with me this evening or—it's all no use."

JEAN: "Really, my dear, that's sheer nonsense. If you drag me there against my will, whom do you suppose you'll be deceiving?"

CÉCILE: "Jean, I implore you, do please come with me this evening."

JEAN, springing out of the bed: "No, I won't! I *will not!* I don't meddle with your beliefs, and you might leave me free to act according to mine."

CÉCILE, with a cry of protest: "Oh! But—but it's not the same thing at all!"

JEAN, gazing down at Cécile, who is sobbing passionately: " 'It's not the same thing!' Yes, that's the source of all our troubles. Never will you bring yourself to respect what you do not understand." He raises his hand. "Anyhow, you can do me the justice of admitting that I never tried to shake your faith by any word I've said. But really, my dear Cécile, there are moments when you make me so angry that I wish you could feel a twinge of doubt one day—just enough to make you a bit less cocksure, less inclined to lay down the law, because you think *your* truth is absolute, infallible!"

His eyes fall on a cheval-glass and he catches sight of his reflected self: barefooted, tousle-headed, hurling denunciations at the tumbled bed. As much disgusted with himself as with Cécile, he flings out of the bedroom, slamming the door.

Jean is alone in his study. Notes are scattered about the desk at which he is sitting. He writes a full page without looking up, then petulantly drops his pen. Try as he may, he cannot settle down to his work; the ideas keep floating away, just out of reach.

It's ridiculous, he thinks. But this morning I can't get down to it at all. And all because of that ridiculous business about the novena— that nine days' wonder! Thrusting aside his notes, he ponders for some moments. No, it would be too damn silly! All the future hangs on incidents like these; I must keep my freedom of action, that's essential. And if I give in today, tomorrow there'll be something else. Out of the question.

He rises to his feet, his nerves on edge, walks to the window, and, folding his arms, gazes vaguely at the rain-blurred sky. But what can she expect to gain by her precious novena? Does she seriously think that her prayers will have some sort of action on God's will? It's all too childish for words! Really, her brand of faith would be worthier of Abbé Joziers' savages. That nine-days' intercession, that mystic number nine! I suppose she's got hold of some formulary for the use of barren women. Fantastic!

He shrugs his shoulders, goes to the bookcase, and seems to be searching for some book. "To thine own self be true." Women don't understand that kind of loyalty. "But what harm can it do you? Just to please me, darling." Self-respect, personal dignity mean nothing to them.

Taking out a book at random, he goes back to his chair.

Luncheon time. Jean takes his seat at the table by himself. He thinks: She'll stay in her room, sulking. She hopes I'll let myself be worked on by her childish antics. In a sudden burst of anger: Oh, damn it, things can't go on like this!

Cécile enters. At the sound of the opening door Jean looks up. He sees a pathetic little face, tear-stained, haggard, leaden-hued. And all his resentment is effaced by an uprush of pity, the pity one feels for a child who has done wrong and is wholly irresponsible; a vast compassion welling up from the depths of his instinctive self, almost a resurrection—but how pallid, joyless!—of the dead love of earlier days.

Quietly, without the least hint of play-acting, she sits down at her usual place. When the maid comes in, she murmurs something about a violent headache. She forces herself to make a show of eating. Long silences.

Jean steals glances at her; observes the clean-cut, wilful curves of the bowed forehead; the swollen eyelids, dry and red; the puffy lips and mouth cruelly disfigured by suffering. And what he sees appals him. I'm torturing her. Whether rightly or wrongly matters little. She is suffering because of me, and it's abominable. Oh, what's the use of trying to make her understand? All I'll ever do is to hurt her. It would be better to give in than to go on torturing her—to no end. After all, what is she asking of me? Little more than what I've often done this summer, when I went with her to Mass on Sundays. So much the worse for her if she can't see the silliness, the ugliness, of what she wants to force me into doing now. No, there's no point in holding out; let her have her way.

A marvellous feeling of relief comes over him, now he has made this decision. There is an almost sensual pleasure in escaping from his egoism, proving himself the better of the pair, the one who understands, forgives—and yields. His eyes grow gentle as he gazes at her. She is eating her meal, like a docile child, without raising her eyes from the plate.

She looks pretty like that, across her tears. But really it's a rotten thing to do, to make a woman cry. Father used to say, "Women are different, and we're much too apt to forget this." He was right. All that comes of treating them like equals is needless suffering. What's happened to Cécile and myself proves how right he was. We must avoid all that makes for estrangement and try our best to cultivate what draws us together. Yes, but for that to be feasible, one would need to be *still* in love.

He rises. Cécile has been waiting, aloof, her eyes fixed on the tablecloth. He thinks: She'll hurry back to her room. I'll follow and tell her that I consent. But, as usual, Cécile goes to Jean's study, where the coffee awaits them. She stands beside the tray, her arms limply drooping.

Jean goes towards her. It has cost him a great struggle with himself; he has had to trample underfoot something of his self-respect, his conscience, and perhaps his future. But he is counting on the coming joy. She will fling herself on his breast, smiling through tears; he will be repaid by the sudden light of gratitude in her eyes.

Bending towards her, he puts his arm round her waist. She accepts the contact passively.

JEAN, with a slight tremor in his voice: "Listen! It's all right; I'll come with you this evening, wherever you want. If only you'll not cry any more."

She frees herself and thrusts him roughly away.

CÉCILE: "Ah, I can feel it; I know you will always, *always,* be my enemy." He stares at her, dumbfounded. "I know too that we shall have to separate one day—in a year's time, in ten years' time, there's no telling. But one day we shall part. It's inevitable. And then how I shall hate you!" She bursts into tears. "Even now I—loathe you." She stretches out her arms uncertainly, as if about to fall; then she steadies herself on the table's edge.

JEAN, glumly: "Very well. I only wished to give you pleasure."

She looks up, as if awaking from a nightmare; the anger leaves her face, and she clutches Jean's arm.

CÉCILE, in an uncertain voice: "Ah, yes. About this evening? That's so, it's very sweet of you." She bends hastily and kisses his hand. "Thank you, darling."

Pressing her handkerchief to her lips, she walks away slowly, dejectedly; in the doorway she tries to give him a smile. Completely baffled, Jean stares at the door which has just closed behind her, then gives himself a shake, walks to the window, flings it open, and, though rain is falling, puts his head outside, like a man who has urgent need of fresh air.

Notre Dame des Victoires. 8 P.M. The church is like a mausoleum; the massed tapers dazzle but shed no light. Here nightly come, from every part of Paris, those whose courage has failed them in their need, those whose hopes were dupes but will not die, and join their prayers in shadows pungent with fumes of burning wax.

Cécile is kneeling, Jean standing; both are bowed beneath the burden of the irremediable.

Later that night, when Jean is sitting in his study, relishing his solitude, the door opens and Cécile tiptoes in, barefooted.

CÉCILE: "Aren't you coming to bed?" Shyly. "Angry with me?" She has a timid, would-be ingratiating smile, like a scolded child's. Disarmed by such guilelessness, Jean cannot help smiling in return. She is in her nightdress. Not a trace of tears remains, and with her hair let down for the night, a big black bow holding it behind, she looks no more than fifteen, the slender little girl he loved at Buis. "I couldn't bear to sleep all by myself tonight—after a day like today. I want so much to feel that all's forgotten—and forgiven." Jean is tired of words; he gently kisses the cheek that coaxingly she bends towards him. This evening, more than ever, he feels an old, old man. "You can't think how cold it is in my room. . . . But I won't keep you from your work, darling. I'll wait for you. You'll let me stay on your knee, won't you? I promise not to fidget."

She nestles against him, fondly yielding. Jean, who has his arm round her, can feel the supple warmth of her young body. Her slippers have dropped off, and he takes the small cold feet in his hands to warm them.

CÉCILE: "You see, I'm simply freezing!"

There is an almost wanton challenge in her laugh. She lets her head sink back, still laughing. Their eyes meet for a moment, and Jean notices with slight surprise a glint of smiling satisfaction between the half-closed eyelids. And then it dawns on him. Obviously. It's the ninth night. So that too was in the programme! But he is not in the least annoyed and continues holding her in his arms.

He has glimpsed the utmost depth of human folly, and he now feels incredibly remote from Cécile, a dweller on another planet. "Women are different . . . ! "

3

Some pages torn from a notebook lie hidden under other papers in a drawer of Jean's writing-desk. They are covered with notes, dashed down in rapid, incisive script:

Women: inferior beings, irremediably.

Like a worm in a fruit, sentimentality at its most virulent is lodged in them, and gnaws at their hearts, disintegrating all.

Women love mystery, with an instinctive, argument-proof adoration. The trouble is, they adore it at the lowest level.

If at night they are afraid of burglars, a night light burning at the bedside reassures them. They need religious belief to make them feel safe, and to soothe the qualms they otherwise might feel about a future state. The idea of asking for "proof" never crosses their minds.

A man should not marry until he has definitely marked out his path in life, has made some headway along it, and is sure of not swerving from it. To change its direction after marriage plays havoc with two lives, not merely one; between two people pledged to live together, it creates a gulf in which all happiness founders—beyond hope of rescue.

4

A year later. The small drawing-room at Mme Pasquelin's house. Jean and Cécile have just arrived for a few days' stay. It is Easter Monday; the hour is noon. Abbé Joziers, who returned from Madagascar two months previously, has come to lunch.

MME PASQUELIN: "Come near the fire. What a disappointing day it's been! It looked so fine when I got up."

The sky has suddenly darkened; hail is drumming on the panes.

THE ABBÉ, standing at the window: "Oh, it's only a squall; it won't last long." He gazes at Jean. "But how my dear young friend has changed in the last five years!"

JEAN, smiling: "Well, how about yourself? You've changed almost beyond recognition. You're so much thinner, for one thing; your cheeks are yellow, and—"

THE ABBÉ, laughing: "Thanks!"

MME PASQUELIN: "Yet he's looking ever so much fitter than he did a month ago. He'd have died amongst his blackamoors if I hadn't got the Bishop to order him back peremptorily."

THE ABBÉ, to Jean: "Yes, my dear boy, that's so. I all but left my bones there. But then our Heavenly Father, warned no doubt by Madame Pasquelin, thought better of it. I imagine Him saying to Himself: 'We've still some work down on earth for that old servant of ours. So back he goes to France!' "

JEAN, gravely: "The first thing, sir, is to repair the damage."

THE ABBÉ: "Bless you, that's been done already. I'm sound in wind and limb." He thumps his chest. "Nothing wrong there, I think. Do you know, the day before yesterday I walked all the way to Saint-Cyr, and felt none the worse for it. Today I intend to walk to Beaumont and look up my friend the curé. So you see there's no need for me to cosset myself." He has been observing Jean as he talks. "Yes, how you have changed!"

JEAN: "So much as that?"

THE ABBÉ: "Well, there's the moustache, for one thing. And then— I can't give a name to it, but there's a great difference in your look, in the whole face, I should say."

MME PASQUELIN, in an aside to Cécile: "And what about you? How are you feeling?"

CÉCILE: "Oh, much as usual."

MME PASQUELIN: "And—there's still nothing?"

CÉCILE, with tears in her eyes: "No."

A short silence.

MME PASQUELIN, lowering her voice still more and glancing at Jean, who is talking to the priest: "And—he?"

Cécile shakes her head and sighs.

Luncheon is over.

THE ABBÉ, going to the window: "Good, it's cleared up. I'd better make a move. As I said, I'm going to Beaumont Vicarage. How about coming a bit of the way with me, Jean?"

JEAN: "With pleasure."

It is a blowy April day. The puddles left by the hailstorm are drying rapidly under a brisk west wind. On the house fronts, bathed in clean, pale light, the wooden shutters, scoured by the hail, make patches of dazzling whiteness.

JEAN: "Shall we take the short cut through the graveyard?"

THE ABBÉ: "Yes." He links his arm in Jean's. "I've much enjoyed this luncheon. Do you know, I was beginning to fear from the tone of your letters, and from what Cécile's mother left unsaid, that all was not *quite* well with you." As in the past, he stresses certain words. "But *now* I see that you are happy, *both of you,* as of course you deserve to be."

Jean gives him a smile, which the Abbé interprets as an assent to his last remark. They take some steps in silence.

JEAN, with a faintly ironical laugh: " 'Happy,' you said. Well, no, I should hardly call it happiness."

The Abbé gives a slight start and halts.

THE ABBÉ: "Surely you don't mean that seriously?"

JEAN, with a wry smile: "Isn't it better to take it with a laugh? What can't be mended . . ."

THE ABBÉ, amazed and somewhat shocked: "Really, my dear Jean!"

JEAN, shrugging his shoulders: "It's too stupid for words, the story of our married life."

THE ABBÉ: "You cut me to the heart, Jean."

JEAN: "I'm sorry—but that's how it is. A deadlock."

THE ABBÉ: "A deadlock! But surely you love each other?"

JEAN, gloomily: "I wonder—"

The footpath narrows and the Abbé moves in front, without answering. As they pass the crucifix he crosses himself. They take a short cut through the graveyard, along paths overgrown with grass. A wicket-gate gives on the open country, and they step forth upon a highroad flanked on one side by telegraph poles, their black recession linked as far as eye can reach by sagging strands of wire. The limpid sunlight of a day in early spring plays on stubble-fields and sodden ploughland. Traversed by silver streaks, grassy meadows slope down towards the Oise, whose banks are still covered by recent floods. Sheltered from the wind, the broad expanse of water mirrors the cloudless pearly grey sky, and willows, submerged to the chin, lift their tousled black heads above the shining surface.

The Abbé comes beside Jean, who is gazing at the countryside. A moment later their eyes meet, the priest's troubled and dark with mute reproof.

JEAN: "Oh, I know that it's my fault. I tried to make good, when I was twenty-two, a boyish dream I had when I was sixteen. And of course it didn't work."

THE ABBÉ: "On the contrary. That affection of your boyhood—"

JEAN, cutting in bitterly: "Excuse me, I know what I'm talking about—only too well. I've had time and opportunity to observe the process working itself out."

The Abbé makes no comment and starts walking again. He is taken aback by the confidence of Jean's tone, that of a man in full maturity. And, guessing this, Jean takes a malicious pleasure in his dismay. The keen air, the sunlight, this country walk, are going to his head, and he lets his tongue run away with him.

JEAN: "A boy of sixteen, you know, has such wildly romantic ideas of love. He indulges in a splendid dream, so remote from all the possibilities of real life that there's not the least chance of his finding anything in the world to match it. So he proceeds to build up a dream figure with the materials ready to his hand; and that's easy enough. He takes any girl who comes his way and invests her with the glamour of his ideal. Of course he's careful not to try to discover what sort of person she really is. No, he enshrines her like an idol in the closed circle of his imagination, he endows her with all the qualities of a Golden Girl. Then, after prudently blindfolding himself, he kneels down before her." He laughs.

THE ABBÉ: "But, my dear Jean, I can—I can hardly believe my ears!"

JEAN: "The spell works slowly but surely. Time passes, but the veil remains over his eyes. And then, one fine day, to prove his gratitude for her embodiment of his dream girl, as they call it, he marries a young person about whom he literally knows nothing, a complete stranger." He pauses. "So, now that he has blundered into —into pledging his whole life to her . . ." He stops and looks the priest in the eyes. "I wonder do you realize what that means: to pledge one's whole life." The priest looks down. "Yes, now that he settles down to live with the girl he has chosen, and whom he intends to love—not in make-believe but in sober earnest—he discovers, too late, that he and she have nothing, *nothing,* in common. She's a stranger; maybe an enemy. And the result, as I said, is deadlock."

THE ABBÉ: " 'A stranger.' Oh, come now! It's no use your talking like that. You two were brought up together."

JEAN: "Yes, and we knew less of each other than young people whose marriage has been fixed up by their parents and who have never met before. Because, in these cases, they devote the months of their engagement to feverish attempts to understand each other and straighten out their problems. That's how it always is in 'arranged' marriages. Whereas we, Cécile and I, never gave a thought to this; we supposed it had all been done in advance."

THE ABBÉ: "Still, to begin with, judging by the first letters you wrote me . . ."

JEAN: "To begin with—yes. But it didn't take me long to discover that we were very different, though I admit that didn't disturb me in the least at first."

THE ABBÉ: "Yes? And then?"

JEAN: "Ah, if you understood the rapture that possesses one in that early phase; it blinds your eyes to everything! I was so desperately keen on attaining that perfect happiness which I'd seen so many other people vainly trying to attain that I really expected my married life would be the exception that proves the rule. And, anyhow, I'd made up my mind to think it perfect.

"Then, too, in the first months of a marriage, everything runs so smoothly for the man. It's child's play for him to establish an influence over his wife. But let him make haste to establish it securely! Even the simplest of women has amazing intuition, and she very soon becomes conscious of her power. With the result that she soon regains all the territory you think you've won. Yes, those first months are quite misleading; a woman has an unconscious genius for remembering and repeating. She holds up a mirror at which— why not admit it?—you look with pleasure. Until the day when you discover that what she's showing you is a mere reflection—of yourself; and already paling, tarnished, fading out."

THE ABBÉ: "Yet, unless I'm much mistaken, you were deeply in love with her?"

JEAN: "I doubt it. I was in love with love, that's all."

THE ABBÉ: "She, anyhow, *she* truly loved you." Jean says nothing. "She loved you and she loves you still. I could see it plainly in the way she looked at you and smiled, just now at Madame Pasquelin's."

JEAN: "You were mistaken. What you saw was a piece of play-acting. We were keeping up appearances." Wearily. "A truce we had agreed on for our stay here, that's all."

THE ABBÉ: "She loved you, Jean. I'm positive of that."

JEAN, shrugging his shoulders: "Yes, no doubt. In her fashion. It was a decorous little passion that for years she nursed in solitude, with the kind permission of her mother and confessor. One of those poetic loves, too ethereal to be quite human."

THE ABBÉ: "Really, Jean!"

JEAN: "Let me have my say; I'm speaking frankly. Well, I don't deny she loved me in that way, but a love like that isn't strong enough to work a miracle. And nothing short of a miracle, I assure you, would be needed to unite our lives."

THE ABBÉ: "But she was so young . . ."

JEAN, with a faint laugh: "Ah, yes, that's so. 'She was so young.'" He takes some steps, then swings excitedly round on the priest. "And that's precisely what I told myself. She's little more than a child, I thought. What I dislike in her will pass in the course of time. Fool that I was! It's quite true that Cécile had the mentality of a sixteen-

year-old girl who imagines she knows everything about the world—
when her whole experience of life, all she has to go on, consists of
gobbets of information she's picked up on Sundays at her Bible
Class."

THE ABBÉ: "Jean!"

JEAN, his voice rough with anger and hostility: "But what I did
not foresee was that this half-baked state was as far as she ever could
develop, her dead-end. So now you know how things are with us."
Jean has stopped walking and assumed a combative attitude, his legs
planted well apart, his breast heaving, head flung back, eyes hard as
flint; his arms are level with his chest, his hands outspread, palms
upward, as though he were testing the weight of some invisible object. "And how proud she was of her little stock of knowledge! Of
course the sources from which she gleaned it were infallible: ser-
mons, conversations with pious small-town worthies, or those books
concocted for the use of Christian girlhood, books packed with
theories none of which has the least bearing on the realities of the
life before them."

The Abbé takes a step forward, places his hand on Jean's arm,
and looks him in the eyes.

THE ABBÉ: "Jean, my dear Jean! You wouldn't speak that way if
you hadn't changed . . . out of recognition." He lowers his voice.
"Am I right in assuming that you're no longer a practising Catholic?"

JEAN, affectionately but composedly: "Yes, you are right."

THE ABBÉ, sadly: "Ah, I now understand *everything*."

The road rises, the spire of Beaumont church comes into view.
The priest quickens his steps, as though wishing to be alone. As
one behind the other they reach the summit of the plateau, they are
greeted by a gentle breeze coming from very far away. The telegraph wires are humming overhead. The hamlet of Beaumont consists of a few cottages dotted about the countryside. The church is
some hundred yards off, guarded by the sentinel pines of the priest's
garden.

Jean sits down on a heap of stones on the roadside, letting the

Abbé go ahead. The sun warms his back, while the cool breeze fans his cheeks. Small dry leaves blow past his feet with a light silken rustle. In front of him stretches the plain.

The shadows are lengthening. Across the stripped crests of the elms, beyond the curtain of a row of poplars, white house fronts and blue roofs sparkle in the level light. Hardly anyone is about. Jean can hear a creak of wheels ploughing through the mud of a sunken road, but the cart itself is invisible. Etched upon the horizon, a grey horse and a bay are drawing a plough across a gently undulating expanse of stubble, the soft brown clods rising soundlessly beside the gleaming share. A belated puddle shines amongst the tree-trunks, where, overhead, abandoned nests crouch like big black spiders in their web of leafless boughs. The ploughman has reached the end of the field; slowly he swings his horses round and starts a new furrow. The grey horse, now coming towards Jean, conceals both the plough and the bay horse, and seems to be advancing by itself.

The wind drops. The creak of cart-wheels has died away. The dead leaves cease rustling. All is still.

The Abbé returns; his head is bowed. Jean gets up and walks towards him. The priest extends both hands, his eyes dim with tears. They go down the hill in silence, the Abbé with his eyes fixed on the ground before his feet.

JEAN, gently: "My dear Abbé, I'm afraid this has been very distressing to you. But sooner or later I had to let you know the truth." The Abbé makes a vague, sad gesture of assent. "I know what believers usually say in such cases: 'You have discarded religion because it prevents you from doing as you like.' But that's not true of me. I've struggled for years; you witnessed my struggles to keep my faith. But now it's over. I have squared up accounts with myself. No doubt it had to be."

The priest turns his head and gazes at Jean curiously, as if trying to discern the new man he has become.

THE ABBÉ, sorrowfully: "To think that *you*, Jean, should have come to this! You, who seemed so true a Christian, so certain to keep to the right road!"

JEAN: "Still, you shouldn't be too hard on me. In the last analysis, it's not the fact of believing or disbelieving that matters; no, what's all important is the way in which one believes or in which one disbelieves."

THE ABBÉ: "But, tell me, *how* did this come about?"

JEAN: "I can't explain. There's no denying that I once was a believer, and now all that is so remote I can't even picture what it means to be one. There are currents of ideas, I suppose, that draw you with them—unescapably. And of course it depends on temperaments. Some men are more inclined than others to make do with ready-made formulas. Like the hermit crab who creeps into the first vacant shell he comes across and shapes himself to fit it. Whereas others prefer to make their own shells."

THE ABBÉ, gloomily: "It's your scientific studies that have warped your mind. That bane of scientific arrogance—ah, how many victims it has claimed! When a man directs his gaze wholly on the world of matter, he develops a sort of blindness to all else; his sense of the supernatural world becomes atrophied, and it's only a short step to disbelief."

JEAN: "I'm inclined to agree. When one practises scientific methods of research, day in, day out, and once one has ascertained time and again how apt they are for the discovery of truth—how refrain from applying them to the problems of religion?" Regretfully. "Am I to blame if religious faith won't stand up to serious critical analysis?"

THE ABBÉ: "So it's your view that the only way to understand is through the intellect? Critical analysis, *logic?* But isn't it precisely by means of logic that theologians demonstrate God's existence and the truth of revealed religion?"

JEAN, quietly: "Perhaps. Yet logic can rebut them too."

THE ABBÉ: "But when it's proved to my satisfaction that the intellect, *unaided,* would be incapable of grasping in its entirety the mystery behind the dogmas of the Church, the qualities of the soul, and the Christian solution of the problem of human destiny—well, differing from you, I see in this a convincing proof of that supramundane Authority which has *revealed* the truth to us." Jean makes no comment, and the Abbé continues, after a pause: "Then, again, can you name a single *fully established* scientific fact that is in *real* conflict with any of our dogmas? For instance, has your science proved to you that God does not exist?"

JEAN, forcing himself to answer: "Well—not quite that."

THE ABBÉ: "Ah!"

JEAN: "Science contents itself with proving that everything takes place in the universe exactly as if your personal God had no existence."

THE ABBÉ: "But, my dear Jean, your science, which is devoted *solely* to the study of the laws of nature proves—for anyone who has eyes to see—in the clearest possible way that God exists."

JEAN, sadly but resolutely: "I'm afraid it's not so simple as all that; we must not confuse the issues. It is true that I believe the universe to be governed by fixed laws, but don't jump to the conclusion that I believe in God. That's a *non sequitur* which has been greatly overworked by Christian apologists. I grant that we're in agreement as to the existence of universal law, but my opinion on the subject— a purely empirical opinion, mind you—has nothing whatever in common with the attitude of the Catholic Church, which regards God as a Supreme Being with personal attributes and exercising personal control over his creation. These are two very different standpoints. Otherwise religion and science would still be identical, as they were at the dawn of human intelligence and"—he smiles faintly—"as they certainly are not today."

THE ABBÉ, vehemently: "So when, *in good faith,* you set up your intelligence against the Christian faith—"

JEAN, breaking in: "Sorry, but I fear we could continue arguing on these lines indefinitely without ever finding common ground." He smiles again. "The truth is, I'm through with those interminable discussions; there's such a gulf between a believer and an atheist that they could wrangle a whole lifetime without ever getting any forrader. I've sometimes been tackled by expert and nimble-witted theologians, and I admit I couldn't think up any really effective answer to their case. But that didn't shake my conviction in the least. I knew that an answer *did* exist, and a mere fluke, like a chance association of ideas—or, better still, an evening's hard thinking—would have enabled me to hit on it. Arguments! One can always find an argument in defence of any theory if one applies one's mind to it." The Abbé looks so crestfallen that Jean steps beside him, smiling affectionately, and takes his arm. "I've come to be convinced, you know, that a man is never converted by any process of reasoning. He merely shores up, with logical arguments, a conviction that he entertains already; and this conviction isn't arrived at, as he fondly thinks, by way of syllogisms and dialectic, but thanks to something much more potent than these: a natural predisposition. I believe that a man is predisposed to belief or scepticism, and all the arguments in the world can do very little about it."

The Abbé makes no answer. Dusk is falling and the air is now quite cold. All that remains of the sun is a streak of orange-red low on the horizon, glowing across a violet haze. Before them stretches a field of young corn, its vivid green faintly silvered by the rising ground mist, and on its silken smoothness the fading glow of sunset mingles with the milk-white sheen of moonlight.

They quicken their pace.

With raucous cries a flurry of crows rises from a stubble-field and settles on the black boughs of an orchard just beyond.

A long silence.

THE ABBÉ: "But there's your wife to be considered. What do you propose to do about her?"

JEAN, quite composedly: "My wife? Well, the opinions you've been hearing are no new development. I've held them for fully three years, and, really, I don't see why we, Cécile and I, shouldn't continue to carry on indefinitely as we have been doing."

The priest gazes at him incredulously.

V. THE RUPTURE

A LECTURE room at Wenceslas College. It is eight o'clock and the students are at their desks. Jean walks in briskly and steps up on the platform.

A STUDENT, coming up to him: "Excuse me, sir, but hasn't the principal given you a notebook to return to me?"

JEAN: "No. I don't quite follow."

THE STUDENT: "Yesterday afternoon the principal asked me to let him see my notes. He said he'd give me back the book this morning."

JEAN: "What notes? The notes you take at my lectures?"

THE STUDENT: "Yes, sir."

JEAN: "No, I've not been given anything. You can go to your place."

An intermittent drone, like that of a seething vat, comes from the rows of benches. Some minutes are needed before the personalities dissociated since the previous day can coalesce again into a studious whole. Heads are raised, then lowered. Gradually order is restored, though some vagrant thoughts, gnat-like, still skim the surface. Then silence falls; a hush of expectation.

Sweeping the lecture room with his gaze, Jean sees fifty pairs of eyes intent on him, and their converging scrutiny seems to rivet him to his chair. His heart beats faster at its mute appeal, his mind grows tense, keyed up to the task before him.

JEAN: "Gentlemen, this morning I must ask you to give particular attention to what I am going to say." He takes a deep breath; there is a glint of triumph in his eyes as he gazes down at the rows of expectant faces. "A few days ago I brought to an end the set of lectures devoted to the origin of species. I am sure you all have grasped the great importance, the paramount importance, of this subject. But I cannot bring myself to close this section of our course without casting a backward glance and briefly recapitulating such points as seem to me . . ."

The door opens and the principal of the college, Abbé Miriel, enters. The priest is in his sixties, but has an easy carriage that belies his age and tendency to stoutness. He has a well-shaped if slightly fleshy face, bald above the temples, with a high-domed, freckled forehead. His upper eyelids rise and fall abruptly, and the gaze that flashes forth beneath them is shrewd, uncompromisingly lucid. A rather boyish smile plays on his lips; an affectation, perhaps, but none the less very charming.

THE PRINCIPAL, to the students, who have risen to their feet: "Sit down, my boys." He turns to Jean. "Forgive me for breaking in on you like this, Monsieur Barois, but I'd forgotten to return this notebook to one of your students." He smiles genially. "And, really, now that I am here, I'm tempted to profit by the opportunity. Will you permit me, Monsieur Barois, to listen to some portion of the lecture you are delivering today? No, no, please don't move." He notices an empty bench at the back. "I'll be quite comfortable there." He seats himself. "And please don't let my presence interfere with any of your habits."

Jean has flushed, then gone pale; the possible significance of this visit has not escaped him. For a moment he struggles with a temptation to tone down the more outspoken passages of the lecture he has prepared. Then courageously, with a tremor of defiance in his voice, he goes on speaking.

JEAN, turning to the principal: "I was about, sir, to recapitulate a series of lectures I have been giving on the origin of species." The priest nods, encouraging him to proceed. Jean turns to the students. "I explained to you the important place we must give to Lamarck and, following him, to Darwin, in the department of science that concerns origins; it owes its existence entirely to those two pioneers; to Lamarck especially. I believe I made it plain that his theory of evolution—or, to use a better term, transformism, which is a wider and less controversial solution than that of natural selection—can now be considered as a scientific truth established beyond all doubt."

He glances at the principal, who is listening, his eyes half closed, his pale hands resting on his knees, betraying no feeling of any kind.

JEAN: "We have seen, in short, that, until Lamarck, science could give no explanation of any of the phenomena of life, and the opinion prevailed that all the species known to us today were separate creations, each endowed from the start with all its present characteristics. We can truly say that Lamarck found the Ariadne's thread to this labyrinthine universe we live in.

"I have set forth to you in detail the facts which prove to us beyond all doubt that all living things are connected with each other in a long line of descent, linking us with the primal matter of the universe. From the initial monad, hardly distinguishable from the molecules of its organic environment—the remote, amorphous ancestor of our cells, compared with which even the simplest forms of life known to us today are infinitely complex entities —from the monad up to the most complicated manifestations of the human body and mind, there has been an unbroken progress lasting over hundreds of thousands of years. And we owe it to that great thinker, Lamarck, that we now can trace and classify the various stages of that progress.

"Next—and this is a point of immediate interest in view of recent developments—I advised you not to attach over-much importance to allegations that transformism is losing ground, in consequence of the discovery that sudden mutations occasionally take place. You will remember my telling you that, after stationary periods, a species may show abrupt variations due to the accumulation of efforts tending in the same direction over a series of generations. I also made it clear that this theory is found to be perfectly compatible with Lamarck's view, if we apply our minds to the facts impartially."

A short silence follows. Since the principal's appearance on the scene Jean has been conscious that his listeners' attention has been wandering. His words fall on an unstable surface and, in his efforts to make an impression on it, he is gradually losing his own assurance. So, abandoning the idea of summing up his previous lectures, he boldly strikes out in a new direction.

JEAN: "I thought it well to begin by this brief summary. But the main purpose of my lecture today is different."

There is now a ring of confidence in his voice, and the surface on which the words impinge seems to grow hard, resilient, like the web of a restrung racquet.

JEAN: "Above all, I wish to impress on your minds indelibly the immense importance of the theory of transformism, and its indispensability for the formation of the modern mind. I want you to understand why we must regard it as the vital core of all our biological knowledge; and how, while keeping within the limits of the most rigorous scientific precision, we find—we are bound to find—that this new manner of regarding universal life has profoundly modified the whole fabric of our present-day philosophy and remodelled most of our previous concepts of the human mind."

As it were, an electric circuit is now established between Jean and his hearers. He can feel them vibrating, thrilling, at his behest. The principal looks up. Jean meets his eyes, which are quite expressionless.

JEAN: "Once we have grasped the fact that all existing things are in a state of constant activity, we can no longer regard life as an active principle originating movement or energizing inert matter. That view was based on a serious misconception, by which we still are handicapped. Indeed, it has falsified man's observation of the phenomena of life since the dawn of human thought. Life is not a phenomenon whose beginning can be posited, since it is a phenomenon always in progress, without intermission. In other words, the universe exists, it has always existed, and cannot pass out of existence. It cannot have been created, inertia being nonexistent.

"Once we realize that an entity can never in any manner be identical with itself at any two moments of its course of existence, we automatically rule out all the arguments which, lured by the mirage of human individuality, men have built up to maintain that precarious theory of free will. In the light of our present knowledge we cannot visualize any being as in full enjoyment of free will.

"And once we also realize that our faculty of reason is no more than an inheritance transmitted through the ages from generation to generation—an heritage handed down to us with all its imperfections by the complex and capricious laws of heredity—we can no longer feel the same confidence in the metaphysics and ethics of the past.

"For transformism is of universal application and governs also the evolution of human consciousness.

"That is why Le Dantec, one of the most enlightened and independent leaders of present-day science, could write: 'For one who believes in transformism, most of the questions which naturally present themselves to the human mind change their meaning; some, indeed, cease to have any meaning.'"

Briskly, despite his bulk, the principal rises to his feet and turns his austere face, the eyes half closed, towards the platform.

THE PRINCIPAL: "Very interesting, Monsieur Barois. You show a commendable ardour in your exposition; it is highly stimulating." He smiles rather sourly. "We will have a talk about it later." He turns towards the students. His tone is genial, paternal. "The lesson, my young friends, of what we have been hearing—and no doubt I am anticipating the conclusions Monsieur Barois was about to draw at the close of his lecture—is the lesson of the perfection of the divine order of the universe. Our earthbound human intelligence can have only an inkling of those transcendent laws; but even that is enough to fill us with awe and admiration. This feeling of humility, when we are confronted by the Creator's stupendous work, is all the more incumbent on us in an age like the present, when the progress of scientific discovery tends only too often to make us forget what a paltry being man is and how relative, at best, is his knowledge." He bows frigidly to the lecturer. "Well, I must leave now. Good morning, Monsieur Barois."

No sooner has the door closed behind him than a ripple of unrest passes through the room, now that the strain of close attention is relaxed. With a quick downward glance Jean gathers to a focus, as it were, the wandering eyes, and once more the young minds strain towards him in an eager, silent communion that no official reprimand can impair.

JEAN, quietly: "I shall now continue . . ."

2

Mme Pasquelin's house at Buis. The summer vacation has begun.

Cécile is standing, half dressed, at her bedroom window. Hardly conscious of what she is doing, she draws her hand across the lower portion of her body. In her eyes is the curiously far-away gaze of all pregnant women. Her features, once vivacious, now confess languor, indifference.

It is nine in the morning. The sky is cloudless and limpid, honey-golden sunlight floods the room.

There is a knock at the door, which opens immediately.

CÉCILE, blinking her eyes: "Oh—it's you, Mother."

MME PASQUELIN: "Yes, it's I." Cécile's eyes widen apprehensively; her mother's tone implies that something is amiss. "Look at this." She holds up a leaflet and, with her lorgnette to her eyes, reads out the address on the wrapper. "Bulletin of the Free-Thought Congress. Monsieur Barois, c/o Madame Pasquelin, Buis-la-Dame." A short silence. "Where is he?"

CÉCILE: "Jean? I don't know."

MME PASQUELIN: "Haven't you seen him yet?"

CÉCILE: "No."

MME PASQUELIN: "He's not in his room."

CÉCILE: "He must have gone out for his morning walk."

MME PASQUELIN: "So it has come to this. Not only have you separate rooms, but he doesn't come to say good morning to you before going out." Cécile sits down; she is looking tired. Mme Pasquelin drops the pamphlet on her knees. "Well, you can give him *this* when he comes back. And tell him from me, that I wish he'd arrange to have things of this sort addressed somewhere else—not to my house. And there's something else that's worrying me." She shows an open envelope. "I got a letter from Abbé Miriel this morning."

CÉCILE: "He's Jean's principal, isn't he?"

MME PASQUELIN: "Yes. He's spending the vacation with his brother, at the Bishop's Palace at Beauvais. He says he'd like to meet me there if I can manage it. He wants to have a private word with me, it seems."

CÉCILE, nervously: "Oh, dear, I wonder what it can be!"

MME PASQUELIN, gloomily: "I haven't a notion, my poor child. But I shall go there this afternoon and find out."

Abruptly she bends forward, takes her daughter's forehead between her hands, and presses her dry lips to it with a little sigh, almost like a sob. Then, frowning darkly at her thoughts, she clatters out of the bedroom.

Two hours later. Cécile is finishing dressing. Jean comes in.

JEAN: "Good morning, Cécile."

CÉCILE: "Have you seen Mother?"

JEAN: "No. I went out early."

CÉCILE, pointing to the leaflet: "Mother gave me this for you."

JEAN, his face brightening: "Ah, yes. I know. I was expecting it. Thanks."

He tears off the wrapper, sits down on the bed, and skims the pages with obvious interest. As she watches him, hostility mingles with curiosity in Cécile's gaze. Looking up, he sees the question in her eyes but he does not flinch.

JEAN: "It's the programme of a Congress that's taking place in London this year. In December."

CÉCILE, on the defensive: "But—but what has that to do with you?"

JEAN: "It interests me, that's all." There is a rough edge to his voice. Cécile makes a fretful movement. "Also, someone has asked me to make a report on it, for a review."

CÉCILE: "Someone? Who?"

JEAN, curtly: "Breil-Zoeger."

CÉCILE: "I could have sworn it! That awful man!"

JEAN, coldly: "Really, Cécile!"

There is a short silence. Jean has resumed his reading.

CÉCILE, piteously: "But—no, Jean, no! I won't have you mixing yourself up with—with all that!"

Jean scowls at her and goes on reading.

JEAN: "What's that you said? You won't have me—? Now, look here!" Stowing the leaflet in his pocket, he walks up to her. "I'll ask you, my dear girl, to allow me to go my own way. This Congress, let me tell you, takes place only once every ten years. It's an international movement, with ramifications far greater than you can possibly imagine." He now is pacing the room, without looking in her direction. "What's more, the subjects down for discussion on this year's programme are ones I'm particularly keen on. Zoeger asked me to take an active part in the Congress, as special correspondent of the *International Review of Ideas,* which is the organ of the movement here, in France. I all but consented." Cécile gives a slight start. "But in view of my duties at Wenceslas College, I felt I must decline. Still, I'm quite determined to attend some of the final sessions which, as it happens, take place during the Christmas vacation. And I shall publish a report of the decisions made at the Congress, for the benefit of the French Section. That much I've decided, and I shall not go back on my decision."

Cécile says nothing. He takes some more steps in silence, then at last turns his eyes towards her. She is lying on the carpet, crumpled up like a slaughtered animal; her pupils are dilated, as if she is on the point of fainting. He hurries towards her, lifts her up, and places her on the bed. And suddenly a rush of overwhelming pity comes over him.

JEAN, in a tone of gloomy resignation: "Very well, then. Have it your own way. I promise not to go."

For a moment she remains quite quiet, her eyes closed. Then she looks up at him with an almost childish smile and clasps his hand.

But Jean frees himself and walks to the window. Yes, she is the stronger of the two. Her suffering is all too real, too manifest—and thanks to it she is invincible.

Jean knows what he stands to lose by this capitulation: a unique opportunity of hearing the ideas which during the past five years have been simmering in his mind and which he has been vainly struggling to fit into a scheme for living—an opportunity of hearing these ideas discussed, combated, defended, and threshed out by men of his own stamp. He is bitterly disgusted. Yes, he can feel pity for her; but for himself no less!

JEAN, without looking round, in a low, embittered voice: "Well, this settles it. I'm doomed to make a failure of my life. And it's not even your fault, you *can't* act otherwise. You don't understand, you'll never even have an inkling of, the ideas that mean all the world to me. You'll always regard them as mere foibles; or, worse still, as shameful, criminal aberrations. You're built like that, and you wouldn't be yourself if you thought otherwise.

"I'm slowly stifling to death in the atmosphere you compel me to breathe. All my energies, all my aspirations, are poisoned by it. The only happiness you can give me, the mild affection of which you're capable, can only do me harm and drag me down to your level. That is the truth, the hideous truth. The mere fact of your presence in my life is enough to wreck it, no matter what I do. And no matter what I do you'll always be here, in my life, year after year! You'll kill my endeavours one by one, and you won't even know what you are up to; just as you will never have the faintest notion of what you yourself are. And you'll spend your days bemoaning your little personal afflictions—being sorry for yourself!" In a burst of anger. "As for me, I'm damned and doomed. And it's your fault."

Cécile has remained quite still; her eyes express nothing but grieved surprise.

He stares at her hopelessly and gives a slight shrug; then, dry-lipped, his shoulders sagging, he goes to the door.

3

Abbé Miriel
　Principal, Wenceslas College
　　Paris　　　　　　　　　　　　　　　　August 17

Sir: I trust you will permit me to begin by expressing my surprise that you should have employed a third party for conveying your opinion of my teaching. Without dwelling further on this unusual method of approach, which (to say the least of it) lacked courtesy, I will proceed directly to your criticisms of my work. As to these, I run no risk of falling into error, since you have been at pains to state your grounds of complaint in a letter which I have been allowed to see and which ends (if I have not misread it) with an unequivocal ultimatum.

This year is the fourth in which you have assigned to me the duty of teaching natural science to seventeen- and eighteen-year-old students. I have not thought fit to confine myself to giving purely practical instruction. A teacher has a more vital duty to his students than that of merely coaching them for an examination. His duty, as I see it, is to raise their general outlook to a higher level and to inspire adolescent minds with a capacity for generous enthusiasms.

I do not wish to disclaim the tendencies to which I have given expression in my lectures. When, in some of these, I ventured beyond the frontiers normally assigned to natural science, I knew what I was doing. In my opinion, the only limit to the human intelligence should be that of its utmost reach, and the farthest flights of thought should be encouraged, not restricted.

Your animadversions have brought it home to me that a man engaged in the teaching of science cannot honestly undertake to abide by any prescribed rule in the course of his duties. For sooner or later he is led to draw independent conclusions, and, when this happens, he is bound to voice the truth that is in him. How, if he has any self-respect, could he fail to impart to his listeners the fruits of his personal experience, the conclusions he has arrived at? Whether we wish it or not, scientific research into the phenomena of life leads directly to philosophy—indeed, to my mind, this is the only philosophy that counts.

Thus, if these problems are to be handled with the broad-mindedness and thoroughness that are their due, a freedom of thought and speech is called for, which, I admit, can hardly be reconciled with the tendencies of the college over which you preside. So, I am quite ready to own that, in this respect, I have, so to say, spoken beyond my brief.

But since I cannot see my way to modifying the tone of my lectures, and since I must definitely refuse to show myself to my pupils as other than I am—a free man addressing free minds—I can see no alternative to tendering my resignation.

Very truly yours,
Jean Barois

Five o'clock. Mme Pasquelin and Cécile are out of doors, sewing in the shade of a big garden parasol. Their chairs are side by side, and they converse in undertones, their lips hardly moving.

Jean appears on the terrace, his letter in his hand. As he approaches the women he is conscious of entering a zone of mute hostility.

JEAN: "I'd like to let you know the answer I am giving to Abbé Miriel. I am resigning my post."

The women are dismayed by the firmness of his tone. However,

Mme Pasquelin, the more combative of the two, begins by conceal-
ing her anxiety.

MME PASQUELIN: "Your resignation? Really, Jean, you can't be
serious!"

Letting her needlework drop to her knees, Cécile looks up at him.
This afternoon the high, smooth curve of her forehead has the look
of a cuirass. For the last twenty-four hours she has been in a haze of
utter misery, now that the principal's peremptory letter has forced
her to face the cruel truth. The fact that Jean is liable to lose his post
is the least of her troubles; what appals her is the menace to his immortal soul—Jean is an atheist!

JEAN: "You seem surprised. Yet I wonder what else you expected
to happen—after that ultimatum."

MME PASQUELIN: "Oh, come now! Don't let's exaggerate. There
never was any question of an ultimatum. Abbé Miriel was much distressed by some of the things you thought fit to say to your pupils,
but he never dreamt of dismissing you. It's the last thing he's wanted
to do—if only out of his personal regard for me. All he asks is for
you to alter your system of teaching, and really"—she smiles—"you
must admit he knows far more than you do about such matters.
Don't forget he's a man of vast experience, and your principal."

Jean averts his eyes, without replying, and Mme Pasquelin hastens
to take advantage of his silence. Assuming an almost genial manner, she tries to keep the discussion from turning acrimonious.

MME PASQUELIN: "Now do try to look at it sensibly, my dear Jean,
like a rational being! Evidently you let your tongue—or your opinions—run away with you. But the principal's a level-headed man, he
doesn't take these—these indiscretions over-seriously, and is quite
ready to overlook them." Her feigned smile is almost painful to see.
"So don't be pig-headed, Jean. Tear up that letter and go and write
him another."

JEAN, wearily: "Please don't let's argue. My mind's made up."

MME PASQUELIN, vehemently: "But you can't, you simply *cannot*
do that. Don't you agree, Cécile?"

JEAN: "It's done."

MME PASQUELIN: "No. I forbid you to send that letter."

JEAN, losing patience: "But, confound it! Suppose someone asked you—you or Cécile—to repudiate your religious convictions so as to keep a job, what would you answer?"

MME PASQUELIN, angrily: "That's absurd. It isn't the same thing."

JEAN: "Ah, yes, that was bound to come. 'It isn't the same thing!' Well, you're mistaken; it is so much the same thing that I didn't hesitate for a moment. I should have realized long ago that my place wasn't in a college run by priests, and thrown it up of my own accord. My one regret is that I shut my eyes so long."

Mme Pasquelin is at a loss. Jean's look, his furrowed brows, the fierce line of his mouth, intimidate her. She crushes down her anger.

MME PASQUELIN: "Jean, I beg you! If you lose your post, what will you do?"

JEAN: "Oh, have no fear! I've heaps of plans, and plenty of ways of employing my energy."

MME PASQUELIN: "Plans! Fine plans too, I'll be bound! All you'll do is to go from bad to worse in your wrong-headedness."

JEAN, seizing the opportunity: "Exactly! Now that I'm a free man"—he brandishes the letter—"I shall stop making the concessions and compromises I've been forced to make hitherto—and of which I'm heartily ashamed. It was a transition period, if you like. Well, I'm through with it!"

Stung to the quick, Cécile stands up and faces him.

CÉCILE: "Now that you're a free man, you said, Jean. And—how about me?"

JEAN, taken aback: "How about you? Well . . ."

They gaze at each other; not a trace of their former love remains in either's eyes.

CÉCILE: "I was deceived—abominably! Deceived by your past, your words, your attitude. Don't forget that."

MME PASQUELIN, intervening boldly: "Yes, and do you imagine she can endure having a husband who's an atheist, an enemy of our religion? Really, it's—unthinkable that, with an upbringing like yours, you should have come to this!"

JEAN, gloomily, answering only Cécile: "What's done is done. You're distressed of course, and so am I. I can't prevent my ideas being alive, evolving. It's not up to me to govern them; it's they that must rule my life."

CÉCILE, sternly: "No. Not so long as I'm with you."

MME PASQUELIN, taking courage from her daughter's unexpected stand: "No, she'd rather leave you. Isn't that so, Cécile?"

Cécile hesitates for a moment in an agony of indecision, then gives a quick nod. Jean, who was watching to see how she would answer, shrugs his shoulders. There is a short silence. Mme Pasquelin gazes at her daughter with a new light in her eyes. In the depths of her maternal instinct something has stirred; a formless hope that, though she is unaware of it, influences what she next says.

MME PASQUELIN: "Really it's too absurd! You insist on making our lives wretched with your ideas. Ideas! Everybody has ideas! Why can't you have sensible ones, like any normal person?" She plays her last card. "If you don't drop this mad notion of resigning your post, and if you refuse to go on with your life as in the past— well, Cécile won't go back to Paris with you."

JEAN: "Do you hear, Cécile?"

CÉCILE, committed by her nod: "Mother's right."

JEAN: "So if I resign my post, you will not return with me to Paris?"

CÉCILE: "No."

JEAN, bitterly, to his mother-in-law: "I congratulate you on your handiwork!" He brings a chair near Cécile and sits astride it. "Now, Cécile, let's have it out between us. And be assured that I'm in earnest." He takes a deep breath. "I could promise to make fresh concessions and patch up a truce between us. But I prefer to continue speaking and acting quite frankly. For your sake I've made compromise after compromise, but I've reached my limit, and it's impossible for me to continue acting thus without abandoning all my human dignity, all decency of mind. What you ask of me is to go on playing a degrading game of make-believe throughout my life and, by a non-committal attitude, by perpetual deceit, to seem to approve of a religion that I can no longer practise. I'd have you understand, once for all, that there are more important things in life than keeping up appearances. No honourable man can undertake to profess all his life long the opposite of what he thinks, even for the sake of keeping his wife's affection. You have no right to make a grievance of my moral honesty, even if it causes you to suffer." He pauses. "Now! Will you come back with me to Paris in October as we'd agreed?"

CÉCILE, with a cry of desperate resolve: "No!"

JEAN, waving away Mme Pasquelin: "Listen well to what I'm going to say, Cécile." He pauses again. "If you refuse to come with me to Paris, if you deliberately wish to break the last links that I wish to keep intact—then nothing will hold me back. I shall go to London during the winter and attend the Congress of which I told you."

MME PASQUELIN, losing all self-control: "But do you mean to kill my daughter? Considering the condition she is in . . ."

Cécile moves to her mother's side.

CÉCILE, to Jean: "I've made up my mind. I'd rather lose you than go on living with a—a heathen."

Jean rises to his feet and, gazing at the two women, is suddenly struck by their likeness to each other. They have the same rather prominent forehead, the same round black eyes, whose slight squint seems accentuated in moments of emotion, the same vacillating gaze that slips aside when challenged in discussion.

JEAN, sadly: "It was your wish, Cécile. You have chosen. But you have till this evening to think it over. If you let me go home by myself, it means an end of all my scruples, and I shall feel free to go my own way in everything. Now I'm going to post my letter."

M. Breil-Zoeger, Editor
  The International Review of Ideas
    78, Boulevard Saint-Germain
      Paris   August 28

My dear Breil-Zoeger: During the last few days a great change has come into my life. I have resigned my post at Wenceslas College, and I am now, in all respects, infinitely freer than I could possibly have foreseen. I can employ the coming months as I think fit, and put in a longish stay in London. So if no one else has been nominated for the front-line duties at the Congress, which you originally proposed to me, I shall be delighted to undertake them.

I shall not be staying in the country until the close of the vacation, as I said I would. I am returning to Paris this afternoon.

Could you keep a morning clear, for us to have a long talk together this week? Ever yours,

Jean Barois

4

A bedroom in a London hotel. Evening. A powerful electric ceiling-lamp floods the room with glaring light. Heavy curtains deaden the noises of the traffic outside.

Breil-Zoeger is lying on his bed. Propped on an elbow, he gazes intently at a woman of fifty, Mme David, who is reading out her shorthand report of the day's session.

Jean is pacing the room, his arms folded, his mind obviously working at high pressure.

MME DAVID: "'. . . as Vinet, a Swiss author, wrote, as far back as 1879: "It is from revolt to revolt that human groups progress, civilization comes into its own, and justice triumphs. Freedom of the press, free trade, free education—all these freedoms, like the fecundating rain of summer, are borne to us on the wings of the tempest." ' "

JEAN, breaking in: "At this point there was some applause, especially from the Swedes, Danes, and Russians. Then the chairman rose to speak and summed up the debate." Puckering his eyebrows, Breil-Zoeger punctuates with a nod each phrase of the sentences that follow. "He explained that you had suddenly been prostrated by a sharp liver attack; then he read out your message, in which you proposed that I should speak tomorrow instead of you. This was voted unanimously."

BREIL-ZOEGER: "Did Woldsmuth give you the exact figures?"

JEAN: "Yes. And I warned Backerston that I wouldn't be attending the Reforms Committee meeting."

Breil-Zoeger nods. He is a man in his early thirties. Though he was born at Nancy, of Lorrainese parents, his face has something Japanese in its formation, which is accentuated by the yellow complexion he owes to his liver complaint; broad cheek-bones, a sparse, straggly moustache, a pointed chin. The deeply sunken eyes, whose pupils always seem dilated, flash out of pits of darkness with a keen, almost feverish intensity, which contrasts oddly with the prevailing gentleness of the face. His voice is toneless, monotonous, pleasant enough to hear, but utterly devoid of warmth.

BREIL-ZOEGER: "Madame David, will you please find the green file marked 'The Religious Problem in France'; it's amongst those papers at the corner of your table. Thanks."

JEAN: "Would you like me to dictate it in your presence, as I did this morning?"

BREIL-ZOEGER: "Yes, that would be best."

JEAN: "I've got the second and third parts into shape, on the lines you indicated, except that some passages are transposed. I'll explain." Breil-Zoeger lets his head sink back on the pillow, his face twisted in a wry grimace. "Are you in pain?"

BREIL-ZOEGER: "Just twinges, now and again."

Some moments' silence.

JEAN, taking some sheets of paper from his pocket: "We'd come to the second part. Heading: Causes of the General Decline of Faith.

Underline, please, Madame David." He turns to Breil-Zoeger. "First cause: the vast development of scientific research during the last fifty years. Now that the field of the Unknown, from which man in earlier days derived his belief in God, is being steadily narrowed down, it follows that the hold of religion is loosening *pari passu*."

BREIL-ZOEGER: "Here you might intercalate . . ."

JEAN: "Take this down, Madame David."

BREIL-ZOEGER: ". . . some scientific truths which go to prove the incapacity of 'their' God to interfere with the inevitable processes of nature, and, therefore, the impossibility of miracles, the futility of prayer, and so forth."

JEAN: "As you wish. Second cause: historical research."

BREIL-ZOEGER: "Make that section brief."

JEAN: "No. It's a very important one. I mean to remind my hearers of the great forward step that was made when it became possible to trace the growth of the Christian legends, stage by stage, and to verify this by the original texts. I shall point out that these legends were built up from beginning to end with purely human elements that crystallized round some incident which had a perfectly normal explanation, but which simple-minded folk endowed with mystery. Leading up to this conclusion: How can anyone be a 'believer' if he studies the history of religions through the ages and observes the various brands of credulity, all equally uncompromising, that have infested the unhappy minds of men?"

BREIL-ZOEGER: "Good."

JEAN: "Then a seeming digression. Scientific progress can influence only cultivated minds. By itself, it would not have been enough to weaken a religion that has struck such deep roots in our national life. Which leads me to"—there is a knock at the door—"to the economic and social factors." He opens the door. "Who is it?"

A VOICE: "From *The Times*, sir. We want information about Monsieur Breil-Zoeger's health and the agenda of tomorrow's meeting."

JEAN: "Ah, yes. Go to Room twenty-nine, and our colleague Monsieur Woldsmuth will give you all the information you require." He returns to the bedside. "Where was I? Yes, Cause Number Three: the social and economic factors. The vast development of industry has drained our countryside of tens of thousands of young men, who have thus broken completely with the traditions of their elders—"

BREIL-ZOEGER: "Drive that point home. It's a decisive factor. We need only think of the immense number of factories operating in every civilized country—a number that will inevitably increase as time goes on, and to an extent none of us foresees today." He looks through his file and extracts a sheet. The movement, slight though it is, gives him a twinge that makes him wince. He reads the opening phrases. " 'The factory worker is almost necessarily a rationalist. Plunged into a busy hive of industry, in which metaphysical speculations are quite out of place; and surrounded by machines whose clangorous tongues announce the triumph of human intelligence, human labour, and mathematics over nature—' Here's what I've written, make whatever use of it you like." He hands him the sheet. "Now go on."

JEAN: "It's here I want to place my description—I remember mentioning it to you—of the French nation today divided into two camps; in one the believers, in the other the unbelievers. Numerically the body of unbelievers is a strong majority, comprising as it does the proletariat, to whom I've referred already, and all the intellectuals. Then—"

BREIL-ZOEGER: "Wait! You should include amongst the unbelievers the half-educated, the little man who has tried to 'improve his mind,' as he calls it. It's high time for a campaign to rehabilitate him. He's too easy game, poor devil, for the ironist. But though he's never had the leisure deeply to study any subject, thanks to his sturdy common sense and the mental balance that comes of decent living, he is drawn irresistibly towards the solutions given by science —in their cruder forms, of course."

JEAN: "Yes, that's very true. As for the believers, they naturally are drawn from the two conservative communities: the peasantry and the middle class. The peasant usually lives far away from a town, in an environment which never changes and in which tradition holds its own unchecked. The middle class are systematically hostile to change; their interests are bound up with the established order, and especially with the Catholic Church, which for many centuries has held in check the cupidities of the 'have-nots.' Also, they are used to interpreting life in terms of ready-made beliefs, and their peace of mind would be endangered if they allowed doubt to rear its head. But, between the two extremes, there is a floating multitude of waverers, those who are in two minds about these matters." There is a knock at the door. Jean shouts irritably: "Come in!"

A VALET: "Here's your mail, sir."

JEAN: "Put it on the table, please." The valet leaves the letters and goes out. "Yes, the *waverers,* those who are in two minds about these matters, torn between the craving for the supernatural they have inherited and the dictates of their reason. And it is their predicament that makes the present religious crisis in France so bewildering and so—so harrowing." He stumbles over his words. His gaze has just fallen on the periodicals and letters lying on the table; amongst the latter is one in Mme Pasquelin's hand. "Would you excuse me?" He opens the envelope.

Buis-la-Dame,

January 14

My dear Jean: Cécile gave birth to a daughter yesterday. . . .

He stops reading. His eyes grow misted; a sudden vision of the past has risen before them.

She wants me to let you know of this and to say that if you wish to see your daughter you can come here. Need I add that, as in the past, a room is waiting for you in my house, and you can stay as long as you desire? Perhaps (as I so greatly hope) you have already learnt what a terrible mistake you made, and are now prepared to make some reparation for your heartless conduct towards Cécile and myself. You will find us in the same state of mind as when you left us—quite ready to let bygones be bygones, once you have realized how mistaken you were.

M. Pasquelin

BREIL-ZOEGER: "Not bad news, I hope?"

JEAN: "No. Now I'll go on. Where were we?" His voice is unsteady; he struggles to pull himself together. "Would you please read out the last few lines, Madame David?"

MME DAVID: "'. . . a floating multitude of waverers'—underlined—'those who are in two minds about these matters, torn between the craving for the supernatural they have inherited and the dictates of their reason. And it is their predicament that makes the present religious crisis . . .'"

But Jean, sitting on an upended valise, hears only a rumble of words, signifying nothing.

5

The railway station at Buis. Jean alights from the train; nobody has come to meet him.

He has the old omnibus with the rattling windows to himself, as it toils up the hill towards the little town. He feels an unexpected thrill as he gazes at the once-familiar streets and shops. Nothing has changed. He sees the town across the mists of childhood, which three months' absence has intensified.

There is a nip in the air, and he buttons up his double-breasted overcoat, which has kept a tang of brine from the Channel crossing.

All doors and windows of the house are closed. A maid, whose face is new to him, holds the door half open, and he slips in almost furtively.

Half-way up the stairs he pauses, tightening his grip on the hand-rail; the sound he has just heard—of a baby crying—has thrown his thoughts into turmoil. Then, steadying himself, he walks quickly up to the landing.

A door opens.

MME PASQUELIN: "Ah, there you are, Jean. Come in."

Cécile is in bed. A big fire blazes merrily in the fireplace. Mme Pasquelin shuts the door. Jean goes up to the bed.

JEAN: "Good morning, Cécile." Her only response is a nervous smile. He bends and kisses her on the forehead. "Is the baby—doing well?"

CÉCILE: "Yes."

JEAN: "And you?" Mme Pasquelin is standing; he can feel the impact of her steely gaze. "When exactly did it . . . ?"

CÉCILE: "Monday night."

JEAN, counting on his fingers. "Six days ago." He pauses. "I got the letter on Thursday. I couldn't be spared at once, but I left as soon as I could." Another silence. "Did you—suffer much?"

CÉCILE: "Oh, yes, indeed!"

Another silence.

MME PASQUELIN, brusquely: "Will you be dining here tonight?"

JEAN: "Well, as a matter of fact, I'd thought . . ."

MME PASQUELIN, with a touch of satisfaction: "Ah! Then you'll be staying here some days?"

JEAN: "If you'd like me to."

MME PASQUELIN: "Very good."

She goes out to make the necessary arrangements. Left to them-selves, Jean and Cécile are tongue-tied, acutely embarrassed. Their eyes meet. Cécile bursts into tears. Jean bends over her again and kisses her affectionately, sadly.

JEAN, in a low voice: "I'll stay as long as you want. Until you're able to get up anyhow. Then—we'll see."

He falls silent, doubtful what to propose. Neither speaks for some moments.

CÉCILE, in a whisper, with a break in her voice: "Jean! You haven't even asked to see your daughter!"

Just then Mme Pasquelin enters with the baby in her arms.

MME PASQUELIN, to Cécile: "We're forgetting the time—what with all this to-do."

The words "all this to-do" flick Jean in the face as he goes up to Mme Pasquelin. He knows what is expected of him—to kiss his child—but cannot bring himself to do it. Partly because his mother-in-law's presence goes against the grain; partly out of a sort of physical repugnance that he cannot overcome. With feigned casualness he strokes with his forefinger the small soft cheek and the pink chin half buried in the moistened bib.

JEAN: "She's—very nice." He steps back, and a new thought waylays him. What Christian name will they give his child? It does not strike him that the official declaration has already been made. "What's her name to be?"

MME PASQUELIN, peremptorily: "Her name is Marie."

As though he were struggling to imprint a difficult name on his memory Jean echoes, "Marie." Then he glances at the tiny fingers squeezing possessively a swelling breast, whose aspect is unfamiliar to him. What eagerness to live is in this small pink lump of flesh! His gaze shifts to Cécile's face, and he is startled by the change. It is fuller, paler, younger-looking, almost her face of years ago.

When she lifts her baby there is the glint of a ring, her engagement ring. He recalls the day when he brought it from Paris, the little square box in his pocket. Cécile was by herself; he went down on his knees to slip that ring, the link, upon her finger.

And the memory rekindles the lost emotions of their youth. How sincerely, how naïvely he had dreamt of giving and receiving perfect happiness!

He is lifting a shroud, violating the sepulchre of their dead selves. Now he is a different being; she too. Irremediably different. And what of the future?

6

Three weeks later. Cécile's bedroom.

CÉCILE: "No! I won't hear of it!"

JEAN: "But, Cécile—"

CÉCILE: "No!"

JEAN: "Here, you are under your mother's influence. Let's get back to Paris, you and I, as soon as we can manage it; I'm convinced—"

CÉCILE: "I refuse to leave before the baptism."

JEAN: "All right. I agree."

CÉCILE: "And I insist on your attending the service."

JEAN, after a short silence: "That, as I told you, I refuse to do."

CÉCILE: "In that case you can go back by yourself."

Another silence. Cécile moves to the window, draws aside the curtain, and gazes out.

JEAN, wearily: "Now, listen! For days and days we have been wrangling—and getting not an inch forrader. Recriminations, innuendoes, hostile silences, fits of weeping—I've had my fill of them, and, well, I'm at the end of my tether. And now you want to start another futile scene!" Cécile remains at the window with her back to him. Jean studiously controls his voice as he continues: "We must try to patch things up, and I repeat that I am willing to resume our life in common, as in the past. Also, I'm ready to make a great many concessions."

CÉCILE, turning to him at last: "That's a lie. You'll never do anything to please me."

JEAN, sadly: "How bitter you are against me, Cécile!" He pauses. "On the contrary, you know quite well that I'm prepared to meet a great many of your wishes, so as to extricate us from our present impasse. Do you want proof of this? Well, were I alone and free, I'd shelter our child completely from religious influences, I'd bring her up in such a way that she'd never have those terrible searchings of conscience that I had to endure."

CÉCILE, passionately: "Oh, please stop! Don't you realize how horrible you are?"

JEAN: "I said that's what I'd do if I were a free agent. But there are the two of us; you have the same rights as I over our child, and I keep this in mind. So I shall leave you free to implant in her the faith that's yours. Only I refuse to help you in this by playing the hypocrite. That, surely, is only fair."

CÉCILE, fiercely: "No! It's all sheer nonsense, what you've just been saying. She's *my* daughter and you have no rights over her, absolutely none. If you ever had any, you have lost them; it's exactly the same as if she had a father who was shut up in an asylum!"

JEAN, in a discouraged tone: "Cécile! Are we really so utterly, so hopelessly estranged, you and I?"

CÉCILE: "Yes, there's nothing left between us now. And, oh, I'm so tired of struggling! And all our life long it will be just the same. Today it's the child's baptism; presently it'll be her confirmation; and then her First Communion—each time the same miserable struggle! In fact I shall have to defend her against you every day, every minute of the day. Against your example, your horrible way of life. Yes, I have now only one duty, and that's to save my daughter—from her father!"

JEAN: "Well? What exactly do you want?"

CÉCILE, coming towards him, her face convulsed with despair: "What do I want? Heaven knows, it's nothing so preposterous; I want an end of all this misery. I don't ask you to change back to the man you were when we were married; I doubt if you could do that —now. All I ask you is to give up parading in public those dreadful ideas that you've picked up—I can't imagine where! I ask you to be present at your daughter's baptism. And I want you to promise me—" She bursts into tears, sways forward, and collapses on her prie-dieu, burying her face in her arms. "Surely it's not asking so very much? I only want to have a husband I needn't be ashamed of. I want us to be a married couple like ordinary married couples. That's all."

JEAN: "And all I ask for myself is to have the freedom that I'm giving *you*."

CÉCILE, rising to her feet in a frenzy of revolt: *"That?* Never! Never!"

JEAN, after a short silence: "Well then?" Cécile says nothing. "I'm afraid that when you married me you expected more of life than life could give you."

CÉCILE: "No, it's you who deceived me. You can't blame me for—for what has happened. I am just as I was when you asked me to marry you."

JEAN, shrugging his shoulders: "I wonder can a man ever feel so sure of the way he will develop in after years as to risk pledging himself irrevocably in such matters?"

CÉCILE, with a cry of horrified amazement: "Apostate!"

Jean gazes at her without speaking. He is plumbing the gulf between them. After pacing to and fro for some moments, he halts, facing her, resolved to force a decision.

JEAN: "Well then?" Her hands locked over her face, Cécile remains silent. "Well then?" His tone is frigid.

CÉCILE, passionately: "Oh, go away!"

A short silence.

JEAN: "Ah, Cécile, don't—don't tempt me!"

CÉCILE, sobbing: "Go away! Leave me!"

JEAN: " 'Leave me?' Do you want a divorce?" Cécile stops crying, lowers her hands from her face, and looks at him aghast. Jean puts his hands in his pockets, his lips curled in an ugly smile. "So you think you've only got to say 'Leave me!' and everything is settled? You seem unaware that before a woman can live as she chooses and keep her child, there has to be a case in court—divorce proceedings, a decree."

He goes on speaking, explaining. And suddenly, unsummoned, striking across the words that it belies, an uprush of hope thrills through him, and a fierce desire for the freedom now within his grasp, for a life at last his own.

He goes on speaking, but in the distance, straight ahead, he sees a rift in the darkness, and, try as he may, he cannot take his eyes off it.

7

February 12

Dear Sir: I am glad to be able to inform you that, after a final interview with Mme Barois and Mme Pasquelin, and under pressure of the threat of divorce proceedings, which these ladies wish at all costs to avoid, their formal assent has been given to all the demands you asked me to formulate. It is therefore agreed that:

(1) You recover your entire independence. Mme Barois has no intention of residing in Paris and will live permanently at Buis with her mother.

(2) Mme Barois will have complete control of her daughter's education; with this single restriction, on which you insisted, that when your daughter reaches the age of eighteen she is to spend a complete year under your roof.

(3) Mme Barois agrees not to reject the allowance of 12,000 francs a year which you insist on her receiving from you. She is, however, resolved not to employ any portion of this income either for herself or on her daughter's education. It will be allowed to accumulate and be settled *in toto* on her daughter.

This last clause gave rise to much controversy, and Mme Barois consented to its inclusion in the Agreement only on my unequivocal assurance that you regarded it as a condition *sine qua non,* and to avoid recourse to a Court of Law. These ladies desired, however, to withhold their assent until I had advised you of the precise effect on your personal income of this deduction (which reduces it to approximately 5000 francs *per annum*). To prevent further delay (which, as I knew, would serve no purpose) I thought fit to inform them that I had already drawn your attention to this fact, but you had declined to go back on your project.

As requested by Mme Barois, I have given her a memorandum of the terms of agreement as set out above.

I trust that my handling of these delicate negotiations has been such as to meet with your approval, and beg to remain,

Faithfully yours,

E. Mougin
Notary, Buis-la-Dame

PART

II

VI. *THE SOWER*

M. L. Breil-Zoeger
  Hotel des Pins
    Arcachon   Paris, May 20, 1895

My dear Breil-Zoeger: Forgive me for my delay in thanking you for the sympathy you so kindly showed me in my recent troubles. The truth is I have been exceedingly busy. Only those who have themselves been through the mill can realize what it means to have to cut those innumerable strands which link a life (even a simple one like mine) to the outside world and to its past. One fails to appreciate the toughness of these strands, their complexity and elusiveness. The task cost me two months' unremitting effort; I threw myself into it with a sort of desperate ardour, and at last I have snapped every link and can call myself *a free man*.

I doubt if you can guess the keen emotion behind this cry of triumph, this paean of Freedom, that rises to my lips; for, unlike mine, your life has always been untrammelled, fancy-free.

And this new Freedom has dawned for me in the prime of life, when my energies are at their highest, after a long, hard schooling in subjection; after two years during which I never ceased longing for it secretly, unavowedly. Yes, Freedom has crashed on me at last, a gift from the gods, given without stint, and I welcome it with every sinew of my being, incorporate it in my life, and, with passionate devotion, vow myself to it for ever!

I have gone to ground without giving anyone my address. For many weeks I have not seen one familiar face or heard a single voice that might remind me of the past. And now everything conspires to crown this new-found joy. Spring has come to Paris, flooding my room with light, with the fragrance of rising sap, with beauty! Never before in my life have I experienced an emotion like this.

Do not write to me, my friend; let me drug myself with solitude until the autumn. But be assured my friendship never falters.

Always yours,
Jean Barois

2

November. An old building with a narrow doorway in the Rue Jacob, Paris.

"Monsieur Barois? Fourth floor, sir. You'll see his card on the door."

A rickety, poorly lit staircase. On the fourth-floor landing there are four doors, but only one doormat.

Harbaroux peers at each door in the dim light; finally on one of them his keen eyes decipher a dusty visiting card, the last two lines of which have been crossed out in pencil.

JEAN BAROIS, M.D.
PROFESSOR, WENCESLAS COLLEGE
80, BOULEVARD MALESHERBES

He rings.

BAROIS: "You're the first arrival, Harbaroux. Come in."

Jean Barois, now in his thirty-third year, is in the full vigour of maturity. His face has greatly changed during the last twelve months; the look of strain has gone, and it has the radiant serenity of a sky swept clear of clouds. He radiates energy and zest for life, freedom, self-assurance, a boundless confidence in the future.

The somewhat austere room is brightly lit by a gas-jet in a plain glass globe. Deal shelves piled with books line the walls. There are half a dozen cane chairs. On the mantelpiece stands a plaster cast of Michelangelo's "Slave," struggling to free his aching limbs and rebellious shoulders from their stony thrall. At the far end of the room a door gives on a bedroom; clothes can be seen hanging in a recess.

HARBAROUX: "Do you know, this is the first time I've set foot here?"

BAROIS: "Yes, I've been living like a troglodyte for the last six months."

Harbaroux glances at the chairs, which are set out in a circle, and his features twist in a brief grin. He is a wizened little man, with a hatchet face, wide at the temples and narrowing down to a sharp chin and a pointed reddish-brown beard; an ugly, ageless face, but almost diabolically intelligent, with upstanding, faun-like ears. His mouth and the deep-set eye-sockets are like holes roughed out in a wax head by a sculptor working against time. His look is keen, unwavering, ungentle. Librarian at the Arsenal, he is an indefatigable worker. His special subject was originally Medieval Law; latterly, however, he has concentrated on the history of the Revolution.

HARBAROUX: "I wanted to see you before it started. Don't you think it would be a good plan for us to settle in advance what subjects should be brought up for discussion with our friends this evening?"

BAROIS, after pondering for some moments: "No, I don't agree."

HARBAROUX, his features tightening, then relaxing, like a hairspring: "No? All the same . . ."

BAROIS: "A meeting like the one we're having tonight is bound to be preparatory. We're not out for any immediate practical result."

HARBAROUX: "Then what's the point of it?"

BAROIS: "In my opinion it will serve its purpose best if it generates, so to speak, a chain of currents between the minds of those who have been asked to attend, and as a result we find a spirit of collective enthusiasm developing from the mere fact of these minds' being brought together."

HARBAROUX: "That's desirable, I grant you—only it doesn't depend on anything we, you and I, can do."

BAROIS: "I agree. But we have a better chance of creating that atmosphere if we let everyone have his say, without keeping to a programme drawn up in advance." He smiles serenely. "It'll pan out all right, you'll see."

Barois weighs his words and rounds his phrases off with the ease of a man used to platform speaking. Though he does not raise his voice, the incisiveness of his diction holds the hearer's attention.

HARBAROUX, shrugging his shoulders: "I wonder! We shall have a spate of noble sentiments. Each of us taking his hobby for a ride! Each in turn inflicting his harangue! And then, before we know where we are, two o'clock in the morning! A wasted evening!"

Barois makes a gesture implying: And what if it is? Then, without answering, he lights a cigarette with the deft precision that comes of long practice. His hard but thoughtful gaze lingers for a moment on the first puff of smoke rising in the clear air of the room.

HARBAROUX: "Hullo! So you've taken to smoking?"

BAROIS: "Yes."

A short silence.

HARBAROUX: "Have it your own way. Personally, I'd have preferred to have the work mapped out, distributed. In my opinion the launching of a review calls for—"

A ring at the bell.

BAROIS, getting up from his chair: "For method. That's what you were going to say, isn't it?" He goes to the door and opens it, while Harbaroux mumbles something with a rather sickly smile.

A HOARSE VOICE, in the hall: "My dear fellow! Would you believe it? An absolute godsend! In Lamennais, of all people! You won't find anything better, I assure you."

Cresteil d'Allize's back shows in the doorway; he is gesticulating, pouring out a stream of exclamations. He does a brisk about-turn to enter the room and blinks when the light from the unshaded gas-jet strikes his eyes.

François Cresteil d'Allize is a tall, slim man of twenty-eight. An exceptionally thin neck emphasizes the proud carriage of his head, a small head with a skull that bulges at the back. A short, triangular face, furrowed cheeks, a wrinkled forehead, gentle yet fervent eyes, a drooping brown moustache hiding a mouth with a disdainful curve, a vacillating, disillusioned smile. He has the commanding accent and bearing of a cavalry officer, and emphasizes his remarks with wide sweeps of his arms. Torn between the conservative principles of his upbringing and a passionate desire to emancipate his mind, he resigned his commission not long ago, cutting himself off from his family and breaking with the generations-old royalist and Catholic tradition of the House of Allize. Thus he has all the rankling bitterness of a recent escapee.

With a brisk, lithe movement he goes up to Harbaroux and, bending his tall body, holds out both hands with impulsive friendliness.

CRESTEIL: "Did you hear, old chap? I found it today in that book called *Words of a Believer*." Ignoring Barois, who leaves the room in response to another ring at the bell, he thrusts a hand into his coat-tails and fishes out a rather tattered volume. Then he declaims from memory: " 'Listen, my friends, and say whence it comes, that strange rumour like the sound of many voices which we hear rising all around us . . .' "

Breil-Zoeger, Woldsmuth, Roll, and Barois enter and halt, their backs to the wall, gazing at the orator in amused surprise.

CRESTEIL, who has not noticed them, goes on speaking: " 'Lay your hands on the ground and tell me why it trembles. Something we know not is stirring in the world today. And is not every man awaiting something, each heart throbbing with expectancy? Son of man!' " He points upward, his voice vibrant with emotion. " 'Son of man, climb to the mountain-top, and declare what you behold!' "

His gaze falls on the new-comers, sweeping them off their feet with a look of rapturous ardour.

CRESTEIL: "I propose to have those lines printed in the cover of our review. They would be the perfect manifesto, concise and eloquent."

BAROIS, from the back of the room, enthusiastically: "Agreed!"

They exchange contented smiles; irony has no place here this evening. Some minutes pass in a general exchange of greetings. Barriers are down; they have come here to impart their various enthusiasms, and this first shared emotion has warmed their hearts.

Breil-Zoeger moves to the centre of the group. His oriental face looks yellower than ever. With his difficult smile and restrained, almost embarrassed gestures, the first impression he gives is one of shyness. But in the shadow of the fine-drawn eyelids, the black, restless, deeply sunken eyes have the hard glow that comes of implacable resolve.

BREIL-ZOEGER: "Suppose we sit down? Let's begin at the beginning. Is there anyone else to come?"

BAROIS: "Yes. Portal."

Smiles are exchanged.

BREIL-ZOEGER: "We won't wait for him."

He has seated himself at Barois' desk, as if he were presiding. Harbaroux, who has the intention of taking notes, draws a chair beside Breil-Zoeger's.

Cresteil remains standing, his back to the bookshelves, so as to be able to gesticulate more freely. His arms are folded, he holds his head high, and in his tight-fitting clothes he has the air of a retired colonel.

Roll is ensconced in a wicker chair. A very young man, who has just set up as a printer, he twiddles his incipient moustache to keep himself in countenance while he observes and listens to the older men.

Silent, his shoulders sagging, Woldsmuth hovers in the background, beside the fireplace. So small is he, one could imagine he is sitting down.

Barois hands him a chair, then plants himself in the middle of the room, sitting astride a chair.

BAROIS, opening a cigarette box on the desk: "Help yourselves. Are we ready to make the plunge?" He smiles. "Right! When you came, Harbaroux and I were having a little discussion. The question was: Should this, our first meeting, be simply a means of getting to know one another better, of exchanging views freely and amicably? Or else—" He signs to Harbaroux to speak.

HARBAROUX: "Or else devoted to real spadework, the drawing up of a concrete plan of action?"

BAROIS: "Personally, I think our right course has been pointed out by Cresteil."

CRESTEIL: "No, by Lamennais."

BAROIS: "We don't want merely to draw up a working programme; that wouldn't be enough. What we desire, above all, unless I'm much mistaken, is—how shall I put it?—to pool our temperaments and enthusiasms. And so, quite obviously, nothing cut-and-dried will meet the case." He warms to his subject. "All of us here are animated by the same aspirations, guided by the same high motives, each prepared to harness the driving force of his personal ideal to the collective effort." He hesitates for a moment. "I seem to have launched out into a regular speech, but I suppose I may as well go on. Whence did it come—the first idea of the formation of our group?"

BREIL-ZOEGER: "From you, Barois."

BAROIS, smiling: "No, it was quite as much your child as mine. But what I was going to say was this: the idea was in the air. It answers to a set of needs we, all of us, feel today. We all believe that we have something to say, a part to play in the world."

CRESTEIL, dramatically: "Yes, the hour has struck for us to give our intellectual activities a social repercussion."

No one smiles at this grandiloquence.

BAROIS: "But whenever we try to express ourselves and to bring our efforts to the notice of the public, we come up against well-established customs, caucuses of literary pundits, who have made writing and thinking their preserve; who monopolize even the humblest organs of opinion and bar the door against outsiders. Isn't that so?"

BREIL-ZOEGER: "There's only one remedy. We must create our own organ of expression."

HARBAROUX: "There you come up against the problem of ways and means—of organizing distribution and enlisting support, without frittering our time away on making approaches and arranging interviews . . ."

BAROIS: ". . . which come to nothing."

CRESTEIL: ". . . and on cultivating friendships in high places—which would degrade us."

BAROIS, quietly: "We're not youngsters of twenty. Most of us are in our thirties or thereabouts. That, to my mind, is a most important point. The fervour we shall devote, first to crystallizing, then to making good and championing our ideas, isn't the fervour of the youngster bubbling over with neophyte enthusiasm. No, it is the fine flower of our conscious selves, a well-considered standpoint towards life, that we have adopted once for all."

All signify approval.

CRESTEIL, with a sweeping gesture: "Ah, what a splendid incentive that will be, to feel we are being read, followed and discussed month by month, or week by week!"

BREIL-ZOEGER, instinctively summing up: "To play an *active* part."

HARBAROUX, with a Machiavellian smile: "Only, my friends, you'll not find it quite so easy, when you get down to brass tacks!"

BAROIS, taking up the challenge: "I don't agree. On the practical side our plan is quite feasible." He pauses. "There are funds—"

BREIL-ZOEGER: "—at our disposal; at *your* disposal, I should say."

BAROIS: "Yes, we have a capital sum available—not a big sum, I

admit, but, I think, ample for our purposes—thanks to the gen-
erosity of our friend Roll." Roll murmurs a protest. "Or, if Roll
prefers to put it that way, to the Collectivist Printing House of
which he is managing director. What's more, we are not paying
for contributions; which means that our production costs will be
quite small. There will be only the paper and printing to be paid
for. So we shall be able to make a flying start and keep going long
enough to win a place in the public eye. After that we'll still have
to put up a fight, no doubt; but by then we shall be better equipped
for holding our own."

BREIL-ZOEGER: "So it's this year, at the start, that we shall need
to put forth our greatest effort."

BAROIS: "Yes. The differences in our temperaments, though of
course our general outlook is the same"—the doorbell rings, and he
rises to his feet—"will ensure the variety so necessary for a review."
He goes into the hall.

BREIL-ZOEGER, curtly, as if giving his verdict on what has gone
before: "We have every chance of success."

CRESTEIL, emotionally: "Yes, we have faith, and our faith will see
us through."

HARBAROUX: "What will see us through is a steady, persevering
effort."

BREIL-ZOEGER, dourly: "Faith has never worked miracles—though
it may have seemed to. But will-power *has*, whenever it's been
strong enough."

Shepherded by Barois, Portal at last makes his appearance. He is
smoking a cigar, and beams affably on the little group in the room.

PORTAL: "Well, here I am! Begun already? No, that's impossible
unless in this part of Paris you dine at six o'clock, like the people
in Balzac."

Pierre Portal is a fair-haired young Alsatian, with mild, china-
blue eyes, and a rather babyish face. The small flaxen moustache
adds but a faint touch of virility to his smile. He has a clear, if
slightly worn, complexion, and in his warm, insistent gaze there

kindles, on occasion, a sudden if discreetly veiled sensuality. Women always take to him.

One detects a certain heaviness in his bearing, gestures, voice; also in his jokes. He has strong, though not violent emotions, based on solid common sense, and a shrewd awareness both of his rights and of his duties. He is secretary to an eminent Paris lawyer, Fauquet-Talon, now a leading light in politics, a man of high integrity and much energy, who has twice held ministerial posts.

BAROIS, introducing him: "Portal. Our good friend Roll."

Roll makes a rather awkward bow. Since sitting down he has kept silent, merely gazing intently at each speaker in turn. His face and bearing convey an average intelligence straining its utmost to keep abreast of the others' minds.

BAROIS, affectionately: "Well, Roll, what do you think of our project?"

Roll goes quite pale, as if he has been rebuffed, then flushes, uncrosses his legs and leans forward to speak. At first he is tongue-tied. Then, abruptly, he musters up his courage.

ROLL: "We print dozens of reviews at our works. Every year there's new ones. But none the least bit like yours."

CRESTEIL: "So much the better."

ROLL: "Reviews for connoisseurs, you know; reviews that don't tackle any problem." There is a curious inflexion in his voice. "They're all dilettanti, the folks that write and read them. Aye, there's a need for a review that keeps in touch with the great movements of the day." He pauses, then thumps his knee with his fist. "That's what we need—men who've got some gumption, who understand what's coming to the world."

CRESTEIL, stepping forward, declaims ecstatically: " 'Something we know not is stirring in the world today . . .' "

BAROIS: " 'Son of man, climb to the mountain-top . . .' "

CRESTEIL, BAROIS, ROLL, together: " '. . . and declare what you behold!' "

They exchange glances, with only the faintest smiles at this rather
boyish outburst, behind which lies deep-felt sincerity.

BREIL-ZOEGER, composedly, in a tone calling them to order: "We
must see to it that within six months our review is recognized as
the ally and mouthpiece of all the isolated groups and individuals
now studying positive philosophy or sociology."

HARBAROUX, screwing up his face and blinking through his cigarette smoke: *"Practical* sociology."

BAROIS: "That goes without saying."

PORTAL: "There are more lonely workers in these fields than one
would imagine."

BREIL-ZOEGER: "And it's for us to bring them together."

PORTAL: "Then there are all the organizers of social leagues,
ethical societies, popular universities."

CRESTEIL: "All the believers without a church."

WOLDSMUTH, timidly: "And the pacifists."

BAROIS: "In a word, all men of good will. It's they for whom our
review will cater. Yes, we have a great task before us. We shall
co-ordinate all the melioristic forces that too often run to waste, and
give them a common direction. A splendid programme indeed!"

BREIL-ZOEGER: "And one which we can realize simply by dissemi-
nating our ideas."

BAROIS: "And by setting an example of complete integrity of
thought and absolute sincerity."

PORTAL, smiling: "That might be risky sometimes."

BAROIS: "I don't agree. I believe that frankness is infectious. Nothing but good can come of bringing every problem out into the
open. For instance, I quite agree with our reactionaries that France
is in the throes of a moral crisis. Well, I shan't hesitate to acknowledge this; I shall admit that morality has lost much of its hold.
That is a fact. So far as this affects the mass of the population, I
attribute it to the prevailing anemia of religious faith; as regards
people like ourselves, to the disfavour and discredit that have be-

fallen those abstract principles which our professors of metaphysics dinned into our ears, as if they were so many self-evident truths." He turns to Breil-Zoeger. "You remember what we were saying the other day?"

PORTAL: "But there's no point in making this admission unless you can suggest a remedy."

BAROIS: "That's another story. Still, even now, we can suggest some palliatives."

BREIL-ZOEGER: "Better still, we can prove that, even at the present stage, it's not impossible to visualize a code of ethics that would meet the case."

PORTAL: "Based on what?"

BREIL-ZOEGER: "For one thing, on the data of modern science; and also on the proofs we have, already well authenticated, of certain laws of life."

PORTAL: "Laws that are still extremely vague—and anyhow it's extremely difficult to see how any ethical system can derive from them."

BREIL-ZOEGER, who resents being contradicted: "No, my dear fellow, not so vague as you think. We can define and classify them. First, the instincts of self-preservation and self-improvement; second, the necessary adaptation of the individual to the social environment with which he cannot dispense."

HARBAROUX, nodding: "Two duties, in short, which every man is bound to recognize."

BREIL-ZOEGER: "Yes. He oscillates between these two poles and finds his moral balance in a give-and-take between the ego and its environment."

BAROIS: "I agree. There, certainly, we have the crux of the matter, and a basis for the ethics of tomorrow."

Cresteil steps forward, his head high, his arms uplifted in a sudden, charmingly unaffected movement of expansiveness.

CRESTEIL: "Ah, my friends, when I hear you speaking like this, I feel sure that if once we can make people realize not only what we want, but what we stand for—if once we succeed in making known the moral quality of our aspirations—we shall draw into our orbit within a very few months all the solitary seekers, all who have something"—he thumps his cavernous chest—"here."

BAROIS, whose fervour tends always to find its outlet in rhetorical exuberance: "And this we shall achieve by exalting the sense of human dignity in all our readers. By helping to restore their meaning to such fine old words as Uprightness and Probity—words that have been allowed to lose their lustre in the lumber-room of romantic verbiage; and, above all, by championing man's right to freedom of thought in every field."

There is an affectionate exchange of looks and smiles, a moment of high emotional tension that gradually relaxes. Barois fills the glasses with frothing beer, whose acrid tang mingles with the cigarette smoke filling the little room.

PORTAL, cheerfully, putting down his glass: "And what's it going to be called?"

BAROIS: "That's settled. We've rallied to Cresteil's suggestion. The name's to be *The Sower.*" He smiles at Cresteil. "Of course the metaphor isn't highly original—"

CRESTEIL: "Thanks!"

BAROIS: "But it's simple and admirably expresses our intentions."

BREIL-ZOEGER: "Has Barois told you about the idea he had for the first number?"

BAROIS: "No, I haven't told him yet. It's an idea, I must confess, on which I'm particularly keen. And I hope everyone present will agree to it, as Breil-Zoeger has done. It's this: I want our first issue to be a tribute to a distinguished member of the previous generation."

SOME VOICES: "Who? Luce?"

BAROIS: "Yes, Luce."

CRESTEIL: "An excellent idea!"

BAROIS: "I've several reasons for this. For one thing, our choice of Luce would be a pointer; it would make the public understand

our slant and the type of man we're backing. Then, again, it would
show that wholesale destruction is no part of our programme, nor
are we mere utopian dreamers—since our ideal has found, as it
were, an incarnation in real life; there's a man living today who
admirably illustrates it."

PORTAL: "I see your point. But mightn't it give an impression
that we're exploiting a prominent figure just to give our review a
flying start?"

CRESTEIL, energetically: "Where a man like Luce is concerned, no
one would ever—"

BAROIS, interrupting: "Listen, Portal. Surely, if those old-fashioned
terms I used just now—Uprightness, Probity, and the like—have
ever been applicable to any man, Luce is that man. Also, there's
no question of asking him to give his blessing to our venture, or
of getting a contribution from him for publicity's sake. No, we
shall pay him homage spontaneously and collectively. In fact I'd
suggest we don't even let him know what we are up to."

PORTAL: "Ah! That puts a different complexion on it."

BAROIS: "None of us is personally acquainted with him. All we know
of him is what he has written and what he has done—his public life.
What's more, he is utterly independent. As a philosopher he owns
allegiance to no school; as a politician—a member of the Senate—to
no party. So our homage will apply only to him personally, to the
man he is. Don't let's forget how much of our moral education we
all owe to him. That's why, on the eve of plunging into the arena,
we cannot do less than make this public statement of our obligation.
Do you agree, Cresteil?"

CRESTEIL, smiling as a memory crosses his mind: "Entirely, Barois.
And I'd like to mention a little personal detail, a memory of my boyhood. Luce had been invited, at short notice, to preside at one of our
school speech days. That was twelve years ago, it was my last term
at school. Luce had just been given some rather important post—I
forget what it was."

BAROIS: "Deputy Professor at the Collège de France, most probably."

CRESTEIL: "I can still see him there on the platform, a quite young man, hardly more than fifteen years our senior, in the midst of an array of greybeards. His face, with its look of noble fervour combined with gravity, made a deep impression on me. When addressing us, he spoke in quite ordinary terms, without raising his voice, but every word struck home with wonderful precision. Within a few minutes he had given us a concise but amazingly vivid picture of the way the universe functions, and man's place in it. The theme fitted in so aptly with the problems that engrossed my mind at the time that I really think the whole course of my life was changed by that short speech. So when, two months later, I started on philosophy, I was forearmed against the transcendentalism so dear to our official pundits."

BREIL-ZOEGER, with a harsh guffaw: "Which Coulangheon called a species of 'delusion of grandeur.' "

CRESTEIL: "Anyhow, I was spared it."

There is a short silence.

BAROIS: "Then, I take it, we agree that our first number shall begin with a 'Tribute to Marc-Élie Luce,' signed 'The Sower.' "

HARBAROUX, to Roll: "Can we get out our first number by January?"

ROLL: "In five weeks' time? It'll be a near thing. Can I count on having the copy in before the tenth?"

BAROIS: "We can do that, I think. A good deal's ready, I believe." He turns to Breil-Zoeger. "Isn't that so?"

BREIL-ZOEGER: "I haven't yet started writing my paper, but I have all my data ready."

PORTAL: "On what subject?"

Breil-Zoeger's gaze lingers on Portal; he seems reluctant to reply. Then his hard eyes survey the faces of those present, all turned towards him expectantly. At last he brings himself to speak.

BREIL-ZOEGER: "Briefly, this." His slow, monotonous voice would pass as forceless but for a curious final intonation that takes one by surprise, a crisp sound flicking the ear like a whiplash. "I think it best for our first number that our contributions should be unequivocally tendentious and make quite clear the position we're taking up." Again he rakes the others' faces with his gaze, to make sure of their assent. "Personally, I intend to publish an article which will pave the way for those which follow. I shall confine myself to setting forth a general idea, the gist of which is this: Since, logically, any study of the human situation of today must begin with a survey of the environment in which the individual is evolving, a truly modern philosophy—the only kind that can breathe new life into the dry bones of past philosophies —is necessarily biological in trend, a philosophy which, operating on the human level, regards man primarily as part of the natural world around him. Such a philosophy has the added advantage of being amenable to new developments, since it derives spontaneously from the existing state of scientific knowledge, and, drawing its data solely from facts that can be verified, is bound to keep in step with scientific progress."

PORTAL: "That will certainly damn our review in the eyes of nine out of ten metaphysicians."

BREIL-ZOEGER, promptly: "And so much the better!"

HARBAROUX, seizing the opportunity: "I say! Wouldn't it be a good idea if each of us gave an outline of his plans, right away? Then our first issue would be more or less mapped out this evening. What do you think, Barois?"

BAROIS, after a moment's thought: "I agree."

HARBAROUX, eagerly: "I've some thirty pages ready—about the Communal movement in the twelfth century and its resemblance to the social troubles of the last fifty years. And you, Cresteil?"

Cresteil has just taken his stand with his back to the chimney-piece. His attitude seems a trifle affected, but once he begins speaking, his glowing eyes, impassioned tone, and spacious gestures carry his hearers away.

CRESTEIL: "I propose to discuss that moot question of 'Art for Art's sake.' In connexion, you know, with Tolstoy's latest manifesto. I want to point out that the problem is often wrongly stated, and to claim for the artist the right—nay, the bounden duty—of giving his mind to nothing else, when the work is in gestation, than to making a thing of beauty. For only disinterested emotion is creative. However, I shall try to reconcile this view with the one set up against it, and prove that the useful is inevitably the outcome of the æsthetic quest of beauty. Thus the artist need give no conscious thought, during his creative work, to what may be its social consequences."

BREIL-ZOEGER, who has been listening attentively: "No more than does the scientist."

CRESTEIL: "Quite so. The task of the artist is to achieve beauty; of the scientist, to achieve truth—two aspects of the same purpose. And then it's for the masses to adjust themselves to these achievements, and"—loftily—"bring their petty social exigencies into line with them."

BREIL-ZOEGER: "That's very true."

BAROIS, to Cresteil: "I thought you wanted to earmark, for your contribution, an article on your quotation from Lamennais?"

CRESTEIL, smiling: "No, I leave that to you."

BAROIS, cheerfully: "Right! I'll take it on. As a matter of fact I had it in my mind while I was listening to you. I can see the makings of an excellent leading article. We could begin by explaining why we have inscribed these words in the forefront of our review, and why they so well convey the spirit of our venture."

CRESTEIL: "Yes, that's just the sort of contribution we need as a send-off for our first number."

BAROIS: "I'm glad you agree."

PORTAL: "What's this quotation you're talking about?"

HARBAROUX, ill-humouredly: "You came too late to hear it."

PORTAL: "Suppose you let us know your idea, Barois?"

BREIL-ZOEGER: "Yes, tell us how you'll handle it."

BAROIS, smiling at his thoughts as he proceeds to do so: "I'll take the passage phrase by phrase.

" 'Something we know not is stirring in the world . . .'

"What is this 'something' that is active beneath the surface? It is the increasing activity of human thought, of progress. You see how that theme could be developed. One might speak of the maturation of a gigantic task, in which each of the emotions we experience, each of our struggles, plays its part. And this movement carries in its womb all the solutions we are groping after, all those truths of tomorrow which still elude us, but which in the fullness of time will fall into our hands like ripe fruit and reveal themselves, one after the other, to the questing mind of man."

CRESTEIL: "Bravo! A hymn to progress! I see . . ."

BAROIS, encouraged to give free rein to his creative fancy: "And I'd say too that some amongst us have a sort of second sight, which enables them to see in advance what others fail so far to see. It is such men that Lamennais is addressing when he exclaims: 'Son of man, climb to the mountain-top, and declare what you behold!'

"Here I'd insert a brief description of our vision of the future. 'Declare what you behold!'

"I see a monstrous aggrandizement of the power of wealth, silencing, crushing under its heel, every attempt made by its victims to ventilate their grievances. But I also see a growing restlessness amongst the workers, and the strident wranglings of political parties can no longer drown the voices of the malcontents.

"And I see the steady, tidal onset of a human majority, rough and brutal, dazed by illusions, hungry for security and material well-being, and up in arms against a blind minority which still retains the prestige of an established order, but whose relative stability depends, for all practical purposes, on the capitalist system. In other words, a steady, concerted drive against capitalist rule; that is to say, against the whole social fabric of the modern world—for all civilized countries are ruled in much the same way at the present time. A formidable drive, for which history has no precedent, and which can't fail to make good, since behind it is a new, vital force that is thrusting up, like sap, in the human family tree—a juvenile enthusiasm defying an old, too civilized world that has outlived its heyday."

ROLL, excitedly: "Bravo! Bravo!"

They exchange smiles. Carried away by the sound and cadence of his own voice and the knowledge that all eyes are fixed on him, Barois feels the uprush of an emotion that has been lacking in his life for many months—the emotion of the public speaker who holds his audience. His head high, his shoulders squared, his feet planted well apart, a gay challenge in his eyes, his face aglow with virile confidence, he resumes the thread of his discourse.

BAROIS: "Next, after these generalizations and in conclusion, I would cast a glance at man, the individual.

"When we look into ourselves, what do we find? Only confusion and uncertainty. The betterment of life on the material plane has pandered disastrously to our weaknesses. Never before have they had such free play or sapped our lives so deeply. An unconfessed dread of the unknown haunts the minds of the majority of cultivated men, and a civil war is raging in the heart of each, now that all that is most vital in the mind has risen in revolt, whether consciously or not, against the survival of those mythical imperatives that once ruled human life. That struggle is in progress everywhere and under many aspects, overt or disguised, and in it lies the explanation of the excessive forms taken by present-day social unrest. What makes the struggle all the graver is that it leads to an all-too-evident decline in the mental efficiency of the individual, and a hideous waste of energy." He pauses, sweeps with his gaze the rapt faces of his little audience, and smiles. "That's all!"

For yet a moment he remains keyed up; then suddenly, abruptly, as if a spring had snapped, his exaltation falls. With an embarrassed smile he sits down awkwardly. A short silence follows.

He opens a bottle of beer, fills the glasses, and drains his at a gulp. Then he turns to Portal.

BAROIS, with forced joviality: "And you, old chap? Have you thought up something for us?"

PORTAL, laughing: "Well, I must confess I haven't. Count me out for the first number. I'll give you something for the second."

CRESTEIL: "Slacker!"

PORTAL: "Oh, come now! I've hit on a subject right enough, only I haven't had time to work on it. So far it's only in my head." He smiles. "You don't believe me? Well, here's my idea. It's not exactly an article I have in mind, but some sketches—pen-pictures, you know —of people I see every day, fellows I rub shoulders with, in the courts, in society, in political circles. Average types, you know."

CRESTEIL: "Ah, *don't* I know! That incorrigibly respectable, worthy, average man!"

PORTAL: "Exactly. Fellows who are right-minded, as they say, because they haven't any minds of their own. The innumerable horde of mildly educated people, rubbed smooth by social contacts, like pebbles in a stream. Most of them have a certain rank in society, often a position of importance, but they live like so many beasts of burden." With a twinkle in his eye. "Yes, they all wear blinkers and go straight ahead like a team of docile horses. Not one has ever thought out anything for himself or had the pluck to overhaul the vague beliefs that were foisted on him along with his first knickerbockers. And when their time comes, they die, conventional and muddle-headed as they've lived, never having once been conscious of their muddlement, or having had even a glimpse of the things that rule our lives, things like instinct, love and death."

BREIL-ZOEGER, fiercely: "Show them up, Portal, don't spare them anything! They're pests, these people, and they foul the air. We'll brush them out of our way, like the noisome rubbish they are."

ROLLS, grimly: "They think they're sitting pretty, like worms in rotten meat. But they're mistaken."

The bitterness of their tone contrasts with Portal's smiling irony, and he is rather startled by the hatred his almost flippant words have conjured up.

HARBAROUX: "They're doomed, anyhow. Only look at them; from father to son they're dwindling away, growing more and more spineless, shapeless, incapable of shouldering any serious task."

BAROIS, cutting into the discussion: "Yes, Harbaroux, that's how they strike you when you see them at a distance or pass them in the street. But when you've lived amongst them—it's a very different story. Yes, you realize then that there's lots of life yet under that shell of seeming death." He raises his fist. "And what's more, of pernicious life."

BREIL-ZOEGER, with an ugly grin: "No, Barois, they're not so dangerous as all that. We've shut them out of everything, isolated them, limited their field of action. In forest fires you cut your losses; the patch you sacrifice is allowed to go on burning while you clear the ground ahead of it to prevent the fire from spreading. That's just how it is with them."

BAROIS: "I doubt it. One needs to have lived amongst these people to realize their massive inertia, the powers of obstruction they still have."

CRESTEIL: "Barois is quite right—and don't I know it!"

BAROIS: "Their mausoleums may be full of cracks, but they're good to shelter many and many a generation yet before that noxious race becomes extinct. We may count ourselves lucky if they don't succeed in issuing from their stronghold once more and hoodwinking public opinion as in the past. Can one ever be sure?"

A short silence.

HARBAROUX, methodical as ever: "Wouldn't it be as well to make a written note of what we've decided on?"

There is no answer; indeed no one appears to have heard the remark. The hour is late. A vague somnolence is damping the generous ardour that fired their eloquence. Reaction has come in the form of an undefinable depression, and a stale smell of cooled-down enthusiasm seems to hover in the air.

CRESTEIL: "Our first number will be a trumpet call outside the walls of Jericho!"

But his voice has grown still hoarser and has lost its triumphant challenge. It sinks into the silence, which closes upon it like a stagnant pool.

ROLL, his eyes puffy with fatigue: "If you don't mind, I'll be going. Got to be at the works at seven, you know."

HARBAROUX: "By Jove, it's nearly two o'clock!" To Cresteil. "Good night."

CRESTEIL: "Oh, we're all leaving."

They make a gloomy exit. Barois is alone. He goes to the window and opens it; resting his elbows on the sill, he draws deep breaths of ice-cold air.

All are silent as they tramp down the wooden staircase, Portal, candle in hand, leading the way. Suddenly he looks round; used to late hours, he alone has kept his spirits.

PORTAL: "And Woldsmuth? We've forgotten all about him. What's our good friend Woldsmuth going to bestow on our first number?"

The little procession halts. All turn with smiles towards Woldsmuth, who is bringing up the rear. Torch-wise the candle is passed up from hand to hand until it reaches him.

Seen against the shadows of the upper landing, his face has a comical resemblance to a spaniel's. Amid a tangle of thick, curly hair, bushy eyebrows, and an unkempt beard, the eyes shine out, gentle yet alert, twinkling behind a pince-nez.

For some moments he is silent. Then, when he realizes the others are waiting on his words, a red stain flushes his cheeks, his eyelids flutter, droop, and then disclose, in rising, a gaze at once piteous and fervent.

WOLDSMUTH, with unlooked-for decision: "I shall simply copy out a very sad letter I've just received from Russia. Six hundred Jewish families have been expelled from a little town in the Kiev district. Why? Because a Christian child had been found dead, and the Jews were accused of killing him—a ritual murder, you know—for making their unleavened bread! Incredible, isn't it? But that's how things are over there.

"There was a pogrom, and the survivors were driven from their homes. A hundred and twenty-six new-born babes died in the exodus, because those who had little children to carry couldn't move as fast as the others and had to spend two nights in the snow.

"Yes, that's how things are over there, and nobody in France has the slightest idea of it."

3

A large house in the Auteuil district of Paris, giving on a garden white with hoar-frost, in which half a dozen children are scampering about. A clock strikes eight.

LUCE, stepping forth onto the terrace: "In you come, all of you! Time for lessons!"

The children race across the lawn towards him, laughing and shouting. The two eldest, a girl of thirteen and a boy of twelve, are the first to reach their goal. They are panting, and in the frosty air their breath forms white haloes round their heads. One by one the others come up, the last in the field being a little girl of six.

The dining-room stove is roaring merrily. Inkpots, blotters, and schoolbooks are set out on the big mahogany dining-table. From his study door their father watches the children getting ready. They help each other smilingly, making as little noise as possible, yet unconstrained. Then, without a word from him, silence falls on the group round the table.

Luce crosses the room and goes up the stairs to the next floor. The curtains are drawn in a child's bedroom; a woman, still young, sits at the bedside. Luce gives her a questioning glance, and she indicates by a gesture that the little girl is just dropping off to sleep.

Some moments pass. Then the mother gives a slight start. There has been a ring at the bell. The doctor?

THE MAID: "There's a gentleman to see you, sir. He says he has an appointment. Monsieur Barois."

Barois is alone in Luce's study, a sparsely furnished room, with a big writing-desk strewn with foreign periodicals, recently issued books, and correspondence. Reproductions, maps, and plans hang on two walls, the other two being lined with well-filled bookshelves. In this calm retreat each sound of the world has its echo.

Luce enters.

Marc-Élie Luce is a small man, with an enormous head out of all proportion to the body. He has bright, curiously sunken eyes, a vast forehead, a fan-shaped beard. There is much charm in the limpid pale-grey eyes. Partly owing to his baldness over the temples, the ample forehead, looming high above the remainder of the face, seems to monopolize more than its share of the skull. The auburn beard is already greying.

Luce is forty-seven. The son of a Protestant clergyman, he began by studying theology but soon desisted, feeling he could not subscribe to any dogmatic creed. All he has retained of his early studies is a keen interest in ethical problems.

When quite a young man, he published a work in five large volumes, *The Past and Future of Belief,* which brought him to the fore and secured his appointment to the Chair of Religious History at the Collège de France. He has won high esteem in Auteuil by his keen interest in the "Popular University," which he founded in that district of Paris, and in local charitable organizations. Elected to the Senate, after membership in the General Council, he is one of the youngest senators. He belongs to no party, though claimed as one of theirs in turn by all the groups seeking to make good some lofty ideal. He has published, in this order: *The Higher Levels of Socialism, The Meaning of Life,* and *The Meaning of Death.*

He goes up to Barois and shakes his hand with simple but compelling cordiality.

BAROIS: "Your letter moved us more than I can tell you, sir, and, as the spokesman of our little group, I'd like—"

LUCE, cutting in with brusque informality: "Sit down. I'm delighted to make your acquaintance, Monsieur Barois." He has the thick, unctuous intonation characteristic of the part of France he hails from, the Franche-Comté. "I've read your *Sower.*" Looking Barois in the face, he smiles, without false modesty. "The praises of men younger than oneself are always dangerous, I think; one's so vulnerable to them." He pauses. He has picked up *The Sower* from his desk and is skimming the pages as he speaks. "That's a good title—*For the Cultivation of the Best in Man.*"

He is sitting with his legs wide apart, his elbows on his knees, *The Sower* open in his hands. Gazing at the massive, beetling forehead bent over their nascent venture, Barois feels a sudden thrill of pride.

Again Luce skims the pages, lingering over some notes he has pencilled in the margins. He seems to be pondering, weighing the sheets he holds. At last he looks up, meets Barois' eyes, and replaces *The Sower* on his desk.

LUCE, with quiet sincerity: "Make what use of me you like; I'm with you."

The slight provincial intonation seems to stress the gravity of this declaration of allegiance. Taken unawares and profoundly moved, Barois finds himself tongue-tied. He cannot bring himself to tender the current coin of gratitude. For some moments the two men gaze at each other, in a silent communion of thought. At last Barois breaks the silence.

BAROIS: "Ah, if only my friends could have heard what you've just said, and the way in which you said it!"

LUCE, smiling: "How old are you?"

BAROIS: "Thirty-two."

Luce observes him with the candid smile, untouched by irony, which expresses his attitude to the world: a sort of childish wonder, an eager curiosity, which finds whatever it lights on rare and strange. The two men are silent for a while.

LUCE: "Yes, you're right. An organ like *The Sower* is badly needed. But you're taking on a gigantic task."

BAROIS: "Why?"

LUCE: "Precisely because yours will be the only periodical that makes a fair and square approach to contemporary problems. You'll be widely read—and that's a tremendous responsibility. Don't forget that every line you publish will have consequential effects that spread like ripples and will be beyond your control. More than that: oftener than not you won't even know about them.

"Ah, yes, one always writes too hastily." He seems to be talking to himself. "The sower goes forth to sow. But he must look to his seed, sort out the good from the bad, so as to make as sure as may be that he scatters only the good grain."

BAROIS, proudly: "We have weighed that responsibility—and accepted it."

LUCE, disregarding Barois' remark: "Are your friends of the same age as yourself?"

BAROIS: "About the same."

LUCE, glancing again at the review: "Who is this Breil-Zoeger? Is he related to the sculptor?"

BAROIS: "His son."

LUCE: "Really! My father knew his father; he was one of Renan's closest friends. Isn't your friend a sculptor?"

BAROIS: "No, he took his degree in philosophy. We worked together for the B. Sc."

LUCE: "His 'Prolegomena for a Positive Philosophy' reveals a highly personal outlook, but"—severely—"the outlook of a sectarian." Barois makes a slight gesture of protest. Luce looks up and gazes at him almost affectionately. "Will you permit me to say quite frankly what I think?"

BAROIS: "Why, certainly!"

LUCE: "I'm inclined to extend that reproach to all your group"—gently—"in particular to you."

BAROIS: "Might I know why?"

LUCE: "In this your first number you've taken up an attitude that's forthright, courageous, but a shade—extremist, shall we say?"

BAROIS: "A fighting attitude."

LUCE: "I'd approve of it whole-heartedly if it were merely combative. But it's *aggressive*. Don't you agree?"

BAROIS: "We're all of us enthusiastic, convinced of the truth of our ideas and ready to fight for them. I've no compunction about showing a certain—intolerance." As Luce makes no comment he continues after a moment's pause. "I believe that any young, forceful theory of life is bound to be intolerant. A conviction which starts by admitting the possible legitimacy of convictions directly opposed to it is doomed to sterility. It has no driving force, no fixity of purpose."

LUCE, firmly: "Yet surely what we should try to cultivate in men is a spirit of mutual forbearance; each of us has the right to be as he is, without his neighbour's forbidding him to be so, on the strength of his personal principles."

BAROIS, with involuntary roughness: "Yes, universal tolerance, freedom for all—it's admirable, in theory. But consider to what the smiling scepticism of the dilettante leads. Would the Church have the power it has in the social order of today, if—"

LUCE, breaking in: "I hardly think I need tell you how heartily opposed I am to all that savours of the clerical! I was born in mid-December 1848, and it's always given me pleasure knowing that I was conceived at a time when the liberal movement was fighting its way up into the light. I detest all that the priesthood stands for, all that sails under false colours, whatever these colours may be. And yet what alienates me from all religious systems, far more than their follies, is their intolerance." He pauses before continuing, measuring his words. "No, I shall never countenance the use of evil methods to counter Evil, when all that's needed is to insist on freedom of thought for all alike—and for oneself to set an example.

"Consider the Catholic Church. It had centuries of supreme authority behind it, and yet all that was needed to shake that tremendous edifice to its foundations was that its opponents should likewise be given the right of openly declaring what they thought." Barois listens, but obviously this attentive silence goes against the grain. Luce now speaks in a conciliatory tone. "Let error have its say, by all means, but let the truth also be free to have its say. And don't let's trouble overmuch about the immediate consequences. Truth will triumph in the end. Don't you agree?"

BAROIS: "Needless to say, I know that, by all abstract standards, you are right. But a man has feelings that he can't control, feelings he simply has to voice." A brief silence. Luce seems to await an explana-

tion. There is an undertone of bitterness in Barois' voice as he proceeds: "Oh, I know quite well that I'm intolerant; I'm through with
tolerance!" He lowers his voice. "To understand, you'd need to know
all I have been through. A young man of independent mind who is
forced to live in an intensely pious atmosphere; who finds himself
becoming daily more and more enmeshed in those supple yet fiercely
tenacious nets spread by the Catholic Church; who feels religion
seeping into his life and into the lives of those around him through
every pore, shaping the hearts and souls of those nearest and dearest
to him, leaving its imprint everywhere—yes, a man who has been
through all that, and he only, has the right to speak of tolerance. Not
a man who has had to make occasional concessions, out of affection;
but a man whose whole life was one long concession. Such a man is
qualified to speak of tolerance. And then"—Barois gazes at Luce with
a wry smile—"he speaks of it as one speaks of perfect virtue, or of
any other ideal which is far beyond the scope of human possibilities."

LUCE, gently, after a brief silence: "You're not—living alone, then?"

Barois' face, darkened until now by memories, lights up; the
anger goes out of his eyes.

BAROIS: "I *am* alone now. Free!" He smiles. "But I've enjoyed this
freedom too short a time to have regained the virtue of tolerance."
He pauses. "Forgive me, Monsieur Luce, for having given way to my
feelings on the subject."

LUCE: "I'm to blame. Quite unintentionally of course, I reminded
you of—of things you'd prefer forgotten."

They exchange friendly glances.

BAROIS, impulsively: "It's done me good. I need advice. There's
more than fifteen years' difference between us. You, Monsieur Luce,
have been *living* for twenty-five years. I have only just broken—after
many painful struggles—all my chains. Yes, all!" His slashing gesture seems to cut his life in two: on this side, the past; on that, the
future. Then he stretches forth his arms. "So, you see, I've a completely new life before me—a vista so immense that it almost makes

me dizzy when I contemplate it. My first thought in launching this
review was to try to get in contact with you. For I see you as the first
landmark on the horizon of my new life."

LUCE, hesitantly: "I'm afraid I can only cite my own experience."
He points to one of the large maps hanging on a wall. "I've always
felt that life is like one of those maps of countries I have never visited; to find one's way one needs only to know how to read the map.
Concentration, orderly thinking, moderation, perseverance—that's all
one needs. It's quite simple, really." He again picks up the copy of
The Sower.

"You've made an excellent start, and you've plenty of trump cards
in your hand. In your team you obviously have men with active, original minds. Nothing could be better." He ponders. "If, however, I
had any advice to give you, it would take this form. Don't let yourself be influenced too much by your companions. Yes, that's often
the danger in groups like yours. Obviously you need community of
thought, and that you have. The impulse which brought you together and started you on your venture was the same for all. But
don't throw your personality into the melting-pot. 'To thine own self
be true'—inexorably. And cultivate in yourself what is truly yours.
Each of us has a quality peculiar to himself, a 'gift' if you like, which
absolutely distinguishes him from everybody else. It's that gift one
must locate within oneself, and promote it, to the exclusion of all
else."

BAROIS: "But isn't that narrowing one's scope? Mayn't it sometimes
be better to act quite differently, and try to get away from oneself as
much as one can?"

LUCE: "No, I don't think so."

THE MAID, putting her head in at the door: "The Mistress asked
me to tell you that the doctor's come."

LUCE: "Right." He turns to Barois. "My opinion is that a man
should remain himself—but develop his mental stature, and try to
become the most perfect specimen of the type of humanity he stands
for."

BAROIS, rising: "But shouldn't he act, talk, write, put forth his utmost strength?"

LUCE: "Oh, a strong personality always manages to express itself. Don't have illusions about the usefulness of mere output at all costs. Isn't a noble life as meritorious as a noble work? I too used to think that one had to keep slogging away at it. But gradually I've come to change my mind about it." He is escorting Barois to the door. As they pass the window, he points outside. "That's my garden. Well, isn't it just the same thing there? We have to see to it that the stock is good and then improve it year by year; and, if the function of the tree is to bear fruit, you'll see the crop increasing of its own accord." They are crossing the dining-room. The small heads, bent over the lesson-books, rise as they enter. "My children."

Barois nods, smiling.

LUCE, guessing what is at the back of Barois' mind: "Yes, quite a handful. And I plead guilty to having two more! There are days when I feel all those eyes fixed on me—and I'm appalled!" He shakes his head. "But life's a strict logician, and its findings will be just; of that I feel assured." He goes up to the table. "This is my eldest, quite a big girl already. And this youngster, Monsieur Barois, is a budding mathematician." He fondles the silken curls of each child as he walks by; then suddenly he turns to Barois. "Ah, life's a glorious thing, isn't it?"

I glimpse a swelling sea, a new day breaking . . .
My heart is like a world . . .

Ibsen

I

A JUNE afternoon in 1896. A *brasserie* in the Boulevard Saint-Michel. The hands of the clock point to five. The ground-floor drinking-hall—a huge dark room in the Heidelberg style, with massive tables, wooden stools, and escutcheons on the walls—is thronged with a noisy crowd of students and young women.

On the mezzanine floor a low-ceilinged room is reserved one day a week for the *Sower* group. Cresteil, Harbaroux, and Breil-Zoeger are seated at a wide, semicircular bay-window extending to floor level. It stands open, and there comes to their ears the hum of traffic in the boulevard below.

Barois comes in, a bulky attaché-case under his arm, and shakes hands with his friends. He sits down and takes some papers from the case.

BAROIS: "Portal not come yet?"

BREIL-ZOEGER: "Haven't seen him."

BAROIS: "And Woldsmuth?"

HARBAROUX: "It's rather odd. I've been going regularly to the Bibliothèque Nationale for the last few days and haven't once set eyes on him."

BAROIS: "He's sent me ten pages on the Education Act—very remarkable they are." He hands a sheaf of papers to Cresteil. "Here are your proofs. They're printed rather close, I'm afraid, but we've so much copy for this number." To Harbaroux. "And here are yours."

HARBAROUX: "Thanks. What date exactly?"

BAROIS: "Roll must have them back at the end of the week." To Breil-Zoeger. "Here are yours. By the way, I'd like to have a word with you about your paper." To the others. "Will you excuse us?" He gets up and goes with Breil-Zoeger to the far end of the room. He speaks in a low voice, affectionately. "It's about your article 'Social Determinism,' old chap. A fine piece of work, incidentally; I doubt if you've ever written anything richer in ideas or more closely reasoned. I took the liberty of reading some of it to Luce last night and he was much impressed by its forcefulness."

BREIL-ZOEGER, complacently: "Good! Did you read out the passage relating to Pasteur?"

BAROIS: "No. And it's about that I'd like to talk to you before you correct your proofs." Seeing the sulky look that crosses his friend's face, Barois feels slightly embarrassed. "Quite frankly, I find that passage a bit too severe."

BREIL-ZOEGER, with a brisk wave of his arm: "I say nothing against the man of science; I deal with Pasteur as a metaphysician."

BAROIS: "I quite understand that. But you judge Pasteur as you'd judge one of our contemporaries, one of his pupils. Far be it from me to say that his philosophical outlook is commendable. But you seem too much inclined to forget how much our modern scientific materialism owes to that incorrigible believer in a spiritual world."

BREIL-ZOEGER, waving his arm again, as if to brush aside an obstacle: "I know as well as you do what we owe him—though this manner of speaking doesn't imply, as far as I'm concerned, any sentimental obligation." He gives a short, cackling laugh, and for a moment a streak of white flashes across the Chinese-yellow face. "Pasteur thought fit to take up, publicly mind you, a perfectly definite metaphysical standpoint, and we have every right to criticize it. Really, there are limits to one's forbearance in these matters! We've heard too much about that speech he made in answer to the address of welcome when he entered the Académie for us to need to feel any scruples regarding Pasteur."

BAROIS: "The family he sprang from and his education prevented him from drawing the philosophical conclusions that flow from his discoveries, as we of a later generation have been able to do—and thanks to him, don't forget. We can't hold it against him if he wasn't young enough to change his views when he made those great discoveries." He pauses, waiting for an answer, but Breil-Zoeger looks resolutely away. "Those opening pages of yours are unjust, old chap."

BREIL-ZOEGER: "You're under Luce's influence, I can see."

BAROIS: "I wouldn't wish to deny it."

BREIL-ZOEGER: "It's regrettable. Because of that mania he has for toleration Luce often lacks firmness, and sometimes insight too."

BAROIS: "So be it." He pauses. "We'll say no more about the matter. You're free." He smiles. "Free and responsible."

Barois goes back to the table and sits down. A waiter brings drinks.

BAROIS: "Are you sure Portal's coming?"

CRESTEIL: "He told me he'd come."

BREIL-ZOEGER: "Don't let's wait for him."

BAROIS: "The truth is that I've some good news to announce, and I'd have liked all of us to be present. Yes, on the material side our *Sower* is doing exceedingly well. I've just made up our half-yearly accounts." He holds up a ledger. "They're open to your inspection.

"We started off six months ago with thirty-eight regular subscribers. This month we have five hundred and sixty-two. Moreover, we sold last month some eight hundred copies in Paris and the provinces. Our June number, of fifteen hundred copies, is all sold out already."

CRESTEIL: "It's certain that Luce's collaboration has been a tremendous help."

BAROIS: "Obviously. Subscriptions have exactly doubled since he gave us his first contribution four months ago. We're printing two thousand copies of *The Sower* for July. I suggest to you that it should contain two hundred and twenty pages instead of one hundred and eighty as in the past."

BREIL-ZOEGER: "Why?"

BAROIS: "I'll explain. We are having more and more letters sent us relating to articles in our review. Indeed, I've had nearly three hundred to read this month. With Harbaroux's help I have sorted them out according to the articles with which they deal, and I shall send to each of you the batch of letters relating to his contribution. You'll find that some of them are highly pertinent. In my opinion we should allot space to such correspondence when we're planning the lay-out of our subsequent issues. These letters show that our readers take a keen interest in *The Sower,* and their criticisms are often valuable. This is something to be proud of, and we should do wrong to bury these letters in our files. So I propose that we should publish every month a selection of them, followed when desirable by"—Portal enters—"by a note written by the author of the article referred to."

Portal seems lost in thought and quite unlike his usual cheerful self. After shaking hands with Cresteil and Barois he sits down.

HARBAROUX: "What's this? Won't you shake hands with me?"

PORTAL, rising: "So sorry!" With a faint smile he shakes hands with Harbaroux and sits down again.

BREIL-ZOEGER: "We'd almost given you up."

PORTAL, nervously: "Well, as a matter of fact, I'm shockingly busy just now. I've only just been able to get away from the Law Courts Library." Looking up, he sees the others' eyes intent on him. "There may be—trouble brewing, something quite unexpected."

BAROIS: "Trouble?"

PORTAL: "Yes. I've recently been having glimpses—only glimpses, mind you—of a very distressing possibility. Of a possible miscarriage of justice, to be precise. It may be rather serious, though so far nothing definite has leaked out."

Greatly puzzled, they stare at him in silence.

PORTAL, lowering his voice: "I'm alluding to that Dreyfus Affair."

CRESTEIL: "Dreyfus innocent? Well, really!"

BAROIS: "Preposterous!"

HARBAROUX: "Some mare's nest, obviously."

PORTAL: "Well, nothing tangible has come out as yet—that I admit. I can only tell you what little I know, and, so far as I can judge, no one else knows more at present. But people are feeling uneasy and inquiries are on foot. I've even been told that the General Staff is looking into it. My chief, Fauquet-Talon, is keenly interested and has asked me for a full report of the trial that took place eighteen months ago."

A short silence.

BREIL-ZOEGER, calmly, to Portal: "Obviously errors may creep into the decisions of a civil court which sits every day and may have to get through a great number of cases within a given time. But a court-martial is a very different affair. The men who sit on it are hand-picked; they're not professional purveyors of justice and, for this very reason, are on their mettle and feel bound to go very carefully into the facts before delivering their verdict."

BAROIS: "Especially in so important a case, when the charge is high treason. No, Portal, you'll find that, as Harbaroux said, it's a mare's nest."

CRESTEIL: "And I've a shrewd idea who's behind it. It's a rumour that's been set on foot by—"

WOLDSMUTH, with emotion in his voice, but unhesitatingly: "By the Jews, I suppose?"

CRESTEIL, coldly: "By the Dreyfus family."

BAROIS: "Hullo, Woldsmuth! Are you there? I didn't see you come in."

HARBAROUX: "Nor did I."

BREIL-ZOEGER: "Nor I."

They shake hands with him.

PORTAL, to Woldsmuth: "Have you too been hearing rumours on this subject?"

Slowly Woldsmuth raises his shaggy face, dark now with a vague distress, and looks at Portal. Then, lowering his red-rimmed eyelids, he gives a brief nod.

BAROIS, quickly: "But surely you agree that, in this case, a miscarriage of justice is practically unthinkable?"

Woldsmuth makes a dubious gesture, as if to say: Who knows?

Anything's possible. All have a feeling of constraint, aggravated by the short silence which ensues.

BAROIS: "Here you are, Woldsmuth. I've brought your proofs."

PORTAL, to Woldsmuth: "Ever met this fellow Dreyfus?"

WOLDSMUTH, blinking his eyes even more rapidly than usual when he is spoken to: "No." He pauses. "But I was present at his dismissal from the Army. And *I saw.*"

BAROIS, irritably: "Saw what?"

Woldsmuth's eyes grow blurred with tears. Without answering, he gazes timidly at his friends, one after the other: at Barois, Cresteil, Harbaroux, Breil-Zoeger. He knows himself alone, and the forlorn smile of the vanquished moulds his lips.

2

October 20, 1896

My dear Barois: It is impossible for me to come to see you, as I have had a slight accident. It's nothing serious but it compels me to stay indoors for some days. Still, I should greatly like to have a talk with you. Could you face the six stories' climb up to my rooms tomorrow, or, at the latest, the day after?

Forgive this importunity, but it's urgent.

Ever yours,
Ulric Woldsmuth

The following day. An enormous old house, more like a block of buildings, in the Rue de la Perle, in the heart of the "Marais" district of Paris. A small attic flat on the sixth floor of Staircase F, numbered 14, stands at the end of a long passage.

A young woman answers Barois' ring and asks him in. There are three rooms opening one into the other. In the first an old grey-haired woman is hanging washing on lines stretched just below the ceiling. In the second are two beds, or, rather, mattresses placed on the floor. The third door is shut. After opening it and peeping in the young woman turns to Barois.

JULIA: "Oh, he's asleep. If you're not in a great hurry . . ."

BAROIS, promptly: "No, please don't wake him. I can wait."

JULIA: "Sleep does him so much good."

Barois, who had no idea that Woldsmuth was married, studies her with interest. There is no mistaking Julia Woldsmuth's oriental origin. Her age is twenty-five. At a first glance she strikes one as very tall and thin. Actually her torso—uncorseted under a black blouse—is thick and short. But her limbs, her arms especially, are extraordinarily long. Her face tapers forward like a knife-blade, and the mass of frizzy jet-black hair bunched on her neck increases its prow-like effect. A pointed nose prolongs the slope of the rather receding forehead. The slotted, half-closed eyes draw upwards towards the temples. The oddly shaped upper lip, which always seems arrested on the brink of a smile, juts out above the lower without touching it.

Briskly she motions Barois to the only chair in the room, and she herself without the least embarrassment squats down on one of the unmade beds.

BAROIS, tentatively: "Might I know how this—this accident happened, Madame?"

JULIA: "No. Mademoiselle."

BAROIS, smiling: "Sorry!"

JULIA, taking no notice of the remark: "We didn't know at the time. It was after midnight and we'd gone to bed, Mother and I." She points to Woldsmuth's room. "We heard a slight explosion, but that didn't alarm us. In fact I was glad to think my uncle had started work again and was beginning to think less about that case. Next morning he called to us; his face had some nasty cuts—from the splinters of glass, you know—and was burnt as well."

BAROIS, much puzzled: "An explosion, you said. Of what?"

JULIA, curtly: "A retort over the Bunsen burner blew up."

Only now does Barois remember that Woldsmuth was once a laboratory assistant. There is a short silence.

BAROIS: "Please don't let me keep you from your work."

Julia is sitting on the tumbled sheets, her legs crossed, her elbows propped on her knees, and is frankly studying Barois' face. Her gaze is friendly and quite unself-conscious.

JULIA: "You're not disturbing me. I'm glad you called today. I've heard so much about you and I've read all your articles and comments in *The Sower*." After a brief pause she adds with a bluntness that seems curiously impersonal: "Ah, what a splendid life you lead!"

She has Woldsmuth's guttural voice, but her free-and-easy manner makes a striking contrast to his shyness. A queer creature! Barois muses, gazing at her.

BAROIS: "I didn't know that Woldsmuth was still interested in chemistry—in a practical way, I mean."

Julia averts her eyes; a sudden glint of fervour has kindled in their moist pupils.

JULIA: "He never tells anything because he is aiming at a great discovery. 'When I've made it, I'll speak out—but not before'—that's how he feels." Barois says nothing but his look conveys his interest. "Still, he has no reason to make a mystery of it with you, Monsieur Barois. You're a biologist." She warms to her subject. "My uncle believes that some day it will be possible to create life by bringing together certain elements under suitable conditions—I'm sorry I can't express it better." She gives him an almost childish smile.

BAROIS: "To create life?"

JULIA: "Don't you think it possible?"

BAROIS: "Well, I know that, theoretically, it's not ruled out. All the same—"

JULIA, quickly: "Uncle's positive it can be done."

BAROIS: "It's a fine ambition in any case. And really there's no reason why it shouldn't be realized some day." He thinks aloud. "We know that at a certain period of the remote past the temperature of the earth was too high to allow of the vital synthesis. So there was a moment when life did not exist; and then a moment when life existed."

JULIA: "Exactly. And the thing to do is to reproduce the conditions of the moment when life began."

BAROIS, puckering his brows: "Wait a bit! I didn't put it quite that way—'the moment when life began.' I'd be more inclined to say, 'the moment when under certain conditions the vital synthesis took place, a synthesis of elements already existing—from all eternity.' "

JULIA, keenly interested: "Why do you draw that distinction?"

BAROIS, somewhat disconcerted by the technical turn the conversation is taking: "Well, to tell the truth, I think that when one uses the expression 'life began,' it's an unfortunate way of putting it. It panders to that all-too-common tendency to insist on a beginning."

JULIA, still squatting on the bed, an elbow on each knee, and cupping her chin with her hand: "But surely the mere fact of knowing that living matter exists obliges us to assume that it came into existence?"

BAROIS, impulsively: "Certainly not! Personally, I simply cannot stomach that notion of a beginning. But I find it quite easy to accept the notion of a substance that exists, that is always undergoing transformation, and will continue to evolve eternally."

JULIA: "The whole universe being included in the process."

BAROIS: "Yes, and forming a single cosmic substance which can transmit life to all that emanates from it." He pauses. "No doubt you help your uncle in his work?"

JULIA: "A bit."

BAROIS: "And you're experimenting with the rays emitted by radium, I presume?"

JULIA: "Yes."

BAROIS, pensively: "One thing's certain: recent discoveries in chemistry have gone far to bridge the gulf that separated life from death in the past."

For some moments neither speaks.

JULIA, pointing to the typewriter: "You'll excuse me if I go on with my work? Anyhow, I hope you won't have to wait much longer."

She sits down at the table; the tick-tack of the typewriter echoes in the room. Her face shows in dark outline against the whiteness of the window; light ripples on her busy hands, which are paler underneath and seem endowed with almost simian agility. The fingers taper off into very long, ivory-yellow nails. Five minutes go by thus.

WOLDSMUTH'S VOICE: "Julia!"

JULIA: "Ah, you're awake, Uncle! Monsieur Barois has just this minute come."

She opens the door and stands aside to let Barois pass. It is a very narrow doorway, and he cannot help brushing against her, but she seems hardly to notice, and there is nothing feminine in her slight movement of recoil. Indeed, she thrusts her head forward, so close that he feels her breath fan his cheek.

JULIA, under her breath: "Don't say I made you wait."

He reassures her with a glance.

Woldsmuth's bedroom has a glassed-in fore-part, formerly a photographer's studio and now used as a laboratory. In the back of the room is an alcove containing Woldsmuth's bed. The body under the sheets might be a child's; indeed, so small is it that the big head swathed in bandages seems hardly to belong to it.

BAROIS: "Dreadfully sorry, old chap, to see you like this. Are you in pain?"

WOLDSMUTH: "No." He still clasps Barois' hand. "Julia will bring you a chair." Barois forestalls her and draws a chair up to the bedside. Julia goes out. Speaking with a proud affection that tries to sound paternal, Woldsmuth adds: "She's my niece."

The tone of voice is the same, but Woldsmuth himself is unrecognizable. Layers of dressing cover his hair, nose, and beard; the only signs of life are a dim smile and the soft brown eyes under the bushy eyebrows.

WOLDSMUTH: "Thank you very much for coming, Barois."

BAROIS: "But, my dear Woldsmuth, that was only natural. What's the trouble?"

WOLDSMUTH, in a changed tone: "Oh, Barois, it's high time that all people of good will should know what's happening. He's exiled over there, he'll die of his privations—and he's innocent!"

BAROIS, smiling at this obsession, due he thinks to illness: "Still harping on that fellow Dreyfus?"

WOLDSMUTH, propping himself on his elbows, excitedly: "I beg you, Barois, I beseech you in the name of all that's just and decent in the world, to clear your mind of prejudice. Forget all you read in the newspapers two years ago and all the stories that you've heard. I entreat you, Barois, to listen to me." He sinks back upon the pillows. "Oh, I know we're always talking about our duty to the cause of human happiness. Yes, it's easy to take an interest in humanity at large, in mankind in the mass, in people whose sufferings will never come under our eyes." He gives a nervous laugh. "But that's nothing, *nothing!* The love one feels for one's real, *literal* neighbour, for those whose sufferings are visible at our door—that's love indeed, the only love that matters." He sits up in bed. "So, Barois, I beg you to forget all you've learnt about this business and hear me out."

All the life of the man, a shapeless lump of bandages, seems concentrated in the restless, ardent eyes, full of mute appeal.

BAROIS: "I'm listening. And please don't overexcite yourself."

Woldsmuth ponders for some moments, then takes from underneath the sheets a sheaf of typewritten pages and runs his eyes over them. But in the alcove where he lies darkness is closing in.

WOLDSMUTH, raising his voice: "Julia! Bring a lamp, please."

The typewriter stops clicking. Julia enters with a small hand-lamp that she places on the bedside table.

WOLDSMUTH: "Thanks." She gives him a frigid smile. The brown eyes, glowing between the bandages, follow affectionately her receding form. Then he turns to Barois. "Let's go right back to the beginning, as if you knew nothing at all about it. The bare facts to start with.

"Well then, a discovery is made at the War Ministry that there has been a leakage of official documents. Next, the head of the Bureau of Statistics, so-called—meaning, of course, the French Intelligence—hands the Minister a letter said to have been found amongst other papers filched from the German Embassy. The letter, written by hand, is what they call the *bordereau* and consists of a list of documents which the writer of the letter is making over to his addressee.

"So much for the initial facts.

"Efforts are made to trace the traitor. Of five documents listed in the *bordereau* three relate to the Artillery. So the inquiry centres on the artillery officers of the General Staff. Owing to a certain resemblance in the handwriting suspicion falls on Dreyfus. He is a Jew, and unpopular. But at the preliminary investigation nothing against him is discovered."

BAROIS: "So you say."

WOLDSMUTH: "What I say is borne out by the fact that the indictment sets forth nothing suspicious either in Dreyfus's private life or in his contacts with outsiders. Nothing, that is to say, but mere guess work."

BAROIS: "Have you read the bill of indictment?"

WOLDSMUTH, holding up a sheet: "I have a copy here, which I'll let you have." A short silence. "The next step is to call in two handwriting experts. One of them does not think that the incriminating letter is in Dreyfus's hand. The other thinks it may be, but his report begins with a very important reservation." He looks through his papers. "This is how it reads: 'If we ignore the possibility that this may be a very carefully executed forgery . . .' Meaning, I think you will agree, that the writing has much in common with that of Dreyfus, but it's impossible definitely to say if it is his or the work of a forger.

"Do you follow, Barois?"

BAROIS, very coldly: "Yes, I follow."

WOLDSMUTH: "On the strength of these two conflicting opinions his arrest is ordered. Yes—without any further investigation, without even keeping the movements of the suspect under surveillance. Everyone is morally convinced that he is guilty—and that suffices. He is arrested.

"Here comes a dramatic incident which I'll describe in detail.

"Dreyfus is summoned one morning to the War Office for a 'general inspection.' He is instructed to attend in civilian clothes—which is contrary to all military precedent. That's the first remarkable feature of these proceedings. Note that, were he guilty, this would have roused his suspicion and he'd have had time to make his escape. He does nothing of the kind. He duly arrives at the appointed hour and finds none of the brother-officers present who would normally have been summoned to attend a meeting of this sort. Another surprise.

"He is promptly ushered into the Chief of Staff's office. The General is not there, but a small group of men in mufti whom he does not know are standing in a corner of the room, all watching him intently. Then, without a word about the inspection, a Major says to him, 'I've hurt my hand. Would you kindly write a letter for me?'

"The moment seems an odd one for asking of a junior officer a friendly service of this kind. There is, in fact, an atmosphere of mystery about the whole proceedings—in the attitude of those present no less than in the things they say.

"Much puzzled, Dreyfus sits down at the desk.

"Then the Major starts dictating to him a letter so phrased as to include some passages from the famous *bordereau*. Naturally they mean nothing to Dreyfus, but the hostility of his superior officer's voice, coupled with the tension in the air of which he has been conscious since entering the room, affects his nerves and, as a result, his handwriting. The Major looks over his shoulder and exclaims, 'Ah, your hand is trembling!' Dreyfus, who has failed to grasp the reason for this remark, which sounds like a reprimand, apologizes. 'My fingers are a bit cold, I'm afraid.'

"The dictation continues. Dreyfus tries to write more steadily.

The Major breaks in irritably, 'Take care! It's serious.' Then suddenly, 'I arrest you, in the name of the law!' "

BAROIS, greatly impressed: "But from where did you get this story of yours? The *Éclair* version of what happened was quite different." Rising, he takes some steps in the dimly lighted room. "What reasons have you for assuming that your version is the true one?"

WOLDSMUTH: "I know the source from which the newspaper got its information. The published description of the incident is a travesty of the facts." He lowers his voice. "Barois, I've had in my hands a photograph of the dictated letter. Yes, I've seen it with my own eyes. Well, the traces of emotion in the writing are very slight and easily explicable. I cannot believe that a traitor who has been found out and is ordered to write the very words he used when betraying a secret to a foreign Power could conceivably show such imperturbability. It's unthinkable!" Barois says nothing. "And there's something else I've discovered. The warrant of arrest was signed a day before the dictation took place; in fact his arrest had been so effectively decided on—whatever might take place that morning—that the prison cell had been got ready on the previous evening."

Barois still keeps silent. He sits at the bedside, his arms folded, holding himself very straight, his head thrown back a little, his eyebrows lifted, his chin thrust pugnaciously forward.

There is a short silence while Woldsmuth peers at his notes. Then, raising his eyes, he leans towards Barois.

WOLDSMUTH: "So Dreyfus is thrown into prison. Though the mental torture would have been enough to drive many a man crazy, for a whole fortnight he was not allowed even to know why he had been arrested, nor was he informed of the charge against him.

"Meanwhile inquiries were being pushed forward in various quarters. He was repeatedly interrogated—without result. Searches were made at his home. His wife was questioned under the most brutal conditions; she was not allowed to know where her husband was, and was even told she'd be signing his death-warrant if she told anyone whomsoever about his disappearance.

"At last, on the fifteenth day, Dreyfus was shown the *bordereau*. With the energy of despair he protested that he knew nothing about it. But all to no avail; the preliminary inquiry ran its course.

"The Court-Martial Board took cognizance of the case, and a second inquiry was set on foot. Dreyfus was interrogated again, plied with new questions, witnesses were examined, accomplices sought—but still to no effect. No solid evidence against him was forthcoming.

"Then, Barois, for the first time the Minister of War publicly entered the lists; in a press interview he declared that the guilt of the accused man was proved to the hilt, but he could make no further statement on the subject.

"Some weeks later Dreyfus was tried *in camera,* found guilty, and sentenced to transportation for life."

BAROIS: "Well, my dear fellow, doesn't his conviction shake your confidence that the man was innocent? If no serious charge had been established against Dreyfus, can you possibly imagine that a board of officers—"

WOLDSMUTH, excitedly: "Yes, I tell you, I *assure* you, that in a four days' trial it was proved beyond all doubt that Dreyfus had never engaged in any treasonable practices, that his alleged journeys abroad, his straitened circumstances, his love affairs, and all the anti-Semitic press had published to rouse popular opinion against him—all these things were so much idle talk, without the least foundation in fact."

BAROIS, shrugging his shoulders: "None the less, two colonels, two majors, and two captains were prepared to . . . Really, my dear fellow, it's preposterous, what you've been saying."

A glint of satisfaction flickers in the sick man's eyes; he is glad that Barois is not yet convinced. The more resistance he puts up now, the stronger will be his conviction, the fiercer his indignation in the end.

WOLDSMUTH, holding up the typewritten pages: "The whole truth is here."

BAROIS: "What exactly have you there?"

WOLDSMUTH: "A report, Barois; a verbatim report of all that happened. Compiled by a man who's practically unknown, a man who has a heart of gold and, with it, a lucid, admirably logical mind."

BAROIS: "And what's your paragon's name?"

WOLDSMUTH: "Bernard Lazare." Barois makes a gesture implying: Never heard of him. "Now you must hear me out. For there's more to tell, much more. I asked you to come to see me so that you should know what's happened. But for another reason too." In a tone whose authoritativeness is as unlooked-for as it is compelling, he goes on: "Barois, we must defeat this conspiracy of lies, of reticences and foul insinuations, which is crushing out the truth. We must see to it that a voice respected by all secures a hearing; that a man whose honesty none dares to question learns the true facts, obeys the dictates of his conscience, and boldly denounces, on behalf of all of us, the wrong that has been done." Shoring himself up on his arms, he is watching his friend's face to see if he has grasped what is expected of him. But Barois' face is hard, impassive. A note of pleading enters Woldsmuth's voice as he makes himself explicit. "In a word, what's wanted is that Luce should give an interview to Bernard Lazare." Barois makes a fretful gesture. "Luce must be induced to listen to him, without prejudice, with all the impartiality of the upright man he is." He waves the typewritten sheets. "A hundred thousand copies of this pamphlet must be printed. This is a crusade in the cause of justice in which neither you nor I nor Luce can fail to take up arms."

Barois begins to rise from his chair.

WOLDSMUTH: "Wait, Barois. Do, please, suspend judgment a little longer. And please, oh, please, don't say anything—yet." In a tone of entreaty. "All I ask is for you to judge for yourself, and not to let your mind be biased by what you may have heard from others. I shall now read out some fragments of Lazare's pamphlet, and you cannot fail, I think, to be impressed by its fervour in the cause of justice—simple, human justice." Feverishly. "Where shall I begin? Yes. Listen to this first.

" 'Captain Dreyfus was arrested after two experts had given *contradictory* opinions.

" 'The inquiry was conducted in a most high-handed fashion. Yet all it revealed was the utter absurdity of the rumours current about Dreyfus, and the falsehood of the police reports, which were flatly contradicted by the witnesses, and on which the prosecution dared not insist.

" 'Thus the whole case for the prosecution rested on a sheet of thin notepaper, a schedule of documents written in a peculiar hand and style, which had been torn in four pieces and carefully stuck together again.

" 'Where did this incriminating document come from? According to Besson d'Ormescheville's report, General Joux, when handing it to the police officer conducting the inquiry, told him that this *bordereau* had originally been addressed to a foreign Power, and had reached its destination. However, under orders from the War Minister, he could not divulge the channel by which the *bordereau* had come to him.

" 'Thus the prosecution has no idea how this unsigned, undated piece of writing was sent by the accused man to its destination; while the defence is kept in ignorance of the channels through which it made its way from the Embassy to the War Office; to whom it was originally addressed; and who it was who purloined it or by some other means procured it.' " Woldsmuth looks up from the page he has just read aloud.

"I should mention that in an earlier page he makes clear the unconvincingness of the document in itself. Just a moment, please. Ah, yes, here it is. I'll read out the passage.

" 'Is the document itself authentic? No.

" 'Let us first consider its origin; or, rather, the origin attributed to it. According to M. Montville, writing in *Le Journal* of September 16, 1894, it was found at the German Embassy by an office-boy who had the habit of making over to the French Intelligence Service the contents of the wastepaper baskets. Was there ever any employee at the Embassy who indulged in these practices? Yes. Was the Embassy staff unaware of this? No. When did it come to the knowledge of the Embassy? A year before the Dreyfus case. Under what circumstances?'" Woldsmuth looks up again.

"I have a report of the trial of Mme Millescamps in the Court of Summary Jurisdiction. You can peruse it later. Meanwhile I'll go straight on with Lazare's summary.

"'Thus, a year before the Dreyfus trial, the staff of the German Embassy was well aware that the contents of wastepaper baskets were being transmitted by some unknown person to the French Intelligence Service. At the time of the trial it was not known whether the person in question was or was not still in the Embassy's employ. Thus they were constantly on the alert and took every possible precaution.

"'This being so, can it be believed that a member of the staff would merely tear into four pieces and drop into a wastepaper basket a document so compromising for a highly valuable agent, a man whose services they wanted at all costs to retain—when they knew full well that these scraps of paper would find their way to the French Intelligence Service?

"'Thus the origin we are asked to attribute to this document lacks all plausibility; unless'—this is important—'it was deliberately concocted by a forger working hand in glove with one of the German Embassy servants, thanks to whose assistance this forged *bordereau* —giving a list of documents which actually have never been delivered to the German Embassy—was dropped into a wastepaper basket, from which it was taken and transmitted to the War Ministry through the usual channels.

"'Now let us examine the verisimilitude of the *bordereau* itself. Can we see any plausible reason why a man who makes a business of malpractices of this kind should attach a superfluous and compromising invoice to the documents he is sending? Normally a spy or traitor takes care not to leave any traces behind him. If he is transmitting documents, he commits them to a chain of intermediaries whose task it is to see they reach their destination. *But never will he put anything down in writing.* Here we should note that the prosecution finds much difficulty in explaining how a document of this kind could have been transmitted. To send it by ordinary post would be the height of folly. Was it then delivered by hand? If so, what was the point of giving a list, what need was there for writing one, instead of handing over the secret documents direct to their recipient?

" 'Indeed, the absurdity of both hypotheses was so patent that the prosecution did not even venture to put them forward.'

"Do you follow me, Barois?"

Barois nods emphatically. He is no longer feigning aloofness. Leaning forward, his elbows on his knees, his chin between his hands, his eyes intently, almost sternly, fixed on the inexpressive bandage-swathed head, none of whose movements escapes him, his nostrils fluttering, his heart thudding, lips parted in tense absorption, he is waiting for what is yet to come, hoping still that what he has just heard is a mere piece of special pleading.

WOLDSMUTH, after a long, silent scrutiny of his friend's face: "Now I'll continue reading.

" 'During the investigation, which lasted two months, was it discovered that Captain Dreyfus had associated with any suspicious characters? No. Yet in that curious missive we find the words: "Unless I hear from you that you wish to see me . . ." Had he then been seeing his mysterious correspondent? His life has been ransacked, all his movements and doings have been scrutinized minutely, yet not a single compromising contact has been alleged against him.

" 'At no stage of the case has the prosecution been able to produce a single fact or make a single allegation suggesting that Captain Dreyfus had any dealings whatsoever with any foreign agent, even in the service of the French High Command.

" 'Then, again, what motives could have prompted Captain Dreyfus to the crime with which he has been charged? Was he short of money? No, he was a rich man. Had he any expensive liaisons or vices? None. Was he a miser? No, he lived up to his considerable means and did not increase his wealth. Is he a neurotic type, liable to sudden, irrational impulses? No, he is an eminently level-headed man, lacking neither competence nor courage. What motive, then, could this happy man have had for imperilling his happiness? None.

" 'So here we have an Army officer with a spotless character, with no bad habits or tendencies, whom the persons themselves who conducted the inquiry found to be honest, industrious, conscientious, and a reliable officer—and suddenly he is shown a piece of notepaper, whose origin is as obscure as its wording is equivocal, and told: "This was written by you! Three experts affirm it, and two deny it!" With the energy inspired by a clear conscience this man denies the odious charge brought against him and protests his innocence. While admitting the blamelessness of his past life, but basing its judgment on the evidence of the handwriting experts, contradictory though this is, the Court sentences him to military degradation and imprisonment for life.' "

There is a long silence.

WOLDSMUTH: "Now I'll read you what Lazare has to say about the 'secret dossier.'

" 'The "evidence" so far produced was obviously inadequate, and General Mercier, the Minister of War, was informed that the Court, having nothing else to go on, leaned towards an acquittal.

" 'And now, despite a definite promise given to the Minister for Foreign Affairs to the contrary, General Mercier thought fit to communicate to the Court *in secret*—even the counsel for the accused man was not permitted to be present—a document he had been keeping in reserve for such an emergency, should it arise. What was this crucial piece of evidence?

" 'It related, according to *L'Éclair,* to the activities of spies in Paris, and contained the phrase, "Definitely that rascal Dreyfus is beginning to expect too much."

" 'Did any such letter exist? Yes. Was it shown confidentially to the judges? Yes.

" 'Was the phrase quoted by *L'Éclair* in that letter? I say it was *not*.

" 'I affirm that the man who handed over to the newspaper in question this highly confidential document—whose divulgation, owing to the diplomatic complications that might ensue, was so much feared that it was produced only in a secret session of the Court—I affirm that this man did not shrink from yet another infamous deed, that of falsifying this highly important document, whose publication was intended to assure the world at large of the guilt of that unhappy victim of injustice who for two years has been undergoing hell on earth.

" 'For the letter shown the Court did not contain the name of Dreyfus, but only an initial *D*.

" 'In its issue of November 10, 1894, *L'Éclair* does not contest my statement; but on this subject I have more to say.

" 'This letter, made public for the first time by *L'Éclair*—despite the veil of secrecy which the authorities had sought to impose—was transmitted to the Ministry of War by the Minister for Foreign Affairs *about eight months before the Dreyfus case*.

" 'So true is it that the letter did not contain Dreyfus's name that for several weeks an employee in the Ministry of War was shadowed and kept under close surveillance because he was unlucky enough to have a name beginning with *D*. Then this trail was abandoned, as were some others subsequently followed, and finally the letter was pigeon-holed and forgotten. No suspicions fell on Dreyfus, and no further thought was given to this letter until the *bordereau* was intercepted and attributed to Dreyfus.

" 'Thus the account given in *L'Éclair* of September 15, 1894, was inaccurate.

" 'We may now consider the plausibility of this letter on internal grounds. Let us suppose that a foreign Power has been fortunate enough to secure the complicity of a staff officer and this officer supplies it with documents of a highly confidential nature. That Power will set a very high value on his services, will do its utmost to safeguard his co-operation, and will take, in consultation with him, all possible precautions to prevent his coming under suspicion. Moreover, obeying the dictates of the most elementary prudence, this foreign Power will be at pains not to compromise by any indiscretion the career of a man so useful to itself; still less will it risk mentioning in a letter, which may go astray or be intercepted, the name of the officer in question.

" 'From which it follows that, unless and until the Government formally denies this, the conviction of Dreyfus, unjustified by any adequate evidence, was secured by the eleventh-hour production of a letter, inspection of which was persistently refused to the accused man and to his counsel. In the course of the trial the letter was not put in evidence; thus there was no opportunity of discussing it, questioning its authenticity or the justification for assuming that the initial *D* should be taken to refer to a man against whom there was no other evidence of any value.

" 'Can we tolerate a man's being thus convicted out of hand, without allowing him access to anything that might serve him to defend his cause? Is it not scandalous that pressure should have been brought to bear, outside the Court, on the minds of the judges, so as to influence their decision? Is it legal for any person whomsoever to enter a courtroom where a case is under trial and to say to the President of the Court, "Forget all you may have heard in favour of the man you are trying. We have documents in our hands which, *for reasons of State* and for the avoidance of diplomatic complications, we have kept secret from him and which we ask you, too, to keep secret. We can vouch for their authenticity and reliability." Yet it was on such grounds as these that the Court delivered judgment! Not one of its members rose and said: "You are asking us to act against the most elementary principles of equity; we cannot do as you wish."

" 'And so effectively had public opinion been misled and the accused man held up to the nation as the most despicable of criminals,
unworthy of any pity, that no one even thought of protesting against
the *manner* in which the "traitor" had been tried and sentenced.
Even those whose patriotism is normally outraged whenever proceedings are taken against an Army officer chose to overlook the
irregularities of procedure in this trial; so convinced were they that,
in the interests of the country, this man, no matter what the means
employed, must pay the penalty of his crime.

" 'Had this feeling not prevailed, many a voice would have been
heard—and perhaps ere long, once the cloud of prejudice has lifted,
such voices *will* be heard—protesting in the cause of justice. We
seem to hear them saying: "If such abuse of authority and such
high-handed methods be connived at, the freedom of every Frenchman is imperilled, placed at the mercy of officialdom. No French
citizen, facing a criminal charge, can feel assured of being permitted
to exercise even the elementary rights of self-defence to which every
man on trial is entitled." ' "

Barois is bending forward, his hands pressed to his forehead. His
look conveys compassion and profound distress. He is staring fix-
edly, desperately, at the bare floor, his gaze focused on a split tile
welded together by dust. Woldsmuth's deep voice, hoarse with fatigue and the stress of his emotion, comes to him again across the
shadows.

WOLDSMUTH, still reading the typescript: " 'There still is time to
make amends. We must not allow it to be said that because a Jew
was on trial, a French court made light of justice. It is in the cause
of justice that I protest; in the cause of the justice that these men
flouted. For Captain Dreyfus is an innocent man; his conviction was
procured by illegal methods, and the case must be reviewed.

" 'And the new trial must not take place *in camera,* the whole
French public must have access to the courtroom.

" 'I therefore lodge an appeal against the judgment of the Court-
Martial. New facts have been elicited; therefore, on legal grounds,

the judgment should be quashed and a retrial ordered. But there are things at stake on a higher level than that of legal quibbles. What is at stake is a man's right to preserve his freedom and to defend his innocence when a false charge has been made against him.' "

Completely exhausted, Woldsmuth sinks back heavily on the pillows. His eyes are closed, and all life seems to have receded from the bandaged head, monstrous as that of the grotesque puppets paraded at *mi-carême*. Only the small hands resting on the sheets and quivering spasmodically seem alive.

Barois rises and takes some heavy steps across the room; then goes up to the bed and halts, his legs planted well apart, his breast heaving, his hands spread open, level with his chest. Before speaking he draws a deep breath.

BAROIS: "Anyhow, we must make inquiries and get at the truth of the matter. This feeling of doubt is unbearable. And I promise that Luce shall see your friend, not later than tomorrow."

October 22, 1896

My dear Barois: Monsieur Bernard Lazare has just left, after spending the afternoon with me. You know what was my state of mind yesterday evening; I am unable to change so quickly, but I must admit I was greatly impressed by what he said to me.

This whole business seems to me of such gravity and so beset with dangers that I feel it would be disastrous to take up a position hastily or decide on any line of conduct without very serious reflection. I therefore refused, for the moment, to lend my name to any project that may be now on foot, but I assured M. Lazare of my good will, which indeed is not only sincere but whole-hearted. One soon realizes that he is one of those men for whom the whole array of the powers-that-be—the State, officialdom, the intellectual, and even the moral arbiters of our present-day world—weighs less than a feather in the balance against the dictates of his conscience. Moreover, he has a lucid, logical mind, and his arguments were most disturbing.

Yes, it is impossible not to be horrified at the thought that so flagrant a travesty of justice may have been enacted under our eyes. And I should find a life, haunted by such an apprehension, quite intolerable.

Therefore I wish to know the truth. I want to be reassured. I am still convinced that there is something behind all this which we do not know, and which will put an end to our anxiety. So I have decided to make thorough and conscientious inquiries on my own account, and of course I shall keep you posted as to their results.

Meanwhile, my dear Barois, please do not speak to me of this most distressing matter; let me retain all the lucidity and detachment I would wish to bring to so difficult a problem. I attach great importance to this request. And, if I may give you a word of advice, avoid this subject likewise when talking to your friends. Opinions are already overheated, and all this stirring up of passions can lead to no good result.

My eldest boy has quite recovered. But now we are worried again by the health of our dear little Antoinette; I greatly fear we shall have to risk the operation. It is a terrible anxiety for me, my dear Barois, and for my poor wife. But, with a large family, peace of mind is always round the corner.

All my good wishes—and meanwhile, I beg you, not a word about that subject.

Yours,
Marc-Élie Luce

3

Luce's study. It is mid-July 1897, and the morning sun is shining gaily, the air shimmering with heat outside the open windows. Beyond the white cambric curtains lies an expanse of vividly green foliage, and the garden is loud with twittering sparrows and the happy cries of children.

Barois is sitting, silent and attentive, facing Luce, who is at his desk, holding himself straight in his chair, but with his head slightly bowed, as though the weight of the big skull were dragging it down. Shaded by the brows, his vision-haunted eyes are fixed on Barois.

LUCE, in a carefully controlled voice: "You understand, Barois, that I would not make these statements without being quite positive about the facts. When you came here eight months ago and arranged for my meeting with Bernard Lazare, I realized at once the risks involved. I had read the *Éclair* article and knew about that story of a 'secret document.'" Bitterly. "But I'd refused to believe it. Then the details given by Lazare shook my confidence; I wanted to *know*." Sadly. "And now I know!" He pauses, then, in a louder voice: "Eight months ago I didn't dare to suspect that the military judges, fully aware of their responsibilities, would have allowed the Minister of War personally to intervene in the trial; still less, that they'd have let him put in evidence secret documents, which neither the accused nor his counsel was permitted to see.

"Since then, alas, I've learnt far more. I've discovered not only that a secret dossier was produced and deliberately concealed from the accused man by his officer-judges, but also that this file did not even contain any evidence of such an overwhelming nature—though this could not excuse the irregular procedure of the Court—that it might at least have set our minds at rest as to the verdict. No, none of the documents in it seriously implicated Dreyfus; they merely raised presumptions which could as easily be interpreted in his favour as against him." He taps the table with his fingers, to emphasize each point. "That, I can assure you, is the truth of the matter."

Barois keeps quite still. His legs splayed out, his hands resting on his knees, he listens. His darkly glowing eyes and set features betray no surprise, only a keen interest in what he now is hearing.

LUCE, placing his hand on a sheaf of documents tied up with tape: "I'll spare you the details, and only tell you that I've spent eight solid months on this investigation, putting all my other work aside." A brief smile lights up his face. "You'll have noticed that I've not been able regularly to supply *The Sower* with the weekly article I promised. Thanks to my seat in the Senate, and with the help of some old friends, I have been enabled to tap the sources and verify all the information given me. Lazare supplied me with photographs of all the essential documents. So I have been able to con them here in my study, at leisure. I've also had them examined by the best handwriting experts in Europe." He lays his hand on a file. "It's all recorded there. I now know all that can be known about the case, and"—he weighs his words—"I no longer have any doubts—not the shadow of a doubt."

BAROIS, rising to his feet: "The world must hear of this! We must make these facts known—to the Ministry of War, to start with."

Luce says nothing for a moment; then he fixes his eyes on Barois. A faint, sad smile flickers over his lips and seems to vanish into his beard. Then, in an impulse of expansiveness, he leans forward.

LUCE: "Let me tell you of a curious experience I've had. Only last Monday—at exactly this hour of the morning, to be precise—I was closeted in one of the offices of the Ministry of War with an old friend of mine, a cavalryman, who now holds a very high post on the staff.

"I hadn't seen him for two years. He welcomed me with many demonstrations of friendship. But no sooner did I mention the name of Dreyfus than he sprang to his feet in a tearing rage! He wouldn't let me put a word in, shouted me down, and behaved exactly as if I'd come there just to pick a quarrel with him! All this gave me a most disagreeable impression, as you may imagine. But I'd made up my mind to see it through and stood my ground. Finally I was able to tell him what I'd come to tell; I set out the facts I'd patiently collected and verified and for whose truth I could vouch. Folding his arms, he fell to pacing his office—with such heavy strides that I could hear his jack-boots creak—but not a word came from his lips. No doubt the medicine I'd been giving him had proved too strong! After a while he returned to his chair and, with all the calmness he could muster, asked me some questions about the feeling on the subject in the Senate, and in the world of university professors, scientists, and others with whom I came in contact. I had an impression that he wanted to size up the potential opposition before deciding what line to adopt. I gripped his hand and begged him on the strength of our long friendship, in the cause of justice, to take action. 'There still is time,' I said. 'A scandal's liable to break at any moment, but so far it's only latent. By acting promptly you may still avert it. Let the Army make the first move and the situation will be saved. The best of men may blunder on occasion, and then the only decent thing to do is to own up to one's mistake and make amends.' But I came up against an obviously uneasy, but none the less obstinate silence. Then brusquely he rose, had a third party come into the office, and showed me out politely—without a word as to his intentions, without a word of encouragement."

Luce's emotion shows in his face; he is silent for some moments.

LUCE: "Then, Barois, I came back slowly, on foot, along the Seine." In a broken voice. "And for quite a while—incredible as this may sound—I wondered if it weren't he who was in the right." Barois gives a slight start. Luce raises his arm, then lets it fall despondently. "I saw so clearly what the result would be once we made public our doubts of Dreyfus's guilt."

BAROIS: "The chief result would be his rehabilitation."

LUCE: "Granted. But don't let's hoodwink ourselves. There would be other consequences, more far-reaching ones. It would mean a bitter conflict between the claims of strict justice and the whole structure of the nation. A war to the knife and perhaps, viewed from one angle, an unholy war."

BAROIS, vehemently: "Really, Luce! How can you—?"

LUCE, breaking in: "Hear me out. If Dreyfus is innocent, as is certain, or practically certain—on whom will the blame fall? Who will take his place in the dock? The General Staff of the French Army."

BAROIS: "What of it?"

LUCE: "And behind the General Staff is the present government of the French Republic, that established order to which we have owed our national life for a quarter of a century." Barois says nothing; Luce pauses before continuing: "Never shall I forget that long slow walk along the river-bank! I was faced by the most horrible dilemma. That of knowing the truth and shutting one's eyes to it; of bowing to an unjust decision because it was made in the due course of law by the Army and by the Government and—this we must admit—with the whole-hearted approval of public opinion. *Or,* of choosing the other alternative: impugning, evidence in hand, a judicial error, stirring up a world-wide scandal and deliberately, like a red revolutionary, launching a direct attack on the established order of our country, the Constitution to which we owe allegiance."

Barois ponders for some moments; then, abruptly, squares his shoulders.

BAROIS: "No hesitation is possible."

LUCE, tranquilly: "Yet I *did* hesitate. I couldn't bring myself to shatter without compunction the relative peace and good esteem which our young republic has been enjoying for a number of years." He gazes intently at Barois. "I quite understand your indignation, your fervour in the cause of the right, of doing justice though the skies fall! But I hope you'll let me say, Barois, that our respective attitudes cannot be quite the same in this respect. Into your ardour to take sides there enters—how shall I put it?—a personal element. Let me know if I'm mistaken. You feel, as it were, a private satisfaction in all this; to put it bluntly, a sense of having your revenge."

BAROIS, smiling: "That's so; you've sized me up accurately enough. Yes, I rather enjoy taking up a position on what 'right-minded' people call the wrong side of the barricade." Earnestly. "For there's no denying it, our adversaries today are the same as those I took up arms against in my youth: routine, despotism, indifference to all that's noble and sincere. And, when you come to think of it, our faith, whether it's founded on truth or on illusion—ah, what an infinitely finer thing it is than theirs!"

LUCE: "I appreciate your feelings. But don't blame me if I hesitate at a moment when we may be called on to lay bare our rottenness to the eyes of all the world." Barois makes no reply, but his smile and the look in his eyes convey: I admire you with all my heart; how can you speak of my "blaming" you? "This whole last week has been a terrible ordeal to me; I've been torn among a host of conflicting motives." Sadly. "I have even caught myself listening to the voice of self-interest. Yes, my dear Barois, I've counted the cost of what I would be risking as a private person if I spoke out, if I elected to cut a figure in this ugly business. And, to my disgust, I felt a qualm of fear."

BAROIS: "You're exaggerating the risk, surely?"

LUCE: "No. There's every chance, given the prevailing mood of the public, that I'd be sunk, irremediably sunk, within a couple of months. And don't forget, my friend, I have nine children." Barois nods. "You see, you know I'm right about the risks. Nevertheless"— a new warmth enters his voice—"such is our predicament today that I cannot 'slink out of the race' without playing false to the whole trend of my life. I have always made truth my ideal and, with it, justice—which is truth put into practice. I've always had a firm conviction—and events have borne it out time and again—that a man's most obvious duty, the one form of satisfaction that never lets him down, lies in the pursuit of truth with all the strength that is in him and in his refusal to allow any consideration whatever to deflect him from that end. And sooner or later, appearances notwithstanding, he discovers that in choosing this path he chose best.

"Each of us must bow to his life principle; mine forbids me to hold my peace today. Indeed, never have I so clearly realized that, while the work of all enables some of us to lead the meditative life, and these solitary efforts are needful since, joined end to end, they further progress—in return this privileged position of the thinker imposes on him duties that he may not, *cannot,* shirk. He must recognize them as such whenever they present themselves; and this is one of those occasions."

Barois nods quietly. Luce rises to his feet.

LUCE: "I've no intention of setting up as a knight-errant. All I want is for my cry of warning to reach the ears of the authorities, and to swing public opinion round towards a saner outlook. Once this is done I intend to hand over the results of my investigations—as a working plan—to whomever it may concern. You follow?" With a look of profound distress. "If only to shake off this incubus of doubt that's stifling me . . .

"If Dreyfus is guilty—and with all my heart I still hope that he is! —let it be proved in open court. But, at all costs, let's have done with this hideous uncertainty!"

He walks heavily to the window and steeps his gaze in the cool green shadows of the garden. Some moments pass. Then, as if suddenly remembering why he had asked Barois to come, he swings round and places both hands on his friend's shoulders.

LUCE: "Barois, if I'm to voice my appeal to all that's decent in France today, I shall need a springboard." Hesitantly. "Would you consent to flinging your *Sower* into the fray?" So revealing is the glow of pride that lights up Barois' face that he makes haste to continue: "No, no, my friend; hear me first and think it over carefully. For two years you've been throwing yourself whole-heartedly into this review and it's making splendid headway. Well, if it becomes my mouthpiece, everything's imperilled and, likely as not, your fine endeavour will fall to pieces."

Barois has squared his shoulders, but he is too much carried away by his feelings to answer. A rush of joy, of fanatic pride, traverses him as he gazes at his friend. Luce understands. The tension in the air increases, and impulsively, their hearts throbbing in the silence of unspoken thoughts, the two men stretch out their arms and embrace each other.

It is the beginning of a phase of supreme, tumultuous emotions.

A week later. The courtyard of the old house in the Rue Jacob, where Barois lives. Inside an open lean-to Woldsmuth and some helpers are sitting at a table, while Breil-Zoeger, Harbaroux, Cresteil, and Portal move to and fro. Behind them, stacked in neat piles, are eighty thousand copies of *The Sower;* a smell of fresh printer's ink hovers in the air.

Other copies, in bundles tied with string, are ready for dispatch to the provinces. Like the line outside a soup-kitchen a hundred down-and-outs are drawn up in single file. At three o'clock the distribution begins. While Barois jots down figures in a ledger, copies of the review, in packets of three hundred, disappear under the arms of the ragged vendors, who promptly start padding down the street in soft-soled slippers.

Soon the first away are outside the zone within which silence is enjoined; only when they have fanned out into the Boulevard Saint-Germain, the Rue des Saints-Pères, and the streets adjoining the Seine, may they give tongue—with a raucous stridence like the sound of a pack in full cry.

"*The Sower*. Extra Special Number. Revelations on the Dreyfus Case. 'Conscience, an Open Letter to the French Public,' by Senator Luce. *The Sower*. Extra Special . . ."

Passers-by stop and turn, shop-doors fly open, children run up, the vendors of *The Sower* ply a busy trade, and the copies disperse like leaves before an autumn gale. Within two hours they have reached the outlying suburbs, coming to rest on dining-tables, on market-stalls, in pockets.

Presently the vendors troop back, empty-handed, thirsty, and, as the courtyard fills, wine flows freely. The last reserves are broached, carried away, exhausted. Again the noisy pack sallies out, shattering the languor of a hot summer afternoon.

There is a stirring in the Paris crowd, a ferment on the boulevards. The eve of battle.

Already in a thousand homes, throughout the great city, French hearts are beating faster, roused to a generous enthusiasm, and thought clashes against thought. Passions are unleashed, clamourous in the warm darkness, like a gathering storm.

VIII. STORM

IIIIIIIIIIIIIIIIIIIIIIIIIIIIIIIIIIIIIIIIIIIIIIIIIIII

I

THE NEW *Sower* office in the Rue de l'Université. Bolted to uprights outside the first-floor windows are two long metal strips, painted white and inscribed in black capitals: *THE SOWER*. The *Sower's* new home is a small first-floor flat. The first two rooms, on entering, are occupied by the clerical staff and other employees, and are devoted to business activities. The third, a larger room, serves as the editorial room. The next, which overlooks a courtyard, is Barois' office, and adjoining it is a recess where a stenographer works.

It is 5 P.M. on January 17, 1898. An animated conversation is in progress in the editorial room, in the centre of which is a big table strewn with inkpots and blotting pads. Pinned to the wall is an unfurled copy of a newspaper, *L'Aurore* of January 13, containing Zola's famous letter *"J'accuse."* Beside it are two posters, printed by Roll, reproducing in thick type the closing passages of the letter.

Barois, Harbaroux, Cresteil, Breil-Zoeger, Portal, and other members of the *Sower* staff are eagerly confabulating. "Cavaignac maintained that Dreyfus made a confession on the day he was cashiered." "Which was a downright lie, needless to say." "Still, I'm convinced Cavaignac spoke in good faith." "Somebody must have told him a document existed to that effect." "Anyhow, he doesn't claim to have seen the document."

BAROIS: "It's grotesque! Can they seriously expect us to believe that as far back as 1896 a piece of wholly conclusive evidence was available—a document whose publication would have promptly put a stop to all the agitation—and yet for all this time no one ever has had the idea of producing it?"

CRESTEIL: "That's self-evident."

BAROIS: "Here are the true facts of that incident." Promptly silence falls on the room. "I have them from Luce, who has been at great

173

pains to ensure their accuracy. Really it's all quite simple, as you'll see.

"On the morning of his dismissal from the Army Dreyfus spent a full hour in the company of an officer of the Republican Guard, Captain Lebrun-Renault. He protested with the utmost vigour that he was innocent. Moreover, he declared that he would see to it that this declaration of his innocence reached the public ear—to such effect that Lebrun-Renault took alarm and, fearing there might be a scandal, felt it his duty to report this to his Colonel.

"Then Dreyfus described a new 'test' to which he had been subjected, somewhat similar to the dictation 'test' of a few days previously.

"The Minister of War, who hadn't lost hope of securing some piece of evidence which would set his mind completely at rest, sent Major du Paty du Clam to the prisoner's cell with instructions to ask Dreyfus if, when offering certain documents to Germany, he was not acting from a patriotic motive, with the object of securing more valuable documents in exchange. This, the Major was to point out, might be deemed by the Court an extenuating circumstance and ensure a lighter sentence. Naturally enough, Lebrun-Renault knew nothing of this manœuvre. Dreyfus was expecting his ordeal to begin at any moment, and, as may well be imagined, his nerves were badly rattled. He kept talking to Lebrun-Renault with feverish volubility, and sometimes incoherently. We can easily see how what he then said may have been misunderstood and garbled in transmission from one mouth to another. This explains how the story got afloat that Dreyfus proposed an 'exchange' of documents with a foreign Power.

"Lebrun-Renault himself never spoke of a confession at the time. That very morning when, after sentence had been passed, General Darras asked him 'if nothing special had transpired,' his answer was, 'Nothing, sir,' and the General reported to the Ministry to this effect. Likewise the written report that Lebrun-Renault sent to the

Commanding Officer of the Paris Garrison, after he had carried out the task assigned to him—a document that Luce has seen with his own eyes—has an entry: 'Nothing special to report.'

"Can we suppose that if Dreyfus had really made an incriminating statement to him, even if not a formal confession, he would not have hastened to report it to his superior officers? And when the vague rumours, circulated next day by the press, came to the notice of the Minister of War, wouldn't he, had there been the least foundation to them, have taken action? Would he not have promptly ordered a further inquiry, so as to secure this conclusive piece of evidence? Would he not have brought pressure to bear on Dreyfus himself, so as to glean more explicit information and to ascertain— a matter of vital importance for our national security—what exactly were the documents he made over to a foreign Power?

"No, really the more one thinks about it, the more incredible it seems, this story of a confession."

CRESTEIL: "You should publish an interview with Luce on the subject."

BAROIS: "He considers the time not yet ripe. He's waiting for Casimir-Périer to give his evidence at the Zola trial."

JULIA WOLDSMUTH, entering: "You're wanted at the telephone, Monsieur Barois."

Barois rises and walks out.

BREIL-ZOEGER: "All things considered, I regard Cavaignac's latest move as definitely helpful."

PORTAL: "Helpful? I don't follow."

BREIL-ZOEGER: "Surely it's obvious. Here we have an ex-Minister of War who gets on his legs in the Chamber of Deputies and formally announces that there exists a document establishing the guilt of Dreyfus beyond all possible doubt. Well, on the day it's proved for all to know that no such document exists, or that if it exists it was deliberately trumped up as an afterthought, and antedated, so as to fill out gaps in the evidence—well, that day public opinion will have a nasty jolt. I'll see to that myself, if needs be! Or, if there's no reaction, it will mean that it's abominably changed, the France we knew."

CRESTEIL, sadly: "Changed abominably! Alas, you've never spoken a truer word."

PORTAL: "All this will be threshed out, anyhow, at the Zola trial."

Barois returns.

BAROIS, a troubled look on his face: "It was Woldsmuth who rang me up. He's just learnt that they're talking of limiting the scope of the proceedings against Zola. The idea is to restrict the charges to his allegations as regards the 1894 Court-Martial, and ignore the rest. I wonder what the idea is."

PORTAL, rising: "It's a very serious matter."

CRESTEIL: "But they've no right to do that."

PORTAL: "I'm afraid they have."

CRESTEIL: "Anyhow, what difference would it make?"

BAROIS: "Let Portal tell us what he means."

PORTAL: "It would be serious for this reason: the Government's trying by every possible means to narrow down the field of this trial and keep off dangerous ground. Now there's a Section of the Criminal Procedure Code which expressly forbids the accused person's offering evidence other than that relating to the facts specified on the charge sheet. In other words, by limiting the range of evidence that can be called, they can limit at their will the points raised at the trial."

CRESTEIL: "And thus whittle down Zola's defence to practically nil."

PORTAL: "Exactly."

BAROIS: "It's scandalous. It means that they can smother up the whole proceedings if they feel like it."

CRESTEIL, indignantly: "It's just one of those damned legal quibbles dear to Government attorneys."

PORTAL, curtly: "Hardly that, Cresteil. It's the law."

General dismay.

BREIL-ZOEGER, quietly: "Personally, I cannot believe they'll take that line. The allegations made were too outrageous to be disregarded. They are simply bound to prosecute the man who dared to write things like this." He goes up to the placard on which Zola's letter is printed in thick type, and reads:

" 'I accuse Lieutenant-Colonel du Paty du Clam of having been the fiendish organizer of this miscarriage of justice.

" 'I accuse General Mercier of having abetted this. . . .

" 'I accuse General Billot of having had in his hands decisive proof of Dreyfus's innocence and of having suppressed it. . . .

" 'I accuse General de Boisdeffre. . . .

" 'I accuse General de Pellieux . . . of having made a scandalously biased preliminary inquiry. . . .

" 'I accuse the Ministry of War of having conducted a foul campaign in the press, with the object of misleading public opinion and covering up its misdeeds.' "

CRESTEIL: "And then that challenge with which the letter ends:

" 'In making these charges I am well aware that I expose myself to proceedings under Sections 30 and 31 of the Code. . . .

" 'I have but one desire, a passionate desire for the light of truth, and I speak in the cause of suffering humanity that has a right to happiness. This burning protest is but my heart-felt cry. May they be bold enough to arraign me, and may the trial take place in the full light of day!

" 'I am ready!' "

BAROIS: "And you think a Government can swallow taunts like that without reacting!"

PORTAL: "In any case, Barois, it would be as well, before the charge sheet is drawn up, to direct public attention to this piece of knavery."

BREIL-ZOEGER: "Yes, and your article must hit Paris like a bombshell, first thing tomorrow morning."

BAROIS: "I'll start on it at once. Portal, would you supply me with the exact wording of that Section of the Code you mentioned?"

PORTAL: "Can I telephone the Law Courts Library?"

BAROIS, opening the door: "Mademoiselle Julia!"

PORTAL: "It's for me, Mademoiselle. Would you call eight-eight-nine-two-one?"

BAROIS, going to his private office: "I'll leave you now. Will you all be at the café this evening?"

SEVERAL VOICES: "Yes."

BAROIS: "Good. I'll show you my article before taking it to Roll, and we'll run over it together. Good-bye for the present."

An hour later. The editorial room is empty. All the staff have gone to their homes and an office-boy is sweeping the floors. Barois is at work in his back-room office.

Suddenly the door is flung open by Julia. She is pale as a ghost, obviously terrified, and with her there enters through the open door a curious buzzing sound.

JULIA: "Monsieur Barois, there's a—a demonstration. Don't you hear?"

Much surprised, Barois goes to the rooms giving on the street, and, opening a window, leans out into the darkness. The yellow flame of a street-lamp dazzles him at first. As his eyes get used to the darkness he sees that the street below is empty as yet, but in the distance, between cliffs of shadow, a black, heaving mass is creeping forward like some sluggish monster. And the confused hubbub of voices and footsteps is steadily growing louder.

Barois' first impulse is to hurry down the stairs to see what is happening. But now there is a sudden increase in the volume of sound outside. Some are singing, some shouting.

"Dreyfus!"

A small isolated group, the vanguard, is now only some fifty yards away. Barois can see faces craning up, arms brandished towards the *Sower* windows.

"To hell with Barois!" "Down with *The Sower!*"

He draws back hastily.

BAROIS: "The shutters! Quick!"

He helps the office-boy, who is half paralysed with terror, to bolt the shutters. Just as they are securing the last window, a walking stick hurtles through the panes, covering Barois and the boy with splintered glass.

The crowd is now immediately below, only four or five yards away; he even can distinguish the different tones of voice.

"Down with *The Sower!*" "Traitors!" "Lynch the bastards!"

Stones and sticks break through the windows and rattle against the wooden shutters. Listening intently, Barois stays in the middle of the room.

"Down with Zola!" "Down with Dreyfus!" "Death to the traitors!"

In the dim light he can just make out the form of Julia beside him. He pushes her towards his office.

BAROIS: "Call up the police station."

Evidently the crowd has run out of projectiles. But the shouts are louder and timed to the rhythm of stamping feet.

"Death to Luce!" "Lynch the traitors!" "Death to Barois!"

BAROIS, very pale, to the office-boy: "Bolt the door and stay in the hall." He goes to his office, unlocks a drawer, and takes out a revolver. Then he goes and stands beside the trembling boy. "If anyone comes in I'll shoot him like a dog." The telephone rings, and he goes to his office again. "Hullo? Is this the Superintendent of Police? . . . Right. I'm the editor of *The Sower.* There's a riot taking place just under my windows, in the Rue de l'Université. . . . What? Already? Thank you, I'm much obliged. . . . I couldn't say. A thousand. Fifteen hundred perhaps."

The noise outside is now continuous: a rhythmic stamping of feet on the roadway, like an army marking time, accompanied by a long, low, feral growling, above which rise shrill cries.

"Death to Dreyfus!" "Down with Zola!" "Lynch the bastards!"

Suddenly the tumult diminishes, there are sounds of scuffling. Evidently the police have arrived on the scene. A few shouts can still be heard, but less distinctly. The noise of footsteps recedes, and within a few minutes dies away altogether. The rioters have been dispersed.

Switching on the light, Barois sees Julia beside him, her hand resting on the table. Emotion has played such havoc with her face that he has to stare for some moments before recognizing her. Her features are convulsed, her skin is ashen-grey, her face has curiously coarsened and is now like that of a much older woman. Its expression is frankly bestial, instinct has come to the surface, and there is something repellent in its blatant sensuality.

That, he thinks, is how she must look in the act of love. And the glance he throws her now is brutal, violent as rape, and she accepts it, like a woman yielding to her ravisher.

Suddenly her nerves give way and, bursting into tears, she sinks into a chair. He leaves the room without a word; his own nerves are on edge and he can feel the fever of his blood. He opens the shutters.

The street is quiet now, little more animated than usual at this hour except for some people standing on their balconies or watching from windows.

Policemen are patrolling the street, under the broken street-lamps, whose gas-flames twist and flicker in the night wind.

THE OFFICE-BOY: "Please, sir, the Police Inspector's come to take your statement."

2

February 17, 1898. The Assize Court on the tenth day of the Zola case.

There has been a short adjournment. The courtroom is filled with a seething, chattering, gesticulating crowd, amongst which one notices a sprinkling of uniforms, gold epaulettes, smartly dressed women. People are eagerly pointing out to each other well-known figures—staff officers, popular journalists, leading lights of the stage

and the political world. A black phalanx of gowned lawyers separates the spectators from the still-empty Bench, over which hangs
Bonnat's melodramatic "Christ."

Sudden and violent as electric discharges, waves of sympathy or
hatred traverse the thick, over-charged air of the courtroom. In
the front row is a small, compact group, talking in undertones:
Harbaroux, Barois, Breil-Zoeger, Cresteil, Woldsmuth, and amongst
the men one woman—the dark, enigmatic form of Julia Woldsmuth.

A clock strikes three and the crowd heaves, as if rocked by a
ground-swell, while a flood of new-comers seeps into the smallest
crannies of the all-but-solid mass. Students in berets, lawyers in
their gowns, clamber over the high barrier separating the public
from the Bench and Bar and perch themselves on window-sills and
ledges.

Patiently Luce worms his way through the crowd, which mutters
his name and scowls at him. At last he succeeds in reaching the
place that Barois has been keeping for him in the *Sower* group.

LUCE, in a low tone to Barois: "I've just been 'over there.' It's
going to be a rough crossing. Most of the jury are in favour of ac-
quitting Zola. The military know this and they're shaking in their
shoes. They'll certainly try to bring off some big coup today or,
anyhow, tomorrow."

An abrupt, short-lived silence falls as the Court enters. The red-
robed judges take their seats; two by two, with the self-conscious
gravity of a Town Council parading in their Sunday best at some
civic function, the jury file to their places.

Émile Zola takes his seat in the dock beside the manager of
L'Aurore; behind them are their counsel, Maîtres Labori and Albert
and Georges Clemenceau, with their clerks.

A low sound, like the rumble of a nearing storm, jars the air;
then abruptly a whistle shrills across it. Zola and Labori glance to
the right, whence the whistle came. Zola's hands are locked on the
knob of his walking stick, his legs are crossed. There is an anxious
look on the deeply furrowed, bearded face, which at some angles

reminds one of a hedgehog's. Whenever he moves his head the pince-nez flashes, intensifying the scalpel keenness of the eyes. Slowly his gaze roves the concourse of his ill-wishers, then lingers for a moment on the *Sower* group.

A man in uniform comes up the central aisle, accompanied by whispers. "Pellieux. That's Pellieux." The General walks firmly up to the witness-box, then halts with military precision.

BAROIS, to Luce: "Ah, so it's Pellieux they're throwing into the breach."

Feelings are running high and the public making such a din that the General swings round and gazes sternly at the culprits. And promptly—such is the soldierly dignity of his bearing, the sense of high authority that emanates from this distinguished officer— they are reduced to silence, if only momentarily.

The Presiding Judge, a burly, moon-faced man whose shaven lips are like a narrow horizontal line drawn between the bushy side-whiskers, scowls darkly and raises his arm in protest against the noise that has broken out again; but to no immediate effect. After some minutes, however, snatches of what the General is saying in his precise, military tones can be heard through the subsiding din. ". . . in a perfectly legal manner . . . the Dreyfus trial . . . I ask the Court to hear me."

VOICES: "Ssh! Ssh!"

GENERAL DE PELLIEUX: "I will repeat that characteristic remark of Colonel Henry's. 'You want light on the matter, do you? Well, you shall have it!'" Steely, challenging, his voice rings through the crowded courtroom, which now at last has quieted down. "When Castelin put his question in the House, something had just occurred which I wish to bring to the notice of this Court. At the Ministry of War—I ask you here to bear in mind that I am *not* speaking of the original Dreyfus trial—conclusive proof had been obtained of Dreyfus's guilt, and when I say 'conclusive,' I know what I am talking about. For I have seen this evidence with my own eyes." He sweeps the jury, then the counsel for the defence,

then the public, with his gaze, and the rugged face lights up with
the smile of the skilled fencer taking his opponent's measure. "Just
before this question was put in the Chamber a document, whose
authenticity is indubitable, was handed in at the Ministry. This
is its exact wording: 'A question is going to be put in the Chamber
of Deputies about the Dreyfus case. Be careful not to mention the
dealings we had with that Jew.' That document, mind you, is
signed. Not by a known name, it is true, but one that is vouched
for by a visiting card, on the back of which is inscribed a trivial
invitation signed with an alias, the same alias as that with which
the document is signed. And the visiting card bears the real name
of the person in question."

There is a short silence. A flutter of excitement runs through
the public; faces turn eagerly towards the Bench, the witness, and
Zola, who has been unable to conceal his indignation; lastly, towards the jury, whose rather commonplace features now wear a
look of satisfaction, as if a load had been lifted from their minds.

GENERAL DE PELLIEUX, in ringing tones: "That is all I wish to say,
Let those persons who have been agitating for a revision of the
trial bear in mind the fact that I have just brought to their notice,
a fact to which I can testify on my honour. Moreover, I now ask
General de Boisdeffre to confirm what I have told the Court."

There is a buzz of voices, through which breaks a thunder of
applause. Luce keeps his arms closely folded on his breast; his face
is pale and drawn as he gazes sadly up at the Bench. His friends
exchange fiercely indignant glances, but none the less they have
been rudely shaken by this bolt from the blue.

BREIL-ZOEGER, in an undertone: "It's a forgery, of course."

BAROIS, with a shake of his shoulders: "That's obvious." He points
to a group of officers, very spruce in their uniforms, raising white-
gloved hands and clapping frantically. "But just try to get those
fellows to admit it!"

Labori has sprung to his feet, squaring up pugnaciously. Indeed,
he looks less like the skilful lawyer he is than a veteran boxer

entering the ring. But even he cannot make himself heard; his voice beats vainly on a solid wall of sound. Opening his mouth to its widest, he rams home his words with whirling gestures, turning towards the Judge, who seems to wish to interrupt him.

At last, in a lull, the Judge's voice becomes audible, shrill with vexation.

THE JUDGE: "But, Maître Labori—"

LABORI, angrily: "Really, Your Honour, I must protest—"

THE JUDGE, stiffly: "The witness has given his evidence. Have you any questions to put?"

LABORI: "Permit me to point out, before proceeding further—"

Like a rapier, the steely voice of General de Pellieux cuts through the altercation.

GENERAL DE PELLIEUX: "I ask the Court to call General de Bois-deffre to the witness-box."

LABORI, so peremptorily that at last silence is imposed: "I request Your Honour—and what has just transpired in this Court carries such serious implications that the defence cannot fail to press the point —I request Your Honour to hear me for a moment, not only with a view to answering the General's statement—though a bare as-sertion does not call for an answer—but also with a view to point-ing out, before things go any further, the effect the statement we have just heard from General de Pellieux must necessarily have on these proceedings. I ask Your Honour's permission to put in a few words."

THE JUDGE, dryly: "A few words, Maître Labori, no more."

LABORI: "As Your Honour wishes."

THE JUDGE: "Unless you have a question to put in cross-examina-tion."

LABORI, vehemently: "How could I have questions to put with reference to an entirely new piece of evidence that has just been sprung on us? Still, I have one question, and shall now proceed to put it."

GENERAL DE PELLIEUX: "It was you who sprang on the Court a new piece of evidence when you read out a charge framed by Major d'Ormescheville, a charge that figured in proceedings heard *in camera.*"

LABORI, triumphantly: "Ah, we're making progress, we're making progress!"

GENERAL GONSE: "I ask to be heard by the Court."

THE JUDGE: "Presently, General."

LABORI: "All I have to say is this. An incident of quite exceptional gravity has just taken place in this Court; that is a point on which we are all in accord. General de Pellieux did not speak about the Dreyfus trial; he spoke of something that happened subsequently to the trial. It is impossible that this happening should not be discussed here—or elsewhere, before another Court. It is clear that after such an incident there can no longer be any question of narrowing down or circumscribing these proceedings. Will General de Pellieux permit me, with all due respect, to point out that no document whatsoever can have evidential value or be treated as proof of any fact in issue, until it has been put in evidence and admitted or traversed by the parties? And will he permit me to add that in this trial—which, whatever we may do and whatever we may wish, is assuming the proportions of an affair of State—we are concerned with two documents or dossiers, equally unsatisfactory, indeed irrelevant, because they are kept secret? One of them, the *bordereau,* served to procure the condemnation of Dreyfus in 1894, without discussion, without hearing the other side, without the accused man's speaking in his defence. And now we have a second document, which, by reason of its secrecy, has served for weeks to prevent anything being given the Court but bare affirmations." He pauses. "Great as is my respect for the statement made by General de Pellieux on his honour as an officer of the French Army, I cannot attach the slightest importance to this document." A furious din breaks out in the courtroom; howls of derision greet the lawyer's last remark. Intrepidly he faces the storm he has invoked and goes on speaking in a tone of contained violence, emphasizing every word.

"So long as this document is withheld, so long as we are debarred from discussing it, and so long as it has not been made public, it can have no bearing on these proceedings. And it is in the name of immemorial justice, of principles that every race has venerated since the youth of the world and the dawn of civilization, that I speak thus." The public is obviously impressed. Opinions are divided, and there are some approving cries of "Hear! Hear!" Labori continues in a quieter tone.

"This leads me to an aspect of the case which has now emerged so clearly that my mind is easier in many respects. One consideration dominates all others in this trial, as I now see it. I refer to its persistent obscurity and the anxiety that is growing amongst the public as the fog enveloping the issues is thickened day by day, I will not say by deliberate lies, but I *will* say by subterfuges.

"No doubt the question whether Dreyfus is innocent or guilty, and whether Esterhazy is innocent or guilty, is one of the utmost gravity. Each of us—General de Pellieux, the Minister of War, General Gonse, and I myself—has, obviously, his personal opinion on the matter, and we may well persist indefinitely in our opinions unless and until this atmosphere of mystery is dissipated and no shadow of doubt remains.

"But the one thing to be strenuously guarded against is any increase or prolongation of the nation-wide anxiety to which this case has given rise. Well, we have here and now a way of getting light, anyhow partial light, on the matter, without giving any loophole for imposing the ban necessitated by proceedings *in camera,* or anticipating any subsequent decision of a competent court. For, come what may, a revision of the Dreyfus trial must and will take place."

There are violent protests. Cries of "No! No! Our country first!" Labori squares his shoulders, then swings round furiously on the demonstrators and rakes them with a gaze of withering scorn. His fist crashes down on the open files in front of him.

"These demonstrators only serve to show that some of you are still blind to the gravity of the issues in this case—from the point of view of civilization and even common decency."

Again there is a din of voices, through which rises some discreet but persistent applause. Labori turns towards the Bench and, folding his arms, waits for order to be restored.

LABORI: "If Dreyfus is guilty and if the allegations of these generals, whom I believe to be speaking in good faith—and this it is that most perturbs me—if their allegations are well founded, sound in fact and sound in law, they will have an opportunity of proving this in open court. If, however, they are mistaken, the other party will prove his case.

"And when once the truth has come to light and the shadows have been lifted, perhaps one or two men will be revealed as those responsible for everything, as criminals and traitors. On whatever side they may be, we shall know them for what they are and hold them up to obloquy. And then we shall settle down, our minds at rest, each to his respective duties, whether those of peace or those of war." He turns to General de Pellieux. "For as to war, General—I think you will agree—it is not when generals who are worthy to speak in the name of the Army they command are standing in the witness-box, it is not at such a moment that anyone need fear war; nor is it by the threat of a war that is not for tomorrow, whatever some people may say, that these gentlemen of the jury will be intimidated.

"I shall end with a question. Your Honour will observe that I have been leading up to something quite definite—and I will take this opportunity of thanking Your Honour for having allowed me to speak at some length. May I say how much I appreciate the consideration shown me by the Court and its awareness of the importance of the issues here at stake?

"The question, sir, is this: Will General de Pellieux state quite frankly all he knows, and will the document he refers to be produced in Court?"

There is tension in the air; the jury stir uneasily, their eyes fixed on the General. For some moments there is complete silence in the courtroom.

THE JUDGE: "General Gonse, what have you to say?"

General Gonse rises from his seat and approaches General de Pellieux, who steps down from the box to make place for him. General Gonse betrays some nervousness, and his voice seems curiously flat after those of General de Pellieux and Maître Labori.

GENERAL GONSE: "Your Honour, I corroborate in every detail the statement which General de Pellieux has made. He took the initiative and he acted rightly; in his place I should have done the same, so as to clear up any possible misunderstanding. The Army has no fear of the fullest light being thrown on the proceedings; nor does it fear, when its honour is at stake, to say where the truth lies." Labori makes a gesture indicating approbation of these words. There is a ripple of applause. The General continues, weighing his words: "Nevertheless, prudence is called for, and I have grave doubts about the wisdom of producing documents of this nature at a public hearing, though they exist and are no less authentic than conclusive."

Coming as an anticlimax after the General's opening phrases, these reservations cause some murmurs of dissatisfaction amongst the public. The majority, however, keep an open mind.

Composedly Maître Clemenceau rises to his feet.

CLEMENCEAU: "Your Honour, may I make an observation at this stage?"

Before he can continue, General de Pellieux walks quickly to the witness-box and, gripping its rail with both hands, addresses the Court in a loud, commanding voice.

GENERAL DE PELLIEUX: "I ask permission to add some words to my statement."

With a wave of the hand the Presiding Judge invites the General to speak. Maître Clemenceau resumes his seat.

GENERAL DE PELLIEUX: "Maître Labori spoke just now of proceedings in revision, with special reference to the document that was produced before the military court. I would point out that no evidence of the production of this document has been tendered."

This statement is so incongruous with the facts—after the dramatic hearing of Maître Salle, whom the Judge had to cut short abruptly when about to divulge what he knew on the subject, and after the explicit statement made by Maître Demange—that the public no longer dares to make any demonstration and listens in uneasy silence to the noisy protests of Dreyfus's friends. Taken aback by this reception, General de Pellieux hesitates.

GENERAL DE PELLIEUX: "I do not know—" He is interrupted by some loud guffaws. Swinging round, he confronts his hecklers with the candour of his soldierly face, the frankness of his deep-set eyes, and an intrepid gaze used to ampler horizons. Spoken in the authoritative tone of an experienced officer who can quell an incipient mutiny with a brief command, his words slash the grinning faces like a whip. "Stop that clownish nonsense!" For some moments he remains quite still, mastering the crowd with his gaze. Then, unhurrying, he turns towards the Bench. "I do not know if due attention was given to the statement made by Colonel Henry some days ago. Colonel Henry stated that Colonel Sandherr had handed over to him an envelope marked 'Secret'; that this envelope had been sealed before the Court-Martial took place, and that it had never been opened. Gentlemen of the Jury, I direct your attention to this point. Next, as to the proposed revision of the Dreyfus verdict on the strength of this document—"

THE JUDGE: "We are not concerned with a revision; that lies outside the jurisdiction of this Court."

GENERAL DE PELLIEUX: "But it is being constantly referred to."

THE JUDGE: "I am aware of that; but, as you well know, an Assize Court is not competent in the matter."

GENERAL DE PELLIEUX: "Very well, I bow to your decision. I have nothing more to say."

THE JUDGE, to General Gonse: "Have you anything to add?"

GENERAL GONSE: "No, Your Honour."

GENERAL DE PELLIEUX: "I ask that General de Boisdeffre be called to corroborate my statement."

THE JUDGE: "Then will you arrange for him to come tomorrow?"

Without answering, the General turns his head and, in the peremptory tone of a man who is used to being obeyed without demur, flings an order over his shoulder to his orderly officer, who is standing in the background amongst the public.

GENERAL DE PELLIEUX: "Major Ducasse, will you go and bring General de Boisdeffre here—immediately."

He is the Army incarnate. His attitude of high disdain impresses all alike—the judges, jury, even his opponents. And the crowd, tamed to submission, fawns on its master, like a whipped dog.

CLEMENCEAU, rising again to his feet: "Your Honour, I wish to make some observations on what we have just heard from General de Pellieux."

Again the General interrupts him, and Clemenceau stops speaking. Then, still standing, squarely planted on his robust limbs, an ironic twinkle in the bright eyes lighting up the rather flat, Levantine-seeming face, he listens to a brief duel of words between Labori and General de Pellieux, relating to the publication of the 1894 indictment.

With his gown billowing round him and his shirt-sleeves visible up to the elbow when he raises his arms, Labori seems to be hurling anathemas at his adversary.

LABORI: "General de Pellieux has sent for General de Boisdeffre; that is very wise of him! But let me warn the Court—and within twenty-four hours you will find I am no false prophet—that nothing General de Pellieux has said, and nothing that General de Boisdeffre may say, will avail to bring the proceedings to an end. For it is not mere oral evidence, however eminent the witnesses, that can replace the secret documents themselves. That is why I say to General de Pellieux: Either produce the documents, or else stop talking about them."

CLEMENCEAU, raising his arm quietly, to the Presiding Judge: "Your Honour, I ask your permission briefly to address the Court." In contrast to his colleague's vehemence his calm assurance makes all the more effect. "General de Pellieux has told us that just before Monsieur Castelin put his question in the Chamber of Deputies, *conclusive* proof of Dreyfus's guilt had been secured. Are we then to assume that until then only *inconclusive* proof had been forthcoming?"

There is a short silence. A faintly mocking smile narrows Clemenceau's slotted eyes. His hands still clasped on his walking stick, Zola turns his head and gives the lawyer an approving glance.

LUCE, to Barois, in a whisper: "Of course he knows the document to be a forgery."

CLEMENCEAU, in the same flat, unemotional voice: "May I ask General de Pellieux: How is it—and this is what a great many people in all walks of life are beginning to ask themselves today—how is it that so important a fact has been divulged for the first time in a Court of Common Law? How is it that when the question was put in the Chamber, General Billot never said a word about these secret documents or warned Members of the danger of war, and that it was only at a hearing in this Court that the startling allegation we heard today was made, and the existence of these documents first disclosed?"

GENERAL DE PELLIEUX, irritably: "All this is mere quibbling. I never said the country was in danger of war. As to why General Billot chose not to mention this document or the others—for, as General de Boisdeffre will inform you, there *are* others—when the question was put in the Chamber—that is none of my business. General Billot is free to do as he thinks fit." He turns to the jury. "One thing, anyhow, is certain. General Billot assured the Chamber, not once or twice but several times, that Dreyfus was justly and legally convicted."

LABORI, aggressively: "Here I really must protest. One, anyhow, of those two words is patently false, and that is 'legally.'"

GENERAL DE PELLIEUX, challengingly: "Prove it!"

LABORI, coldly: "It *has* been proved—to the hilt!"

CLEMENCEAU, in a more conciliatory tone: "We have made persistent efforts to prove this fact but have always been prevented from so doing. If General de Pellieux wishes me to make my meaning clearer, I ask for nothing better."

THE JUDGE, curtly: "Unnecessary, Maître Clemenceau."

LABORI, losing all self-control: "It has been proved by Maître Salle! It has been proved by Maître Demange! It has been proved again and again by statements in the newspapers which have never been officially denied. It was proved by General Mercier, who did not dare, when I confronted him with the facts, to say the contrary. On the previous day I had issued a challenge through the newspapers, and his only response was to draw a pettifogging distinction, which in itself sufficed to prove the point beyond all doubt. When I said, 'General Mercier handed in a certain document to the Court-Martial and then went around boasting of having done so,' General Mercier's answer was, 'That is not true'—thus fogging the issue again, I will not say deliberately; more likely he spoke without thinking. So I followed up with the question, '*What* was untrue? that you tendered a certain document or that you went around boasting of having done so?' To which General Mercier replied, 'That I went around boasting of having done so.'

"I maintain that, for anyone whose mind is free from prejudice, my point is proved. Its proof is that, in spite of the feelings the Dreyfus case has aroused throughout the country, no one has come forward to say what General de Pellieux has not dared to say—and what I defy him to say!" He pauses, then smiles. "So I make bold to say my point is proved."

GENERAL DE PELLIEUX, haughtily: "How do you expect me to say what happened at the Dreyfus trial? I wasn't present at it."

Labori gazes first at the jury, then at the judges, then at the public, as though inviting them to take note of this evasive answer. After this, he bows politely to the General, with a smile of triumph.

LABORI: "Very good. Thank you, General."

CLEMENCEAU, intervening: "Your Honour, we have a witness now in Court who has it from the mouth of one of the members of the

Court-Martial that a secret document was handed to the President of the Court. But we have not been allowed to put him in the box."

LABORI: "I have two letters to the same effect in my brief. And I also have a letter emanating from a friend of the President of the Republic. He declines to give evidence, as he has been warned that, were he to depose to the true facts, other witnesses would be called to controvert him."

CLEMENCEAU: "And why did General Billot say nothing on this point to Monsieur Scheurer-Kestner when he came to ask him about it? Had he done so, the whole matter would have been cleared up by now."

THE JUDGE, fretfully: "All that can wait, Maître Labori, until we have finished with the evidence and you are addressing the Court."

GENERAL GONSE, coming forward again: "I have something to say regarding the deposition made earlier in the proceedings, in which certain notes were referred to. I informed the Court that those notes were of a secret nature. Such documents *always* are secret. All correspondence between the various departments of the Ministry of War is conducted by way of 'minutes,' and these are invariably marked 'Secret.' So when we speak of a memorandum on this or that point, its secrecy is taken for granted.

"Next, when you were told that Dreyfus did not know what took place in the office of the General Staff in September 1893, this, too, was incorrect. For one thing, Dreyfus began by spending six months—"

THE JUDGE, brusquely intervening: "The Court is not concerned with the original Dreyfus case." To Generals de Pellieux and Gonse. "You can return to your seats, both of you." The Judge takes advantage of the amazed silence that follows these words to give a peremptory order to the Clerk of the Court. "Call the next witness."

The Clerk hesitates. Labori has risen to his feet and stretched his arms wide, almost as though he were setting up a physical barrier against the continuation of the hearing.

LABORI: "Your Honour, it is absolutely impossible after what has just transpired—"

THE JUDGE, resolutely: "The hearing will proceed."

LABORI, indignantly: "But, Your Honour, that's impossible. You are well aware that when an incident of this kind has taken place the trial cannot proceed unless and until the matter has been threshed out. Therefore we are obliged to hear the evidence of General de Bois-deffre."

THE JUDGE: "We shall hear it in good time." To the Clerk. "Call the next witness."

LABORI, tenaciously: "Your Honour will permit me to point out—"

THE JUDGE, peremptorily to the Clerk: "Go and call the next witness."

The Clerk goes out.

LABORI: "With all due deference, I submit that the hearing should be suspended at this point."

Major Esterhazy enters the courtroom, escorted by the Clerk of the Court.

THE JUDGE, to Labori: "I will give my ruling on your application when the witnesses have been heard."

Esterhazy walks to the witness-box; he has a pronounced stoop, a sallow complexion with red patches over the cheek-bones, and rest-less, feverish eyes. Very thin, he has all the appearance of a consumptive. He is loudly applauded by the public as he enters.

The Judge is about to address him when Labori intervenes for the last time, boiling with indignation.

LABORI: "But I have asked the Court that the hearing of other witnesses should be stayed until General de Boisdeffre has given his evidence. The Court cannot postpone its ruling on my petition until after the witnesses have been examined."

Uncertain how to act, the Presiding Judge glares at him in silence. To keep himself in countenance, Esterhazy folds his arms and waits, obviously embarrassed and puzzled by what is happening. Labori has resumed his seat and is busy writing his petition.

THE JUDGE, harshly, almost truculently: "Will it take you long, drawing up your petition?"

LABORI, surlily, without looking up: "Ten minutes."

The hearing is suspended. The Judge signs to the Clerk to escort Esterhazy back to the witnesses' waiting-room. Nerves are on edge, and the public goes on cheering Esterhazy until he has left. Without seeming to notice the noise in the courtroom, the judges rise and, unhurrying, vacate the Bench, followed by the jury, the defendants, and their counsel.

The growing exasperation of the public, so far kept partially at bay by the presence of the judges, at last has free vent. Shouts, excited comments on the evidence, angry retorts, fill the over-heated air, now tainted with the smell of packed humanity. The noise is deafening.

The *Sower* staff gather round Luce. Portal, who is in his gown, joins them. His blunt, candid face, now showing signs of his vast disappointment, seems chubbier, more pink-and-white than ever under his lawyer's cap.

PORTAL, sinking wearily into a chair: "Another secret document!"

BAROIS: "What exactly is it, do you know?"

BREIL-ZOEGER, in his iciest, most cutting tone: "This is the first time it's been heard of, to the best of my knowledge."

LUCE: "No, I knew of its existence. But I didn't think they'd ever dare to use it."

BREIL-ZOEGER: "Who's it written by?"

LUCE: "It purports to have been written by the Italian Military Attaché, and it's said to have been intercepted in the German Attaché's mail."

BAROIS: "Anyhow, it stinks of forgery!"

LUCE: "Naturally. It's a palpable fake. For one thing, it reached the Ministry—by what channel, I have no idea—at a strangely convenient moment, the very day before the Minister was due to answer that awkward question in the Chamber. And, also, just at the time when the General Staff was beginning to grow anxious about the turn the Affair was taking."

BREIL-ZOEGER: "And then the way it was worded."

JULIA: "We don't really know what was in it. The General was quoting from memory."

LUCE: "Still, he assured us that the name of Dreyfus was there in black and white. That in itself casts doubt on its authenticity. It's straining credulity too far to ask us to believe that, at a time when the press was beginning to take an active interest in the case, these two attachés would have spoken openly of Dreyfus in their correspondence. Even assuming that they actually had dealings with him, they'd never have made such a blunder as to mention him by name, especially after the formal denials made by their respective governments."

BAROIS: "That's obvious."

PORTAL: "But who the devil can be forging documents of that sort?"

BREIL-ZOEGER, with a ferocious guffaw: "Why, the Army Staff! Who else should it be?"

HARBAROUX: "Yes, our Ministry of War has a team of expert forgers on its pay-roll, that's certain."

LUCE, quietly: "No. There I can't follow you."

The frankness and assurance of his tone carry conviction. Only Breil-Zoeger lifts his shoulders incredulously.

BREIL-ZOEGER: "Still, surely, the facts point—"

LUCE, firmly to all the group: "No, my friends, you're wrong. Don't let yourselves be carried away. The General Staff's no more a gang of forgers than we are, as some people think, a gang of traitors. Never will you make me believe that men like General de Boisdeffre, General Gonse, General Billot, and the others would conspire to fabricate false evidence."

Cresteil d'Allize has been listening to the dispute with a wry smile, fretfuly tugging at his long moustache.

CRESTEIL: "I quite agree with Luce. I used to know General de Pellieux; he's the soul of honesty."

LUCE: "Indeed, you need only see and hear him to feel sure he believes what he says. There's a ring of complete sincerity in his voice.

And until the contrary is proved, I'll hold this true of the other generals as well."

CRESTEIL: "They were easy game, and they've been hoodwinked."

BREIL-ZOEGER, with a tart smile: "You attribute to them a gullibility that's hardly credible."

CRESTEIL, promptly: "Quite credible, I assure you. Take my word for it, old chap, if you'd had as much to do with Army officers as I have. Wait! Turn your head a moment. See that group behind us? Now, study them without prejudice, and what do you see? A look of stolid self-assurance, I grant you; it comes of always being obeyed and the officer's prerogative of being infallible *vis-à-vis* his men. But they're honest faces, fundamentally honest."

LUCE: "Yes, look round the courtroom, Zoeger. Most revealing, isn't it? The truth is that men of the officer class aren't used to predicaments which call for subtle thinking. So they're at a loss when someone springs a dilemma of this kind on them. If there's a guilty man about, who is he? Are they to look for him in the Government or in the Army, amongst those staff officers who have affirmed on their honour that Dreyfus was justly sentenced? Or is the criminal that obscure Jew, a mere nonentity, who was convicted by a tribunal of seven brother-officers, and at whom so much mud has been slung during the last three years that some of it inevitably has stuck?"

BREIL-ZOEGER, superiorly: "Surely it's obvious even to the meanest intelligence that whenever the military authorities were asked for definite proof of Dreyfus's guilt they balked at producing it? Everyone, even an officer, has brains enough to draw his conclusions from that."

JULIA: "And then what weight can those precious 'words of honour' they're so fond of have as against solid arguments like Lazare's book, or Duclaux's pamphlets, or your letter, Monsieur Luce?"

BREIL-ZOEGER: "Or even Zola's letter, over-emotional though it is?"

BAROIS: "Patience, my friends! We're getting near our goal." To Luce. "Today we've made a great step forward."

Luce does not reply.

PORTAL: "'A great step forward!' You're easily satisfied, Barois."

BAROIS: "Surely you see my point? General de Boisdeffre will be here any moment; they've sent to fetch him. With his first words Labori will put the General's back to the wall, and he'll be *obliged* to produce that secret document in court. Once that's done, it will be open to inspection, and it won't stand up long under any serious examination, that's a certainty. So the military authorities will be convicted of having tendered a forgery in evidence, there'll be a prompt swing-round of public opinion, and within three months a retrial."

He makes his points with slashing gestures, his eyes blazing with exultation. His whole bearing radiates strength and optimism.

LUCE, carried away by his friend's enthusiasm: "After all, who knows? Perhaps you're right."

BAROIS, with a boisterous laugh: "There's no 'perhaps' about it! This time, I'm certain, we have them at our mercy!"

BREIL-ZOEGER, tartly: "And suppose General de Boisdeffre finds a way of wriggling out of it? It wouldn't be the first time."

WOLDSMUTH, who slipped out when the adjournment was announced, has returned to his seat: "Here's the latest! General de Boisdeffre's just arrived in a carriage. The hearing's going to proceed."

BAROIS: "Did you see him?"

WOLDSMUTH: "Yes. I recognized him at once. He's in mufti. One of the officers of the Court was waiting for him on the steps. He went straight to the witnesses' room."

JULIA, to Barois, clapping her hands: "You see!"

BAROIS, exultantly: "This time, my friends, they've no loophole left. It's an open fight—and we're going to win it!"

The lawyers and members of the public who had left the courtroom bustle back to their places. In the midst of the confusion the judges and jury resume their seats. The defendants are brought in.

Labori steps briskly to his place, remains standing for a moment, his clenched fist resting on his hip, then bends towards Zola, who whispers to him, smiling.

Silence falls, unbidden. All nerves are strained to breaking point. There is a general feeling that at last decisive battle is about to be joined. The Presiding Judge rises to his feet.

THE JUDGE: "The hearing will continue." Quickly, without sitting down again. "In the absence of General de Boisdeffre the hearing is adjourned till tomorrow." A short pause. "The Court will now rise for the day."

At first nobody seems to take in this announcement, and in the amazed silence which ensues the judges make a dignified exeunt. The jury have remained at their places. Taken by surprise, Zola turns to Labori, who continues standing with his back to his chair, in an attitude of defiance that now serves no purpose.

At last the meaning of what has happened sinks in: the battle is postponed, it will not take place today. And now cries of disappointment fill the air, merging into a confused din. The crowd is out of hand; everyone is standing, stamping his feet, emitting catcalls, whistles, objurgations. No sooner is the Bench empty than there is a general rush to the exits. Within a few moments these are blocked by the surging mass; women faint, faces stream with sweat, all self-control is cast to the winds in a blind, insensate stampede.

The *Sower* group remain at their places, appalled by what has happened.

JULIA: "The cowards!"

BREIL-ZOEGER: "Humpf! They prefer to wait for orders."

LUCE, sadly to Barois: "You see! They've the whip hand."

BAROIS, boiling with rage: "Ah, but this time they won't get away with it without a scandal, unscrupulous dogs that they are! I'll see to that in my article of tomorrow. Whom do they expect to fool? When Parliament takes the matter up and forces the authorities concerned to show their hand, they get the answer: 'This isn't the place. Go to the Law Courts and everything will be cleared up.' Then, when the case comes on, whenever any attempt is made to get to the bottom of the matter, whenever the truth seems to be on the point of emerging—slowly, laboriously—at long last, it's kicked back into the mud and trampled underfoot. 'The point cannot be raised'—and so forth. No, all that has got to stop, the country must realize the damnable way in which its wishes are being flouted."

Shouting is heard outside the doors.

WOLDSMUTH: "Listen! Something's happening. Let's go and see."

CRESTEIL: "Easier said than done! We'll never get through."

BAROIS: "Try for that gangway." To Julia. "Follow me."

BREIL-ZOEGER, starting to climb over the benches: "No, this is the quickest way."

BAROIS, shouting: "Same rendezvous as yesterday! At Zola's side!"

They hurry pell-mell out of the courtroom.

Wild cries are echoing in the vaulted corridors of the Law Courts; it is as if another Revolution had broken out in Paris. A cordon of Republican Guards, elbow to elbow, tries to contain the onrush, but without success. Yelling groups charge through the barrage, clash and mingle in the dimly lit passages. The air is loud with cries. "Traitors!" "The swine!" "Three cheers for Pellieux!" "Bravo, the Army!" "Down with the Jews!"

Just as Barois and Luce are joining the small, compact group of Zola's friends, a sudden eddy of the crowd, breaking through the line of police officers, pins them against the wall. Barois tries to shield Julia. Portal, who knows his way about the building, hastily opens the door of a cloak-room; Zola and his companions pour in precipitately.

Zola leans against a pilaster, bare-headed, very pale, the lids of his shortsighted, ferrety eyes half closed. Apparently he has lost his pince-nez in the scuffle. His lips are set in a hard line, and his gaze shifts uneasily from side to side. Catching sight of Luce and Barois, he shakes hands with them hastily, without a word.

At last the police succeed in clearing a passage. The Chief of Police has appeared on the scene and personally directs operations. The small, faithful band starts off again, joined now by Breil-Zoeger, Harbaroux, Woldsmuth, and Cresteil.

A dense crowd fills the courtyard and adjoining streets; the demonstrators are in occupation of the whole district round the Law Courts, up to the walls of the great hospital, the Hôtel Dieu. They form a grey, heaving mass, dappled here and there with blurs of yellow light from the gas-lamps, which have just been lit, as a wintry dusk falls on the city. Now and again strident police whistles cut through the yells, catcalls, and concerted volleys of abuse. Across the din comes a persistent, rhythmic call, a leitmotiv. "Death to the traitors! Death!"

At the top of the flight of steps Zola pauses and bends towards his friends, his face convulsed with horror and disgust. "The cannibals!"

Then, with a sinking heart but at an even pace, he walks down the steps, leaning on a friend's arm, to where his carriage is waiting, surrounded by an escort of mounted police, who keep the crowd at bay.

When he turns to shake hands with some of his group, the yelling swells to a roar. "Chuck him into the Seine!" "Death to the traitor!"

The Chief of Police, fearing the worst, orders the coachman to drive off at once. As the carriage rumbles away at trotting pace a volley of missiles splinters the windows. Like a pack of hounds in full cry, the crowd surges forward, shrieking at the top of their voices, in pursuit of the receding carriage, which disappears into the dusk.

LUCE, in a broken voice to Barois: "If a drop of blood were shed just now, there would be a shambles."

Major Esterhazy comes down the steps, followed by a general; they are cheered all the way to their carriage. The police cordon is broken again. Barois tries to extricate Luce and Julia, but the crowd is too dense.

Zola's friends are recognized and loudly hissed. "Reinach! Luce! Barois! Death to the traitors! Long live the Army!" Strings of young fellows holding hands, students and well-dressed youngsters from the fashionable districts, wind their way snake-wise through the gaping crowd. Each of them has a paper badge, like the numbered labels worn by conscripts when reporting for military training, fastened to his hat, a badge that has been distributed by the thousands in the streets, inscribed· *"What every Frenchman says to Zola:* TO HELL WITH YOU!"

Officers in uniform thread their way through the mob, acclaimed by bursts of cheering.

Some individuals with Jewish noses are rounded up and roughly handled by boisterous youths, who do a war dance round them, brandishing torches made of rolled-up copies of *L'Aurore*. In the gathering darkness the effect is eerie, like some savage witch dance.

At the corner of a street, on the Seine bank, Luce and Julia halt to wait for the others. Suddenly a smartly dressed woman rushes towards them. Supposing she is being pursued, they make room for her, to offer their protection. But she heads straight for Luce and, gripping the lapel of his coat, tears off his Legion of Honour rosette. And, as she runs away, she flings contemptuously over her shoulder, "You rotter!"

Luce watches her receding form with a smile of infinite sadness.

An hour later. Luce, Barois, Julia, Breil-Zoeger, and Cresteil are walking slowly along the railings of the "Infanta's Garden." Night has fallen and a slight drizzle wets their shoulders. Barois links his arm affectionately in Luce's but Luce says nothing.

BAROIS: "Oh, come now! Why feel so discouraged? Nothing's lost, and the fight goes on." He laughs.

Luce turns and studies his friend's face under a street-lamp. With his virile zest for action, vast reserves of dynamism and confidence, Barois makes him think of an accumulator charged with vital energy.

LUCE, to Breil-Zoeger and Julia: "Look at him! You can almost see the sparks flying out of him!" Wearily. "Ah, how I envy you, Barois! Personally, I'm at the end of my tether, I've lost hope. France today is a drunk woman who can't see straight or walk straight; she can't distinguish false from true, she's ceased to know what justice means. No, really she's sunk too low—and it's heart-breaking."

BAROIS, with a vivacity that whips up their drooping spirits: "You're wrong, Luce, utterly wrong. You heard those shouts, didn't you? You saw those excited crowds? Well, a nation that still can work itself up to such a pitch of excitement over ideas—ideas, mind you!—is very far from being down-and-out."

CRESTEIL: "Good old Barois! He's hit the nail on the head as usual."

BREIL-ZOEGER: "That's obvious. Granted things have taken a nasty turn—but why should that surprise us? It may well be the first time in our history that morality has taken a hand in politics, so there are bound to be ructions."

BAROIS: "Really, it's a sort of *coup d'état,* what's happening."

LUCE: "Yes, from the very start I've had the impression that we were witnessing a revolution."

BREIL-ZOEGER: "Not 'witnessing'—making one."

BAROIS, exultantly: "And like all revolutions it's being launched by an enlightened few, a little group that pulls it off, unaided, by dint of passion, will-power, perseverance. Ah, what a damned fine thing it is, a fight like the one we're putting up!"

Luce shakes his head evasively.

Impulsively Julia comes up to Barois and clings to his arm; but he does not seem to notice her.

BAROIS, with a boisterous, almost boyish laugh: "Yes, I admit that, just at present, the situation is as ugly, as bestial, as imbecile, as it well can be. But what matter? It's from this vile substratum that truth and beauty will flash forth one day." To Luce. "You've always told me that sooner or later lies find their punishment in the mere course of things. Well, I too believe in the inevitable triumph of truth, and though this afternoon we seem to have lost again, that's no reason for despair. Perhaps we'll win on the next round."

3

August 31, 1898. Paris is comatose, half empty. The *Sower* group has met on the first floor of the café in the Boulevard Saint-Michel. It is nine in the evening.

The windows stand open on the hot darkness, and immediately

beneath them the canvas awning over the café terrace glows softly, lit up from below. On all sides stretches the Latin Quarter, silent and abandoned by its gay fraternity of youth during the vacation. Empty streetcars, all their lights on, clang and clatter up the rise towards the Luxembourg Gardens.

Barois has tipped out the contents of his big attaché-case onto the table. Seated round him, the others are delving in the pile, running their eyes over pamphlets and newspapers.

PORTAL, to Cresteil: "Any news of Luce?" Portal has just returned from a holiday in his home town in Lorraine.

CRESTEIL: "Yes, I saw him last Sunday. Really I was most distressed. He has aged terribly in the last three months."

BAROIS: "I suppose you know that he's been asked—oh, very tactfully, needless to say—to discontinue his lectures at the Collège de France as of the beginning of next term? They'd been creating too much of a stir, towards the end of June, for the taste of the authorities. In fact everyone's cold-shouldering him these days. At the last session of the Senate hardly a dozen of his colleagues deigned to shake hands with him."

PORTAL: "It's unbelievable, the stupidity of the public at large!"

HARBAROUX, scowling darkly: "It's that damned nationalist press that's responsible for everything. Those people won't give the public a moment's breathing space to come to its senses."

BAROIS: "On the contrary, they're wantonly crushing out all the generous emotions that are normal to our people; all those fine qualities which placed France—at her risk and peril but to her glory!—in the vanguard of civilization. And in acting thus they profess to be combating anarchy and anti-militarism, which they have the impertinence and dishonesty to identify with the most elementary instincts of justice and human decency. And the masses are only too ready to be fooled."

WOLDSMUTH, shaking his fuzzy head: "Ah, yes indeed! You can always do what you like with a nation if you set them on to Jew-baiting."

CRESTEIL: "What makes the success these people have with the general public so amazing to me is that their arguments are really quite beneath contempt. A moment's reflection is enough to show their hollowness—when they tell us, for instance, that the Dreyfus case is a huge conspiracy engineered by the Jews."

BAROIS: "As though a complicated operation of this sort could have been thought out in advance and every step foreseen!"

CRESTEIL: "And even when you ask, 'But what if Esterhazy were the writer of that precious *bordereau?*' they take it in their stride. 'That only shows,' they reply, 'that the Jews bought him over, and got him to copy Dreyfus's handwriting so perfectly that you couldn't tell the difference.' Really it's too childishly absurd!"

BREIL-ZOEGER: "The trouble comes from the endless complications that have been dragged into the case. A spate of investigations, of inquiries into side issues, has completely hidden its true significance, submerged the basic facts. All sorts of hares have been started, and off they've gone in every conceivable direction, along the most preposterous by-paths. What's needed now is some dramatic incident that will swing public opinion right around, and get people to take a saner view of the case as a whole."

CRESTEIL: "Yes, a dramatic incident—I agree."

BAROIS: "And perhaps we're on the way to one, thanks to this talk about the High Court's taking action." He produces a letter from his pocket. "Here's something I got in this morning's mail." He smiles. "An anonymous letter full of kind intentions."

HARBAROUX, who has taken the letter from Barois, reads it out: " 'I have it on good authority that the Minister of War has submitted to the Government a proposal to indict before the High Court all the leaders of the party seeking a review of the Dreyfus case. Your name, with that of M. Luce, figures on the list.' "

BAROIS: "A flattering propinquity!"

HARBAROUX, reading on: " 'Their arrest is to take place on September 2 at an early hour. So you still have time to make your escape. A Friend.' "

BAROIS, laughing heartily: "Priceless, isn't it! A nice little billet-doux to get first thing in the morning!"

BREIL-ZOEGER: "It's that article of yours on Saturday that moved your 'friend' to action."

PORTAL: "I didn't read it." To Cresteil. "What was it about?"

CRESTEIL: "About that famous sitting of the Chamber when, in his innocence, the Minister of War thought fit to produce from his pocket five 'highly important documents'—and in reality produced five forgeries. Barois proved convincingly that these documents are false."

The manager of the café comes in.

THE MANAGER: "Monsieur Barois, there's a gentleman waiting to see you below."

Barois follows him out. At the foot of the stairs he sees Luce.

BAROIS: "Hullo? What brings you here at this hour of the night?"

LUCE: "I've news for you."

BAROIS: "About the High Court?"

LUCE: "No. Who's upstairs?"

BAROIS: "Only our *Sower* friends."

LUCE: "Right. Let's go up."

On seeing Luce, all show signs of surprise and some anxiety. In silence he shakes their hands, then sinks wearily into a chair. With his face so drawn and wasted, the massiveness of the forehead is even more impressive.

LUCE: "I've just heard some news of grave importance." They gather round him. "Either yesterday or the day before there was a startling development at the Ministry of War. Colonel Henry fell under suspicion of having forged the documents produced at the trial." All gaze at him in stupefaction. "Henry was promptly called and questioned by the Minister. Did he confess? That I don't know; but I *do* know that for the last twenty-four hours he's been under arrest at Mont-Valérien."

BAROIS: "Henry arrested! But that means—!"

Such is their excitement that they can hardly think coherently for some moments; only utter stifled exclamations of delight.

BREIL-ZOEGER, in a voice hoarse with emotion: "That means the whole case will be reopened."

BAROIS: "It means revision obviously."

HARBAROUX, meticulous as usual: "But what documents exactly did he forge?"

LUCE: "The letter to the Italian Military Attaché which contained the name of Dreyfus written in full."

BAROIS: "What? That precious letter General de Pellieux made so much of?"

BREIL-ZOEGER: "The letter the Minister read out six weeks ago to the Chamber of Deputies!"

LUCE: "Yes, it's a complete forgery, except for the heading and the signature, which were got, it seems, from a letter on some routine matter."

BAROIS: "It's almost too good to be true!"

WOLDSMUTH, like an echo: "Too good to be true—yes. I don't feel easy about it."

LUCE: "But it's only a start. Once the inquiry takes this turn, a number of other questions will need answering. For instance: Who invented the tale that Dreyfus had confessed? Why wasn't a word breathed about it until 1896—two years after he had been cashiered? Then, again, who erased the original address and wrote in Ester-hazy's on that incriminating letter, the *"petit bleu,"* so as to raise the presumption that Colonel Picquart was trying to shield Dreyfus and inculpate Esterhazy by means of a document he'd tampered with?"

WOLDSMUTH, his eyes full of tears, repeats: "It's too good to be true. I don't feel easy about it."

LUCE: "In any case, this arrest has already had important conse-quences. Boisdeffre, Pellieux, and Zurlinden are leaving their posts. And I hear that the Minister too is tendering his resignation—which I can well understand. After having read out to the Chamber—albeit in good faith—a forgery, he can hardly do less."

BAROIS, laughing: "But it's *they* who should be arraigned before the High Court, not we!"

LUCE: "What's more, Brisson has swung round completely."

PORTAL: "At last!"

BAROIS: "That confirms what I have always said. Once an old-school republican like Brisson has his eyes opened, he'll move heaven and earth to have the case reviewed."

WOLDSMUTH: "I should say he must be feeling pretty sick at the thought of those million copies of Henry's forgery he had printed and posted up all over France."

HARBAROUX, with a loud guffaw: "Good Lord, yes! I wouldn't care to be in Brisson's shoes. That famous piece of evidence is on show in every town hall; it's fresh in every mind, and our patriotic papers gloat over it in every issue. And now, all of a sudden, it turns out to be a fake. Well, well!"

PORTAL: "The game is up, and they know it."

WOLDSMUTH, gloomily: "I wouldn't be too sure. I don't feel easy in the least."

BAROIS, laughing: "Oh, come, Woldsmuth! Really you're carrying your pessimism too far this time. The Government thought twice before ordering Henry's arrest, you may be sure. It means they couldn't see their way to hushing the matter up; they knew the truth would out, and there was no stopping it."

WOLDSMUTH, gently: "But Henry isn't even in the military prison.

BAROIS: "But surely—?"

CRESTEIL, breaking in with a sudden look of discouragement: "Yes, Woldsmuth's right, confound it! The fellow's only under open arrest, at the Mont-Valérien fort—which isn't the same thing."

They gaze at each other in consternation; the reaction is all the more pronounced because their hopes had run so high.

LUCE, dejectedly: "Perhaps they only wanted to gain time, so as to devise some way of getting out of the difficulty."

CRESTEIL: "And treat the forgery as a mere breach of military discipline? That's possible, I fear."

WOLDSMUTH, mournfully: "No, I haven't much confidence."

BAROIS, angrily: "That's enough of it, Woldsmuth! This is no time for pessimism." Firmly. "Our duty's plain. We've got to stir up such a rumpus about what's happened that they won't be able to hush it up."

LUCE: "Ah, if only Henry had confessed in the presence of witnesses!"

Shouts echo up the boulevard, newsboys are crying the day's "Late Specials." Though there is little traffic, the confused din of voices makes it almost impossible to distinguish what they are shouting.

PORTAL: "Ssh! That sounded like 'Colonel Henry.' "

LUCE: "What? Have they learnt of it already?"

Impulsively all have moved to the open windows and are hanging out, craning their necks, trying to catch what the boys are saying.

BREIL-ZOEGER, running to the door: "Waiter! The evening papers! Quickly!"

But already Woldsmuth has dashed down the stairs and out into the street. The shouts are growing fainter; the boys have turned off into side streets. Some minutes pass.

At last, breathless, his hair in disorder, his eyes sparkling, Woldsmuth appears at the head of the stairs brandishing a newspaper with headlines in large type:

"SUICIDE OF COLONEL HENRY AT FORT MONT-VALÉRIEN"

BAROIS, with a shout of triumph: "There we have it—our confession!"

He turns to Luce, and in a rush of emotion the two men embrace each other silently. Portal, Breil-Zoeger, and Cresteil try to snatch the newspaper from Woldsmuth, but he quietly hands it to Luce, who, jerkily adjusting his pince-nez, his face very pale, reads in a voice shaken by emotion.

LUCE: " 'Last night, at a meeting at the Ministry of War, it was ascertained that Lieutenant-Colonel Henry was the author of the letter in which the name of Dreyfus appears in full. The Minister gave orders for Lieutenant-Colonel Henry's arrest, and he was removed to Fort Mont-Valérien.

" 'This evening, on entering the cell at 6 P.M., the orderly assigned to the Lieutenant-Colonel found him lying on the bed in a pool of blood, his throat cut in two places, a razor in his hand. Death had taken place some two hours previously.

" 'The forger had paid the penalty of his crime.' "

The paper drops from his fingers. The others snatch it up, and it passes from hand to hand; each wishes to see the great news with his own eyes. And then a long, fierce cry of exultation, shrill with an almost insensate glee, breaks from their lips.

LUCE, in a choking voice: "Now that Henry's dead, it's over; there are some aspects of the Affair that will never come to light."

But his words are lost in the general excitement. Only Breil-Zoeger has heard and sadly nods his head. Woldsmuth has moved, unnoticed, to the window and, leaning out into the darkness, is shedding tears of joy.

4

A year later, August 6, 1899, the eve of the Rennes trial. The *Sower* office, a Sunday afternoon. Barois, who is in his shirt-sleeves, paces his office, his hands in his pockets, thinking out an article. His mind is at its most alert; the strong features that twitch now and again, the faint smile of satisfaction on his lips, vouch for his confident assurance of success. The bad days are over.

BAROIS: "Come in. Ah, it's you, Woldsmuth. Good." Woldsmuth looks even tinier than usual in a light dustcoat. He has a satchel slung over his shoulder and a big attaché-case under his arm. "We haven't met for several days. What have you been up to?"

WOLDSMUTH, settling into the nearest chair: "I've just come back from Germany."

BAROIS, without surprise: "From Germany?" After a moment's silence. "Anyhow, I knew you'd turn up today, to take over the management, as we'd agreed."

WOLDSMUTH: "Are you all leaving by the night express?"

BAROIS: "No, the others reached Rennes this morning. Luce had things to do there, and they went with him. I shall take the night train."

WOLDSMUTH: "When is Luce giving his evidence?"

BAROIS: "Not until the fifth or sixth day's hearing. I stayed behind so as to hand over to you, and also to write a final article which will appear tomorrow."

WOLDSMUTH, eagerly: "Ah? So there's a number coming out tomorrow?"

Barois, who takes Woldsmuth's interest for curiosity, gathers up some loose sheets on the desk.

BAROIS: "Oh, something quite short; just a few lines by way of prelude to the trial. Look here! I'll read out what I've written:

" 'Our goal is well in sight at last; the long-protracted nightmare is drawing to a close. We are no longer interested in the last act, the verdict which is a foregone conclusion, inevitable as the triumph of justice.

" 'All that remains to us today is the memory of having lived through an historic drama, unique of its kind, a drama in which thousands of characters played their parts and whose stage was the whole world. For its issues were at once so poignant and so universal in their appeal that first the entire nation and then all civilized mankind followed it with breathless interest. For what is assuredly the last time, humanity, divided into two unequal groups, joined vital issue; on one side was organized authority, which always turns a deaf ear to the voice of reason, and, on the other, the spirit of honest inquiry, which proudly disdains all social considerations.

" 'Generations to come will speak of "the Affair" as we today speak of "the Revolution," and will welcome as the happiest of coincidences that the dawn of a new century is also the dawn of a new era. And how glorious is the promise of a century ushered in by such a victory!'

"As you see, my dear Woldsmuth, a mere ebullition, a trumpet call!"

Woldsmuth gazes at him in stupefaction, then timidly draws his chair nearer.

WOLDSMUTH: "Tell me, Barois. Are you really so confident as that?"

BAROIS, smiling: "Why, of course!"

WOLDSMUTH, putting more energy into his voice: "Well, personally, I'm not. I don't feel confident at all."

Barois, who now is pacing the room with a look of almost gloating triumph, stops abruptly, then shrugs his shoulders.

BAROIS: "I seem to have heard that before! What a wet blanket you are, old chap!"

WOLDSMUTH, quickly: "So far facts have proved me right, I fear."

BAROIS: "But the conditions are very different today. There's been a change of government and our new government is convinced of Dreyfus's innocence and determined to clear the matter up. This time the trial will take place in public; there'll be no scope for hole-and-corner work. Why, really, to feel any doubt about the verdict is tantamount to assuming Dreyfus's guilt." He ends with a hearty laugh, a boisterous affirmation of common sense and certitude.

Woldsmuth gazes at him silently. The small, stubborn eyes glow darkly in the hairy, dust-stained face.

WOLDSMUTH, affectionately: "Do sit down, Barois. I want to talk to you seriously. I see a great many people, you know." Half closing his eyes, he goes on speaking in a muffled, toneless voice. "And I pick up lots of information."

BAROIS, sharply: "So do I."

WOLDSMUTH, in a conciliatory tone: "Then no doubt you've noticed. Well, consider the nationalist press. All the forgeries have been shown up, all the illegalities of the trial revealed, and yet their newspapers aren't climbing down. They've been forced to give ground on the facts, but they are having their revenge. They're slinging mud at all their enemies, indiscriminately. That report by Ballot-Beaupré—a completely honest summing up of the Affair—do you think any of their papers published it? Not they! They described it as the report of a man who'd been corrupted by Jewish gold—as were Duclaux, Anatole France, and Zola."

BAROIS: "What of it? Do you suppose their readers are so gullible as that?"

By way of retort Woldsmuth produces a sheaf of nationalist papers from his pocket and flings them on the table.

BAROIS, growing irritated: "That proves nothing. My answer is that during the last two months three thousand new subscriptions to *The Sower* have come in; you know it as well as I. The truth is that a great wave of enthusiasm—for public honesty and fair-dealing—is sweeping France today."

WOLDSMUTH, morosely: "It may be. But it hasn't yet reached our Ministry of War."

BAROIS, after reflection: "That's so. I admit that the judges, decent men, perhaps, but military-minded, are all against the agitation for revision of the case. But don't forget that the eyes of Europe, indeed of the whole civilized world, are fixed on Rennes today—and the military judges know this." He rises to his feet. "Well, there are some situations that compel, and these worthy officers will be forced to recognize that all those early allegations won't bear a moment's serious inspection, and"—he laughs—"there aren't any new ones."

WOLDSMUTH: "That depends."

Thrusting his hands in his pockets, Barois shrugs his shoulders again and once more starts pacing up and down the room. But the firmness of Woldsmuth's voice has taken effect, and presently he comes to a halt, facing him.

BAROIS: "Depends on what?"

WOLDSMUTH, with a wry smile: "Do sit down, Barois. You make me think of a caged lion." Frowning, Barois goes back to his seat behind the desk. "You remember that story about some tremendously secret documents?" Barois' look invites him to explain. "No? Then let me tell you. This is the story that's being circulated now. That a whole series of letters between Dreyfus and the Kaiser were somehow stolen." He smiles. "Grotesque, isn't it? But let that pass.

"According to this legend, the real *bordereau* formed part of this correspondence. It was written by Dreyfus on ordinary notepaper, and the German Emperor made some notes in the margin in his own hand. When Wilhelm II learnt of the theft he insisted on the return of the stolen letters, threatening to declare war if they were not restored. So as to have documentary evidence of Dreyfus's guilt, the Ministry had a tracing made of the *bordereau* on thin paper, before complying with the Kaiser's request. The marginal comments in his handwriting were, of course, omitted. Thus the whole affair was built up on this tracing of the original—a counterfeit in one sense, but a faithful reproduction of the incriminating original."

BAROIS: "A grotesque story! So grotesque, in fact, that never to my knowledge has it been formulated officially or even semi-officially."

WOLDSMUTH: "I know. But all the same it's going round, passed from mouth to mouth in gatherings attended by officers, magistrates, lawyers, and society people. None claims first-hand knowledge of course. What's said is: 'A well-informed friend gave me to understand . . .' and so forth, to the accompaniment of knowing winks and smiles. And gradually it has taken effect and paved the way. So to-morrow when the case starts at Rennes and the defence tries to force the staff officers to show their hand, they'll play their little parts. All they'll need to do is to make a show of embarrassment at certain points, to pause and stammer—you see the tactics? And everyone will take this to mean: 'Draw your own conclusions. Anyhow, we'd rather be accused of forgery than bring about a European war.' "

BAROIS: "A war! But at this hour of the day there can't be any question of a danger of that sort. Considering all that's been said and written about the foreign military attachés, about German espionage and counter-espionage, who can be such a simpleton as to think that any 'dangerous' diplomatic documents still remain to be made public? Did any such document exist, it's obvious that the General Staff would have produced it long ago, just to put an end to all the trouble."

WOLDSMUTH, gloomily: "It's not quite so simple as all that, I fear. All along I've been worried about the 'diplomatic' issue—it's the thread that runs through the Affair from end to end, and though it's kept invisible, everything, every incident, links up with it. That's where the danger lies, a very real danger." About to speak, Barois thinks better of it; his look betrays his deep concern. "But, happily, there's still time to forestall their machinations. I've been compiling a kind of 'brief,' containing nothing but facts for whose veracity I can vouch. During my recent visit to Germany I have verified those about which I felt the slightest doubt."

BAROIS: "Ah, that's why—"

WOLDSMUTH: "Yes." He opens his attaché-case. "I've material here that will blow their 'State Secret' arguments sky high. But there's no time to lose. Here is my 'brief.' Publish it tomorrow."

BAROIS, after pondering for some moments: "Thanks, Woldsmuth. But I think the publication of evidence of that kind today would be most unwise." Woldsmuth makes a discouraged gesture. "It would draw attention to a feature of the case which, whatever you may think, has been deliberately relegated to obscurity. They might feel moved to fall back on it, by way of a reprisal, and that would have a bad effect on public opinion.

"No, publication would be a tactical blunder as things stand. For there is bound to be an acquittal. Let's have our triumph in beauty, without raking up old animosities." His shoulders drooping, Woldsmuth begins to close his attaché-case. "No, leave your notes with me."

WOLDSMUTH: "What's the good? If they're to serve any purpose they must be used at once, preventively."

BAROIS: "I'll take them with me to Rennes and show them to Luce. If he thinks as you do, I promise—"

WOLDSMUTH, with a gleam of hope: "Yes, do show them to Luce, and please repeat exactly what I've told you." He thinks for a moment. "But you can't possibly take them as they stand. They're in such a muddle. I shall have to go through them carefully. You see, I'd hoped we could do the job together for tomorrow's issue."

BAROIS: "Your niece is here. If you dictate to her, it shouldn't take long."

WOLDSMUTH, his face lighting up: "Oh, Julia's here?"

Barois gets up and opens the door.

BAROIS: "Julia!"

JULIA, from the next room, without moving: "Yes? What is it?"

The familiarity of her tone is so noticeable that Barois flushes and glances hastily at Woldsmuth, who, poring over his papers, has betrayed no surprise.

BAROIS, controlling his voice: "Would you come here for a moment, to take down some notes?"

Julia enters. On noticing Woldsmuth, her eyelids flutter slightly—no more than that. Her rebellious air seems a reminder to her uncle: "I'm my own mistress anyhow!"

JULIA, curtly: "Good afternoon, Uncle Ulric. How was your trip?"

Woldsmuth raises his head but does not look at her. And now she notices the twisted, disconcerting smile, the strained look on his face. She guesses something she had never even suspected until now. When at last Woldsmuth looks towards her, it is she who lowers her eyes.

WOLDSMUTH: "So you're here, Julia. All's well with you, I hope. And with your mother."

JULIA, with an effort: "Yes, we're both quite fit."

WOLDSMUTH: "Then would you . . . ? I've some notes to be taken down . . . for Barois."

BAROIS, who has noticed nothing: "Go to her office, Woldsmuth, you'll be more comfortable there. And meanwhile I'll finish my article."

Rennes,
August 13, 1899

My dear Woldsmuth: I assume you have read the shorthand reports for yesterday and the day before. How right you were, my friend! Yet who could have suspected it at the time?

All these last days our enemies have been eagerly awaiting the "conclusive" evidence against Dreyfus that they have so often been promised. The generals had their say; disappointment all along the

line! Then, as public opinion obstinately refused to admit that no
such conclusive argument existed, they interpreted the reticences of
the General Staff exactly as you foresaw. Which was what the General Staff intended. A rumour has actually being going round that at
the last moment Germany forced this heroic silence on our officers!

I am sending herewith the notes you dictated to Julia before I
left; they are, alas, of vital importance as things stand today. Breil-
Zoeger, who is going back to Paris to take over from you, will hand
them to you this evening with this letter.

Get in touch with Roll at once and see that your article appears
tomorrow on the front page. Also, before leaving Paris, please arrange for a wide distribution of this issue. Bring two thousand copies
to Rennes; that will be enough.

Sadly and sincerely yours,
J.B.

Next day, on the front page of *The Sower:*

WILHELM II AND THE DREYFUS CASE

"During the last few weeks we have been surprised to observe that
an ingenious legend, which, to the minds of simple persons, seems
to solve the mysteries of the Affair, has made its reappearance. It is
the story that a French agent purloined from the Kaiser's desk a
bordereau on stout paper annotated by the Kaiser himself. Under
the threat of war the French authorities were compelled hastily to
restore the original document, and the *bordereau* we know (on
thin, transparent paper) is a tracing of the original, which was made
at the Ministry of War in view of the 1894 trial.

"We need not trouble to point out the glaring improbabilities of
this romantic tale, and shall limit ourselves to asking three questions.

"(1) If the *bordereau* is a tracing of words written by Dreyfus,
how is it that the handwriting is little if at all like that of Dreyfus,
but identical with Esterhazy's?

"(2) If Henry's forgeries can be accounted for by the necessity of substituting diplomatically harmless documents for those in which the German Emperor's handwriting appeared and which therefore could not be made use of, how was it that Henry, when questioned by the Minister of War just before his arrest, did not clear himself by explaining that his forgeries were reproductions of authentic documents? Several generals were present when he was questioned, and General Roget took the statements down in shorthand. Henry did not attempt to justify his forgeries by any allegation of the kind.

"(3) If the story of the annotated *bordereau* is true, how was it that when Brisson, greatly shocked by Henry's suicide, manifested intentions of making a public confession of his mistake and securing a revision of the Dreyfus verdict—how was it that the Minister of War, who took such pains to argue Brisson out of this resolve, did not simply inform him of the German Emperor's intervention, and thus bring the swing-round of opinion, which was causing the anti-revisionists such dismay, to an immediate stop?

"After asking these pertinent questions we shall confine ourselves to setting forth in chronological order certain facts whose significance seems so obvious that no comment is called for.

"(1) On November 1, 1894, the name of Dreyfus appeared for the first time in the newspapers, with the allegation that he was a spy in the service of Germany or Italy. The German and Italian Military Attachés were amazed; the name was wholly unfamiliar to them both. This is proved by the fact that on June 5, 1899, the Italian Ambassador forwarded to the Minister for Foreign Affairs, for transmission to the Court of Appeal, a code communication dated 1894 from the Italian Attaché (who was working hand in glove with the German Attaché) in which he secretly informed his Government that neither of them had ever had any dealings with the Dreyfus in question. At the same time the General Staffs of Germany, Italy, and Austria had inquiries made in their respective secret services and failed to elicit information regarding anyone by the name of Dreyfus.

"(2) On November 9, 1894, the German Attaché was implicated by name in a French paper. After another inquiry the German Embassy issued a formal *dementi* in the form of a press communiqué. It should be noted that this denial cannot have been made without due care and caution, since Germany would not have run the risk of making a statement, under such conditions, which might thereafter be proved false in the course of a public trial. Moreover, at the same time the Imperial Chancellor instructed the German Ambassador in Paris to make an official declaration, *suo motu,* to this effect to the French Minister for Foreign Affairs.

"(3) On November 28 the interview with General Mercier was published in *Figaro.* Five days before the conclusion of the inquiry, which was to lead to the indictment of Dreyfus before a military court, the Minister stated that there was 'conclusive proof' of the guilt of the accused man, and that Dreyfus had offered his documents *neither to Italy nor to Austria.* The inference that Germany was implicated was obvious, and a new and strongly worded protest was made by Germany through diplomatic channels.

"When the French press failed to take this into account, the Kaiser, the German General Staff, and the German press were greatly incensed at finding that the veracity of their formal declaration was being questioned. Accordingly, on December 4, on the Kaiser's orders, another interview took place between the Ambassador and our Minister for Foreign Affairs. An official communiqué was issued, vigorously protesting against all allegations tending to implicate the German Embassy in the Dreyfus Affair.

"(4) The trial took place. As regards the 'secret dossier' shown the trial judges, without inspection of it being granted to the accused man or his counsel, we are in a position to state that there was nothing in this dossier bearing out the tale of a *bordereau* annotated by the German Emperor. This can be verified by questioning the members of the 1894 Council of War, now present at Rennes, on this point.

"(5) At the close of December 1894, after the verdict, the press openly accused Germany of having insisted on a trial *in camera,* because Germany was directly involved in the circumstances of

Dreyfus's guilt. This also was tantamount to giving the lie to the Ambassador's statement. On December 25, immediately after the sentence, the Ambassador made a further official statement to the press. But the newspapers continued their campaign, talking about a document returned to Germany so as to avoid the risk of war.

"(6) On January 5, 1895, the day on which Dreyfus was formally 'degraded,' the German Ambassador received a very important dispatch from the Imperial Chancellor. In the absence of our Minister for Foreign Affairs he took it directly to our Premier. This dispatch, now published for the first time, ran as follows:

" 'H.H. the Emperor, who feels the utmost confidence in the good faith of the President and Government of the French Republic, requests Your Excellency to inform M. Casimir-Périer that, if it is proved that the German Embassy was never implicated in any way in the Dreyfus Affair, His Majesty hopes that the Government of the Republic will not hesitate to make this publicly known.

" 'Without a formal declaration to this effect, the rumours that the press continues to circulate regarding Germany will persist, and compromise the position of the Emperor's representative in Paris— Von Hohenlohe.'

"Thus the Kaiser, at the end of his patience, made a direct appeal to the French President himself.

"The Ambassador was received by the President at his official residence, and we have it on unimpeachable authority that M. Casimir-Périer chose to regard the incident as a private rather than a diplomatic order, since the German Emperor was asking him to intervene personally. In fact, as he himself subsequently stated, 'an appeal was made to his good will in his private capacity.'

"In this connexion we may refer to the evidence given by M. Casimir-Périer before the Supreme Court of Appeal and Revision. He began by stating explicitly that he had no secrets of any kind to conceal. 'I have observed,' he went on to say, 'that my silence (at the Zola trial) seemed to countenance the notion that I—and perhaps only I—had knowledge of incidents, of facts, or of documents which

might influence the course of justice. I feel it my duty, in view of
the present unhappy state of dissension and unrest prevailing in
France, to place myself at the disposal of the Supreme Court *un-
reservedly* . . .'

"This puts an end to any suspicion whatsoever that (as some have
alleged) the President was bound by a pledge of secrecy. A declaration of this sort coming from a man of his high integrity is conclusive. He went on to describe the diplomatic conversation that en-
sued, leading to an official communiqué through the Havas Agency,
which definitely exonerated all foreign embassies in Paris. And on
the next day but one the Kaiser expressed his satisfaction.

"Nor must we overlook the statement made by M. Hanotaux, the
Minister for Foreign Affairs at the time of the 1894 trial. To the
question, 'Have you any knowledge of certain letters from a foreign ruler, which were written at the time of the Dreyfus trial and
tended to prove the guilt of the accused man?' he gave a perfectly
definite answer: 'I have never seen any such letter, nor have I ever
heard of one. Nobody ever offered me anything of the kind. I have
never been consulted as to the existence or the value of any such
documents. In short, the whole story is completely mythical; moreover, it has been denied in communiqués to the newspapers.'

"Let us cite, in conclusion, the evidence given before the Appeal
Court by M. Paléologue, who was liaison officer between the Min-
istry of War and the Ministry for Foreign Affairs at the time of the
Dreyfus trial.

" 'Neither before nor after the Dreyfus trial did I hear anything
about the existence of a letter from the German Emperor, or of letters from Dreyfus to that monarch. The allegations to which the
Presiding Judge has alluded seem to me completely unfounded. The
nature of my then duties authorizes me to say that, had documents
of this kind existed, I would certainly have known of their existence.'

"(7) On November 17, 1897, the German Ambassador informed
our Minister for Foreign Affairs that the German Military Attaché,

Colonel von Schwartzkoppen, affirmed on his honour that he had never had any dealings, direct or indirect, with Dreyfus.

"(8) In 1898, just before the Zola trial, the Emperor was extremely anxious to make a decisive, *personal* intervention, but his advisers discouraged him from doing so. They knew how high feelings were running in France and feared some personal insult might be levelled at the Kaiser, leading to grave complications. However, he insisted that an official statement should be made publicly, at a sitting of the Reichstag.

"This is the statement made accordingly, by the German Foreign Secretary, at the session of January 24, 1898:

" 'You will understand that I must approach this subject with extreme prudence. Any indiscreet approach might be regarded as an unwarrantable intervention on our part in matters concerning France. I deem it all the more incumbent on me to maintain a wise reserve on this subject since we may anticipate that the trials being held in France will throw the fullest light on the Affair.

" 'Therefore I will confine myself to affirming, in the most formal and categorical manner, that no relations or contacts of any kind whatsoever have ever existed between ex-Captain Dreyfus, now undergoing penal servitude on Devil's Island, and any German agent whatsoever.'

"(9) Five days later the Emperor himself called on our Ambassador in Berlin, gave him his personal declaration on the subject, and asked him to communicate it officially to our Government.

"(10) Finally, at the present moment, the state of mind prevailing in the Emperor's entourage is the same. The Kaiser himself is fervently desirous of making a personal 'gesture.' But his advisers dissuade him from it, and will continue to dissuade him, so as to avert a serious danger—that, by reaffirming Dreyfus's guilt, France might once again give the Kaiser the lie direct, and thus create an intolerable position which would lead to the breaking off of diplomatic relations. However, the German authorities are prepared to confirm, through the usual channels, all the declarations already made.

"If we are prepared to believe that the Kaiser was really compromised in an affair of espionage, we may, at a pinch, assume that, for political considerations, he might feel called on to deny the truth in an official statement. But is it credible that, once this diplomatically necessary lie had been told and put on record, he would have voiced his protest again and again on every possible occasion, with such deliberate emphasis and such extreme insistence?

"Even if we leave out of account the temperament of the German Emperor and his well-known touchiness regarding points of personal honour, is it to be believed that a monarch would dare to make such vehement and plain-spoken declarations if there were the slightest risk of his being one day, as a result of the discovery of some conclusive piece of evidence, shown up to the world as having lied?

"Who can fail to see in the Kaiser's attitude anything other than a very simple, heart-felt sense of duty? He knows, better than anyone, that Dreyfus is innocent, and he does his best to proclaim this knowledge as emphatically and frequently as is possible without exposing his country to the risk of diplomatic complications.

"None are so deaf as they who will not hear!"

M. Marc-Élie Luce
Auteuil   Rennes, September 5, 1899
My dear Luce: We are utterly despondent. To all intents and purposes ours is a lost cause. The past fortnight has put the seal on the Affair. The judges have made up their minds and they know well that the majority think as they do.

Woldsmuth blames me for having published his article belatedly. I too blame myself, though I doubt if earlier publication would have made much difference. How combat a myth which no one has ever clearly formulated? Anyhow, there would have been no way of coming to grips with it, since all agree that those alleged marginal comments in the Kaiser's hand cannot be verified. Under such conditions anyone's word is as good as another's, and in this war against mere phantoms we were helpless, doomed from the start.

Had a swing-round of public opinion been feasible, it would have been brought about on the day after you left Rennes by the attitude of Casimir-Périer, the man in France best qualified to know whether or not the Kaiser was involved in the Affair. I saw this man, whose character is spotless, facing the Presiding Judge, and his voice rang true when he made his statement. This is what he said:

"You ask me to tell the whole truth and nothing but the truth. I have sworn to do this, and I shall speak out without withholding anything. Despite what I have reiterated in the past, some people persist in believing, or in saying—which, alas, is not always the same thing—that I alone know of certain incidents or facts which might throw light on the case, and that I have not yet revealed all that, in the interests of justice, should be known. That is false. I do not wish to leave these precincts until I feel satisfied that everyone present is convinced, unshakably convinced, that I know nothing as to which I am bound to silence, and that I have frankly and completely stated all I know."

I don't question the good faith of the military judges. I believe them to be as impartial as they can be. But they are soldiers. The newspapers they read have seen to it that they, like the whole Army, are kept in complete ignorance of the inside history of the Affair. These worthy officers have been confronted by an outrageously simplified pair of alternatives, a most damnable dilemma: "You have to choose between finding Dreyfus guilty and blackening the Army's good name."

There might be some hope, if they were kept apart from outside influences and left to themselves to judge the facts, according to the promptings of their consciences. But unfortunately every evening, when the hearing ends, they still frequent circles in which the accused man's betrayal of his country is a foregone conclusion.

I wouldn't say they are determined to find Dreyfus guilty, but I feel quite sure they will bring in a verdict to that effect. How indeed could these men, whose natural dispositions have been vitiated year after year by the exigencies of their profession, act otherwise? They have been, as it were, crusted over by twenty-five years of wearing uniforms, a quarter of a century during which, day in and day out, they have had the virtues of military discipline, the sense of Army hierarchy, drubbed into them. And in the high officers who appear before them they see living symbols of the Army to which they have dedicated their lives. How could they decide in favour of a Jew, against the General Staff? Even if, in their heart of hearts, they have an uneasy feeling that they should act thus, it is *physically impossible* for them to do so.

Moreover, I am bound to admit that the figure Dreyfus cuts in Court has nothing to counterbalance the fine presence of the men in uniform opposing him. Yes, the majority even of his friends are disappointed in him. Wrongly, to my mind. For four years we have been fighting for ideas, and have made Dreyfus, so to speak, their figurehead. All of us had conjured up in our imagination a picture, none the less precise for its capriciousness, of the stranger we were championing. He returns to France and, as might have been expected, the reality doesn't conform to our expectation. And a good many of us have not yet forgiven him for our disillusionment.

Dreyfus is a simple man, all of whose energies are of the introversive order. He is also an invalid; long confinement and the ordeal he has been through have sapped his vigour. A few pints of milk are all he can digest; you can see him shivering with fever. How could he rise effectively to the occasion, when confronted by an excited mob of people three-quarters of whom regard him as the blackest of traitors, and the remaining quarter venerate him as a symbol? Surely, under such conditions, no one could play the heroic part we asked of poor Dreyfus! He no longer has strength enough to proclaim his innocence in the proud, defiant tone he used at the first trial. What little energy is left him he husbands, using it not against his accusers but against himself, to prevent himself from breaking down, and to put up a show of courage.

The true nobility and tragic grandeur of this attitude are completely lost on the average man. He might perhaps have won over the crowd by striking a more theatrical pose; but the self-control which he strains every effort to maintain is regarded as mere apathy, and the men who have been fighting in his cause for the past four years hold this up against him.

Personally, I confess that when I saw him at the first hearing— I had never set eyes on him before—in spite of my friends' enthusiasm and the high hopes I had voiced so proudly that very morning in *The Sower,* my heart sank, and I had a foreboding of defeat. I hid my feeling then even from you. But I can now see that I realized, with a conviction as absolute as it was abruptly come by, that we were fighting in a lost cause—lost, moreover, in an ugly way. Nothing would remain in hearts once fired with generous emotion but a residue of sordid memories. And now this odious thought is always present at the back of my mind.

You did well to leave Rennes; your place was not here, in this maelstrom of absurdity.

We are at the end of our tether. Don't forget that for many of us this is the second sweltering summer we have to live through in an atmosphere oppressive as a nightmare. Picture to yourself our days of long-drawn-out suspense in the stifling atmosphere of that courtroom, listening to evidence that reeks of prejudice and hatred. And picture, too, those evenings, even worse than the days, when, to escape our suffocating hotel bedrooms where sleep is out of the question, we forgather in streets or cafés and reckon up for the nth time our chances of victory or defeat! If we have managed to see it through so far, it is because the conviction that justice would prevail steeled our endurance. But, though we are nearing the conclusion of yet another phase, the end still seems as far off as ever. And how long the road before us yet—there is no knowing.

It is sad indeed to see our admirable country sunk so low, both intellectually and morally. To think that at this moment there is a truly world-wide stirring of the human conscience, a movement of revolt, and for the first time in centuries France lags behind!

Please tell Breil-Zoeger that if he wishes to return to Rennes, Harbaroux can go to Paris to take over at the office.

Au revoir, my dear friend, and ever yours,

Jean Barois

P.S. I have just learnt that Labori intends to make a personal appeal to the Kaiser, with a view to obtaining, before the close of the trial, yet another declaration from the Emperor of Dreyfus's innocence. What's the use? Considering how things are, it's bound to be too late.

Telegram to:

Barois, 103 Lycée, Rennes.   Paris, September 8, 11:30 A.M.

Have just received telegram reporting new protest by German Government in this morning's *Imperial Monitor,* in response Labori's appeal:

"We are authorized to renew declarations made by His Majesty's Government to safeguard personal dignity and obey dictates common humanity. On Emperor's instructions, Ambassador, January 1894 and January 1895 handed to Hanotaux, Minister Foreign Affairs, to Premier Dupuy and President Casimir-Périer, repeated declarations that German Embassy in France never entertained relations direct or indirect with Dreyfus.

"On January 24, 1898, Secretary of State von Bülow stated before Reichstag commission: 'I declare in the most solemn manner that no dealings or intercourse of any kind took place between ex-Captain Dreyfus and any German organization whatsoever.'

"Minister Foreign Affairs has undertaken officially to transmit this protest to the judges before verdict rendered."

Still have hopes. Spread the news through all local newspapers.

Luce.

Telegram to:
 Luce, Auteuil.   Rennes, September 9, 6 p.m.
 Guilty of treason with extenuating circumstances. Ten years' imprisonment. A nonsensical self-contradictory verdict. But we're not
beaten yet. On with the fight for justice!   Barois.

5

September 9, 1899. The evening of the verdict. At Rennes station
three successive trains have been boarded at a rush. A fourth, composed of ramshackle cars collected from various sidings, gets laboriously under way amid the seething turmoil on the platforms. Barois,
Cresteil, and Woldsmuth have squeezed into an ancient third-class
car divided into compartments by partitions reaching half-way up
to the roof. Two oil lamps do duty for the whole car.
 There is not a breath of wind. The open windows give glimpses of
the night-bound countryside. The engine crawls along, trailing
through the sultry darkness a din of voices like that of an election
meeting. Heated comments flash back and forth through the foul air
of the compartment in which are Barois and his friends.
 "Of course those damned Jesuits were behind it!"
 "That's no thing to say. What about the honour of the Army?"
 "Anyhow, it's a death-blow to the trade-union movement, I should
say."
 "They were quite right. The safety of the country would be endangered if an officer who's been sentenced by seven brother-officers
and declared guilty by the High Command were to be reinstated.
It would be infinitely worse than a miscarriage of justice."
 "You're right. And I'd go further. Suppose I'd been one of the
judges and suppose I *knew* that Dreyfus was innocent. Well, sir, for
the safety of our country, for the maintenance of order, I'd have
sent him to the firing-squad without a moment's hesitation."
 CRESTEIL, springing up impulsively and making his raucous voice

heard through the din: "There's a French scientist, Duclaux, who has answered that argument about the safety of the country. This is what he said, more or less: 'No reason of State can hinder a Court of Justice from doing justice.'" Cries of "Traitor!" "Blackguard!" "Dirty Jew!" Cresteil strikes an attitude of challenge. "Gentlemen, I am ready to meet you wherever you may desire." There is another volley of abuse. Cresteil remains standing.

BAROIS: "Oh, let them be, Cresteil!"

Gradually, as a result of the stifling heat, the murky light, the jolts and lurches of the decrepit car, everyone grows drowsy. The noise becomes localized, diminishes. Huddled together in their corner, Barois, Cresteil, and Woldsmuth converse in undertones.

WOLDSMUTH: "The saddest thing is that this quite laudable idea of serving the country's best interests has been, I'm positive, behind much of the opposition we came up against."

CRESTEIL: "You're wrong there. You're much too fond, my dear Woldsmuth, of giving people credit for noble sentiments. Oftener than not they're guided by self-interest, consciously or unconsciously, or by mere blind deference to convention."

BAROIS: "Talking of convention, I was greatly struck by a little scene I witnessed at the second or third hearing. I came a bit late and entered by the press corridor just as the officer-judges were arriving. At the same moment four witnesses, four generals in full uniform, came up, a little behind them. Well, the seven judges stopped dead, lined up along the wall and stood to attention. And the generals, mere witnesses, walked past them, as if they were on parade, and the judges automatically saluted."

CRESTEIL, impulsively: "That has its beauty!"

BAROIS: "No, old chap. That was the military college cadet you once were speaking, not the Cresteil of today."

CRESTEIL, sadly: "I suppose so. Still, really it's excusable when you come to think of it. To make a man of action, proud of his vocation, discipline asks so much at every moment of the day that you can't lose the habit of valuing it at the price it costs."

BAROIS, following up his train of thought: "The verdict we heard given, you see, fits in with that little scene in the passage. On the face of it, the conviction of a traitor 'with extenuating circumstances' seems sheer idiocy. But consider the facts: the conviction was a military necessity—to save the Army's face—and their sense of discipline obliged them, though they were unaware of this, to vote for it. The 'extenuating circumstances' meant that, after all, as decent private individuals, they couldn't altogether square their consciences."

The train reaches Paris at daybreak. A gloomy silence fills the cars, which disgorge their draggled, shivering denizens upon the platform. Luce is there, waiting, his gentle eyes searching for his friends amongst the crowd. Breil-Zoeger, too, has come. Silently they all shake hands, their hearts filled with a vast affection, a vast sadness. Weeping, Woldsmuth kisses Luce's hand.

BAROIS, after a brief hesitation: "Julia isn't with you?"

BREIL-ZOEGER, looking up quickly: "No."

They move away, in a compact group, without speaking.

BAROIS, with a shade of nervousness, to Luce: "Any news?" He is troubled by Luce's silence. "Any talk of an appeal?"

LUCE: "No, it seems that, on technical grounds, there's no possibility of an appeal."

BAROIS: "So—what then?"

LUCE, after some moments' silence: "Perhaps a pardon."

CRESTEIL and BAROIS, together: "He'll refuse it."

LUCE, firmly: "No."

It is the last, the knock-out blow. They halt on the pavement, stunned, unseeing, their shoulders sagging.

WOLDSMUTH: "Try to put yourselves in his place. Should he go back to that island and endure that hell on earth again? And to what purpose?"

CRESTEIL, dramatically: "To remain a symbol."

WOLDSMUTH, doggedly: "It would kill him. What would be the good?"

LUCE, with deep compassion in his voice: "Woldsmuth's right. At least we shall rehabilitate a living man."

The evening of the same day. Barois has left the *Sower* office early and walks blindly ahead, gripping in his pocket the note from Julia which he found on his desk.

You are coming back from Rennes and you will be surprised at not finding me in the office.

I don't want to deceive you. I gave myself freely; I take back my freedom on the same terms. So long as I loved you, I belonged to you without reserve. But now that I love someone else, I must tell you quite frankly that you have ceased to count in my life. I make no secret of this change, it is my way of proving the respect I have for you, to the end.

By the time you read this note, I shall have regained the liberty to dispose of my life as I think fit. You're brave enough and intelligent enough to understand me, and not to waste your energies on vain regrets.

But I shall always remain your friend.

Julia

Once back in his room in the Rue Jacob, he stretches himself fully dressed on the bed. A morbid, personal, and poignant grief has been grafted onto the grief he felt before, the bleak discouragement that had already sapped his energy. His head is burning, heavy as lead. And suddenly, in the darkness of the bedroom, memory rekindles past emotion, and he feels a sudden uprush of sensual desire, a longing to recapture, cost what it may, certain unforgettable thrills he has experienced in this very room. He springs up, biting his lips, wringing his hands, his features working convulsively; then, as abruptly, he lets himself fall back, sobbing, upon the bed.

For yet some moments he struggles, like a drowning man caught in the undertow. Then he founders into dark, dreamless sleep.

A ring at the bell awakes him and plunges him headlong into his despair. The sun is high; a clock strikes ten. Opening the door, he sees Woldsmuth on the threshold.

WOLDSMUTH, startled by Barois' haggard, dishevelled appearance: "Sorry! I'm disturbing you."

BAROIS, irritably: "No. Come in. Come in."

WOLDSMUTH, refraining from looking at him: "I tried to find you at the *Sower* office—about that information you wanted." He raises his eyes. "I managed to see Reinach." Awkwardly. "I'm very—I mean, I wanted . . ."

He cannot get the words out. The two men gaze at each other, and Barois realizes that Woldsmuth knows all. Somehow he feels relieved. He holds out both hands to his friend.

WOLDSMUTH, shyly: "Yes. And to think that Zoeger, a friend . . ."

BAROIS, who has gone quite pale, in a choking voice: "What? Breil-Zoeger?"

WOLDSMUTH, taken aback: "Well, I don't know for sure. I thought . . ." Barois is seated, his fists clenched, his head thrust forward, his mind void of thoughts—like a figure hewn in stone. Woldsmuth is alarmed by his silence. "I'm dreadfully sorry. I'm meddling in something that's none of my business. But I thought I'd come round. I'd like to—to help you to feel less badly about it."

Without answering or looking at him, Barois thrusts his hand into his coat-pocket and hands him Julia's letter. Woldsmuth reads it with a sort of forlorn eagerness, and his lips begin to tremble weakly; his breath comes in short, wheezy gasps. Then, folding the sheet of notepaper, he seats himself at Barois' side and clumsily puts his short stumpy arm round his friend's shoulders.

WOLDSMUTH: "Ah, that girl Julia! I know. It hurts, hurts horribly, one feels like killing." With a wistful smile. "And then it dies down."

Suddenly, without moving, he begins to sob quietly, persistently, letting the tears flow down his cheeks unchecked, as one weeps for a personal distress. As Barois watches, noting his tone, his words, his tears, he knows what so far he has but dimly surmised. And suddenly, before pity comes, he feels a morose satisfaction; he is less alone, another shares the blow. But then a wave of sentimental compassion brings tears to his eyes. How cruel life can be!

BAROIS, humbly, as if words could erase the past: "Ah, Woldsmuth, my poor friend, how I must have made you suffer!"

6

May 30, 1900. At the Paris Exposition. In one of the lath-and-plaster restaurants, beflagged and lavishly beflowered, that have been run up for the occasion on the banks of the Seine, some thirty young men are seated round a dinner-table.

Waiters have just lit the candelabra; bathed in a soft yellow glow, wine-glasses and drooping flowers glimmer in the gathering dusk. The banquet is ending on a mood of languid, reminiscent calm.

Luce, who is presiding, rises. Over-shadowed by the massive forehead, his limpid gaze, serene yet searching, lingers for a moment on the group around the table. He smiles, as though in humorous excuse of the written sheets he produces from his pocket.

The slight provincial burr adds colour to his diction and imparts a note of geniality, at once simple and compelling.

LUCE: "My friends, exactly a year ago we had great occasion for rejoicing. Monsieur Ballot-Beaupré had just read his report at a public meeting, and we had seen the whole Affair come to life under our eyes in his admirable summing-up. It had a clean-cut precision of detail and an eloquence which made it a model for all time of what such a résumé should be. The approving silence which greeted his speech was proof of the great change of heart of that very same public which, only a year before, was hurling abuse at Zola. And, now that the incubus which had been weighing on us for three years was lifted—by official hands—we felt a limitless confidence as to the future.

"Ever and again there rose to our lips those words pregnant with hope with which Monsieur Mornard concluded his address to the Court: 'I await your verdict as the dawn of a new day that will flood this land of France with the light of truth and amity.'

"It is to commemorate those glorious hours—which, I think you will agree, were the last unsullied hours of the Affair—that we have gathered here tonight. I will not dwell on the painful memories of last summer. Already the details are growing blurred for most of us. The generous desire shown by the Government to nullify the half-hearted verdict of the military judges justifies us in awaiting, with a patience that is new to us, the moment when, by the sheer force of things, truth will sweep away the last traces of injustice. For truth is invincible and always ends by bending events to its will.

"The worst, we may be sure, is over. As one of our friends wrote recently: 'Mass violence is like the storm-winds of spring; like them it swells and blusters, then calms down and dies away, leaving the growing seeds to thrust their way up to the light.'

"This is a difficult time, I know, for all those who for several years have been living in a ferment of activity. Panting like hounds at the end of the day's run, they have to halt, once the arduous pursuit is over and their work is done. But now a new anxiety begins to haunt them, when they survey the havoc and the victims strewing the battlefield. Am I not right in saying that this anxiety is shared by us all? For how could it be otherwise when we see the plight of France today, a land rent by dissension, a house divided against itself?

"In the thick of the fight we gave little thought to its aftermath. That was what our enemies reproached us with. We did not burke the issue, but retorted that national honour must rank before public order and that an act of flagrant illegality, even if its pretext be the national security, spells infinitely worse evils than a transient period of unrest. It imperils the one achievement for which a certain pride is justified on our part; those noble ideals of freedom with which French blood has enriched the world at large. Nay, I would go further: it jeopardizes justice and fair-dealing throughout the whole civilized world."

There is a ripple of applause.

"Nevertheless, now that we have gained the day, we can but rec-ognize the predicament into which the obstinacy of public opinion plunged the country; we are living on the morrow of a revolution.

"In the chaotic period that immediately preceded the climax, and under cover of our final onslaught, a whole horde of partisans, men we had never heard of, attached themselves to the group of militants and intellectuals that we had constituted hitherto. They snatched from our hands our humble but unvanquished flag and brandished it in our stead, for all to see. They swarmed over the terrain we had opened up in our task of social scavenging. And now that the bat-tle's won, it is they who hold the field as conquerors. May I here draw a verbal distinction—a matter of jargon, if you will; yet one on which I set much store? *We* were a handful of 'Dreyfusites'; they are an army of 'Dreyfusards.'

"What kind of men are they? I have no idea. They exploit certain false identifications, which we rigorously forbade ourselves; thus they identify militarism and the Army, nationalism and France. What is their programme and what are they capable of building on the ruins we left behind our advance? Of that too I have no idea. Will that splendid future whose promise lit our dreams dawn at their bidding, as they profess? I wonder!

"No, I greatly fear that in some respects they are no better than the men whom we defeated. Still, it's a consolation to think they cannot be worse.

"As for us, our task is ended; the achievement of what we so pas-sionately longed for is in the hands of others. Deliberately we ini-tiated a vast upheaval, and most of us are paying the price of this today—in the loss of peace of mind and personal happiness.

"It's hard, my dear friends, very hard—I know it as well as you. I have lost my hearers at the Collège de France, and, though I have been re-elected to the Senate, I have no illusions. No committee in-vites me to sit on it, and I play no active part in national affairs.

"Those who are deriving the most obvious benefits from our crusade are, for the most part, cold-shouldering us, and they view us with the greatest suspicion. They are wrong. Their conduct almost suggests that, now they know the danger we present to anyone who has not—shall I say?—clean hands, they feel slightly nervous in our company." He smiles.

"Less to be pitied are the younger men, those who have time ahead of them for reshaping their lives. That baptism of fire, on the threshold of a life of high endeavour, has, I feel convinced, done them a world of good. It has burnt away the overgrowth of false sentiments and make-believe from their personalities, leaving only the essential substance—solid rock! How salutary for them was the necessity of choosing once for all their course in life, their loyalties! Yes, I know many such younger men who will have come out of this ordeal the better for it." Smiling, he raises his eyes for a moment from the sheet he is holding and turns towards Barois, who is sitting next him. "Our friend Barois, for instance, whose generous enthusiasm and fine courage never faltered, and who was a pillar of strength when things were at their worst." He goes on reading.

"Yes, Barois is the guardian of our vestal flame, *The Sower,* his creation, and, come what may, we must stand by him. Only consider the great work he has done and still is doing, and let his example be our inspiration and our safeguard. For many years he has devoted himself whole-heartedly to *The Sower,* scattering abroad all his ideas and projects without stint, without the sordid fear that someone might filch them from him and put them into execution first, and obeying no dictates but those of his own conscience. At his side there will always be work for men of good will. After enjoying a sensational circulation—which will go down in journalistic history—*The Sower* has settled down to a more normal one, better fitted to its aims, for it's addressed to a minority, and that intellectual minority will never fail in its allegiance. Let us support it, gentlemen, in every way we can; let us bring to it those fruits of experience to which even the youngest of us can lay claim today—for those crowded years have taught them as much as a whole ordinary life-time. And let Barois continue to centralize our efforts and give them the widespread influence that at once encourages and justifies them.

"But, above all, my friends, let us steel ourselves against that sterile defeatism which is already making insidious progress. Oh, I know as well as you how often one is tempted to despair!" He speaks very earnestly. "Who of us has not been appalled by the difficulties in which our unhappy country has entangled itself? Who has not felt a sense of personal responsibility weighing on his mind? How, indeed, could it be otherwise? When one considers the ordeal we have lived through, is it surprising that a certain pessimism has left its mark on us, indelibly? For inevitably our path has been strewn with lost illusions." He raises his head.

"But we must not let feelings of this sort, however poignant, darken counsel. We know our sacrifice was in a noble cause, and this should suffice us. What we did, my friends, we *had* to do; nor would we hesitate to do it again if the need arose. Let us remind ourselves of this in our moments of perplexity and doubt.

"France today is a land divided against itself—a grave predicament, but not beyond redress. The worst that can befall our country is a material and momentary setback. But, as against this, we have kept France loyal to her ideal, to that sense of national honour without which no people can survive.

"Let us remember, too, that fifty years hence the Dreyfus Affair will be no more than one of many minor battles in the long conflict between human reason and the passions which blind it; a moment, no more than that, in the slow but glorious progress of humanity towards a better world.

"Our present conceptions of truth and justice will be superseded in times to come; of that we may be sure. But, far from damping our ardour, this certainty should be a spur to our activity today. It is the duty of each successive generation to advance along the path of truth to the farthest limit of its capacity and strain its eyes towards the vision far ahead—aspiring, vainly, no doubt, but resolutely, to the ultimate light of Absolute Truth. That, in fact, is the *sine qua non* of human progress.

"The value of a generation consists in the effort it puts forth, an effort paving the way to higher and still higher achievement. Well, my friends, our generation has made its effort—worthily.

"May peace be with us all."

Luce sits down. A long silence follows, vibrant with emotion.

IX. CALM

SEVERAL years later. An entire five-floor building in the Rue
de l'Université is now occupied by *The Sower*. The entrance hall is
stacked with bales of paper; the ground and first floors house the
printing press; in the upper floors are the editorial offices of *The
Sower* and the premises of Sower Publications.

A clerk enters one of the offices on the fourth floor.

THE CLERK: "A gentleman wants you on the phone, sir. 'Harry'
was the name he gave."

THE SUB-EDITOR: " 'Harry'? Don't know him."

THE CLERK: "He's on the *New York Herald*."

THE SUB-EDITOR: "Ah, Harris you mean. Put him through." He
picks up the receiver. "Yes, that's quite all right. I mentioned it to
Monsieur Barois and he agrees. But no writing up, please; no boost-
ing. Just the bare facts. . . . Certainly. What do you want to know?
. . . Since the Dreyfus Affair?" He laughs. "Why not since 1870,
while you're about it? . . . Yes, what he's doing at present, that would
be better. . . .

"With pleasure. . . . Well, he has lecture courses in the evenings at
three town-halls; in the Belville, Vaugirard, and Panthéon districts.
They're largely attended by the working class. At the Panthéon
Hall, mostly students, as might be expected. . . . Yes, stress that. It's
something he's very keen on, raising the mental level of the masses
and directing them towards freedom of thought. . . .

"Twice a week he lectures at the Institute of Social Studies. . . .
This year? The title is 'The World-Wide Crisis of Religion.' It
works out to a book a year.

"Then, of course, there's *The Sower*. That's his biggest chore.
Two hundred pages every fortnight. . . . I wouldn't know. At least
fifteen articles of his own a year, at a rough guess. And there's a

'Notes and Comments' section in each issue—all the ideas that have come to him during the fortnight. . . .

"No, the *Sower Conversations,* that's something quite different. I'll explain. Every week we have a meeting here, articles are handed in and plans made for the next issue. Monsieur Barois had the idea of getting these conversations taken down in shorthand and publishing under the title 'Memoranda' any passages that seemed of general interest. Then our subscribers began to take a hand in it; they wrote proposing topics for discussion. An excellent development—it keeps us in touch with the public and we learn what subjects are of immediate interest. Then the 'Memoranda' blossomed out into *The Sower Conversations,* which appears in book form every three months or so.

"Gladly. . . . But you could have found the list anywhere. Firstly, his books on the Affair: *For Truth's Sake,* First, Second, and Third Series, not to mention a host of pamphlets. Next, his public speeches, a collection of which is published at the end of each year. There have been six volumes so far, under the title *Fighting Speeches.* The seventh is on press. Then there are four volumes of his lectures at the Institute. Want to know their names? . . . Right. *The Progress of Popular Education, Free Thought Abroad, A Study of Determinism, The Divisibility of Matter*— Wait! It would be a good idea to say that the lecture he's giving next Sunday at the Trocadéro is something quite exceptional. It's not his habit to address large audiences of this kind; in fact Barois has never done anything of the sort before. Stress that, please. . . .

"No, I couldn't tell you. About three thousand seats, I think. Half of them, it seems, are booked already. . . . Yes, the name's a draw, and so's the subject: 'The Future of Unbelief.'

"Thanks. . . . Always ready to help. . . . Good-bye."

2

The afternoon of the following Sunday, at the Trocadéro. There is a large crowd; cabs and carriages arriving in a steady stream disgorge

their occupants at the foot of the steps leading up to the huge building. The police have turned out in force to keep order.

Suddenly a ripple of excitement traverses the group of young people gathered at the entrance giving access to the platform of the
great hall. Barois and Luce alight from their carriage. Many by-
standers take off their hats. The two men walk briskly into the
building, accompanied by some friends.

At three o'clock the auditorium is packed, the exits blocked by
people who have failed to get seats. Slowly the curtains are drawn
aside, disclosing an empty platform. Almost immediately Barois
makes his appearance; he is greeted by a vast clamour of applause,
which rises, falls, and rises massively again, with a buzz like that of a
swarm of bees about to take wing, then abruptly gives place to dead
silence.

Unhurrying, Barois climbs the steps leading to the raised platform. The spacious proscenium dwarfs him, and his features can
hardly be distinguished, but the manner of his entrance, the dignity
of his bow to the assembly, the calmness of the gaze with which he
slowly sweeps the thousands of faces aligned concentrically below
and around him, testify to the assurance of a man who knows the
tide is running in his favour. His eyes still fixed on the audience, he
sits down.

barois: "Ladies and Gentlemen . . ."

He has a brief access of nervousness, a tightening of the heart.
But then the silence of the crowded auditorium and the look of
friendly expectation on all those rows and rows of faces turned towards him break the tension. Yielding to a sudden inspiration and
abandoning the opening he has prepared, he lets fall his notes and,
smilingly, drops into a tone of friendly conversation.

"My dear friends, I see you have turned out in force today. You
have not hesitated to give up your normal programme for a Sunday
afternoon, so as to come and hear a talk on 'The Future of Unbelief.' Obviously its title was enough to draw you here. I find this
deeply moving and significant of the age we're living in.

"All civilized nations are undergoing today the same religious crisis. In every land where culture or intelligence has taken root, the same questions are stirring in men's minds; rationalism and unbelief are undermining the authority of the fables taught by the priests; the same drive towards emancipation of the mind is shattering the tyrannous prestige of all the gods that be.

"Thanks to her innate love of freedom, her sense of logic, and her demand for positive proof, France has for two centuries led the way in the world-wide movement towards free thought. It was France, indeed, that set that movement on foot. All the Latin countries in which Roman Catholicism once reigned supreme—Italy, Spain, and South America—have followed France's lead. A similar change of heart is taking place in the Protestant countries—North America, England, and South Africa. So general is this movement that the more enlightened elements of Islam and Buddhism are being affected by it, and the same applies to the civilized parts of India and Africa, and the whole of Japan. Throughout the world the Churches have been forced to give up the temporal power they had exercised for many a century, and which was skilfully directed to shoring up their spiritual authority. They have seen their privileges withdrawn one by one, and have found themselves forbidden to meddle in non-religious matters. In fact, to all intents and purposes, State religions have ceased to exist. Everywhere the State is non-sectarian and observes a strict neutrality towards the various faiths whose practices it tolerates.

"This concerted drive against the embattled forces of religion covers too wide a field for me to deal with it in detail in my talk today. I shall confine myself to pointing out again that it is *world-wide;* for I would not have you think, as you may have been inclined to think, that the irreligious evolution of our country is a local development and goes no farther than our frontiers. On the contrary, it is bound up with an awakening of the critical spirit in all the nations of the world."

He pauses. Before, he had a miscellaneous concourse of men,

women, and young people; this now is welded together into an audience, synthesis has been achieved. His eyes, voice, and mind are now in direct contact with a uniform mass, a single entity pregnant with thoughts from which his own thought is distinct no longer, but of which it forms the nucleus, the dynamic core.

"The Catholic Church, which claims to be above all man-made laws, put up a stubborn fight against being subjected to the law of the land. However, it has had to capitulate and to transfer what influence it still possesses to the field of spiritual things. That is its last stronghold, and even there the rising tide, whatever some may think, is steadily, ineluctably, sapping the foundations. For the modern mind is ever less and less satisfied with dogma—and this aversion is growing prodigiously with each new generation. Every advance of science adds yet another argument against religious dogmatism, which, moreover, has long ceased to gain any support, however flimsy, from contemporary research.

"In its struggle against the implacable advance of knowledge, I can see only one potential hope for the Church, if it is to survive at all—and that is to evolve and bring its tenets into line with modern thought. For the Church this is a matter of life and death. If it refuses to adapt itself, we may feel certain that, within the space of a few generations, there will be no believers left.

"But at this point I wish to make it clear to you that it's literally impossible for the dogmas of Catholicism to be modified, even to the most trifling extent. Thus nothing can save it from extinction; not only can we count on this as a foregone conclusion, but we can almost fix the date of its decease!

"A philosophical doctrine can develop; its texture is the stuff of human thought disposed in a manner which is necessarily tentative and therefore capable of revision. But a revealed religion starts with tenets which cannot be amended, since, by definition, they were divinely inspired when first enounced. Thus a religion of this kind can change only at the price of self-destruction. For any alteration would be tantamount to an admission that its earlier form fell short of perfection; that it did not come directly from God, and no 'revelation' ushered it into the world. This, indeed, is so obvious that the Catholic Church has never ceased pointing to its immutability as a proof of its divine origin. Quite recently the 1870 Vatican Council did not hesitate to affirm that 'the doctrine of the true faith revealed by God was not bestowed as a philosophical instrument for the betterment of the human intellect, but has been committed to us as a *divine endowment.*'

"Thus Catholicism is irrevocably committed; change is ruled out by its first principles.

"But we may go still further. Even were it possible for the Church to modify its tenets without contradicting itself, this would give it only a brief reprieve, for the following reasons.

"Even the most cursory study of the origins of the various religions shows us that all were born of the curiosity primitive man felt when confronted by the universe. You will find that all begin with a set of myths which embody the childish theories concocted to explain natural phenomena. So true is this that, strictly speaking, there has never been a primitive religion, in our sense of the term. From the dawn of human life up to our times there has been only one persistent train of thought: the train of *scientific* thought, which began as a jumble of nature myths. Thus what we call 'religion' is really one of the early stages of scientific progress, when the deist explanation was accepted, for want of a better one. And, absurdly enough, this early phase in the long history of research has left after-effects persisting to our times, owing to man's dread of the supernatural. In a word, man has never been able to discard that legacy of mystical hypotheses which were invented in those early days to 'explain' the mysteries of nature. This fortuitous crystallization, as we may call it, held up the advance of science for many centuries. And thereafter the paths of science and religion diverged irrevocably.

"I will now revert to what I was saying a moment ago. Religion is simply a relict of an extinct type of science, a dead husk that has taken on the form of dogma. It is no more than the shell of a scientific hypothesis which has long since been superseded and in this process of drying up has lost whatever life it may once have had. Thus, if religion were to try to change itself and to catch up with scientific progress—which stands for what it would have been had not its development been arrested—well, it would be bound to fail. It has contrived to last out so many centuries only because it comforted man's troubled heart with lies; allayed his dread of death with specious promises; and dulled his speculative instinct with assertions both unfounded and impossible to check. Were the Church one day to renounce all that flummery which puts it on a level with a Christmas pantomime, not an iota would survive of that substructure which, for some, gives it a semblance of vitality. For the religious instinct in man, on which the Church could reckon in earlier days, has no place in the truly modern mind. It would be quite wrong to regard man's natural craving to understand and investigate as a residue of the mystical beliefs of our ancestors. Actually, it existed long before religious emotion was known to man, and it has found full and ample satisfaction in the triumphs of contemporary science.

"Thus, as you see, we can have little doubt that a dogmatic religion like Catholicism is irrevocably doomed. The absolute rigidity of its tenets makes it less and less credible to modern minds, which are too well aware of the relativity of their knowledge to accept a doctrine purporting to be unchangeable and infallible.

"Moreover, the forces undermining it do not all come from without; Catholicism is languishing internally as well, attacked by a creeping paralysis which unfits it for the contemporary world.

"In fact the tide is flowing strongly towards a godless society and towards a purely scientific conception of the universe."

No sooner has he uttered this last phrase than he realizes it has given a fillip to his hearers' interest. Their gaze grows more intent, he feels the impact of a collective will urging him in a certain direction. And he understands. After following his destructive arguments to the end, they are now eager for some vision of the coming world; like children, they are waiting for their fairy-tale. He has no notes on this subject, but he obeys. His eyes grow luminous, a visionary smile plays on his lips.

"What form will it take, this irreligion of the future? Who of us can answer this question with any confidence? But one thing's certain, it will not be, in any sense whatever, a 'deification of science.' We are often, too often, told that our scientists are the high priests of a new cult and are replacing one faith by another. It may be that, in the confusion of a transitional age, some men of science transfer a remnant of the religious emotions they have inherited and for which they have no ready-made outlet, to the science which they serve. But that's a mere aberration. Actually there's no scope for new idols, and anyhow science cannot possibly be set up as one. For intelligence is negative; this is a truth to which even the most idealistic temperaments have sadly to resign themselves.

"My personal belief is that the union of men's intellects and hearts—and the latter are still groping for their way—will come relatively soon, and that it will find fruition by way of social solidarity on the one hand and scientific knowledge on the other. I foresee the possibility of moral laws based on a searching analysis of the individual and his relations with his environment. This will bring satisfaction to the heart of man, since the new order will give free play to his altruistic instinct. Faced by the crushing indifference of nature, men are bound to feel the need to get together, and from this need ethical compulsions will naturally ensue. It seems to me more than likely that these duties, inspired as they will be by the mutual affection that draws men into fellowship, will establish, anyhow for a time, a reign of social peace.

"Of course these are mere flights of fancy. I know how dangerous it is to play the prophet." He smiles. "And, as we know, a prophet is 'without honour' in our midst.

"Anyhow, one thing's certain; there will be nothing metaphysical in the principles on which the new social order is founded. The day has come when nothing but factual demonstration can satisfy our minds. Those religions which claimed to solve the riddle of the universe will be replaced, I feel certain, by a philosophy as positive as it is strictly unemotional, a philosophy nourished continually by scientific discoveries; variable and transient, shaped to the changing trends of thought. Thus we can be pretty sure that it will never cease enlarging its frontiers—far beyond the narrow conceptions which limit our field of vision today. Only think how incomplete and paltry it now seems, the so-called scientific materialism of fifty years ago! Our age, more truly scientific, is already tending to rise above the outlook of the world that satisfied our fathers; the next generation will carry the process a stage farther. The mind of man today is blazing trails through the unknown, and the new methods of research we now employ are highly promising. But as yet we cannot even guess at the new aspects of reality our progressive discoveries will open up to us."

A short pause. His look changes. His eyes regain their wonted hardness, and his voice its characteristic "edge." Looking down, he fingers the loose sheets lying on the table.

"But enough of visions of the future, tempting as these may be! Time is passing, and there is a second point I'd like to dwell on in this talk, before I leave you.

"What steps can each of us take towards the more or less rapid attainment of our hopes?

"A vast field of activity lies open to us all. Thankless as it may sometimes seem, man's task today, by contrast with the future I have just been picturing, this task is of capital importance and on no account must we neglect it.

"Ours is one of those generations to whom has fallen the duty of actively furthering scientific evolution. We are living in one of those tragic periods of world history when an outworn age is in its death throes.

"Ah, my friends, when once we realize what hideous moral torture is the lot of a generation such as ours, an epoch in which men's consciences are, as it were, stretched on a rack, torn between an age that is dying and an age that is coming to birth; and when we remember that the energy with which we make and proclaim our choice may determine the duration of the agony these suffering sensibilities endure—how grave is the responsibility that falls on each and all of us!

"Briefly speaking, we have two means of taking action: by our personal attitude, and by the education of our children. Suppose we now, as the Church would put it, 'examine our consciences' in this respect?

"How many of us, whose convictions are definitely hostile to any kind of religious faith—how many of us, none the less, allow religion to preside at the most important occasions of our lives, from the marriage rite to the death-bed!" Sadly. "Oh, yes, I know, I know as well as you—better than some of you, perhaps—all the excuses we can make for these concessions. I know the cruel self-humiliation of the free man who deems it his duty to submit himself to these ritual observances. Only too well I know those inner conflicts, the cruel ordeal of a conscience that is torn between the desire to keep faith with itself and all the forces sapping its integrity: family ties, affection, respect for others' feelings. But we must not throw dust in our own eyes. To give in on such occasions is an act of flagrant immorality that nothing can condone. In the age of moral crisis we are living through nothing is more momentous than a public declaration of faith; not only as regards the man who makes it, but also because of its possible effect on others whose minds are not yet made up. Honesty towards ourselves and towards those whose eyes are on us—that, as things are, should be our guiding principle, the most inflexible of moral laws. Those who palter with their personal integrity, or by a non-committal attitude impede, in their environment, the progress of evolution, are committing a crime against society, a crime infinitely more serious than all the sentimental grievances their families might feel, did they choose the harder path—of honesty!

"More unpardonable still is their offence as regards the education of their children. The child's mind is uncritical. The notion of doubt comes only after long experience of the everyday world; it implies acquaintance with the possibility of error, mistrust not only of one-self and one's own sensations, but of other people too, and their advice. Like all primitives, the child is credulous, he has no sense of probabilities, a miracle would not surprise him.

"If you confide this wax tablet, a young mind, to a priest, he will easily make an indelible imprint on it. He will begin by inspiring the child with an irrational fear of God; then he will impart to him the mysteries of his cult as so many revealed truths, which sur-pass, and always *must* surpass, the human understanding. The priest is ever ready with assertions; never with proofs. The child is readier to believe than to apply his intellect. So they get on well together. Reasoning is the opposite of faith; a mind that faith has formed remains for a long while, perhaps always, incapable of draw-ing rational conclusions.

"Can you, then, expose a personality as innocent and defenceless as a child's to religious influences?"

He has risen to his feet, carried away by the violence of his in-dignation, vibrant with memories of his own childhood. The man of action is awake in Barois; the polemics of his daily life have made him conscious of his power, he feels the zest of battle. So impetuous is his onrush that he sometimes overthrows an obstacle on his path before it even meets his eye; his is a blind force sweep-ing all before it.

"Only think! The Church inveighs against us, it launches its anathemas at all that constitutes the most vital part of our being, and yet, fools that we are, we hand our children over to the priest! How account for such obtuseness? Is it that we nurse a secret hope that they will rid themselves of superstition as they grow up? If so, what name is bad enough for such hypocrisy?

"And what, indeed, could be more fatuous than the belief that the mind, as it matures, will necessarily dispel those fumes of pious poison? Do you not realize how tenacious a child's faith can be? No, we must face the facts. A man on whom religion has set its mark in childhood cannot discard it with a mere shake of his shoulders, like a garment that has worn out or become too small for him. In the child, religion finds a soil made ready for it by eighteen centuries of voluntary servitude. It twines itself inextricably round all the other elements of his mental and moral growth. The process of disentangling himself, if it be possible at all, is tedious, laborious, often inconclusive, and always painful. And how many people living under present-day conditions have either leisure or energy enough to set about this reshaping of their whole personality?

"Moreover, I have so far limited the issue; I have spoken of the dangers of religious education only in so far as it affects the individual. But it also directly threatens the social fabric as a whole. At a time like ours, when religious beliefs are tottering everywhere, there is a very real peril in letting the moral law be linked up with religious dogma in the minds of the younger generation. For once they have got it into their heads that the rules of social morality have a divine origin, and once the day comes, as come it must, when they begin to feel unsure of God's existence, their whole moral structure will promptly collapse, and they will be like ships without a rudder.

"There, briefly, you have the dangers we run when we act as shortsighted or time-serving parents. And what are the would-be noble principles with which we disguise our spinelessness?

"I can hear your answer: 'We take the broad-minded view; we declare our neutrality.'

"Oh, I know it's hard to see where one's duty lies. But don't let's be deceived by words. That vaunted neutrality—our opponents do wrong in accusing us of often violating it; for can any sort of teaching be absolutely neutral?—yes, it's we alone who are hampered by that declaration of neutrality! In fact neutrality today means simply deference to the propaganda, the tireless propaganda, of the Church.

"Well, this one-sided compromise has lasted far too long. Let us openly take up our position in a conflict that is now inevitable, the greatest conflict of our age. And instead of conducting it surreptitiously, let us fight in the open, in the light, and on equal terms. By all means leave the priests free to open schools and teach our youngsters that the world was created out of nothing in six days; that Jesus Christ was the Son of God the Father and a Virgin; that his body came forth, unaided, from the tomb three days after his burial, and ascended into heaven, where he has been seated ever since on God's right hand.

"But, my friends, let us, too, be free to open schools in which we have the right to prove, with science and common sense as our allies, how preposterous are the superstitions on which Catholicism is founded. Give truth and lies a fair field, and it's not the lies that will win! Freedom, yes, but not only for the priest and his catechism; freedom for the intellect, freedom for the child!"

He walks to the front of the platform, his arms outspread, his eyes aflame with enthusiasm.

"Yes, my friends, I would like to conclude with that appeal: Freedom for the child! I want to feel that I have quickened your consciences, and to see in your eyes a light of new, unshakable resolve. Let us remember all that we have gone through to cast out of ourselves the 'old' man. Let us remember those fires of anguish that laid waste our souls. Let us remember our night fears, our tremulous revolts, our agonized confessions. Let us remember our prayers and tears and terrors.

"And have pity on our sons!"

3

The same year, some months later. The Place de la Madeleine. Barois steps into a cab.

BAROIS: "The *Sower* office, Rue de l'Université." He slams the door. The cab does not move; the driver flicks the horse with his whip. The horse tosses his head, but refuses to start. "Get a move on, cabby! I'm in a hurry."

The cabman lays on vigorously with his whip. The horse, a young, restive animal, hesitates, rears, jerks up its head, then starts off like an arrow. The vehicle whisks down the Rue Royale, crosses the Place de la Concorde hell-for-leather, swerves left along the Boulevard Saint-Germain.

It is four in the afternoon, and the traffic is at its thickest. Leaning well back, the cabby tries vainly to hold in his horse; the utmost he can do is to direct its course to some extent.

A broken-down streetcar bars the way; to avoid it, the driver swings round to the left where the road is momentarily empty, but he has failed to see another streetcar bearing down on him in the opposite direction. It is impossible to slow down; equally impossible to pass between the two streetcars.

Pale with terror, Barois huddles back against the cushions. A sense of utter helplessness, shut up as he is in the swaying, box-like cab, and the certainty of disaster flash like lightning through the chaos of his thoughts.

He utters a low cry. "Hail, Mary, full of grace . . ."

A crash of shattered glass, a violent shock. Then all the world goes black.

In Barois' apartment, some days later. Shadows are gathering in the room. Sitting quite still at the window, Woldsmuth is reading. Barois lies on the bed, his legs in plaster up to the waist. He regained full consciousness only a few hours ago; for the tenth time he is mentally recapitulating his experience.

There'd have been room, he thinks, if that damned car on the right hadn't put on speed. . . . Had I time to realize death's nearness? Can't remember. All I know is that I was in a panic. And then that hideous screech of brakes!

He smiles to himself; the joy of life regained sweeps through him. A close shave—but I brought it off! Curious how scared one is of dying. Why dread the extinction of all thought, all pain, all sensation? Why this horror of mere not-being?

Perhaps it's just one's fear of the unknown. That business of dying is obviously the only sensation utterly unknown to us. No one has anything to tell about what it really feels like.

And yet anyone with a scientific training, given a few seconds to think it out, should manage to resign himself to death without much ado. He knows quite well that life's no more than a series of transformations, so why be frightened of *that* one? It's not the first and, presumably, not the last incident in the *processus* of becoming.

Then, again, when one has led a useful life, put up a good fight, and has something to leave behind one—why repine? Personally, I feel sure I shall say good-bye to life quite calmly.

Suddenly a look of dismay settles on his face. All his confidence is dashed. It has come back to him, that dramatic moment just before the crash, and he has recalled the cry that sprang instinctively to his lips: "Hail, Mary . . . !"

An hour goes by. Without moving, Woldsmuth turns the pages of his book.

Pascal brings a lamp, closes the shutters, and comes to his master's bedside. The flat, Swiss face, with its close-cropped hair and big blue eyes, is comfortably reassuring. But Barois does not see it; he is gazing straight in front of him, his brain working at a prodigious speed. And his thoughts are fantastically clear, pellucid as mountain air after a thunderstorm. After a while his features, tense with the mental effort he is putting forth, slowly relax.

BAROIS: "Woldsmuth!"

WOLDSMUTH, jumping up hastily: "Are you in pain?"

BAROIS, curtly: "No. Now listen. Bring your chair up."

WOLDSMUTH, holding his wrist: "You've a touch of fever. Keep quite still and don't tire yourself speaking."

BAROIS, freeing his arm: "Sit down and listen, I tell you!" Angrily. "No, I insist on speaking. I didn't remember all. I was forgetting the last bit! Listen, Woldsmuth! When I saw a smash was inevitable, what do you think I did? Well, I prayed to the Virgin Mary! Grotesque!"

WOLDSMUTH, soothingly: "Don't think about it any more. You've got to rest. The doctor—"

BAROIS: "No, my wits aren't wandering. I know very well what I'm saying and I want you to hear me out. I shan't be able to rest until I've done what I have now to do." Woldsmuth sits down. Barois' cheeks are flushed, his eyes unnaturally bright. "At that moment I, Jean Barois, had only one idea, a crazy hope. I put up a prayer—a heart-felt prayer, mind you!—to the Holy Virgin, beseeching her to perform a miracle." He guffaws. "A miracle, I tell you! Well, my dear fellow, you can imagine how little confident one feels in one's mental equipment after an experience like that." He sits up in bed. "So, as you'll understand, I'm haunted by the thought that this may quite well happen again—this evening, tonight, at any moment—there's no knowing. I want to get something down in writing and forestall that possibility. And I shan't feel quiet till I've done it."

WOLDSMUTH: "Yes, we'll see to it tomorrow, I promise you. You shall dictate to me, and—"

BAROIS, with a vehemence that sweeps all before it: "At once, Woldsmuth, *at once.* I insist. I shall write it all out in my own hand, this evening. Otherwise I couldn't sleep." He taps his forehead. "It's all in here, all ready, and writing it down won't tire me in the least. The hardest part is done."

Woldsmuth yields and, after propping Barois up on two pillows, hands him his fountain-pen and some sheets of paper. Then he remains standing at the bedside.

Barois writes steadily, without raising his eyes, in a firm, clear hand.

This is my Last Will and Testament. What I write today, in my early forties, in the full mental vigour of my prime, should ob-

viously outweigh anything I may say or think or write at the close of my existence, when my intellect and judgment may well be impaired by the infirmities of old age. I know nothing more harrowing than to see an old man, whose whole life has beeen devoted to the furtherance of some noble idea, go back in his declining years on the principles that inspired his life's work and play traitor to his past.

When I reflect that conceivably this may be my fate, and my life's work end with a betrayal of this nature, and when I picture the use to which those whose lies and malpractices I have combated with so much ardour will not fail to put this final, miserable lapse of mine, my whole being is up in arms, and I protest in advance, with all the energy of the man I now am, the living *man I shall have been, against the groundless repudiations—even, perhaps, the prayers* in extremis!*—of the dotard I may then have become.*

I deserve to die, combatant and defiant, as I have lived, without capitulating, without whoring after idle hopes, without fearing my return to the primal matter that nourishes the slow processes of evolution.

I do not believe in an immortal, independently existing soul.

I do not believe that mind and matter are mutually exclusive entities. The "soul" is a complex of psychic phenomena, and the body is a complex of organic phenomena. Consciousness is a by-product of life, an attribute of living matter. I see no reason why that universal energy which produces motion, heat, and light should not also produce thought. Physiological functions and psychological functions interlock; like all other activities of the nervous system, thought is a manifestation of organic life. I have never found thought existing apart from matter and a living body; and I am aware of one universal substance only, living substance. Whether we regard it as "life" or "matter," I believe it to be eternal. Life had no beginning, and it will go on producing life for ever. But I know that my personality is but an agglomeration of particles of matter, whose disintegration will end it absolutely.

I believe in universal determinism; that we are conditioned by circumstances in all respects. Everything evolves, everything reacts; men and stones alike. There is no such thing as inert matter. Thus I have no reason to attribute more individual liberty to my acts than I attribute to the slower transformations of a crystal.

My life is thus the product of an endless struggle between my organism and my environment. Because at every moment I act in accordance with my personal reflexes—in other words, for reasons applicable to myself alone—a spectator has the illusion that I am free to behave as I like. In reality none of my actions is free in that sense; none of my responses could be other than what it is. Free will would imply the power of performing miracles, of tampering with the relations between causes and effects. It is one of those metaphysical notions which only prove the ignorance, under which we laboured for so long (and indeed still labour), of the laws which govern our existence.

Thus I deny that a man can exercise the slightest influence on his destiny.

Good and Evil are mere arbitrary distinctions. I admit, however, that these distinctions will retain their practical utility so long as that illusion of the mind, the idea of personal responsibility, is needful for the maintenance of our social structure.

I believe that though all the phenomena of life have not yet been analysed, they will be analysed one day. As for the first causes of these phenomena, I believe they lie outside our range, and no research, however thorough, can elucidate them. Owing to his limited place in the universe, man is by nature a relative and finite being, incapable of forming conceptions of the Absolute and the Infinite. He has invented names for what transcends himself, but these have not got him any further; he is a victim of his terminology, for those words and names do not, so far as human understanding is concerned, correspond to any cognizable reality. He is a mere element of the whole and, naturally enough, that whole lies beyond his apprehension.

To revolt against these limitations is to revolt against the planetary conditions of the world we live in.

Thus I consider it a waste of mental energy to try to explain the unknowable by mere hypotheses which have no empirical backing. It is high time for us to cure ourselves of our metaphysical moonmadness and to cease troubling about those unanswerable Whys *which our mystic-ridden heredity leads us to propound.*

Man is confronted by a practically limitless field of observation. Gradually science will thrust back the frontiers of the unknown so far that, if man applies himself to understanding fully all the real world within his compass, he will have no time left for mourning over all that lies ineluctably beyond his mental reach. And I am certain that by teaching men to accept their ignorance of the unknowable, science will give them a peace of mind such as no religion has ever been able to provide.

Jean Barois

His hand is heavy on the pen as he slowly writes his signature. Then abruptly the tension of his will breaks like a snapped violin string. His flushed face suddenly grows deathly pale and he sinks back, exhausted, into Woldsmuth's arms.

Sheets of manuscript flutter across the counterpane.

Alarmed by this sudden collapse, Woldsmuth has called to Pascal. But already Barois is opening his eyes and smiling up at the two men.

Some moments later his steady breathing shows that he has sunk into deep, tranquil sleep.

PART

III

X. THE FLAW

FIVE years later. Barois has just finished breakfast.

PASCAL: "There's a priest come to see you, sir. He's in the study."

BAROIS: "A priest?"

PASCAL: "He wouldn't give his name."

Barois goes into the study. An aged priest is standing there, his back to the light: Abbé Joziers.

THE ABBÉ: "I didn't give my name. I wasn't at all sure if you'd want to see me." Noticing the friendliness of Barois' smile of greeting, he lowers his eyes. "Good morning, Jean."

More than ten years have passed since any familiar voice called him by his Christian name. His eyes fill with tears, and he holds out both hands. The priest grasps them, and the two men remain without speaking, their hands clasped, for some moments.

Abbé Joziers is in his sixties. The tall, wiry body has kept its alertness, but the face is an old man's. His hair has gone quite white, his skin is yellow, criss-crossed with wrinkles, and a deep furrow runs down each side of his nose. One has an impression that the flesh underneath has wasted away, leaving only a thin tissue above the bones.

Barois motions him cheerfully to a chair, and the priest sits down, but with a certain stiffness in his manner.

Barois, too, has changed. He has grown thinner, his gaze is more thoughtful, the black moustache, now streaked with white, hides the harsh line of his mouth.

THE ABBÉ: "As you may well suspect, this is no friendly visit. I have come because I was asked to see you, and there was no one else to undertake the duty.

"No doubt you can guess what brings me here." Barois shakes his head; he is obviously puzzled. The Abbé has come, full of indignation, but, impressed by the unmistakable sincerity of the man before him, he feels more indulgence. Irresponsible! he thinks. Nevertheless he braces himself to his task, crushing down his natural affection for Jean, and his tone is frankly hostile as he continues. "A short time ago you delivered a public lecture—on what occasion I do not know—entitled 'Psychological Case Histories Illustrating the Evolution of Present-Day Faith.' "

BAROIS: "That's so."

THE ABBÉ: "In that lecture you deliberately quitted the field of general ideas and gave your hearers details whose autobiographical nature was only too obvious. The passages I have read—reluctantly enough—describe incidents of your youth, even of your married life, with a complete lack of decency."

BAROIS, sarcastically: "You put it rather strongly. The incidents in question were referred to anonymously and were presented in a scientific and objective form which excluded all personal considerations. I had studied a large number of psychological case histories, some of them supplied to me by correspondents, mostly doctors in the provinces. But some details, I admit, related to my own life."

THE ABBÉ, raising his voice: "There, Jean, you are mistaken. Those details were not solely your affair." Bitterly. "Alas, I've lost many illusions about you in these last years; but never did I think it would be my duty to remind you of the most elementary rules of decency. There are certain details of his married life an honourable man instinctively keeps secret. How could you sink to gratifying public curiosity—no matter what the public—by laying bare in a lecture hall, for any reason whatsoever, the feelings of a woman who was, and is, your wife—and the mother of your child?"

Barois flushes deeply, but he makes no protest. A stream of memories has flickered into consciousness, a whole past come back to life.

THE ABBÉ: "One of the local newspapers—it's the freemasons' organ—has published passages from your lecture, and these could not fail cruelly to hurt your wife's feelings, and . . ."

Barois has ceased listening. With a tense yet far-away look in his eyes he gazes at the Abbé. "To hurt your wife's feelings!" Never once since they separated has it occurred to him that she could still be wounded by anything he said or did.

He has been badly shaken; stumbling across to his desk, as to a haven of refuge, he sinks heavily into his chair, grasping its arms with nervous fingers.

BAROIS: "Yes, I see it now. But it was so—so unintentional." The Abbé looks frankly incredulous. "You don't believe me? Well, try to put yourself in my place; I've been living here, alone, for over ten years. I never see anyone except a few friends, the men who work with me. I'm terribly busy, I never have time to look back on the past—and, anyhow, retrospection isn't a habit of mine. The only news I ever have from Buis is the letter a lawyer's clerk sends me once a year, informing me that the allowance has been paid. Not a word more than that." The priest is obviously dumbfounded. "Do I surprise you? Well, it's perfectly true. The past is the past, I've left it far behind; it's dead to me, and I never give it a thought.

"When I prepared the lecture you mention, my sole object was to collect all the relevant data to which I had access. Some of these came from my own life, and I didn't hesitate to use them. Obviously those memories were not mine alone, I'm bound to admit it." As if talking to himself. "Yes, quite likely I acted like—like a cad." He stares at the floor; his fingers twitch slightly.

"My dear Abbé, I bitterly regret having been the cause, even quite unintentionally, of—" Impulsively. "Please explain to her; do, please, repeat to her what I've told you."

THE ABBÉ, disarmed by such insouciance: "No, Jean, it would be better for me not to repeat what you've said."

There is a short silence. The priest picks up his hat.

BAROIS: "You're not in a hurry, I hope." He hesitates. "May I have some news—of how things are with them? Is Cécile still living with her mother?" The Abbé nods; he is obviously reluctant to engage in a conversation. "And are they still leading the same sort of life? Charitable societies, parochial meetings, and all the rest of it?"

THE ABBÉ, frigidly: "Certainly Madame Barois gives to these most of the time she does not devote to her daughter."

BAROIS: "Ah, yes, the child. She's—wait a bit!—she's just turned thirteen, hasn't she?" Naïvely. "What's she like, the child, I mean? Is her health all right?" He catches the Abbé's eye and smiles uncomfortably. "I'm afraid I must strike you as a monster of heartlessness. I'm sorry, but"—he makes a sweeping gesture—"I've blotted all that out, you see. It's all so utterly remote. My life's work is all that interests me now. Why should I try to humbug myself or others? After all, I'd already left for England when the child was born. She's a complete stranger, and I've no reason to be interested in her; she has nothing of me."

THE ABBÉ, gazing intently at his face: "That's not so. In fact what struck me most when we met today after all these years is how much she is like you in appearance."

BAROIS, in a different tone: "She takes after me, you mean?"

THE ABBÉ: "Yes. Her eyes, her chin, her general expression—they're almost exactly yours."

Another silence follows. The priest rises. He begins to walk away, dissatisfied with Barois, and with himself. He has left unsaid so much he had wished to say; the visit has been a failure, another bitter memory to add . . .

BAROIS, escorting him to the door: "And—are you still residing at Buis?"

THE ABBÉ: "Yes, the Bishop appointed me to the living four years ago, come next Corpus Christi."

BAROIS: "Oh, I didn't know."

They are standing in the hall.

THE ABBÉ, with an uprush of resentment: "Ah, we've been cruelly treated at Buis by this new legislation of yours!"

BAROIS, smiling: "Don't imagine that I approve of all that's happening in France today because I made a stand for freedom of

thought and have always combated injustice." The priest has started
to open the door of the flat but closes it gently and faces Barois. "If
the review I'm running ever comes your way"—the priest makes a
vague gesture of distaste, which again brings a smile to Barois' lips
—"you'll realize that I've always applied to the Church the same
principles as actuated us during the Affair; exactly the same principles." Sadly. "And, let me tell you, this attitude has lost us quite
a number of subscribers. Still, that's a side issue. I voiced a protest,
as vigorous as I could make it, when I saw the Government enlisting the support of the 'Dreyfusards' of the new school in order to
pervert the laws for which our Deputies had voted and have them
carried out in a spirit wholly different from that in which they had
been promulgated."

THE ABBÉ, coldly: "I am glad to hear you speak thus. But I regret
that, though you see the vileness of what is taking place in France
today, you fail to see its cause, and to realize how grave is the responsibility you share with your friends for this state of things.
Good-bye."

BAROIS, shaking the Abbé's hand: "May I say that it's been a very
great pleasure to me, seeing you today? Though I deeply regret the
—the circumstances that brought you here. Please let them know
this at Buis." With a forced smile. "In any case, have no fears for
the future. Yes, it seems my health is breaking up; the trouble's
here." He presses his hand to his heart. "No more public speaking,
no overwork—that's the doctor's orders. It's been a great blow."

THE ABBÉ, affectionately: "I'm so sorry, Jean. But it's nothing serious, surely?"

BAROIS: "Not if I'm careful."

THE ABBÉ, impulsively: "Well then, you *must* be careful. Your life
isn't ended yet; it mustn't end—like this."

BAROIS, peremptorily: "I'm more confident than ever of having
chosen the right path, and that it's my duty to follow that path to
the end."

THE ABBÉ, shaking his head sadly: "Then, good-bye, Jean."

2

A spring afternoon in Luce's garden in Auteuil. Luce is sitting in
the shade of the chestnut trees. Flecks of golden light play on his
forehead and white beard. He is gazing mournfully into the middle
distance. An open newspaper, splashed with big headlines, lies on
his knees:

> "ZOLA'S REMAINS TRANSFERRED TO THE PANTHÉON.
> *The Official Ceremony. President and*
> *Cabinet in Attendance. Police*
> *Precautions. Many Arrests."*

Suddenly his face lights up. Barois is coming towards him. The
two men shake hands; words are superfluous. And when they are
seated they still remain silent; neither feels inclined to voice his
feelings. But the same thought shows in the eyes of both; their disgust with this theatrical parade, from which they have been excluded; with these vulgar demonstrations in the so-called honour of a
man of Zola's stamp; with this exploitation of a name that stands
for probity and justice as cover for political self-advancement. At
last Luce brings himself to speak.

LUCE, dejection sounding through the banality of the remark: "A
perfect spring morning, isn't it?" Barois nods vaguely; the words
have little import. Some moments pass before Luce makes another
effort. "And how are you feeling, my dear Barois, these days?
Better, I hope."

BAROIS: "Yes. In fact I may say I've been keeping fit ever since I
stopped lecturing."

LUCE: "And how's *The Sower* faring?"

BAROIS, chuckling to himself, after a quick glance at Luce: "Do
you remember your surprise when a number of people cancelled
their subscriptions after my campaign against the nonsense talked
by our rabid anti-militarists?"

LUCE: "Yes. What about it?"

BAROIS: "Well, it may interest you to hear of a little experiment I made recently." He laughs, then checks himself as though he fears his laughter may end on a sob. "I chose twenty names on our list, those of people who'd been with us from the start and given us active support, and for three months I stopped sending them *The Sower*." With bitter emphasis. "Not one of them even noticed it, we didn't get a single letter of complaint." He pauses. "Like to see the list of names?" Luce brushes it aside. Barois gets up and paces to and fro along the garden path. "A trifle, of course. The sort of thing one takes in one's stride—provided one's as enterprising, as young, as we were in the good old fighting days. Now, however—"

LUCE, impulsively: *"You,* Barois, to talk like that! Absurd!"

BAROIS, smiling, with an involuntary thrill of pride: "Thanks, Luce. But it's a fact that for some months I've been detecting symptoms in myself that rather worry me. A tendency to grow slack, sceptical, too easy-going." Languidly. "There are some evenings when I feel terribly alone."

LUCE, adroitly: "You're never alone when you're seated at your desk."

BAROIS, straightening his shoulders: "That's so. And I've still so much to do." He runs his fingers through his hair, and takes some steps. Then all the fire dies in his gaze. "Wait a bit, though! I've noticed something that's a bad sign. Whenever a pretext arises for leaving the office, a visit to make, for instance—an excuse, you see, to quit—I don't get irritated as I used to. Indeed, I rather welcome it. I'm sure you, my dear Luce, haven't reached that stage."

LUCE, smiling: "No, I can't say I have."

BAROIS: "And at times I have an impression that I'm growing more inclined to linger over memories than to strike out in new directions. I fight against this, of course; I make a point of reading everything that comes out. But, all the same, I feel less supple mentally —as if some dead weight cramped my energy."

LUCE: "The dead weight of experience."

BAROIS, pensively: "Perhaps. The feeling that I still am capable of understanding—lots of things; but somehow I'm handicapped physically—as though my reflexes were getting out of hand." Luce smiles incredulously, but Barois ignores it. "In one's best years one pictures life as a long straight road extending as far as the eye can reach towards two opposite points of the compass. But gradually one discovers that the life-line isn't straight or continuous, it curves and its two extremities tend to meet each other." He too smiles. "Thus the wheel comes full circle. You develop into an old man who can only turn like a squirrel in its cage."

LUCE: "Oh, come now! Really, Barois, you—" He springs to his feet. "There they are, our good friends, all of them!"

Three men have just appeared under the vaulted entrance leading to the garden: Breil-Zoeger, Cresteil d'Allize, Woldsmuth.

LUCE, to Barois in a whisper: "Hullo! Has Cresteil lost some near relation?"

BAROIS, also in a low tone: "None of us knows. But he's been in full mourning for a fortnight."

The five men shake hands warmly, but at first no one speaks.

LUCE, after some moments of uneasy silence: "Did any of you go there?"

BREIL-ZOEGER: "No."

CRESTEIL, his voice hoarse as usual: "They realized that a choice had to be made: it was either they or we."

Cresteil looks gaunter than ever. He has become quite bald, and the baldness emphasizes the haughty carriage of his head. Drawn tight over his cheek-bones and nostrils, his skin looks like a film of yellow parchment.

WOLDSMUTH, voicing the thought of all: "When one remembers Zola's funeral, the *real* one!"

LUCE: "Yes, those who gathered round his bier were true mourners, a faithful few."

BREIL-ZOEGER, with a sardonic chuckle: "And we didn't need police protection for a bevy of cabinet ministers!" His pupils are contracted, hard as flint. He is fighting down the stomach trouble that is always gnawing at his vitality, like a hungry foe within.

BAROIS: "And do you remember our thrill of pride and courage when Anatole France rose to his feet? You recall how he began? 'I will not say only what it is right to say, but I shall say *all* that it is right to say.' And then he reminded us that France is the motherland of Justice."

WOLDSMUTH, pondering: "Wait! Yes, I remember the exact words. 'There is only one country in the world in which such things could take place. How noble is the soul of this our people, which in bygone ages taught Law and Justice to Europe and the world!' "

They listen, their eyes fixed on the tangle of greying hair within which the tinted spectacles he now wears make two blobs of glaucous light. Cresteil breaks the spell.

CRESTEIL, with a bitter laugh: "Yes, we had our fools' paradise, all right, while it lasted! And what's come of it, I ask you! We lanced the abscess, we counted on a cure—and now gangrene's set in." Luce makes a deprecating gesture, Breil-Zoeger's shoulders lift. "A golden age indeed! Commercialism rampant, policies bought and sold in the market-place, organized looting by the anti-clericals, stark nonsense from the anti-militarists, the collapse of all good government."

BREIL-ZOEGER: "I hold no brief for the political methods of today. But I will say this: they're no worse than those we had to put up with before the Affair."

BAROIS, thoughtfully: "Well, I wonder!"

LUCE, quickly: "Oh, come, Barois! We've no reason to regret those bad old times."

BREIL-ZOEGER: "If the government of those days had done its duty, it wouldn't have left to us the task of seeing justice done."

LUCE: "I'm sorry for you, Cresteil. You see only the dark side; you shut your eyes to the promise of better things. The Republic of today has at least one merit: it is the only form of government that has in it the seeds of self-betterment. You must give democracy time to set its house in order."

CRESTEIL: "What's so abominable is that those very people whose activities are one long betrayal of our programme have the nerve to set themselves up as our political heirs. The men who thought fit officially to encourage delation in the Army dare to take shelter behind our principles when called to account in Parliament."

BREIL-ZOEGER: "As you might expect of politicians!"

BAROIS, sadly: "But, of course, it's a well-known historical phenomenon; the victors promptly acquire the vices of the vanquished. Really it would seem that power engenders a special, highly contagious brand of immorality, and there's no escaping it."

CRESTEIL, gloomily: "No, the truth is that everything connected with the Affair, and everything that's come of it, is tainted, rotten to the core."

LUCE, indignantly: "Really, Cresteil!"

CRESTEIL: "Why fly in the face of the facts? From the production of the secret dossier of 1894 up to the final proceedings in revision, by way of the Esterhazy trial and the Zola case, the whole course of the Affair was strewn with breaches of the law." Angrily. "And that wasn't the worst of it. When we were up against that grotesque sentence given at Rennes and the equally grotesque pardon"—he seems to find pleasure in reopening the old sores—"such of us as hadn't utterly lost heart still hoped against hope for a final victory. But that, of course, was aiming too high; we were doomed to be let down on every count, and relegated to the scrap heap. And so all the meaning of the Affair, all the ideals for which we'd fought so hard and worked ourselves till we dropped—everything fell to pieces when that final illegality closed the Affair for good; the quashing of the sentence by a Court of Appeal which had no legal right to set aside the verdict but did not hesitate, in the interests of justice, to play fast and loose with the provisions of the law. What a miserable farce!"

LUCE: "But, Cresteil . . ."

BREIL-ZOEGER, dryly, with contained irony: "Do you seriously suppose that a new court-martial, presided over by seven officers chosen at random, would have been better qualified than the Supreme Court of Appeal, the court of highest jurisdiction in the land?"

CRESTEIL: "No, Zoeger, that's the wrong way of putting it. Actually, the story goes that the Supreme Court of Appeal was being steadily 'packed' during the two preceding years—and it's certain that an exceptional number of new judges was appointed to it during the period. But that's beside the point I wish to establish." His tone is fastidiously precise. "My point is that there was a more honourable way of settling the business, without all those endless wrangles between lawyers about the interpretation of Article 445 of the Code. For it was possible to keep clear of the civil court and all these legal complications. To wipe out the injustice done at Rennes, what was needed was a straight verdict of acquittal by another military tribunal. And for lack of this, the Affair remains, and will remain for ever, a stain on our public life, a festering wound that nothing can ever heal."

BAROIS, dubiously: "That would have meant reopening the whole case."

CRESTEIL: "No doubt. But it was worth it!"

BAROIS: "Don't forget there are limits to human endurance."

CRESTEIL: "Barois, you think exactly as I do on the subject. You've made that clear time and again in *The Sower*." Barois smiles and lowers his eyes. "And then—only think of the sensational effects a new court-martial would have had! The same generals whose reticence had led to Dreyfus's conviction in 1899 had just repudiated in the preliminary inquiry the whole story about a *bordereau* annotated by the Kaiser. So all they had to do was to repeat their depositions before the officer-judges, and an acquittal was inevitable."

LUCE: "Oh, what's the use of raking up the dead ashes? And anyhow, Cresteil, you push your pessimism much too far, bad as things are today."

BAROIS, rising: "Really, a listener might have thought we'd come together here just to air the grievances of our middle years!"

BREIL-ZOEGER, with a harsh laugh, pointing to the newspaper lying on the grass: "It's our Ash Wednesday."

Barois goes up to Luce, to take leave of him.

CRESTEIL, abruptly to Barois: "Going back through the Bois de Boulogne? If so, I'll come with you."

LUCE: "The root of the trouble, to my mind, is that we French aren't a moral nation. And why is that? Because for many centuries politics and self-interest have ranked before the true interests of the country. A complete re-education was needed, obviously; but, though we didn't bring off as much as we expected, we mustn't jump to the conclusion that we've failed all along the line. No, we're making headway slowly but surely." He shakes Cresteil's hand. "Say what you will, Cresteil, but it was a wonderful century, which began with the Revolution and ended with the Affair."

CRESTEIL, in a weary, disillusioned tone: "It was also a century of utopian dreams and muddled aspirations, of jerry-building and patched-up solutions. We can't be sure, of course, but I shouldn't be surprised if it comes to be called the 'gimcrack' age."

An avenue in the Bois de Boulogne. The afternoon is drawing to a close, the air is mild. Cresteil, whose nerves are frayed, is setting the pace.

CRESTEIL, in a changed, confidential tone: "When I'm with the others, you see how I behave; I get worked up, I seem very sure of myself. But when I'm alone—ah, it's a very different story. No, old chap, it's over. I can't gull myself with fine phrases any longer. I've been through too much; only too well I know life for the damned raree-show it is! Duty, virtue, goodness—they're all just make-believe, you must know it as well as I do. Fine-sounding names to cover up selfish instincts, the only real things in our mental make-up. What dreary humbugs we all are!"

BAROIS, greatly moved: "But, my dear Cresteil, what's come over you? I'm most distressed to hear you say such things."

CRESTEIL, fiercely: "A man is—as he is. That too is something I've fully realized only quite recently. I never asked to live, least of all to live the life I've led."

BAROIS, as a last resource: "Haven't you any work in hand just now?"

CRESTEIL, with a burst of laughter: "My books, you mean? Yes, there too you see in me the perfect failure, the typical misfit. What's Art with a capital 'A'? Like Justice and like Truth. One of those pompous words that mean nothing; that are hollower than a rotten nut. And to think I used to work myself up into frenzies of devotion for those fatuous words! Art! Man, that wretched impotent, fancies he can add to nature, can create! A nincompoop like that create! Why, it's the acme of absurdity."

Sick at heart, Barois listens to his friend, as one listens to a storm in the forest, the groaning of twisted branches, the shrilling of the gale.

CRESTEIL: "Do you know, Barois? If I had to start life again, I'd begin by killing off all my ambitions. I'd train myself not to believe in anything. I'd make a point of loving life solely in its smallest manifestations, the only ones that haven't too much bitterness to be swallowed at a gulp. The one way of getting any happiness is to pick up what crumbs of comfort lie on one's path. That's the one chance a man has of gleaning a little consolation on the road that leads to 'dusty death'—for all roads lead to the same place, the same dark hole."

So poignant is the tone in which he utters the last word that Barois gazes at him in wonder. Cresteil has fallen silent. Abruptly, after taking some steps beside Barois, he stops, as though his breath and will-power have given out; then points to an avenue leading to the right.

CRESTEIL: "I'll leave you now. That's my way."

Barois watches the lanky figure, all in black, coat-tails flapping and shoulders bowed, speeding awkwardly away under the long shadows of the trees.

XI. THE CHILD

I

Abbé Joziers
  The Vicarage
   Buis-la-Dame   December 26

My dear Abbé: At Madame Barois' request Maître Mougin has written reminding me that, under the provisions of our agreement, I am now entitled to require my daughter to spend a year with me, since she will reach the age of eighteen in a few weeks' time. I would prefer not to reply through a lawyer, and I trust I am not asking too much if I request you to transmit my answer.

Would you please thank Madame Barois on my behalf for making this proposal and convey to her, in the manner you think best, my reasons for declining it.

I will state them quite frankly; as you will have noticed, frankness has become a second nature with me.

At the time we parted, I wished to reserve for myself the possibility of intervening, at a suitable moment, in my daughter's education. But conditions have changed. For eighteen years, as you know, I have not seen my wife or my daughter. Really I should be presuming on my rights, were I to ask today to be allowed to play a part in a life in which I have hitherto had no place, and shall never have any place. In any case it seems to me that the feelings my daughter may be presumed to entertain for a father who is a complete stranger would make a meeting of this kind as distasteful to her as, indeed, it would be to me.

So there is no need to make any change in the present arrangement, and I hope you will kindly convey to my wife that she is released from any obligation towards me in this respect.

Please accept my gratitude, dear Abbé Joziers, and believe me,

Always yours,
Jean Barois

New Year's Day. It is nine in the morning, and Barois, who has risen late, is dawdling over his dressing. He has no engagements in view. Pascal brings some letters and cards on a tray.

PASCAL: "Will you be dining in, sir?"

BAROIS, who is sorting out his mail, looks up: "No. You can take the evening off." Glances at him hesitantly. "I suppose you've a family or friends you'll be looking up today?"

PASCAL, placidly: "No, sir, I can't say as I have. If you are going out, sir, I'll dine early and go to the movies."

BAROIS, calling him back: "In that case, Pascal, I think I'll dine here. That all right? At any time that suits you, and make the meal as simple as you like. I shall stay in all day. Restaurants are always so noisy and tiresome on days like this."

He glances through some letters, then picks up an envelope postmarked Buis and slowly opens it.

> The Vicarage,
> Buis-la-Dame
> December 31

My dear Jean: I shall always be willing, in memory of the past, to act as your spokesman. And I carried out your request with all the more readiness since any other solution would have seemed to me particularly inconsiderate.

Your decision spared Mme Barois new causes of distress, and you owed that to her. The poor lady deserves some recompense for the life of noble self-abnegation she has led.

However, I should feel that I was failing in my duty towards you, were I to conceal the fact that it was Marie who persuaded her mother to communicate with you through Maître Mougin. So you can see for yourself how different are the filial sentiments you attribute to your daughter from those which a profoundly Christian education has caused her to develop.

> Affectionately yours,
> M. L. Joziers

Barois is standing at the window; he gazes at the envelope, then at the room, then at the street below. It takes him some moments to master his emotion. Then, picking up the letter again, he makes a great effort to concentrate his thoughts on its contents.

Why exactly did Joziers use that particular expression: "I should feel that I was failing in my duty towards you"? Presumably because he realized that what he says in that last paragraph might change my whole attitude. Now if the move had come from me, and I'd been acting on some caprice, I should certainly answer "No." Also, if I'd had the idea of trying to influence her in some surreptitious way. But that's not the case. The suggestion came from her. And, that being so, why not . . . ?

He smiles. How odd that it should be she who makes a point of holding me to our engagement! And against her mother's wishes obviously, since my refusal has spared Cécile "new causes of distress." So Cécile's great fear is that I may insist on my rights under our agreement, and the girl must have had to make a firm stand—which means she's definitely bent on coming here.

Still, I'm damned if I can see why! Curiosity? That's unlikely. The mere thought of leaving Buis, her mother and grandmother, the home she's lived in all her life must be rather alarming—especially when it means coming to Paris. What on earth has been going on inside that eighteen-year-old head?

In any case, it must have needed a lot of determination to persuade Cécile to agree. Which proves she has a strong will, her own ideas. It's very perplexing. Joziers, I remember, gave me to understand that she was rather like me in appearance. Perhaps we have some mental qualities in common too; the same tenacity of purpose? Yes—who knows?—she may have something of my turn of mind and wants to check up and review what they've taught her. Perhaps she's going through the same spiritual conflict that I went through at Buis in my young days. And this prompts her to make a move to Paris, so as to breathe more freely, emancipate herself.

As he lingers on these agreeable speculations, he discovers in himself a capacity for personal affection the existence of which comes as a surprise. But presently he shrugs his shoulders. No, that won't do! The Abbé writes about the sentiments which "a profoundly Christian education has caused her to develop." Evidently they've got her in their grip!

He makes a fretful gesture. Really, it's too absurd! Here I am getting into a state of irritation because a girl I've never set eyes on is in the enemy's camp! And ten minutes ago her piety was a matter of supreme indifference to me. I must be losing my wits! Presumably—he smiles to himself—that's because she entered my life only ten minutes ago; until then she'd been no more than a name—and what a banal name at that! Just another "Marie"!

He picks up the letter for the third time. And, reading it, he realizes that the voice of reason is powerless against the irrevocable decision that each word of this letter engraves upon his mind.

2

A February afternoon. Hearing a key turn in the lock, Pascal hurries to the entrance door.

BAROIS, entering: "Well, Pascal, is everything ready?"

Pascal smiles understandingly and nods.

Barois walks round his study, inspecting it with a critical eye. All is spick and span with the exception of the desk, on which confusion reigns. Michelangelo's "Slave" stands on the mantelpiece straining his muscles in his vain, eternal struggle to break free.

Next Barois walks quickly to the other end of the flat, where there are two bedrooms with a small dressing-room sandwiched between them. The larger room is papered in a pale blue and has been newly furnished.

His look conveys satisfaction, tempered by vague apprehension. He straightens a lampshade, feels the heat of the radiator, glances at his watch, and goes back to the study.

BAROIS: "Pascal! We've forgotten something! Run out and buy a bunch of white flowers. This size." He indicates it with his hands. "Mind they're white."

Five minutes later there is a ring at the bell. Barois, who is pacing up and down his study, goes quite pale. And that fool isn't back yet, confound him! He goes to the hall and, after a moment's hesitation, opens the front door.

Abbé Joziers is the first to enter. He is followed by a girl and a plainly dressed woman of fifty.

BAROIS: "My man's just gone out." He opens the study door. "This way."

The priest enters, then the girl. Barois is about to follow, but the maid brushes past and gets in front, resolutely dogging the footsteps of her young mistress.

THE ABBÉ, quietly: "Good afternoon, Jean. I bring you your daughter. And Julie—the faithful Julie." Smiling, he makes a priestly gesture. "Two of my best parishioners."

Barois takes a timid step towards Marie, who is holding herself very straight, blushing deeply. She is small, dark, clear-complexioned. And suddenly a picture forms before him of Cécile when she was twenty.

Marie holds out her hand, and Barois clasps it firmly. A short silence follows. Then the door opens and Pascal appears, bouquet in hand. He stops, smiling, quite at his ease.

BAROIS: "I sent him out to get some flowers." To Marie. "A man's flat is always rather—rather austere, you know."

All have remained standing and seem embarrassed. Marie lowers her eyes. Julie keeps hers fixed on Barois. The priest casts a disapproving glance round the room. Barois feels that, at all costs, this vaguely hostile silence must be broken.

BAROIS, to Marie: "Shall I show you your room?" He moves towards the door, then turns to the priest. "Won't you come with us?" His look implies: Come and see where she is going to be, so that you can tell about it when you get back.

Sunlight is streaming into the bedroom, and somehow they feel even less at ease here than in the sombre-hued study. As before, they stand planted in the middle of the room at a loss what to do or say. Barois tries to dispel the constraint by launching into explanations.

BAROIS: "Your dressing-room's over there. And that is—er—Julie's room. So you won't feel isolated." To Pascal, who is bringing in the luggage. "Put it in front of the window." His cheerfulness is ebbing before a growing sense of discouragement, and his one desire now is to get it over. He turns to Marie, who is gazing listlessly at the window. "Well, we'll leave you to yourself—you'd prefer that, wouldn't you? I expect you want to unpack."

THE ABBÉ: "In any case I've my train to catch. So, my dear child, I'll now say *au revoir.*"

Marie gazes at him and her eyes grow misted. Though she makes no movement, one feels she is about to fling herself into the old Abbé's arms. Then, stepping forward, he kisses her paternally on the forehead and repeats, "*Au revoir,* Marie." His tone is affectionate but firm; it has the indifference towards this present life of those who have always lived for the other. It conveys to the girl: I am sorry for you, but you yourself invited this test, and can you doubt that God will see you through?

Barois leads the priest back to the study. His hands are shaking, his nerves at breaking point. Somehow he conjures up a friendly smile.

BAROIS: "What time's your—?"

But before he can get the last word out he breaks down completely and sinks into a chair beside his desk, burying his face in his hands, his body racked by sobs. That vision of Cécile as a girl, of the irrecoverable past, has risen again before him. Those wistful, timid eyes! And a sudden uprush of love, a yearning for what cannot be, has broken through his defences, and with it a sense of the responsibility of having brought into the world another human being capable of suffering!

Impassively, with folded arms, his fingers buried in his sleeves, the priest watches. He is thinking of the rock struck by Moses, but deliberately withholds any show of compassion.

At last Barois raises his head, and wipes his eyes.

BAROIS: "Forgive me for behaving like this, but it's been a shock, you know. And my nerves are none too good nowadays." The Abbé has picked up his hat and breviary. "What time does your train leave?"

Two hours later. All this time Barois has been pacing his room, from door to window and back again, listening eagerly to every sound in the flat. At last, unable to bear it any longer, he walks quickly to Marie's bedroom.

All is silence.

He knocks at the door. There is a sound of hurried movements in the room; then Marie's voice. "Come in."

In the gathering dusk, outlined against the glimmering window, are two dark forms. Evidently, at his knock, Marie and "the faithful Julie" rose hastily to their feet; two chairs stand derelict in the centre of the room. Barois feels a curious sinking of the heart.

BAROIS: "So you were sitting in the dark?" He turns on the light and encounters Julie's watchful gaze. A chaplet dangles from her fingers. Marie makes an awkward gesture; her eyes are red, he notices, as if she has been crying. "You've done your unpacking, I see. Have you everything you require?" To Julie. "Don't hesitate to ask if you need anything. Pascal's a very obliging fellow and he'll do all he can to make you comfortable here." To Marie. "Well, suppose we make a move to my study until it's time for dinner?"

She follows him meekly. Looking round, he is struck by her dejected air.

BAROIS: "Really one would think I was leading you to the scaffold!"

She tries to smile, but the note of affection in his voice makes her, for some reason, want to cry. Barois turns on all the lights in the study, then briskly draws an armchair forward. Marie settles into it uneasily. He feels as embarrassed as she—and ridiculous too, because of his age.

Marie has a low, slightly prominent forehead; an olive complexion with translucences of pink and sudden glints of dusky red, the bloom of a moss-rose. Under the black eyebrows, which have the same tortuous line as her father's, the pale grey-blue eyes come as a surprise. They lack gentleness, and her chin too is stubborn, like a man's. But the delicately moulded nose, the childish smile that flickers on her lips, redeem the face from harshness. Marie has the charm of healthy, unsullied youth.

BAROIS: "Yes, I quite understand how hard it is for you, being uprooted like this from your home surroundings and parted from your mother. I expect you find Paris, this flat, everything here in fact—myself included—a bit alarming!" She makes a shy, deprecating gesture. "No, no; I can guess how you're feeling. Why even I—well, I hardly know what to say to you, how to begin." Seeing her friendly smile, he is emboldened to continue. "Yet, after all, it was you who had the idea of spending a couple of months here; I'd never have dared to ask it of you myself. And, now you're here, there's no reason why we shouldn't get on quite well together. Don't you agree?"

MARIE, with obvious constraint: "Yes . . . Father."

An ironic thought crosses his mind. That "father"—it's how she says it in the confession box! Then his look grows earnest.

BAROIS: "I don't know what—what you've been told about me." She blushes, makes a protesting gesture, and a stubborn look comes into her eyes. There is more warmth in his voice as he continues. "Anyhow as you wished to—to make my acquaintance, I think it's up to me to explain things quite frankly. I may seem to have behaved abominably towards your mother and towards you, and I won't deny that I'm to blame in a good many respects. Still, there's something to be said on both sides. You're very young, Marie, to be mixed up in—in things like this. I'll try to explain matters as tactfully and honestly as I can."

At the word "honestly" Marie raises her head.

PASCAL, on entering, in a solemn voice: "Dinner is served, Mademoiselle."

She turns and looks at him in surprise.

BAROIS, laughing: "You see, I've ceased to count. You are the mistress here." He rises. "Shall we make a move now? If you're not too tired we'll talk about—all that after dinner."

Dinner is over. The ice has been broken between them. Marie leads the way to the study, and her eyes fall on the flowers still wrapped in tissue paper.

MARIE: "Oh, dear! They should have been put in water."

BAROIS, to Pascal, who is bringing the coffee: "Here, Pascal. You'd better give these to Julie and ask her to—"

MARIE, quickly: "No, no. Give them to me. Have you a big enough vase?"

Pascal brings her one and smilingly watches her arrange the flowers.

BAROIS: "Marie, I can see you've made a conquest of Pascal." She laughs. "No coffee?"

MARIE: "No, I never take it."

BAROIS: "Well, as you're the lady of the house, would you pour mine? Only half a cup; that's all I'm allowed now. Thanks." They smile, like two children playing at being grown up. "Do you know, Marie, I've been asking myself a question all evening: 'Why did she want to come here?'" Marie remains silent. Barois' voice is affectionate but insistent. "Yes, *why?*"

Marie has ceased smiling. She does not flinch from Barois' gaze. Then she shakes her head, as though to say: No. Later on, perhaps. But not tonight.

3

Six weeks later. The editorial office in the *Sower* building.

THE SUB-EDITOR: "What about Monsieur Breil-Zoeger's article on lay education?"

BAROIS, glancing at the clock: "Oh, put in something else instead."
He rises.

THE SUB-EDITOR: "Well, it's been hanging fire for four months, and—"

BAROIS, who has risen from his chair: "Perhaps it has. But I can't
publish that article in its present form. I must see Breil-Zoeger about it."

THE SUB-EDITOR: "Shall I put Bernardin's paper in this number?"

BAROIS: "If you like."

THE SUB-EDITOR: "Oh, and I'd also like to know what answer we're
to give to Merlet."

BAROIS: "That can wait, my dear fellow. It's not urgent, and I must
be off now. We'll see to it tomorrow." He takes his hat and overcoat
off the peg.

As he walks past the Gare d'Orsay he glances up at the station
clock. Only a quarter to four. I leave the office a bit earlier every day.
I'll end up by staying at home all the time. I'll *end up?* No; she'll be
leaving in three weeks . . . A spasm of anguish grips him. He quickens his steps. A picture has risen before him of the study, a girl's
head bent under the lamplight, the forehead in shadow, soft light
playing on the glossy hair. And he smiles to himself as he walks on.

She has settled down, he thinks, just as if it were her home. It's
quaint, that mixture of shyness and self-assurance she has. Anyhow,
she always knows what she wants. Yes, she impresses one, definitely.
There's something so healthy, so well-balanced about her; she gives
a sense of harmony and wholeness that's very rare and restful.

No, my feelings aren't a father's, really; they're paternal, but that's
not quite the same. A father feels he has authority, certain rights. I
don't. I'm nearly fifty and she's eighteen—that's where the paternal
element comes in. In fact what I have for her is, absurdly enough, a
sort of sentimental attachment, almost like—why boggle at the word?
—a lover's.

He climbs the staircase, smiling happily to himself. Like a lover's!
In the doorway, Pascal's moonface.

BAROIS: "Is my daughter in?"

PASCAL: "No, sir, she's not back yet."

A stab of disappointment, then profound depression; soon it will be thus day after day. Ten minutes pass.

MARIE: "Here I am, Father!"

She is wearing a dark dress, her cheeks are cool and pink, her eyes sparkling.

BAROIS, smiling with pleasure: "You're awfully late today, Marie."

No sooner has he spoken than he regrets the remark. His gaze has fallen on the gilt fore-edge of the prayer-book she is laying on the mantelpiece, preparatory to taking off her hat.

MARIE: "It's the first day of the Retreat." She goes out, comes back with two bound volumes of *The Sower,* and puts them on the desk. "What will you give me next, Father?"

BAROIS: "Well, I'm wondering. What would you like?" His tone implies: You know quite well I've no ideas of your tastes in literature.

MARIE, smiling: "Why, the next numbers, of course."

BAROIS: "That second volume contains the year's issues, up to December last. There have been only eight since then." He goes on to a set of pigeonholes. "Here they are. But if you want to read only articles by me, you needn't bother to look at them. I haven't published anything since January." He laughs. "You can guess why."

MARIE: "Do I really prevent your working?"

BAROIS, smiling: "No, you don't prevent my working; it's not that. Only, since you've been here I work less, it seems. I haven't the same desire to work as I used to." He looks at Marie, who seems genuinely remorseful. Yet what importance can it have for her whether he works or not? Indeed, she should feel glad of having checked his output of pernicious literature! Then he reverts to the thoughts that were in his mind on his way home. "I don't see why I shouldn't tell you, Marie. You've brought into my life something which it lacked, something of whose preciousness I'd never had an inkling. Companionship, affection—call it what you like. Of course, when I say 'affection,' I'm speaking only for myself." She makes as if to correct him, then blushes. "So the thought that you'll soon be leaving me is painful, terribly painful."

MARIE, gently: "I'll come again."

He thanks her with a smile, an elderly smile, and is silent for some moments.

BAROIS: "I've become very deeply attached to you, my dear. And yet you're still a mystery to me; I simply cannot understand you." She frowns, on the defensive. Barois points to the prayer-book. "I'm conscious of a gulf between us, and that's the cause of it. I feel it every morning when you come back from Mass. And at other times, when you're sitting with me here in the evenings, hunting out all I've written in *The Sower,* reading my books, asking for explanations and listening to them quite calmly—yes, at these moments I have an idea you're not so very far from me. And yet! No, definitely I can't understand you."

Marie is standing, one knee resting on a chair, her hands folded on her skirt, in an attitude of languor. But her eyes are alert. She gives a quick glance at the volumes of *The Sower* she has brought back, then seems to come to a decision and ensconces herself in the armchair.

MARIE: "Well, I wanted to read everything, first."

She pauses. The hour has struck for the long-deferred explanation, and her voice conveys the tension of a young, immature mind at grips with something outside its range. Noticing the far-away look in the limpid blue eyes, Barois guesses she has paused to make a silent prayer for courage. He tries to help her.

BAROIS: "If only I knew *why* you wanted to come here!"

She gazes at him, pondering deeply for some moments.

MARIE: "As a test." He cannot conceal his bitter disappointment. She flushes deeply and lowers her head. The smooth, rounded forehead brings to his mind a buckler. Then the words come with a rush. "Father, I want to take the veil." Barois gives an exclamation of amazement. She looks up. "I knew you'd lost your faith. So I wanted to make your acquaintance, to share your life, study your work, come under your influence. It was the crucial test of my vocation." Proudly. "And I'm glad I came."

BAROIS, sadly: "So you wish to become a nun, Marie?" He is struck by the way she smiles, a twisted, joyless fluctuation of the lips, attended by a gaze that has a faintly ironical self-assurance, and yet seems lifeless, almost hopeless. Barois raises his arm, then lets it fall despondently, and avoids meeting her eyes as he continues. "Well, I hardly expected that! I often asked myself, Why's she here? And I formed all sorts of theories. Finally I decided, She's going to try to convert me."

Marie gives a high-pitched laugh, the laugh of a nervous child.

BAROIS, irritably: "Why laugh? Surely that wouldn't have been such a bad idea—for a nun-to-be?"

She grows serious again and, rising, fetches her prayer-book. After hunting for the page, she hands it, open, to her father.

BAROIS, reading: " 'I would that all men were even as I myself. But every man hath his proper gift of God.' "

MARIE, smiling: "I'm not so conceited as you seem to think. If God wanted you for Himself, would He need my help? He has other plans for you, Father." She shakes her head. "No, everyone finds his appointed path as best he can. Personally, I've been given the happiness of finding it quite simply and easily; I had only a few steps to take. You haven't had that happiness, and I'm sorry for you. Yes, Father, I can only be sorry for you, terribly sorry. For how could somebody like me try to convert somebody like you?"

BAROIS: "And you weren't afraid when you exposed your faith to my influence?"

MARIE, shaking her head again: "No. For one thing, I knew that if you had those ideas you had them in—I don't know how to express it—in a noble, high-principled way. So one couldn't really blame you for them."

BAROIS: "How did you know that?"

MARIE, smiling to herself: "I knew it."

BAROIS, with a sudden curiosity: "Tell me, Marie. Was it your mother who ... ?"

Marie reddens, then gives a slight nod. Barois does not insist. He

goes to his bookcase, opens it, takes out some volumes, and gazes at
them thoughtfully.

BAROIS: "Let's see, Marie. You've read my 'Reasons for Disbelief,'
eight consecutive articles, haven't you?"

MARIE: "Yes."

BAROIS: "And this one, 'Science versus Dogma'? And this one, 'The
World's Religions: Their Origins Compared'?"

MARIE: "Yes."

BAROIS, closing the bookcase door: "You've read all that and applied
your mind to it. And, afterwards, all that you'd believed in hitherto
didn't seem . . . ?"

What he had meant to say was: You can't convince me that a childish faith like yours can stand up against the onslaught of a life like
mine, devoted to combating religion with clean-cut arguments. But,
seeing Marie's quiet smile, the gentle obstinacy of her eyes, he holds
his peace.

MARIE: "But don't you see, Father, that if my faith could be shaken
by arguments it wouldn't be faith?"

She smiles again, this time with charming naïveté. And Barois
glimpses an aspect of the human mind quite new to him. So, he
muses, there are certainties proof against all argument. Still, I don't
quite understand. Does she mean that the difficulties I see in religious
belief don't exist for her because she has an *a priori* certainty? In
other words, that she has definitely placed her faith above all reasoning and, even if she let herself be convinced intellectually by my
arguments, they wouldn't affect her faith in the least, because she is
above them, immunized against them? It's childish, that attitude—
but unassailable.

BAROIS, gently: "But, Marie, what's the basis of this certainty of
yours?"

Her distress is obvious, but she refuses to shirk the issue.

MARIE: "When once one has felt what I have felt—oh, Father, it's
hard to put it into words, that wonderful experience. You feel God's
very presence, you feel him pouring into your soul like a great flood,

filling it with joy and love. When you've had that experience, even if only once in a lifetime, all the arguments men build up to prove to themselves that their souls are not immortal, not given them by God—yes, all *your* arguments, Father—are dust before the wind." A serene smile lights up her face.

Barois ponders in silence for a while. "What I have *felt*," she said. Obviously there's no countering that, and there never can be. But if only I could prevent her making an irrevocable decision!

BAROIS: "Does your mother approve of the step you intend to take?" A look in which sadness struggles with obstinacy settles on the girl's face, and she lowers her eyes. Barois is dumbfounded. "What! You haven't told her yet?" Marie does not answer. "But why? Have you reason to think she'd try to dissuade you?" She still is silent. "Surely that, if nothing else, should warn you. However great your desire to take the veil, you realize that you'll be causing so much suffering that you haven't even dared to . . . ?"

MARIE, on the brink of tears: "Why should I hurt her like that before the time comes? I'm so sorry for her, you know. She has never been happy, poor Mamma."

She blushes; that last remark slipped out involuntarily. But Barois does not seem to have grasped its implications. He bends towards her.

BAROIS: "Please listen to me, Marie. I don't want to argue with you; this has nothing to do with your religious faith. You've read in my writings all the reasons I could bring forward. Well, they haven't convinced you; let's say no more about it." He draws a deep breath. "So you see it's not the free-thinker who's speaking to you; only the man of fifty, a man who has learned some wisdom, a man who has seen how one's ideas can change in the course of a lifetime. It's rash, terribly rash, to bind oneself, to pledge one's whole life, when one's as young as you are. Don't forget that all sorts of things can modify your ideas, that the passing years and wider understanding and new experiences may bring changes of which you haven't an inkling as yet." Marie makes a gesture conveying: Oh, I've no fears on that score! "Why, your heredity alone should give you pause! All those instincts which led me when I was your age to make my bid for freedom exist in you. Do what you will, they're there, beneath the level of your conscious mind; you may keep them under, more or less, but there they'll stay, and at any moment they may thrust their way up into the light and play havoc with your life.

"Really, Marie, how can you be so positive you'll never come to doubt? Can you, indeed, assure me that you've never, *never* felt the slightest doubt? Try to look into yourself, my dear. Really it's incredible that after studying that"—he points to the bound volumes of *The Sower*—"that not even the shadow of a doubt has crossed your mind."

MARIE: "Yes, Father, I can say that. It's perfectly true." Her eyes are bright with happy faith, and he gazes at her wonderingly. After a short silence Marie speaks again. "No, the world's too empty. Nothing's great, nothing lasts."

BAROIS: "Do you think that here on earth a heart that strains towards better things can find no scope?"

She observes him for some moments, respectfully, compassionately.

MARIE: "Yes, Father. I've thought a lot about you since I came to Paris. You haven't had the privilege of being touched by grace, you have not known what it means to feel God's nearness—and yet you are so kind and good. But how you must have striven—when it's so much simpler to be good just by loving God!"

BAROIS: "Do you really believe it's a noble thing to shelve responsibility, all the difficulties of the workaday world, and take refuge in the lifelong reclusion of the cloister? Do you regard that course as nobler than bravely taking up the task that lies to your hand and carrying it through? than leading the good life amongst your fellow men and women? What you're choosing is a sort of suicide—the suicide of thought and action."

MARIE, her face radiant with an inner vision: "No, the gift of myself to God."

BAROIS: "And what does it amount to, that gift of oneself, on the threshold of a life that's bound to be difficult, like every human life?

What is it but a shirking of the most elementary duties? No, don't talk to me about the virtues of submission! It's an opiate that dulls the pain, that's all. You, Marie, are young, intelligent, brimming over with vitality—how can you desire that blank negation, the contemplative life? Are you acting worthily of yourself?"

MARIE: "You talk like all the others; you can't understand the first thing about it." With rising emotion. "I've been given privileges, and privileges impose duties. All are not chosen, but those whom God has called and chosen should give themselves without reserve. They have to pay the ransom for all those who give the smallest possible portion of their lives to God—and for those who give nothing whatever of their lives to him."

BAROIS, brusquely: "Ah, I'm beginning to see! It's my ransom you wish to pay?"

MARIE: "I don't expect you to understand me, Father. But, yes, the vows I shall take will pay a little of the family debt, they will make some compensation for—for what your books have done." Affectionately. "Who knows if God has not laid on me this vocation, in exchange for a soul, a very noble soul, which, but for it, would have been lost?"

Her eyes are faintly glassy, a smooth, hard surface from which the gaze of others, others' questionings and doubts, glance off, without penetrating.

Barois thinks: How amazing is a religion which can swing human minds so far away from realities and hold them there! There's absolutely no foundation for it. The least touch of common sense would overthrow it, if the human mentality had not been conditioned to faith by centuries of blind obeisance.

It simmers in children's minds, kept at the appropriate temperature by the emotive figments of the catechism, the ardours of a First Communion. And it can rise to such a pitch of artificial heat that a whole life may be transmuted by it. And this it is that gives Marie that fine serenity which has won my admiration ever since she came to live here. How many years must pass, how many generations grope their way towards the light, before scientific knowledge brings peace to the troubled minds of men? Who can say? Perhaps it never will.

4

M. Marc-Élie Luce
Auteuil

My dear Luce: I hoped to see you at our weekly meeting this afternoon and tell you that I am taking a fortnight off during the Easter holidays. But I have so many things to attend to before leaving Paris that I may not be able to come to say good-bye. Hence this letter.

And yet there was so much I'd have liked to tell you *viva voce*. During these last weeks I have had an emotional experience as painful as it was shocking. My daughter wishes to become a nun.

Her announcement came as a bolt from the blue and you can picture my consternation. Indeed, the eagerness she has always shown, since she came to live with me, to become acquainted with all that I have written against Catholicism quite misled me. I remember telling you of the impression I had at first, a grotesquely false impression as the event has proved. My present view is that, strong-willed and intuitive as she is, she suffered from the cramped conditions of provincial life, and her reaction took the form of an intense, highly introverted mental activity. For her the Church has provided merely a framework, clean-cut but supple, within which her personal emotions can expand. What dominates her sensibility today is not dogmatic religion, but the spontaneous yearning of a young, untried soul towards the infinite—and, perhaps, the illusion that she has attained it.

One thing is certain: that, given the perfect health of mind and body which is hers, her childish faith might well have evolved, had she attached the same importance to dogma as she does to the emotional side of religion. But this was not to be, and the promptings of the mystical state she has now attained are so imperious as to give her complete assurance of the existence of a spiritual world, an assurance no rational arguments could shake.

People trained as we are to subordinate their sensibilities to the guidance of the intellect can have no notion of certitudes like those. Marie has *experienced* contact with God and can no more combat an auto-suggestion of this kind than we can convince a mental case of the unreality of his hallucinations. Nothing could persuade Marie that this supernatural world into which she has projected all that is best in her—and which, thanks to her moments of ecstasy, she has actually seen—is no more than a mirage, a trick played on her by her imagination, a fairy-tale she has been telling herself since earliest childhood.

I know, my dear Luce, that you won't approve of this. But, now I realize that I am up against a hopeless task, the plans I made when I talked things over with you, and the advice you gave me for bringing this young girl little by little to replace her delusions by a progressive awareness of the truth—all these plans and that advice seem to me of no avail. I recognize both my own inability to convince her and the immutability of her self-deception. My conclusion is that she has been shaped by religion and for religion. The position being too strongly entrenched, I have beaten a retreat. Obviously her faith is rooted in a lie, but it is also a source of human happiness, *her* happiness. You who are a parent—far more amply so, indeed, than I!—may perhaps understand how I feel. In the old days I'd have said, "Truth before everything, even if it brings suffering." Now—well, I'm not so sure. I keep silent and I believe I love her more in keeping silent, however much this goes against the grain, than in trying to destroy the mainspring of her life.

I have arranged to spend the Easter holidays with her. And I propose to end my daughter's visit, which will have been an unexpected, delightful oasis in my life, by a trip to a land of flowers and sunlight. We leave the day after tomorrow for the Italian Lakes.

I am prepared for some bitter moments when I revert to my solitude, but I prefer not to think about that. I shall need you greatly, my dear Luce, and I know you will come to my rescue. This knowledge alleviates the prospect of my return to Paris, alone.

So *au revoir,* my very dear friend.

Affectionately yours,

J.B.

5

At Pallanza. It is six o'clock of an April evening. A row-boat is creeping out across the lake. Marie and Barois are seated in the stern, their backs to the town, whose sounds have died away into the distance. There is hardly a ripple and, bathed in a silvery light at once intense and misted, the boat cuts slowly through the silken smoothness. A full moon rides near the zenith, one has to crick one's neck to see it. They seem infinitely remote from the world of men, floating in a limbo of spectral silence, of mist and moonshine.

In the bow the oarsman's shoulders rise and fall in a steady rhythm; his shirt and canvas trousers are palely gleaming patches, while his hands and bare feet seem black as an icon's.

Barois cannot take his mind off the impending separation. Marie, gazing upwards, out of space and out of time, steeping her soul in the limpid sheen of sky and lake, seems lost in a secret dream, as though nothing at this moment stood between herself and God.

Suddenly a waft of heavily scented air, warm as a human breath, drifts to them over the lake, from the roses, wallflowers, lemon groves, and eucalyptus trees of the Isola San Giovanni. Leaning back, Marie trails her bare arm in the ripples of the wake; Barois' hand seeks hers, and the smooth coolness of the water caresses their two wrists.

Seven o'clock chimes in a campanile and from the farther bank the echo sends back the seven strokes, thudding like a distant gong.

They are rowed back to Pallanza. Julie awaits them at the entrance of the hotel, two telegrams in her hand.

The telegrams announce the death of Mme Pasquelin.

Nine that evening. His suitcase packed and strapped, Barois is leaning on the balcony of his bedroom. Before him stretches the lake, bathed in pearly light. Immediately below is the public square, shrill with life. Somewhere a band is playing, streetcars clang, shouts and laughter fill the air. Ablaze with lights, a big lake steamer disgorges its human cargo on the landing stage.

Dear child! This fortnight she has given me—ah, what happiness! . . . But how lonely I'm going to feel now!

Suddenly all the lamps on the steamer go out, and from a black mass spangled with lights it becomes a white mass pitted with black holes, like the floating carcass of some sea monster. As small waves lap the hull, it slowly sways, and exhales its little life remaining in wavering puffs of smoke.

In the death chamber at Buis the customary death vigil is taking place. The light from two tall tapers falls on the coifs of kneeling nuns. Utterly worn out, Cécile is slumped in an armchair, her smarting eyelids half closed. Her thoughts speed towards Marie, now on her way back. She'll be here first thing in the morning and then I shan't be alone. But in the background of her mind another thought is hovering: *They* will be here quite soon.

She recalls all that she has learnt about Jean from her daughter and from Julie. She draws her hand across her forehead. He'll find me terribly changed. Why, it's eighteen years since we last saw each other! And suddenly memory casts across the screen a picture of the man he was in his early thirties.

Hastily she rises to her feet, and, to fix her wandering thoughts on the dead woman, goes back to the bedside and kneels down.

Since his coming to Buis, Barois has not left his hotel bedroom. The walls ooze moisture, which settles on his shoulders like a clammy mist. He has been crouching over the fire all day; his cheeks are burn-

ing and cold shivers run down his back. Now and again he casts a
glance at Marie's letter.

My dear Father: The funeral service will take place tomorrow
morning, but Mother says she would rather you did not attend. She
is greatly touched by your sympathy and asks me to tell you that if
you are still at Buis tomorrow afternoon, she would greatly like to
thank you personally for your kindness to me. Please come at six;
everyone will have gone by then.

Your affectionate daughter,
Marie

At nightfall a fit of restlessness comes over Barois and he goes out
into the gathering darkness. He begins by walking in the Lower
Town, as if deliberately avoiding the place that lures him like a mag-
net. That evening calm he knows so well broods on the streets. Here
nothing has changed for many years; the movable counters on the
pavements are being taken in for the night, the same decrepit omnibus lumbers past, the same shop signs creak in the wind at the street-
corners. As it was in the beginning . . . !

He walks rapidly up the hill towards the church. The road seems
steeper than in the past and he is out of breath, his heart is thudding,
when after passing the presbytery he enters "his" street.

It is empty and that same cold wind is sweeping it. That was his
grandmother's house. His gaze lingers on the windows, those of the
room where his father died, those of his old bedroom. On the portico
is a notice-board: To let. The black church tower looms in the background.

A few steps bring him to the Pasquelins' house. Cécile is there,
and Marie. A yellow glow filters between the slats of the shutters at
one window; that of the death chamber, no doubt.

A flood of childhood memories sweeps over him as he stands and
gazes. A clock strikes in the church tower. Familiar chimes! Tears

come to his eyes. The wind is freshening, he shivers and turns up the collar of his overcoat. Then, his teeth chattering, he hurries back to the hotel.

The fire is out. He rings, and has it relit; then stretches his legs towards the glow. Pictures form in the leaping flames—of Cécile, of Abbé Joziers, of his wedding day. What a blunder that marriage was!

He is trembling with cold and nervous exasperation, beset by sombre memories. Ah, how hard it is to shape one's life aright!

Next day, at six in the evening, Barois rings the bell at the Pasquelins' house. He is feverish, coughing. The door is closed. The bell has exactly the same timbre; the clatter of clogs on the tiles as the maid comes to the door is exactly the same. A local provincial phrase comes to his mind: "The 'wont' of the house."

Wearing deep mourning, Cécile is sitting at her bureau in the small drawing-room. In front of her is a pile of mourning cards to be sent out to friends, and she is addressing the envelopes. She is so unlike what he expected that he finds it easy to behave like a stranger.

BAROIS: "Need I say how deeply I sympathize with you, Cécile?"

She has risen to her feet and is gazing at him. He is much thinner than she had expected, and there is something new and baffling in his expression.

CÉCILE: "Thank you, Jean."

She holds out her hand. He presses it with the discreet warmth appropriate to a visit of condolence.

He too is startled at finding her so greatly changed. Somehow he had failed to realize that on her, as well, the wear-and-tear of eighteen years must have left its mark. Still, this middle-aged woman in black is unmistakably the Cécile he knew; she has the same big forehead, the same slight squint, the same faint, nervous lisp. A moment ago he could not even have pictured the Cécile of today in his imagination; but now he cannot conceive her having aged otherwise.

Marie breaks the silence.

MARIE: "Here's a chair for you, Father."

CÉCILE, sitting down: "I must thank you for the welcome you gave Marie. You were very nice to her, Jean, and I'm most grateful."

BAROIS, impulsively: "But that was only natural!" He feels suddenly embarrassed and adds hastily: "Was your mother conscious in her last moments?"

CÉCILE: "No. But she was prepared for death. She had partaken of the Sacrament so often after her first attack. Anyhow, on the last day she was almost completely paralysed, and her mind had gone." She weeps. "She didn't recognize anybody, not even me."

The whimper in her voice evokes unlooked-for echoes in his mind.

MARIE: "Mother, we must give Father one of Grandmother's last photos."

Cécile casts a hasty glance at Jean, who lowers his eyes.

CÉCILE, rather doubtfully: "Certainly, darling, if you'd like to."

Marie goes out. They are alone for some moments. Their eyes meet, then turn uneasily away. Each is obscurely hoping for the word of healing, of reconcilement. But then the door opens and Marie steps between them. The moment has slipped away, and now they can part, there is nothing more to say.

6

Paris, April 25

Mademoiselle: I make bold to write and let you know that Monsieur Barois has been seriously ill since his return to Paris, with pleurisy, and has got so weak he hardly speaks at all. The doctor came to see him this morning with two other doctors. They stayed a long while with Monsieur and told me they would send a nurse. They also asked me if Monsieur had any relations. I feel it my duty, Mademoiselle, to let you know of this.

Yours obediently,
Jules Pascal

Two days later Marie is at Barois' bedside, with the doctor. Cécile has stayed behind in the hall. Since there is now no urgent reason for her presence at Buis, she has decided to come to Paris with her daughter. In view of her father's serious condition Marie has settled into her old room. At a loss what to do, Cécile has taken a room in a near-by boarding-house, which she leaves only to come to the flat for news of the invalid.

The doctor leaves the bedroom, followed by Marie.

MARIE: "Please come back soon, Doctor. We feel so helpless when you're not here." She looks utterly worn out and wearily buries her head on her mother's shoulder. Cécile no longer dares to question her. "It's terrible how he's changed since only yesterday. The doctor is very anxious and he's arranging for another consultation this evening. He doesn't want to risk tapping the pleural cavity again without a colleague's opinion."

CÉCILE, in a broken voice: "Is he in much pain?"

MARIE: "A little less now." She bursts into tears. "But the nurse says it's a bad sign. No, let me be; it does me good to cry. Oh, it's simply heart-rending. He called me by name just now, and he spoke your name twice." There is a short silence. Then, impulsively. "Mother, go in and see him."

Cécile does not refuse; it's the last time, death is on the threshold. She is aghast at the thought of this irreparable event that is to put the seal on their rupture, for all eternity. But never has she felt her wrongs so poignantly. She walks through the study, carefully refraining from looking round her, and enters the bedroom. Her eyes fall on the bed, the haggard face upon the pillow.

He opens his eyes, and shows not the least surprise at seeing her here. She clasps his hand and is about to press her lips to it. But he draws her near him and, raising himself a little, puts his arm round her. His eyes are full of horror and dismay.

BAROIS: "Cécile, my dear, I'm going to die."

Crushing back her tears, Cécile shakes her head.

The nurse comes in with cupping-glasses. Pascal props up his master while Marie peels off the layers of cotton-wool. The three of them bend over the sick man. Cécile has a glimpse of white skin.

She moves away. A sense of profound discouragement has come over her; she feels so useless here, a mere visitor, with her crape veil, black gloves. She casts a last glance at the bed, hurries to the door, and, once she is outside, her tears flow freely.

Three weeks later. Wrapped in a heavy rug, Barois is lying on a sofa in his study. He gazes up anxiously at Breil-Zoeger, who is standing at his side.

BREIL-ZOEGER, continuing the description he has been giving: "We all attended."

BAROIS: "Who was the chief mourner?"

BREIL-ZOEGER: "Colonel Cresteil, his father—in full uniform."

BAROIS: "Ah, so his father was still alive! He never said a word about him."

BREIL-ZOEGER: "He was always secretive about his private life."

BAROIS: "And you still haven't discovered why he made that journey to Geneva?"

BREIL-ZOEGER: "No. But I assume he went there simply to kill himself. Cresteil was bound to end like that. Rather touching in their way, the precautions he took. He burnt everything that might lead to his identification; he even shaved off his moustache, in the train. It took the police four days to find out who he was. Curious, isn't it, that fixed resolve of his, not merely to die, but utterly to vanish from the face of the earth?"

BAROIS, his eyes full of tears: "Ah, my dear Zoeger, sometimes life seems too, too . . ."

He leaves the phrase unfinished. Breil-Zoeger makes no comment. With his shrewd yellow eyes he is busily assessing the havoc pleurisy has wrought on Barois.

Barois used to have a thick crop of curly black hair; within a few weeks much of it has fallen out. His eyes are deeply sunken, void of energy, and the eyelids weigh heavy upon them. He lies huddled limply on the sofa; the hands resting on the rug look flabby, inert.

BAROIS, with a wan smile: "I suppose you find me greatly changed?"

BREIL-ZOEGER, in the quietly trenchant tone that is his wont: "I do." A short silence.

BAROIS: "I've had a rotten time, you know."

Breil-Zoeger scrutinizes him coldly, without commenting. Then he rises, preparatory to leaving.

BREIL-ZOEGER: "Woldsmuth's undertaken the obituary notice. I'll tell him to bring it to you."

BAROIS: "No, he needn't bother. I'm not fit for any work yet. I leave everything in your hands. By the way, before you go, would you give me a volume of *The Sower?* Nineteen hundred—the second half-year. Thanks."

Left to himself, he flutters the pages impatiently; his obsession has come back again. At last he finds the article whose memory has been haunting him, skims through it, then slowly rereads the concluding phrases:

Why fear death? Is it so different from life? Human existence is no more than a continuous sequence of states of being; death is but one more transformation. Why, then, fear it? What is there so dreadful in ceasing to be that temporarily assembled whole which we are at each successive moment? How can we fear the restitution of our elements to the inorganic stuff of the universe, since this is also a sure return to complete unconsciousness?

For me, personally, once I understood the nothingness awaiting me, the problem of death ceased to exist. Indeed, I find that the thought that my personality is not immortal, and the certainty that my span of consciousness is limited, give me all the more zest for living, while life lasts.

He lets the book fall on his knees, amazed at what he once dared to write, *without knowing.*

Pascal opens the door. Cécile enters; then Marie.

MARIE: "How are you feeling today, Father?"

BAROIS: "Better, my dear, much better. Good morning, Cécile. It's very kind of you to come to see me." Marie stoops towards him; he kisses her, then says with a smile: "There's nothing like illness for teaching us how much we need others."

Cécile has settled into a chair, in the full light of the window, and Barois is struck by the forlorn look on her face. Marie is standing near her; she too has been weeping.

MARIE, noticing her father's inquiring look: "I've spoken to Mother about my vocation. And I told her you'd given your consent."

BAROIS, quickly: "My consent? But, Marie, there was no need for that."

Cécile shows surprise.

CÉCILE: "So you knew about Marie's intention before I did, Jean? Surely you tried to dissuade her?"

MARIE, looking earnestly at Barois: "Please, Father, say exactly how you feel about it."

BAROIS, mustering his ideas with an effort, turns to Cécile: "I raised objections, of course. But really it's too remote from me, the call that Marie's heard, for me to understand what it means to her. So when I saw how set on it she was, and how happy at the prospect, well—"

He breaks off; to have completed what he meant to say would have reopened old wounds, whose scars he now respects. He gazes sadly at his wife and daughter, each of whom is suffering through the other.

Marie is still standing. In her gaze is no vitality, only a tenacity of purpose, to which the stubborn little chin lends emphasis. A picture rises before Barois—of Cécile in the year of the final break between them.

It is only now he realizes how vastly Cécile herself has changed; all the obstinacy has gone, the lethargy given place to simple human grief. Tears flow down her cheeks. She is cruelly torn between two emotions, her motherly instinct up in arms against her faith. She cannot bring herself to yield up her daughter, even to God.

CÉCILE, in an uncontrollable rush of emotion: "Oh, it was easy enough for you to give in to her, Jean! What did it matter to you whether she lived with me at Buis or in a convent? But think what it means for me! What's to become of my life if she goes away and I am left alone in the world?"

Involuntarily Marie makes a vague gesture, and her gaze roves from Barois' face to her mother's. They understand and look away uneasily. Neither speaks.

XII. THE CRITICAL AGE

Nostra vita a che val?
Leopardi

I

EIGHTEEN months later, at the *Sower* building. It is a Thursday, the editor's reception day. Barois is in his office, talking to Portal.

PORTAL: "You write in it much less, of course."

BAROIS: "Quite true, but I'm not so conceited as to think that's the real reason. And don't forget *The Sower* has plenty of new blood nowadays, and some of our younger contributors are really brilliant."

PORTAL: "The truth, no doubt, is that you have against you what I call 'the new reaction.' It's the same thing in all fields of thought."

Barois, who seems to feel the cold, draws nearer to the fire. His shoulders hunched, his elbows resting on his knees, he huddles up in a low chair wedged against the fender.

BAROIS: "Yes, we're back numbers, that's the truth of it. And why not? Change is a law of life." He stretches his hands to the flames. "Even I can feel it when I write, I haven't the old fire. Not that I bring less conviction to what I say, but—how shall I put it?—owing to the mere lapse of time, my sincerity has become something ready-made, a technique, almost a mannerism."

A short silence follows.

PORTAL, to give the conversation a more cheerful turn: "How about that study of modern youth you've been working at? I hope you haven't dropped it."

BAROIS: "No. In fact I'm expecting a visit today in connexion with it." Wearily. "But really I was wrong to embark on it at all. Frankly these young people baffle me. I haven't written a line on the subject

303

for a month. But of course the business of moving has thrown all my work into arrears."

PORTAL: "Have you fixed up your new quarters to your liking?"

BAROIS, gloomily: "More or less." He walks over to the window. "You see those three windows up there? It's cramped, but I'll get used to it. The old apartment was becoming a bit of a burden." He smiles. "It's a period of financial stringency, as they say in official circles." He obviously takes pleasure in imparting to a friend these details of his private life. "Really, my dear fellow, it was a stroke of luck, my finding those rooms. When I was in my old quarters I had to stay at home in wet or foggy weather. But now I'm living up there, I can step across in any weather, provided I wrap myself up well."

PORTAL, moving towards the door: "Well, good-bye for the present. I'll pay you a surprise visit in your eyrie one evening soon and we'll have a good long talk."

BAROIS: "Do, old chap. It'll be like old times."

Left to himself, he stares at the fire for some moments; then rises, takes some papers from a filing-cabinet, and settles down at his desk.

Some minutes pass. He jots down notes in the margins, then abruptly pushes away the sheets of paper and rings.

BAROIS, to the office-boy: "Would you see if Monsieur Dalier is in the editorial room?"

The man who enters some moments later is a youth of twenty-five, of small stature and short-legged, but with a sturdy chest and a strikingly large head. His clean-shaven face is glabrous, the thin lips have a slightly disdainful twist, his eyes twinkle ironically behind pince-nez.

Barois leans back in his chair and gazes thoughtfully at the young man.

BAROIS: "I've just read your article, my boy, and, to speak quite candidly, it won't do, it won't do at all. I wouldn't say it's badly constructed, but it cannot possibly be published, as it stands, in our review." Dalier remains standing, puzzled, on his guard. Barois selects some pages and hands them to him. "Look at these passages. If they really convey your ideas regarding the religious emotion—well, so much the worse for you! *The Sower* certainly cannot endorse them."

DALIER: "Sorry, sir, but I simply don't follow. That was the angle from which Monsieur Breil-Zoeger told me to—"

BAROIS, with a sharpness unlike his normal self: "Monsieur Breil-Zoeger is entitled to his own ideas. But I am the editor of the review. And, so long as I remain in charge of it, I shall certainly not allow so narrow-minded, so bigoted, an article to appear in its columns." A flush has come to his cheeks, followed by a sudden pallor. Dalier makes a move towards the door. Barois slowly draws his hand across his forehead, then motions Dalier to a chair. He now speaks in a friendly, no longer hectoring, tone. "Can't you understand, Dalier, that in this article you've deliberately shut your eyes to one aspect of the truth? Of course that made things easier for you—but it's not playing fair. I too have insisted all my life long on the bankruptcy of religion; indeed, I believe I have contributed to it. But the bankruptcy of *dogmatic* religion, not that of the religious emotion." He hesitates. "Well, it's possible that I may on occasion have failed to draw a clear distinction; the reason was that I hadn't realized what the religious emotion really is and that, by its very nature, it lies outside the ambit of the critical intellect." He looks Dalier in the eyes. "It's the dogmatic side of a religion that's founded in futility. But religious emotion is a very real thing and—believe me, my dear Dalier—it's sheer nonsense to deny its reality. I'm entitled to say this, as I too once denied it. Any given art form becomes out of date, but art itself survives, isn't that so? Well, it's much the same with religion."

Dalier says nothing, but his look conveys total dissent.

BAROIS: "For one thing, you're too young to be able to pass a balanced judgment on such matters. You've only just come through your first religious crisis, if I may call it so, and naturally you're all for complete, unqualified emancipation."

DALIER, with calm self-assurance: "There's never been the least religious crisis in my life so far, and I think I'm safe in saying there will never be one."

Barois smiles incredulously.

DALIER, sulkily: "I assure you, sir, that you quite misjudge me. Atheism is in my blood. My father and grandfather were atheists. So there was no occasion for a conflict between my intellect and my emotions. I *knew* that heaven was empty, and never had a qualm of doubt about it. And when I reached the age of reason I realized without an effort that all events are linked up as causes and effects, that the law of causation operates blindly, aimlessly, and that nothing in the universe justifies us in supposing there is any directive power behind it or any progress along a given line. Things just happen—and that's all there is to it!"

BAROIS, after gazing at him curiously: "I grant you that people may exist who are utterly devoid of any religious sense—just as, for instance, colour-blind people exist. But obviously these are exceptions, and they have no right to generalize on the strength of their own—peculiarities. Indeed, since you have no idea what religious emotion means, why write about it? What can you have to say on a subject which lies wholly outside your range? Your logic leads you to conclusions which may seem to you self-evident, conclusive; and yet every religious mind will reject them, I assure you, as being utterly incapable of accounting for certain intensely real forms of human experience."

DALIER: "But, sir, I've heard you say, yourself, dozens of times—"

BAROIS, regretfully: "Perhaps. But today I tell you this. Though dogmas may have had their day, the religious emotion will persist. Under another form, I grant you. You've only got to look around you and you'll see that all the attacks of rationalism have failed to eradicate it. On the contrary, religious sentiment is permeating our civic life more and more. You will also find it present in the attempts that are being made all over the world to defend the cause of justice, to ensure a happier future for all classes and a fairer distribution of property and duties. Faith, hope, and charity. These are precisely the virtues which, though I mayn't have used these names, I have tried my best to put into practice ever since I freed myself from the dogmas of my upbringing. Surely, then, it's only a question of words. What's the obscure force that urges me towards right conduct if not a deep-seated religious feeling which has survived my loss of faith? And whence do they come, our aspirations towards self-improvement and the betterment of the world, if not from some such source?

"No, say what you like, the human mind is fundamentally religious. That we must accept as a datum. That craving to believe is as much part of our make-up as the need to breathe." He notices that Dalier seems to want to put in a word. "Yes? Tell me what you think."

DALIER: "That craving you speak of has been invoked, time and again, to justify prejudice and sheer delusion."

Barois gazes at him earnestly and seems momentarily doubtful how to proceed.

BAROIS: "Well, let's grant that there have been erroneous beliefs, but don't forget that these beliefs, mistaken as they were, often promoted the well-being of humanity at that stage of its evolution. Can we not say that, viewed from a strictly human angle, these errors may seem uncommonly like truths?"

DALIER, with a faint grin: "Well, Monsieur Barois, really I'm surprised to hear you, of all people, championing the cause of error!"

Barois does not reply at once. Then, leaning forward and gazing at the floor, he continues.

BAROIS: "That, my dear Dalier, is because I've learnt that there are people—people who nobly live and love and are beloved—to whom illusion is infinitely more necessary than truth; for the good reason that it is something they can assimilate *in toto,* it enables them to carry on. Whereas, given pure truth, they'd die of inanition, like fish on dry land. And, in dealing with people of this kind, we aren't justified, no, we have not the right—" He looks up and sees

Dalier's eyes intent upon him. "Yes, I can guess what you're thinking. 'The chief's a back number! His brain is going!'" He smiles
without bitterness. "You may be right, who knows? And yet—!

"Truth at all costs, and nothing but the truth—that's always the
slogan of eager youth. But with more experience we become less
categorical; we allow for the possibility of provisional, personal
error, we prefer indulgence to strict justice." He pauses. "What
else can you expect? A man is bound to modify his views as he
grows older. One gives thirty consecutive years to a long effort to
make life fuller, richer, more harmonious—and then, looking back,
one sees how pathetically little has been accomplished. Sometimes
one even wonders if, on a long view, any new order is really better
than the old one. All these things are so relative—how can one help
contradicting oneself? When a man is honest and when, year after
year, he has acquired a solid apprehension of realities, it's impossible
for him to be merely logical."

DALIER, harshly: "You mean, I take it, that a man's incapable of
following the dictates of pure, unemotional reason to the end?"

BAROIS, who has not noticed this interjection: "One's young—and
don't I know what youth is!—and one goes forward happily, confidently, until a moment comes when one understands that all this
has an end. And once that hour has struck . . . ! Oh, you've had
good notice, there's plenty of time to get used to the idea. Yet it's
so gradual you hardly know what's happening, to start with. You
find your self-confidence, your enthusiasm, waning, and you ask
yourself, 'What's wrong with me nowadays?' And then you feel
you're being dragged backwards, gently but persistently—and there's
nothing to be done about it! When that process starts, my boy, as
you'll discover for yourself, one takes a very different view of life."

He smiles forlornly. Dalier, however, feels a thrill of youthful
triumph, the zest of the young athlete snatching the torch from
trembling hands.

DALIER, briskly: "Anyhow, I can't see my way to making changes in
the article, to bring it into line with your present views."

The office-boy enters and hands Barois a visiting card.

BAROIS: "Tell him to wait. I'll ring."

DALIER: "I'd have to rewrite the whole thing, and that I can't bring myself to do."

BAROIS: "Very well. Have it your own way."

When Dalier has left Barois goes to the fireplace, pokes the fire, and rings. Suddenly he shrugs his shoulders. I behaved like a fool. I should have put my foot down, firmly!

Two young men of twenty or thereabouts are ushered in.

BAROIS: "Monsieur de Grenneville?"

GRENNEVILLE: "That's I. May I introduce my friend, Maurice Tillet, who's at the École Normale?"

De Grenneville is a slim youth of middle height, dressed with quiet distinction. He has well-shaped if rather commonplace features. There is something typically French in his appearance. He has a small, fair moustache and candid eyes, but there is a hint of self-complacent irony in the curve of his lips. Generally he shows that mixture of assurance and reserve which a good student at a religious institution retains—until his first love affair.

Tillet is much taller, robust almost to the point of ungainliness. His face is all angles, with shrewd, alert brown eyes, a long nose, large mouth, and an incipient black beard. He has a trick of thrusting his big hands into his pockets when he is about to speak, and then, on second thought, taking them out abruptly.

DE GRENNEVILLE: "The letter you received in answer to your questionnaire was written jointly, by both of us."

BAROIS: "Please sit down, gentlemen. It's kind of you to come to see me." To de Grenneville. "As I told you in my letter, I intend to publish your paper *in extenso*. It's quite the most interesting one that has come in so far. But as I have to supplement it with"—he smiles—"some critical comments, I am very glad of the opportunity of having a talk with you." To Tillet. "Are you still at the École Normale?"

TILLET: "Yes, sir. I'm just beginning my second year."

barois: *"Literae humaniores,* I suppose?"

tillet: "No. Science."

barois, to de Grenneville: "And I presume you're working for a professorial degree in philosophy?"

de grenneville: "No, sir. At present I'm studying law and doing my last year in political economy."

Barois glances through a bulky file that is lying on his desk; then, with some effort, concentrates on certain pages.

barois: "There's one thing in your reply which, I must confess, gave me a most disagreeable impression, and it's the complete contempt you seem to have for your elders, whatever they may have achieved. Please take my word for it that I'm not voicing a personal grievance; it's the principle behind it that dismays me. For it's not just that juvenile bumptiousness with which we are familiar. No, your arrogance has something solid, well thought-out, behind it." He smiles. "The young men of my generation, too, were convinced that they were right, but we showed more deference, or so it seems to me, to pioneers of the older generation. We had, in fact, a sort of modesty behind our cocksureness; or, to speak more accurately, a feeling that possibly, just possibly, we might be mistaken. You, however, seem quite positive that you alone represent all that is best in modern French youth.

"Well, that's an open question. Don't forget that the nationalism you preach is, if you look closely into it, an anomaly. It's not a normal attitude for a nation; it's a fighting attitude and involves rattling of the patriotic sabre."

de grenneville, with boyish truculence: "Precisely. I agree it is regrettable that, at the moment, France has to make a painful effort to dislodge from her system a germ which might well prove fatal— like a healthy organism getting rid of a foreign body lodged within it."

barois: "Yes? And what is the germ you have in mind?"

de grenneville, aggressively: "Just—anarchy!"

He pauses, waiting for a brisk reaction, but Barois gazes at him placidly.

DE GRENNEVILLE, with a faint smile: "I believe you will agree, sir, that a wave of anarchy is sweeping the country. A controlled, intellectualized anarchy, which makes no stir but is making steady progress and sapping our national energy. There's no question as to its origins. When the majority of the nation abandoned its traditional beliefs, it also lost its criteria of judgment, all that makes for a stable national life."

BAROIS: "But what you call anarchy is simply the manifestation of a nation's intellectual vitality. Dogmas are as out of place in ethics as in religion. The moral law is simply an an aggregate of social conventions, which, if it's to serve any practical purpose, has to evolve along with the social order to which it is applied. And this evolution is only possible if there exists within the social order that ferment which you call anarchic, the intellectual leaven that gives rise to progress."

TILLET: "If you can call it 'progress'—the series of futile social convulsions which are enfeebling France!"

BAROIS: "If the transitions are abrupt, that's because the phases follow each other at shorter and shorter intervals. In the past morality changed from one century to another, now it changes with a single generation. That's a fact we've got to face."

There is a short silence. The youths exchange glances.

TILLET: "We're not greatly surprised to hear you defending the present state of anarchy. Like most men of your generation, you went to school with our revolutionary writers, men who detested every stable institution."

BAROIS, jestingly: "Taine, for instance?"

TILLET: "Yes, Taine. From Goethe down to Renan, Flaubert, Tolstoy, Ibsen—they're all tarred with the same brush!"

Still smiling, Barois shrugs his shoulders.

DE GRENNEVILLE, with quiet pity: "In fact the whole nineteenth century, from the '89 Declarations to Jaurès, not to mention Lamartine and Gambetta *en passant,* was doped with that romantic humbug. All through the century you'll find the same highfalutin verbiage —picturesque, I grant you, but devoid of any guiding principle or common sense."

TILLET: "Or, as I should say, bursting with good intentions, but without the faintest inkling of realities. Not the ghost of a logical argument; the merest vapourings! Not the least relevance between the terms employed and social facts!"

BAROIS, conciliatingly: "But don't you agree that *all* words, whatever they are, are bound to have their meanings rubbed away when they've been bandied on the market-place for a hundred years? And though you may reject those 'romantic' words as drained of all content, yet you too, whether you wanted to or not, have absorbed from them all they had to give."

Both young men make protesting gestures.

BAROIS: "Well, take your own case. Don't you think that you too may be doping yourselves with pretentious words?" He picks up the file of answers to the questionnaire and shows it to them. "Look there! And there! 'Discipline.' 'Heroism.' 'Reconstruction.' 'Our national prestige.' May it not well be that fifteen years hence all that high-flown jargon will seem equally devoid of any useful meaning?"

DE GRENNEVILLE: "Quite possibly those terms may go out of fashion; but the realities they stand for will remain. Nationalism and classicism aren't vague expressions; they stand for clean-cut ideas, in fact the clearest, most inspiring ideas current in France today."

TILLET: "I suspect that the misunderstanding arises from our using the word 'idea' in a different sense from yours. To our mind, any notion which isn't rooted in active life so solidly as to form a vital part of it isn't worthy of the name of an idea. It's nothing, a mere empty sound. I grant you we may say that life is governed by ideas, but these governing ideas are worthless unless they spring from life itself, are fed by it and ruled by it."

DE GRENNEVILLE: "Your generation, Monsieur Barois, unlike ours, was satisfied with abstract theories, which not only failed to inspire it with the desire to *do* things, but did much to—to sterilize it." Self-complacently. "Well, that sterile, navel-gazing contemplation may be good enough for Orientals, but, let me tell you, contemporary France, the France that has been through the Agadir crisis and lives under the German threat, has no use for it!"

BAROIS, goaded beyond endurance: "But why do you young people always regard your elders as mere dreamers, incapable of coming out into the open, *doing* things? It's so flagrantly unjust; no, I'd go further, flagrant ingratitude.

"Can you say that the generation which played an active part in the Dreyfus Affair shrank from action? No generation since the Revolution had to fight so hard for its opinions as ours had to; to take such personal risks. Many of us were heroes. If all this is new to you, I suggest you take a course in contemporary history. Don't run away with the idea that because we had analytic minds we were mere dilettanti. No, our enthusiasm for words like Truth and Justice—which seem to you today mere sound and fury!—was, in its time, a spur to action."

A short silence follows.

DE GRENNEVILLE, coldly respectful: "You certainly stake high claims on a brief episode, when some of you thought fit to leave your ivory towers and join in a crusade. And what a crusade, I ask you! But I'd have you note two things: how short the crisis was, and the disillusionment that followed on its heels."

Barois makes no comment.

DE GRENNEVILLE, gently: "No, Monsieur Barois, that generation of yours was not a fighting generation. Therefore its influence was doomed to be short-lived."

TILLET: "Yes, you've only got to see how it behaved in the stormy days of the Affair. All its activities were haphazard, undirected. So much so that today the Dreyfus Affair gives those who were too young to follow it closely the impression of a windy war of leaderless, aimless rowdies, flinging big words at one another's heads!"

DE GRENNEVILLE, sticking to his point: "And look at the results! Look at the charming state of parliamentary government in this country! Why, you yourself have admitted in *The Sower* that your hope came to nothing; that what your precious friends have been doing is a travesty of your intentions."

Barois makes a fretful gesture but finds nothing to say. They are using weapons he himself has forged. And, anyhow, how prevent these raw youths from judging the tree by its fruits alone?

TILLET, summing up: "The people responsible for the degradation into which modern France has sunk are those men who persistently, year after year, have been blind to the true spirit of the country. It's high time for us to discipline ourselves; what we need is a republic in which rights and duties are assigned on a totally new basis."

BAROIS, with evident surprise: "Then you're republicans, you two?"

TILLET: "Certainly."

BAROIS: "Well, I shouldn't have thought it."

TILLET: "Though opinions are terribly divided, and though the royalists are certainly making headway, most of the younger men are staunch democrats."

BAROIS: "I'm glad to hear that."

DE GRENNEVILLE: "Indeed, the country as a whole is democratic."

BAROIS: "Well, I'm surprised to learn that you can reconcile our republican government with your ideas of hierarchy and authoritarianism."

DE GRENNEVILLE: "Why not? It's only a matter of tightening up the present form of government."

TILLET: "It's a matter of making a sweeping reform of parliamentary methods and getting the political virus out of our system. We must divert the conception of popular government—which, incidentally, has no relation to the actual facts—towards a government by groups representing the various professions and other organized bodies. Really it will come to much the same thing, but with order and moderation thrown in."

BAROIS, smiling: "Well, *there* anyhow we can meet on common ground. I greatly hope the rising generation will succeed in setting our political house in order, and see to it that plans for social progress take precedence over inter-party wrangles."

DE GRENNEVILLE, confidently: "That, sir, we shan't have any difficulty in accomplishing, once we have gone further towards bringing the country back to the paths of our traditional morality."

BAROIS, still smiling: "What exactly do you mean by 'our traditional morality'?"

DE GRENNEVILLE: "Catholic morality, obviously."

Barois ceases smiling and gazes at them intently.

BAROIS: "So both of you are Catholics? Practising Catholics?"

DE GRENNEVILLE: "Yes."

BAROIS: "Ah!" He pauses, and now a note of anxiety enters his voice. "Tell me frankly, gentlemen; is it a fact that today the great majority of young people are Catholics?"

DE GRENNEVILLE, after a slight hesitation: "I couldn't really say; all I know is that there are a great many of us. Amongst the youngest, and those who have just left school, there's a definite majority of practising Catholics. Amongst us, who are a few years older, I think I can safely say that there are about as many believers as unbelievers. But most of those who don't believe regret it, and invariably act as if they did believe."

BAROIS: "To speak quite candidly, what you've just said proves to my mind that the latter are, and will remain, impervious to Catholic propaganda."

TILLET: "You say that because you can't enter into their feelings on the subject. If they defend a faith in which they do not share—but which they'd like to share—this is because they have recognized its active virtues. They have personally put these virtues into practice and they find that the fact of being enlisted amongst the defenders of religion gives more scope to their activities. So quite naturally, as reasonable beings, they do their best to further a system of morality which they well know to be the best possible system."

BAROIS, after pondering for some moments: "No, I can't approve of the advocacy of a religion one doesn't believe in; it seems to me a complete *non sequitur*. Your explanation sounds plausible, but it doesn't incline me to judge less severely those chiefs of yours who preach this bogus gospel. What's only too obviously behind it is the aristocratic contempt the masses inspire in them. Indeed, whenever they're hard pressed, they fall back on that line of defence, which is tantamount to saying: 'Religion is made for the masses, like the saddle for the horse; *we*, however, are not beasts of burden.' In other words, they regard Catholicism as an excellent guarantee of social peace. But they prefer to keep the privilege of truth to themselves." He warms to his subject. "Personally, I've always advocated an exactly opposite principle. I consider that our first duty is to make the truth known to all and sundry. We must give men the maximum of freedom without bothering to decide whether or not they are yet qualified to use that freedom as it should be used. For we should bear in mind that freedom is a boon which men learn to turn to good account only by slow degrees, and only by making an excessive use of it to start with."

A polite but hostile silence greets his words. Barois shrugs his shoulders.

BAROIS: "Sorry! I must apologize for this digression. My personal beliefs are neither here nor there. We've met to discuss this letter"—he points to the file—"which you sent to *The Sower*.

"It shows pretty clearly why Catholicism has an inevitable appeal for you; but it doesn't show why you are actually members of the Church. May I assume that you were brought up as Catholics and have kept your faith intact?"

DE GRENNEVILLE: "Yes, that applies to me, anyhow. I had a Catholic education; in fact as a child I was fervently religious. However, in my sixteenth year, my faith underwent an eclipse. But it never failed altogether and it returned to me, quite spontaneously, when I was studying philosophy at the Sorbonne."

BAROIS: "When you were studying philosophy, you say?" He sounds surprised.

DE GRENNEVILLE: "Yes, Monsieur Barois."

Barois makes no comment and turns to Tillet.

BAROIS: "And have you too, Monsieur Tillet, always been a practising Catholic?"

TILLET: "No. My father was a science teacher in a provincial town, and I was brought up in an aggressively free-thinking atmosphere. So it was only later in life that I came to Catholicism, while I was studying at the École Normale."

BAROIS: "Ah! One of those sudden conversions, I suppose?"

TILLET: "Oh, no, there was nothing dramatic about it, no mystical revelation. After trying various ports without success, I 'made the haven where I would be.' That's all. And, once there, I realized that mere common sense would have saved me all the false moves I'd made before. For really it's so obvious that Catholicism, and Catholicism only, provides our generation with what it needs."

BAROIS: "That's where I find it difficult to follow you."

TILLET: "Yet it's quite simple, really. What's indispensable to us, if we are to keep our will to action vital and alert, is a moral discipline behind it. Yes, what we're out for is a fixed, time-proved system, which will definitely rid us of those germs of intellectual unrest we have inherited from you and, try as we may, can't get out of our blood by any other means.

"The Catholic religion provides exactly what we require. It buttresses our personalities with its power and its wisdom, which have stood the test of twenty centuries. The Church exalts our zest for action, because it adapts itself to every aspect of human sensibility and gives a wonderful access of vitality to all who join it without niggling or reserve. Indeed, that's the whole point; what we need today is a faith capable of inspiring us to action and heightening our energies."

BAROIS, who has listened very attentively: "Quite so. But surely this distaste for the speculative intellect that you show so plainly—and, might I add, complacently?—surely it doesn't go so far as to lead you to ignore certain discoveries of modern science that strike at the very heart of the dogmatic religion you profess? How, then, can you believe it as it stands? How reconcile, for instance—"

TILLET, breaking in: "But there's no question of reconciling anything with anything! Religion moves on one plane; science on another. Scientists can never touch religion; its truths lie far outside their reach."

BAROIS: "But, don't forget, modern criticism attacks religion directly, at its very sources."

DE GRENNEVILLE, smiling indulgently: "No, Monsieur Barois, we're not talking the same language. These difficulties you speak of simply don't exist for us. What value can assertions made by some professor of Greek who draws his arguments from a comparison of ancient texts —what value can these have against the certainties our faith has given us?" He laughs. "I assure you I'm staggered by the thought that arguments of that order could have had a decisive influence on our elders' faith."

TILLET: "When all is said and done, the cogency of such historical or philological arguments is only superficial; they can't do anything against the logic of the heart. Once one has personally experienced the practical efficacy of faith—"

BAROIS: "Excuse me, but surely as regards this efficacy on which I notice you keep harping, there are several other philosophical systems which—"

TILLET: "Oh, we've looked into those systems which you have in mind—from your fetish-worship of evolution to the romantic mysticism of your atheist philosophers. No! None of these systems can answer to the spirit that is stirring in France today. We are ready to devote ourselves passionately to a cause, but we insist on its being worth while. Your generation has bequeathed us nothing that can solve any of the problems of practical life."

BAROIS: "Practical life! That seems to be an obsession with you young people. You don't seem to grasp that this pursuit of palpable and immediate ends is bound to play the devil with your intellectual integrity. We of my generation were more disinterested."

DE GRENNEVILLE: "Excuse me, Monsieur Barois, but you've got our meaning wrong." He smiles. "We too, I can assure you, use our brains, and I'd even say that our thoughts sometimes reach a very high level.

But they never lose themselves in the clouds—and that's undoubtedly an improvement on the past. We adjust our speculations to actual needs, and we loathe sterile abstractions. We regard them as a cowardly retreat from life and the duties it imposes."

BAROIS: "But that means the death of the intellect!"

TILLET: "No, merely of intellectualism."

BAROIS: "I can only say I'm sorry for you if you've never known the thrill of intellectual adventure, of purely speculative flights of thought."

TILLET: "Anyhow, we knew what we were doing when we elected for the idea of duty, the duty ready to one's hand, instead of those cloudy lucubrations whose only effect is to turn men into pessimists and sceptics. We, Monsieur Barois, have complete confidence in ourselves."

BAROIS: "So I've noticed. We too had confidence in ourselves."

TILLET: "But your confidence hadn't the staying power of ours; you soon lapsed into doubt."

BAROIS: "You seem to think that doubt involves a purely negative attitude. Well, you're greatly mistaken. Or are you going to hold it up against us that we didn't solve the riddle of the universe? Researches made during the last fifty years have proved that most of the dogmatic statements which set up to convey the truth about the natural world were quite beside the mark. There was, anyhow, some merit, even though the truth itself was not attained, in charting out the places where it was *not* to be found."

DE GRENNEVILLE: "In short, you came up against the unknowable, but you failed to assign to it the importance that was its due, as a potential source of energy. You started out from a blind assumption that unbelief was necessarily superior to faith and—"

BAROIS: "So you're so little conscious of your own position as to talk about 'blind assumptions'! Can't you see that you yourselves are indulging in one, the first convenient, ready-made theory that came your way? You remind me of the hermit crab which settles into the first empty shell available. You found yours in Catholicism, and you've shaped yourselves to it so precisely that you now imagine, and make others imagine, that you grew the shell yourself!"

DE GRENNEVILLE, smiling: "Anyhow, it's a method that has its advantages. Why, the mere fact that it makes us feel surer of ourselves speaks in its favour!"

TILLET: "One needs a guiding principle. The great thing is to choose one that has stood the test of time, and then stick to it through thick and thin."

BAROIS, thoughtfully: "Still, I don't see what you gain by it."

DE GRENNEVILLE: "We gain the peace of mind you never found."

BAROIS: "Nor can I see what new or useful contribution you are making to human progress. But I can see quite clearly the harm you're causing—with a deliberately subversive propagation of unrest which interrupts and jeopardizes the good work done by your forerunners and may well hold up their programme without giving anything by way of compensation."

DE GRENNEVILLE: "Our contribution is our zest for action, which, and which alone, can regenerate the soul of France."

BAROIS, losing patience: "But, damn it, you keep on talking of 'action' and of 'life' as if you had a monopoly on them! I assure you no one ever loved life more passionately than I. And yet this zest for life has led me to a position exactly the opposite of yours. It gave you a craving for religious faith, while it led me away from faith, irrevocably." There is a long silence. Barois sounds disheartened when he speaks again. "After all, maybe it's too much to expect humanity to follow the dictates of reason for several consecutive generations."

He falls silent. His last remark had come almost unthinkingly, and now he recognizes it as an echo of something Dalier had said to him reproachfully earlier in the afternoon. Quoting from Dalier! Sadly he wonders: Is it enough that someone contradicts me, no matter from what angle, for me to flare up promptly and start refuting him? Is truth, then, always a mirage? He draws his hand across his forehead and gazes at the two callow, self-assured youngsters. No, *their* truth isn't the last word.

BAROIS: "The wheel turns. I'm old enough to be your father, and there's now no question of our understanding each other. That's normal, after all."

The young men exchange smiles, which wound him to the quick. He stiffens, faces them squarely, and at last sees them for what they are.

BAROIS: "But have no illusions, gentlemen, about the part you're playing. You are reactionaries pure and simple. And the present reaction was so inevitable that you need not pride yourself on being its pioneers. It was bound to come—the swing of the pendulum, the backwash of the wave. But wait and see! The tide is making, slowly but surely."

DE GRENNEVILLE, truculently: "Unless we are at the first stage of an evolution of whose consequences you haven't even an inkling, Monsieur Barois."

BAROIS, harshly: "That's nonsense. An evolutionary process never takes that abrupt, arbitrary, defensive form." He has risen to his feet, chuckling to himself, for he feels the old combative spirit of his youth awake again. He falls to pacing the room, his clenched hands in his pockets, his eyes glowing with the old fire, a mocking smile on his lips. "I don't deny you represent an active group, but yours is an isolated movement without allies and without a future. Your influence is merely episodic. You talk big, you're out to reform the world and start a new era whose Year One will correspond, you naïvely hope, with the beginning of your twentieth. You dogmatize before you've given yourselves time to look around and form any useful opinions.

"Will you allow me to go still further?

"At the origin of your attitude lies an emotion you won't acknowledge—perhaps because it's not a very flattering one, but more probably, I think, because you do not recognize it for what it is. It is a latent sense of fear."

The young men look genuinely outraged.

"Yes. Behind those fine words, 'order,' 'discipline,' 'national spirit,' there's a trace of what you see in them; but there's something more, and something less exalted—the vulgar instinct of self-preservation.

"From your earliest days you have had a presentiment that the established order was doomed to break up under the steady pressure of the movements set on foot in the nineteenth century. You feared that, by dint of hewing at the base of the half-dead tree on which you had your nests, those doddering old impotents, your elders, would one day bring it down with a crash and pitch you head-foremost into a future too precarious for your liking. So, instinctively, you exalt all that can shore up that tottering tree a few years more. Up with the priests! Up with the police! What the country needs is a strong hand—and so forth! Everything, in short, that can serve as a barrier to the freedom of others. For their freedom, as you well knew, would mean inconvenience to you personally; their gain would be your loss. Progress was rolling on a bit too fast, so you jammed on the brakes. Your heads are none too good, and the speed was making you dizzy.

"All that talk about 'activity' is an attempt to cover up the present enfeeblement of French thought—which seems to need a spell of rest after blazing so many trails into the unknown. Moreover, it's not the first time this has happened; there once was another group of over-privileged persons who did not dare to join in the Revolution; and some of them paid for this with their necks."

The young men have risen to their feet, and their hostile, if deferential, attitude infuriates Barois. All that his outburst has evoked from these impertinent youngsters is the condescending smile bestowed by adolescence on an "old fogy." All are silent for some moments.

DE GRENNEVILLE: "I hope you will excuse us for not sharing your views on this subject. . . . Well, I think we've said all we had to say."

BAROIS, shaking hands with them: "Thanks for coming to see me. Your letter will appear in its entirety. And it will be for the public to judge."   ,

DE GRENNEVILLE, as he is going out: "So you are convinced, sir, that your generation 'blazed new trails into the unknown'?" He smiles. "That's just as well, otherwise you and your friends would have a dismal old age in store. I'll merely venture to remind you how little

those famous truths of yours, which were to free men's minds, actually freed those of most of your contemporaries."

BAROIS, coldly: "You may be right. But they'll bring complete freedom to our children." He smiles. "And to yours too, gentlemen."

2

On her way up the *Sower* staircase Marie encounters a little old man
coming down.

MARIE: "Good afternoon, Doctor."

THE DOCTOR, raising his hat: "Mademoiselle . . . ?"

MARIE: "I'm Monsieur Barois' daughter."

THE DOCTOR, affably: "Oh, excuse me, Mademoiselle Barois. I didn't
recognize you."

MARIE: "I'm glad we've met, Doctor. I want to know your impression of my father's health." She opens the door of an empty office.
"Can you spare a few minutes?"

THE DOCTOR, following her into the room: "Really you're wrong to
feel alarmed. His present condition is satisfactory—I might say, very
satisfactory. In a few days' time—"

Marie signs to him to stop and holds him with her forthright gaze.

MARIE: "Please speak quite frankly, Doctor. And, first, let me explain how things stand with me. I am entering a convent in Belgium
very shortly. Within a few months I'll be seeing my father for the last
time." She masters her emotion. "Forgive me for mentioning these
personal matters, but I want you to understand. I'm not thinking so
much about the present attack. But I realize that my father has something seriously wrong with him; he's changed so terribly within the
last two years."

THE DOCTOR: "I fear there's no denying that Monsieur Barois' general condition is far from satisfactory." He pulls himself up. "Still,
the disease he suffers from need not prevent his having many years
of life ahead, provided he looks after himself and runs no unnecessary risks. And don't forget it's normal for a man of your father's age to have troubles of that kind."

MARIE, her face hardening: "I wish to know the truth. There's no hope of his recovering, is there?"

The doctor hesitates; then, seeing the insistence of her gaze, decides at last to be frank and shakes his head. A short silence follows.

THE DOCTOR: "But, as I said before, a sufferer from this complaint may have many years of life before him. Overwork and especially public speaking have gradually weakened his heart. We must remember, too, that as a child your father showed symptoms of—er—anemia. Drastic measures were taken then, and it's clear they were successful; for over forty years there was no recurrence of the symptoms. Then, unfortunately, he had that attack of pleurisy—how many years ago was it?"

MARIE: "Two."

THE DOCTOR: "And something happened then which often happens in such cases. The inflammation of the bronchi makes it easier for the germs to infiltrate and suddenly revives the latent tuberculosis." He notices Marie's look of surprise. "Yes, this often happens even after forty years' respite, and the old lesions become active again. But let me repeat, my dear young lady; with persons of your father's age diseases of this kind progress very slowly. The symptoms are attenuated, and there are long periods of quiescence between attacks."

MARIE, gazing earnestly at the doctor: "Then what he's just had was one of these attacks?"

THE DOCTOR: "Yes, a very mild one. Your father caught cold the other day and it was enough to affect his general health."

MARIE: "I'm much obliged, Doctor. That was all I wanted to know."

Barois' flat consists of two small rooms and a kitchen. He is lying on a sofa at the window, watching the people moving about in the courtyard below. Her sleeves rolled up, an overall covering her dress, Marie is tidying the room.

BAROIS: "Please don't bother, Marie. My charwoman will see to all that tomorrow morning."

MARIE: "Doesn't she come in the evening?"

BAROIS, smiling: "No."

MARIE: "Then who cooks your dinner?"

BAROIS: "That worthy woman, the concierge." He smiles again. "For a man by himself, you know, the evening meal's a very simple affair."

MARIE, after a short silence: "Own up, Father; you miss Pascal. Didn't I tell you you would?"

BAROIS, awkwardly: "Not a bit of it! I'm well looked after, I get everything I need. Anyhow, there's no room here for a servant."

For some moments neither speaks. Marie goes on tidying up; Barois follows her movements with his eyes. When at one moment she passes near the sofa, he takes her hand and presses his lips to it. She smiles. But the eyes of both are dark with unspoken thoughts.

BAROIS, fondling Marie's hand: "I'd been looking forward so much to this week of yours in Paris, before you begin your novitiate. And now it's all been spoilt by this wretched illness; you've had to spend your time nursing a sick man."

MARIE: "You'll come to see me at Wassignies?" She reddens; the mere thought of the convent has quickened her emotions.

BAROIS: "But surely novices are cloistered like the nuns?"

MARIE: "Yes. But their relations are allowed to come to say good-bye to them the day before they take the veil."

BAROIS: "I wonder if I should come? I expect your mother would like to have you to herself that day." His tone is indifferent, but stealthily he watches her with keen attention. Marie shakes her head emphatically. Barois sounds more cheerful when he speaks again. "And, anyhow, my dear Marie, it's highly problematic if I'll be up to making a trip to Belgium."

3

A sparsely furnished flat in the Passy district of Paris. Luce is sitting at his desk. Seeing Barois enter, he hastily takes off his glasses and goes forward to meet his friend.

LUCE: "Your news was a great shock, my dear Barois. And I simply cannot understand . . ." Barois, who is out of breath after the three flights of stairs, sinks heavily into a chair, pressing his hand to his heart. His smile is a tacit request for a few minutes' breathing space. Luce continues speaking after a brief pause. "Your letter didn't give any real reason for your decision. It seems so—so uncalled for."

BAROIS: "No, old chap, don't try to argue me out of it. My mind's made up." Luce makes an uncomprehending gesture, then goes back to his chair behind the desk. "It was no hasty resolve, I assure you. I've had it in mind for quite a while."

LUCE, gazing earnestly at him: "Start on some new work, Barois, and you will see, you'll soon be your old self again."

BAROIS: "I'm not up to making plans." He frowns. "And in any case I shall soon be going away for a while. That ceremony in Belgium, you know. My daughter . . ."

LUCE, quickly: "Ah, yes. Well, take my advice and wait a bit; don't commit yourself to anything before your return."

Barois guesses the thought behind the words and smiles wryly.

BAROIS: "No, that's not it. The truth is that I'm no longer physically or mentally qualified to run *The Sower*. I've lost that first fine rapture. The public's noticed it, and so have our contributors. The reins are slipping from my hands; it's more and more the young men who are giving the lead. As for me, I'm a mere has-been; what's more, an object of suspicion." He makes a faint grimace. "And friend Breil-Zoeger's been waiting to step into my shoes quite long enough." He takes from his pocket a thick wad of manuscript. "I'd like you to have a look at this when you have time. It's a sort of confession—a swan song, if you prefer. I propose to give an entire number of *The Sower* to it. So as not to slink away like a whipped dog, you see. Yes, a whole number, all to myself. And thereafter I shall hold my peace."

LUCE: "That you'll never be able to do!"

BAROIS: "But why not? As it happens, my doctors advise me to leave Paris and settle down somewhere in the suburbs. I need good air, they say."

LUCE: "A man like you can never resign himself to silence."

BAROIS: "Excuse me, but he can! There comes a stage in a man's life when he must have the sense to call a halt, to look around and take his bearings."

LUCE, bending forward: "Suppose the situation were reversed, and I'd come to you and said, 'I'm throwing up everything, fading out of the picture'?"

BAROIS: "Oh, *you*, my dear Luce! Well, you wouldn't have the right. But that's not *my* case."

LUCE: "There's nothing about me that you can't claim for yourself."

BAROIS: "No. You have the wisdom of the man who takes what comes as it comes. And that makes the difference between happiness and unhappiness."

LUCE, smiling: "But it's so easy to find one's happiness in the satisfactions of the intellect."

BAROIS, savagely: " 'In satisfactions of the intellect'? They've ceased to satisfy *me*. No, I'm sick and tired of the unavailing struggle to make some sense of life."

Luce, who has been seated, his arms folded, gazing at the floor, raises his head at the last remark and lets his thoughtful gaze linger on his friend's face before replying.

LUCE: "Ah, so that's the sore spot? But why be so set on discovering an absolute and final meaning in life? Why spend your days brooding over problems that cannot have a solution?"

BAROIS, with sudden violence: "Why? For the simple reason that, if I personally disappear before finding the key to the mystery, all my efforts will have been wasted. What consolation can it give the living man, Jean Barois, to think that other men, two thousand years hence, will know perhaps a little more than we? It's I, personally, who am tortured by the riddle of existence."

LUCE: "Don't forget that Moses never entered the Promised Land."

BAROIS, with a bitterness he cannot control: "Ah, Luce, I simply can't make you out! Really one would think you'd never given death a serious thought. Still, you've known sorrows and bereavements—after your wife's death, surely."

LUCE, in a toneless voice: "Yes, when that happened, I felt quite desperate. For many, many weeks." He raises his head. "But then one morning in the garden—we were still living in Auteuil at the time—I looked up and saw again the trees, the sunlight, the children. And gradually I climbed up out of the pit."

BAROIS: "But I—well, ever since I felt my end approaching, I have not known a moment's peace. In the old days I told myself, 'Yes, death will come and take me like everybody else.' But"—he presses his hand to his heart—"but now I know *where* it will enter, and everything's different. I feel its claws fixed in me here, in this patch of ailing flesh, and dragging me down into the darkness—me, my work, the joys I'd still have got from living. No, I can't resign myself to that plunge into a never-ending night."

LUCE, after a moment's silence: "We don't see these things from the same angle. Personally, I've always regarded life and death as indivisible, two aspects of the same mysterious process. I've held this view for so many years that I no longer feel the least inclination to rebel."

BAROIS: "Your humility is more than I can manage."

LUCE: "I'm not humble; but I don't rebel either. My spark of being is so infinitely small; I'm used to being a mere fragment of the universe that's working out its destined course. I'm linked up with the past and with the future, and I regard those who will carry on my work after my death as so many prolongations of my personality." He smiles. "As I said just now, I set the highest value on intellectual satisfactions; and the *reasonableness* of death, when one views it thus, makes me accept the fact of dying as readily as the fact of birth."

BAROIS: "I envy you!"

LUCE: "But this acquiescence is within everybody's reach." Barois shakes his head. "I can assure you"—there is now a note of reproach in his voice—"that I'd force myself to react if I felt as paralysed as you do by the thought of death. We men are only a small element of the life of the universe, but perhaps the only element that's conscious of itself; and this consciousness makes it our duty to use life to the utmost. But why should I have to talk like this to you of all people—you who loved life so much?"

BAROIS, despondently: "But, my dear fellow, I love it more than ever, and there's the rub! I can't bear to think of its ending. In fact it's my love of living that makes me rebel against the terms on which life is given us. Why should man have consciousness if it serves only to show him the nonentity awaiting him?" Luce gazes at him without answering. "It's that appalling nothingness I can't get out of my thoughts, try as I may."

LUCE: "You're letting your ego get the whip-hand, as often happens when a man is ageing. His personality becomes more compact, impervious, and the outer world interests him less; he concentrates on his self. But one can, and must, resist that hardening of the mental arteries."

BAROIS, breaking down completely: "But, oh, my friend, how can one help despairing of everything and everyone? Only consider what all our efforts have led to. Ever since the Affair we've had nothing, *nothing,* but disillusionments. Everywhere lies, selfishness, injustice, flourish exactly as they did before. Where can you see progress? Is there a single one of our convictions that has managed to make good? No, the tide has set the other way, against us. The younger men have no use for us; they've taken a stand against all the ideas we fancied we'd established. It's heart-breaking! A great many of them are becoming fervent Catholics. Is it because they're unaware of our attacks on religion? No, but they've found solutions to these problems which answer better to their needs, and now they're just as —as dogmatic as we were. Why they've even thought up specious arguments for raising Free Will—dead and buried as we thought it—from the grave, and taking action on the strength of it. These, my dear Luce, are facts we cannot blink away.

"Try as we may to bring freedom to our fellow men and to better their lot, human nature is against us. With each new generation all the old mistakes, the same injustices, rear their ugly heads; it's always the same dreary struggle, the same victory of the strong over the weak, of the young over the old—and ever shall be!"

LUCE, resolutely: "No, I can't follow you there; your picture of the world is far too black. On the contrary, in spite of setbacks which I deplore as much as you do, it's decency and progress that slowly gain ground all along the line. Yes, on the whole humanity is progressing; that's obvious, and no honest man can deny it."

BAROIS, laughing: "Why not be frank, Luce, and admit that a healthy faith in progress is essential to your peace of mind?

"I agree that on the technical and purely scientific side—as in all things that depend on observation and experiment—there have been advances. But, when you get down to fundamentals, what new truth has been discovered since the days of the Greek philosophers? We don't know an iota more than they did about life and death. Like them, we grope our way. We can neither positively affirm nor deny the existence of a soul, of personal freedom, and the rest of it."

LUCE: "Anyhow, it's something to have proved that things go on exactly as if the soul and freedom didn't exist."

BAROIS: "That sort of negative, hypothetical discovery has ceased to satisfy me."

LUCE, sadly: "So you too, Barois, have become infected! Oh, I know the mental confusion and distress of the times we live in. But don't you feel these are the birth-pangs of a better future? 'In sorrow thou shalt bring forth.' So far you haven't used the fashionable slogan, 'the bankruptcy of science,' but it was hovering on your lips. A convenient slogan, I admit. For ten years the morons have been exploiting it, and the younger men have taken it over blindly. Of course it's easier to make assertions than to verify." Proudly. "But all the while this so-called bankrupt science has been marching serenely on. Our savants are daily improving on the hypotheses they put forward tentatively and are consolidating them with new discoveries. Yes, science forges ahead implacably, without deigning to answer its opponents— but it's science that will have the last word." He rises and takes some steps across the room, his hands behind his back. "This reaction was inevitable. People foolishly asked of science more than it could furnish in those early days; more, perhaps, than it will ever give. They thought there wasn't any limit to research. And now some scientific-minded people, like yourself, allow their temperaments to get the better of them. When they're in their sixties they lament, ingenuously enough, 'I've been in harness now for thirty years and during all this time my life has been crowded with activities. What has science done during that period? Hardly progressed at all, so far as I can see.'

"This notion of the bankruptcy of science, my dear Barois, is due merely to the disproportion between the span of our human lives and the slow evolution of our knowledge. You, and those who think like you, are victims of appearances. You are like our ancestors who believed for many centuries in the absolute inertia of the mineral world because they failed to see any changes taking place in the structure of a stone during their lifetimes."

Barois has heard out the homily with cool indifference.

BAROIS: "Yes, those arguments used to content me—once. Now they don't. I can see the logic behind them, but, as for bringing back the peace of mind I've lost, they're worse than useless." He is silent for some moments. Tears come to his eyes. "Ah, how ghastly it is, growing old!"

LUCE, briskly: "You, old! Why, you're years younger than I!"

BAROIS, gloomily: "I feel terribly old, my dear Luce. I'm like a broken-down machine which doesn't respond to the controls. My heart's sounding the 'Dismiss!'" He taps his chest. "It's like a punctured bellows, here. The slightest chill sends me to my bed with a temperature. Yes, I'm played out; I feel incapable of getting down to work again."

LUCE, vainly trying to sound convincing: "Oh, it's only a passing phase. Just now you're run down, but you'll turn the corner."

BAROIS, bitterly: "But *you*, Luce, do you never feel the burden of the years? the mental debility that comes with age, the feeling one is settling into a rut? And then that sense of remoteness, that growing atrophy of the emotions, which makes it impossible to take anything to heart? Well, I'm conscious of all that—damnably conscious. My life has reached a dead-end, and it's a horrible sensation. I'm not up to any activity, and yet I've only one keen desire: to have the desire to act!

"And when I look back on the past, what do I see there? What have I really done?" Luce makes as if to protest, but Barois hurries on. "Obviously I've written, strung words together, built up theories. I'll leave behind me books and articles that have had their heyday. But do you suppose I'm taken in by this? that I've any illusions about the futility of all I've done in that line?"

LUCE: "You underrate your life's work, Barois, and you've no right to do that. You have made researches, discovered fragments of reality, and broadcast them generously. You have helped to uproot certain errors and to maintain certain truths that were tottering. You have stood up for justice with an inspiring fervour which made you for fifteen years the life and soul of a great movement. Well"—his tone is simple, friendly—"that's to my mind a very fine record."

Barois' eyes glow with pride; smiling, he holds out his hand.

BAROIS: "Thanks, Luce. In the old days it would have done me a world of good to hear those words. They are exactly the funeral oration I'd have wished for.

"But now . . ." He falls silent for some moments, then gazes at his friend's face. "What's in your mind, Luce?"

LUCE: "I was thinking, as I looked at you, that many of our predecessors must have gone through the same Slough of Despond. Yes, those men—to whom we owe whatever success we have achieved—felt, I'm pretty sure, the same despair, and imagined that their struggles had been in vain." He pauses. "But you're wrong, Barois, just as they were wrong. No good seed is wasted or sterile; there's no idea that does not germinate one day, not a scrap of honestly thought-out knowledge that is wholly lost. How can we be sure that one of those ideas that we've put forward, you and I, will not be the starting point of some discovery which will bring wider freedom to the men of to-morrow? To have played a worthy part in the world, all that's needed is to have given it the most and the best of oneself throughout a life-time; to have sown the good seed to the best of one's ability. And then one can depart in peace and make way for the new-comers."

BAROIS, sadly: "But, alas, I'm not sure of having sowed the good seed." Luce gazes at him with profound discouragement. "My atti-tude towards the universe has wholly changed, and I've lost my bearings.

"There are days like today when I can no longer believe in what I've championed up till now. Of course I don't expect to reach the point of satisfying myself logically that all my earlier convictions were mere moonshine. But—I don't quite know how to put it—I feel an almost physical distaste for them, the reason being, I suppose, that they have brought me nothing but disappointment."

LUCE: "But that's irrational!"

BAROIS: "Oh, a man can be rational to his heart's content when he is thirty; when he has a whole life before him in which to alter his views if need be; when he's in the full flush of his mental vigour and his blood runs warm with hope and happiness. But when he's near-ing his end, he feels so small, so pitiable, when confronted by the infinite." A far-away look comes into his eyes, and he seems to be speaking to himself. "Above all, one feels vague longings, longings for one knows not what, for something that would put an end to all these inner conflicts. A little peace, a little reassurance—something on which to lean, so as to be less miserable during the brief span that yet remains."

He raises his head. Luce, who was smiling sadly, meets his gaze, and the smile dies on his lips. There is a long silence. After a while Barois seems to pull himself together. He hands his manuscript to Luce.

BAROIS: "Here you are. I'd like you to read it."

Twenty minutes go by. The light is failing and Luce has risen and moved near the window. A symphony in varying tones of white: pale window-panes, the muslin curtain, Luce's beard and forehead, the sheets of manuscript.

Dusk is flooding the corners of the room.

Barois sits waiting, gazing at his friend.

Luce turns the last page and reads it attentively, to the final line. The hand holding the sheets is lowered, he takes off his spectacles, and, screwing up his eyes, peers into the shadows, trying to make out Barois' face.

LUCE: "My dear fellow, what would you have me say? I can do nothing to help you—now." He pauses, then murmurs sadly, "I'm sorry, but—I can do nothing."

4

The carriage rumbles by the wall of the convent at Wassignies-sur-Lys, near Gand, and draws up at a big postern-gate, which promptly swings half open. Barois crosses an empty courtyard, hesitates, then approaches a wide flight of steps. When he is on the topmost step another door is opened in the same curiously furtive manner.

Once he is across the threshold the door swings to behind him. A shadowy form, a nun whose face is closely veiled, comes forward and signs to him to follow. She walks quickly, rattling a wooden clapper all the time. After leading him down several passages, the nun opens yet another door, stands back to let him enter, and locks the door behind him.

The convent parlour is a large room paved with highly polished tiles and bisected from end to end by a lattice-work partition.

Like an effigy of antique grief, a woman in black is crouching motionless on a wooden bench, her hands pressed to her eyes. Barois goes up to her. Cécile shivers and holds out her hand, but is unable to utter a word.

He sits down beside her. Some silent minutes pass.

Then in the courtyard a clock strikes four silvery chimes. At once, on the far side of the lattice-work partition, three nuns, all of much the same height, their faces veiled in black, come into view. Two of them move towards a statue of the Holy Virgin and kneel before it, while the third goes up to the partition and unlocks a sliding panel. Then she goes back to the others, and they repeat a decade of *Aves*.

Cécile and Barois are standing, their nerves stretched to breaking point. Cécile's lips are parted, as if she were gasping for breath.

The rosary ends. One of the nuns crosses herself and comes forward. She draws aside her veil.

Cécile gives a stifled cry and clasps her passionately to her breast; then abruptly stands back and gazes at the girl, as though fearing she may have been mistaken. A moment later her arms are round Marie again, and she is uttering little whimpering cries of love.

Marie straightens herself up and without freeing herself from her mother's embrace holds out her hand to her father. He kisses it, making no effort to keep back his tears. Then their eyes meet, and Barois sees on Marie's face that look of tremulous ecstasy and the nervous smile which are the outward and visible signs of the faith that burns within her. Only, in the past, it seems to him, her eyes had not this starry radiance.

MARIE: "Please, Mother, please don't cry. God will give you strength and consolation." Her voice is dim, remote. "If only you knew how happy I am!"

Cécile has buried her face in Marie's shoulder and is lisping broken phrases.

CÉCILE: "But, oh, Marie darling, what's to become of me? How can I live without you?"

Marie puts an arm round her mother and gently strokes her forehead.

MARIE, turning to Barois: "Father, I've just read the last number of *The Sower*, your 'swan song' as you call it. Yes, I asked them here to let me read it, as a last favour." Her gaze sinks into his. Then her face lights up with hope. "Father, in every line you wrote, I realize that you are seeking God."

Barois shakes his head.

Cécile has not heard; she goes on sobbing, murmuring forlornly, "What's to become of me?"

Marie's eyes move from one to the other and a wholly human pity wells up, for the last time, perhaps, in her heart. Bending forward, she clasps her father's hand, then gently draws it beside her mother's.

MARIE, very softly: "Ah, I've prayed so often . . ." Her voice sinks to a whisper. "Please stay together now."

The nuns in the background have risen to their feet and now come forward.

When Marie hears their approaching footsteps, a tremor runs through her body, her features stiffen with apprehension. She frees herself from Cécile's arms and slips into her father's. But he has scarcely time to feel the silken smoothness of the small, rounded forehead under his lips before she releases herself. In a last, desperate rush of affection she embraces her mother, who gazes at her with hungry, distraught eyes. Then she steps away hastily; the veil falls back across her face. A nun closes the sliding panel and turns the key.

No one will ever again see that living face.

Cécile seems turned to stone, her arms stretched forth, her lips parted in a soundless cry. Suddenly she totters and would have fallen, had not Barois steadied her with his arm. She clings to him.

CÉCILE, faintly: "Please don't leave me, Jean. Don't leave me."

The door opens. The nun who ushered them in approaches, sounding her clapper. Barois helps Cécile to the door.

An hour has passed. They are sitting in the inn-parlour. Two armchairs have been drawn up by the fire; the light from a hanging-lamp falls on an untouched meal.

Barois, whose chair is slightly behind Cécile's, observes her bent back, the hat askew on her dishevelled hair. Sometimes she turns and presses her handkerchief to her swollen 'lips, to crush back a new access of sobs.

He is prostrated by fever, each heart-beat gives him a twinge of pain, his nerves are raw. That choked sound of sobs has wakened far-off memories. But there is no bitterness in this evocation of the past. Yesterday's loneliness, the loneliness of the days to come, weigh more heavily than misunderstandings of long ago.

He thinks: She said, "Don't leave me, Jean." A mere cry of despair perhaps. But suppose she really meant it? From a practical point of view it would be hard to manage. She might settle down with me in the suburbs, of course, but she would be out of her element there and she'd miss the parochial activities which mean so much to her. Is there any alternative? Definitely I can't see myself settling down in the Pasquelin home.

Unconsciously he utters aloud the conclusion of his musings.

BAROIS: "It would be possible only if you agreed to leave your place and come and live with me at my grandmother's."

Cécile looks round. Barois flushes. She hesitates, letting the words sink into her mind. Under the stress of emotion her slight squint grows more pronounced. Then, still seated, in a rush of gratitude she stretches out her hand and clasps his.

XIII. TWILIGHT

. . . like a man using a lamp he himself is holding to guide his steps.   André Gide

Do not blow out the smoking taper. Its very fumes will serve to guide us.   Ibsen

I

IT IS ten o'clock in the morning of an early summer day. Cécile is in her bedroom in the old Barois home. She has installed in it the furniture from Mme Pasquelin's morning-room.

Cécile is seated at her desk. She is wearing a black frock; her hair is smoothly dressed in bandeaux. A ledger lies open before her. Beside it lie registers inscribed "Church Expenses," "Parish Funds," and the like.

CÉCILE: "Come in." Jean enters. She jots down the total of a column of figures, then turns to Jean with an affectionate smile. "How are you feeling this morning?"

JEAN: "Not too bad."

CÉCILE: "It's a lovely day."

Jean goes to the window. The sill is warm to the touch; the court-yard is flooded with sunlight.

JEAN: "It must be delightful out of doors."

Cécile is arranging her registers with neat, methodical gestures. Then she puts a hat on and slips a register under her arm.

CÉCILE: "I'm taking this to Abbé Lévys."

Jean follows her down the stairs. The hall door stands open, the terrace shines dazzling white. He takes some steps uncertainly, half blinded by the glare. The sun bakes his shoulders.

The first peonies and strawberries of summer glow in the borders, and the vine arbour is a mass of vivid green.

The church clock strikes the half-hour.

338

He raises his head and, slipping past the yellow-ochre wall, his gaze loses itself in the blue beyond; a sky that comes from very far away and passes, circling the world.

Slowly he makes his way to a wooden bench beside the arbour and, sitting down, stretches his arms along its warm back-board, letting the light and warmth seep into him. His hands glow pink with sunlight. Peace descends on him.

He thinks: I'm here and this is spring. I don't understand it, but somehow it grips me, bends me to its will. There must exist vast tracts of knowledge into which our thought has not yet ventured. Ideas that range far beyond all our vague theories about the soul and God; ideas which would resolve all our discords. I wonder . . .

Some minutes later, when Jean is slowly walking back to the house, the bell at the street entrance tinkles. A priest steps into the courtyard and, seeing Jean, goes up to him.

JEAN: "I'm afraid my wife has just gone out."

THE ABBÉ, after a momentary hesitation: "May I introduce myself? Abbé Lévys."

JEAN, standing on the top step: "My wife will be most disappointed. I know she wants to see you; in fact she went out with that object."

THE ABBÉ, with a gesture seeming to relegate Mme Barois and parochial matters to the background of his thoughts: "I should much regret it if I didn't take this opportunity. I came to Buis only quite recently. But, ever since I've been here, I've wanted to meet you."

Jean makes a slight bow.

THE ABBÉ: "Oh, I know you prefer to keep to yourself. But I hope I may claim the right of intruding on you when I mention that for twelve years I've been, not a subscriber"—he smiles and points to his cassock—"but one of your constant readers."

JEAN, taken aback: "What! You read *The Sower?*"

THE ABBÉ: "Regularly." He lowers his eyes. "I've even been one of your contributors—with unsigned letters, several of which you published."

JEAN, coming down the steps: "Well, you amaze me. I'd never have dreamt that—but I'm keeping you standing in the sun. Won't you come in for a moment? My wife will be back soon."

He leads the priest to what used to be the drawing-room and is now his study. It is furnished with the salvage of his active life: bookshelves, his desk, and, in lonely eminence, the naked, suffering form of Michelangelo's "Slave."

Abbé Lévys is tall and thin. He has clean-cut features whose regularity is marred at times by a nervous twitch. His skin is gnarled and yellow, his gaze vacillates between aloofness and keen attention. His mobile lips set occasionally in a joyless, almost bitter smile.

JEAN, his curiosity aroused: "Well, it's news to me that we had a priest amongst our correspondents. May I know in what spirit you read our *Sower?*"

THE ABBÉ: "Oftener than not with reservations; but always with interest and frequently with some measure of agreement." Jean frankly shows his astonishment. "Don't you think that at a certain level of intelligence, when a man has once decided to have no palterings with the truth and to obey his conscience, it is hard to be on one side without being—a little—on the other?" Jean gazes at him without answering. The priest is silent for some moments. "It's Monsieur Breil-Zoeger who has taken over from you, if I'm not mistaken?"

JEAN: "No, the present editor is a young fellow named Dalier—a bigot, with very narrow views. But to all intents he is merely Zoeger's mouthpiece. Zoeger has always preferred to lie low and pull the strings."

THE ABBÉ: "So you're no longer connected with *The Sower?*"

JEAN: "Not in any way whatsoever. And I'd like you to know that I thoroughly disapprove of the increasingly anarchistic trend they're giving the review." The priest makes no comment. "Anyhow, I have nothing more to do with them. It's a clean break." He picks up some copies of *The Sower*. "They send me copies by force of habit, but as you see I haven't even cut the pages of the last few numbers. What would be the use? They'd only get on my nerves." He frowns, drops the copies on his desk, then tries to change the subject. "The only colleagues I've kept in touch with are Luce and Ulric Woldsmuth, a very old friend, who shared the struggles of our early days."

THE ABBÉ: "Woldsmuth? The scientist, you mean?"

JEAN: "Do you know him?"

THE ABBÉ: "I've read his book."

JEAN, smiling with pleasure: "What a splendid fellow he is! Think of it, for thirty years he's been trying to discover the origin of life. Thirty laborious years, without once losing heart!"

THE ABBÉ, glancing round the room: "And how about you? Are you still working?"

JEAN, shrugging his shoulders: "No, I wouldn't call it working. Just now I'm translating—for my own benefit—the diary of an English mystic." He smiles mournfully. "It took me some time to get used to this hermit-crab existence. But my health doesn't permit any other. I can just hang on, by taking precautions; spending my winters at the fireside and my summers basking in the sun." But the ardour of his gaze belies the resignation of the words. "Such is life, of course—and grumbling won't mend matters." He picks up some copies of *The Sower* and lets them drop one by one on the desk. "Yes, the young fellows of today have a short way with their elders." He stares at the carpet. "Do you know, I think the world's a bit unfair to failures. True, their efforts may not show any definite results, but they're not wasted, for all that. Don't you agree? No effort can be wholly futile."

THE ABBÉ, much surprised: "Surely, Monsieur Barois, you can't be alluding to a personal experience?"

Jean thanks him with a smile. The Abbé gazes wonderingly at this man, so different from the Barois he had pictured.

JEAN, harking back, after some moments' reflection, to a thought that is almost an obsession with him now: "I made the mistake of thinking that science would suffice in itself to bring peace and goodwill to men. Well, it has completely failed."

THE ABBÉ, cautiously: "Still, if you confine yourself to the creation of goodwill between nations, science has done as much in less than a century as Buddhism—or even Christianity—did in twenty centuries."

JEAN: "Perhaps. But look at the practical results. What has the mass of the people gained through science? An earthbound materialism, ugly and, what's even worse, sterile." *The priest is about to answer, but thinks better of it. Surely it's not for him to plead the cause of science! Jean goes on speaking in a meditative voice.* "And it seems to show that man does not live by work or by truth alone; he needs his Sunday—little matter how we may define it."

THE ABBÉ, *with sudden vehemence:* "Yes, little does it matter, since no definition can be vast enough to include the Perfect, the Infinite, God. And all these are but different names for one and the same conception—of that something behind everything for which all men yearn, whatever they may call it."

JEAN, *gazing at him intently:* "Then, if I take your meaning, you wouldn't condemn, out of hand, a man who, all his life long, had preferred his definition to yours?"

THE ABBÉ, *impulsively:* "Certainly not." *He has heard the note of anxiety in Jean's seemingly casual tone. He pauses before continuing.* "I remember something to the point in one of Björnsen's plays. One of the characters says—" *He rises. Cécile has just entered the room. She is careful not to betray her surprise.* "I hoped to save you your errand, Madame Barois, but I started too late."

CÉCILE, *handing him the account-book:* "Here are the Church Accounts brought up to date." *She feels embarrassed at speaking of these matters in Jean's presence and in this forbidding room, whose threshold she so rarely crosses.* "There are some points to settle about the school subscription as well. Would you come upstairs for a moment?"

THE ABBÉ: "Certainly." *To Jean.* "I hope you will excuse me, Monsieur Barois, for having trespassed . . ."

JEAN, *eagerly:* "Not a bit! I've much enjoyed your visit." *Cécile has gone out, leaving the door open. He continues in a different* tone. "You haven't yet told me what that character of Björnsen's said."

THE ABBÉ: " 'As for faith, that's God's affair. Meanwhile our whole duty is to be sincere.' "

JEAN: "Yes, that's well said."

2

From Abbé Lévys' Diary:

October 12 (after a long talk with Barois). I went to see him, prompted by a feeling which it is my duty to deplore, a wish to meet the famous polemist whom I had come to regard as the very symbol of free-thought. I went to him because I saw in him the one person in this small town with whom I could discuss freely my spiritual troubles.

And I met an unhappy man, more to be pitied even than myself, even more sadly torn by mental conflicts!

But it took me time fully to realize this. At first I thought it more discreet not to intrude too often on his self-imposed seclusion. But then it was he who invited me to come—for no specific reason, merely to see me.

I soon noticed his tendency to make the conversation veer towards religious problems, and I did not shirk them. Indeed, I even tried to let him see something of my own difficulties in this respect. But he seemed unable to visualize the man beneath the priest; apparently what drew him to me was my priestly function. None the less, he persisted in an aggressive attitude towards Catholicism. He kept on bringing arguments of a scientific order to bear—arguments whose cogency I know only too well! But he went about this in an oddly tentative way, almost as if he quite expected these arguments to be refuted. And this I did instinctively.

Gradually I came to see how the land lay. Physically he is wasted by a slow consumption; he is a mere spectre of a man, with un-naturally bright eyes, his strength sapped by constant bouts of fever and onsets of congestion, each of which does further damage to his lungs. Psychologically, his condition is still worse; he is harassed by doubts of what he held to be the truth and by his fear of death. He clings to his old convictions, but now they bring him nothing but mental torment.

I had thought to get helpful advice from him; but it's rather I, it seems, who can give him help!

I should not dream of evading the unlooked-for task that is imposed on me, but there is something tragic in my predicament. How strange that the priest called to lead this atheist to God should himself be a poor wretch who is in an almost equal plight, and has been wrestling with his own doubts for many years!

And yet perhaps this is as well; perhaps I am better qualified than many another to minister to this ailing soul.

I shall put my whole heart into this ministration, and see to it that he never suspects how unsure are the hands bringing him the solace that he seeks, the peace that is in God.

November 2. He has phases of terrible lucidity, whenever the fever leaves him for a few days. This morning he cut across what I was saying with a queer look in his eyes. "There are times—as a matter of fact this is one of them—when I manage to stand outside myself and one part of me judges, as I'd have judged fifteen years ago, the man I have become. And then I wonder if, from all eternity, I wasn't doomed to bondage." He pointed to the cast of Michelangelo's "Slave" which stands on his mantelpiece. "Look at him! Try as he may he can't raise a free arm. Perhaps, like him, for all these years I've been putting up a mere show of emancipation.

"I've had enough," he added, "of negations. Scientists have no more authority for denying than others for affirming. But your religious dogmatism jars on me for the same reason. I know too much about it; I was taken in by it so long."

January 16. I found him lying on his bed, utterly despondent. In front of him lay a copy of *The Sower* which had just come in, and for once he'd read it. "Look," he said. On the last page was a short article headed, "Another Conversion"; a scathing personal attack on him. He shrugged his shoulders, but I could see he was cut to the quick.

Then he dropped the subject and we had some desultory talk which petered out into a longish silence. When I turned to go he looked me in the eyes. "At bottom I'm a mystic. And yet I don't believe in anything."

"You don't believe in anything?" I said. "But one always believes in something. There's not one of us but has his God—hidden away, perhaps, in the depths of his being—to whom he bends in worship and daily offers himself in sacrifice."

But he shook his head gloomily. "No, I assure you I don't believe in anything. I'm groping in the dark, but I'd like"—he spoke so low that I only just caught the words—"to find peace before I die."

January 25. I had occasion to come back to this subject. We were discussing once again the proofs of God's existence.

"Your proofs show nothing," he said, "except that you, Lévys, believe in God. That's all they prove—the personal equation. If they had any value, do you suppose there would be atheists?"

"But there aren't any absolute atheists," I answered. "Why, you yourself have never ceased being a believer! Your trust in progress and the future of science, yes, even your belief in the triumph of atheism—what were these but manifestations of faith?

"You believe that Nature is moving towards a goal and that there is a system of universal law; well, that system produced human consciousness, your consciousness, and thus brought into the universe the idea of justice. That eternal order of things is God."

He pondered for some moments before replying, "Yes. But an impersonal God. Yours is personal. And that's where superstition begins."

How answer that?

March 7. Every time I say good-bye to him I reproach myself for having failed—owing, maybe, to my own vacillating faith—to light on the right thing to say. And yet each time I see him again I am dumbfounded by the amazing results my feeble words have produced.

Not that my arguments have convinced him. But they are an answer, of sorts, to the objections he puts forward. I now see that the greatest mistake would be to keep silent and that, however weakly, I must parry all his attacks. What he really wants of me is a simple, clean-cut, and, above all, positive solution.

Nothing has ever made me realize so clearly that faith isn't merely an intellectual conclusion, a matter of proof, but a function of the will and the emotions, of trustfulness, and a desire to submit.

March 19. The Gospels are coming to play a great part in his inner life, and he is always quoting them. He has formed a habit of resorting to them daily; they are the well-spring of poetic emotion that, alone, can quench his thirst. But, generally speaking, he reads less and less. I usually find him sitting in an armchair with his feet to the fire and an unread newspaper lying on his knees.

June 3. Hitherto in our conversations I have chiefly dwelt on such emotive reasons for believing as the need of consolation; our feeling that justice must finally be done and compensation made for life's frustrations; and our desire for guidance in our lives.

He is particularly responsive to the beauty of the Christian life, and I often cite examples. On these occasions I see a hungry look in his failing eyes. The other day he said that "beauty alone would be enough to justify faith—if the fruit could be held to justify the tree. And, after all, why not?"

Our conversation today was unusually animated; he is feeling more cheerful now that the weather has turned warmer and he can go out of doors. We strolled together in the sunlight, talking. He asked me to define certain dogmas, and seemed much impressed when I explained that theology includes a host of doctrines of greatly varying importance; that we must not confuse the essential dogmas —relatively few in number—with the unessential, though commonly accepted, doctrines; that by and large there are many questions— as to the efficacy of indulgences, for instance—regarding which

Christians are allowed to hold widely differing opinions. I went so far as to assure him that the dogmas concerning purgatory and hell are far less explicit than is commonly supposed, and even the most orthodox believers are given much latitude in the interpretation of these dogmas.

Unwittingly I may have overstressed the point, so conscious was I of the comfort my words were bringing him. Still I don't think I went beyond the limits assigned to modern apologetics.

June 28. I have just come home, profoundly saddened, such was the pity he inspired in me today. I found him in bed, much weakened by the night's bouts of fever. This muggy weather we have been having during the past week has brought on a cough which, though slight, alarms him.

However, Mme Barois tells me the doctor has no particular anxiety and feels sure that when summer has set in this relapse will pass. But Barois looked absolutely worn out. He said to me with a shudder, "Last night I thought I was going to die." And then added, in a tremulous voice, "I'm afraid of death, you know."

Never until then had he broached the subject so directly. Standing at the bedside, gazing down at him, I found myself infected by his terror; but I took care not to show this. He had clasped my hand and would not let it go.

"The first time I was frightened by it was when my grandmother died. I was a boy of eleven or twelve, and had just been through a very serious illness. I was standing beside my grandmother's bier— it was placed out there, in the courtyard—gazing at the masses of wreaths and the candles, when suddenly an awful thought came to me: 'And suppose she doesn't exist at all, not one tiny bit of her?' "

Then he added in a curious voice, "What does death mean? The disintegration of the being that I am, which is held together by my consciousness. What follows then? Does my consciousness—my 'soul' if you prefer—vanish as well?"

I could see him watching me; he had reached that stage of mental prostration in which comforting assurances are all one can endure to hear. Never before that had I realized so intensely the efficacy of the sacerdotal office with which, unworthy as I am, I am invested.

"I too," I told him almost fiercely, "yes, I too would be at my wits' end, had I not complete faith in a future life. Without it the mere thought of death would paralyse all my energies. But a belief in immortality is part and parcel of my consciousness, and all the arguments, even the strongest that can be brought against it, are easily overcome." He was still holding my hand, and it was painful to see the anxiety in his gaze as I continued. "What is the source of my consciousness? Is it a mere by-product of the nervous complex of my brain? But isn't it obvious that those words 'the brain,' 'the nerves'—like life and death—are, in the last analysis, but names for unsolved mysteries? They are mere labels; they explain nothing.

"I feel within myself intimations of the divine, I have glimpses of perfection, which cannot possibly be mere secretions of that imperfect and perishable organ, my brain. I feel within me the stirrings of an ideal life, and I cannot trace their origin to any given part of my physical self. I am conscious of two quite distinct varieties of experience—my contacts with the world of matter, through my senses; and those I have with the spiritual world. By disintegrating the physical elements of my brain, death puts an end to the first field of experience; but it can have no effect on the second. And it is on this category of experience that I base my faith in personal immortality."

But then he turned to me with a beseeching look that made me understand his need for a decisive answer, and said in a low voice, "Still, a personal consciousness exists only in virtue of *both* types of contact. How can we conceive of a consciousness which has ceased to have any contacts with the world of matter?"

Unfortunately I had no answer ready. "There's no need," I told him, "to have a clear idea of the life beyond the grave; all that matters is that there assuredly is a future life."

He let go my hand.

I realized that I had cruelly disappointed him. And my pity inspired me to make a last effort.

Bending towards him, I answered his thought more than his words. "You're hot for certainties, my friend. And, since the limitations of our human intelligence deny you that supreme vision of the truth you long for, why not ask God to grant it to you?"

He shook his head despondently. "As a priest," I continued, "I can only give you arguments. But God can touch you with his grace." Then, speaking with all the authority I could muster up, I added, "Hope, my friend; never lose hope. Do not harden yourself against believing. Open your heart to the infinite love and understanding of the divine Creator."

Then I picked up the New Testament and turned to the Fourth Chapter of St. Mark. "So is the Kingdom of God, as if a man should cast seed into the ground; and should sleep, and rise night and day, and the seed should spring and grow up, he knoweth not how."

As I read the words, I could see his features relaxing, his anguish passing. And, letting his head sink onto the pillow, he wept.

I could not take my gaze off the wasted face. So to this end it has come, I thought, all that fine enthusiasm, a life of high endeavour! Betrayed by that stricken body which is playing him false when his course is but half run! Betrayed by his intellect, which rashly urged him towards the unattainable! But are not all lives thus betrayed?

The same day, later. What a blessed thing is our religion, which alone provides a remedy for these sick souls! Nothing else can give us courage to live and die, and transform our terrors of the mysterious Beyond into a sublime expectancy. Most men have a craving for peace of mind that is greater than their craving for the truth, and the gift that religion brings them is better far than all that science has to give. And what a noble vocation is mine, to be a bringer of hope!

No, I shall not leave the Church. I could not live without it. It would be monstrous to break with a tradition which has done so much for suffering mankind. I must have been crazy even to think of forsaking Catholicism merely because it lags behind human science. I hadn't taken into account that deep-seated emotional bond between me and my calling that no mere impulse of the will could ever break.

Obviously I find it as hard today as I did a year ago to accept the literal meaning of our dogmas. But I realize that only under their auspices can I bring unity and harmony into my life. So I shall content myself with clinging to the spirit rather than the letter, and this will reconcile my conflicts. And thus the moral efficacy of my faith will never fail.

Ah, yes, I have given too much of myself to the Church; I have known too poignantly "the agony and bloody sweat" of the Garden of Olives to think of breaking away. The Church has made me shed too many tears, has laid such heavy burdens on me—and wrought me so much good! And thus we are bound each to each irrevocably.

3

It is a warm morning towards the close of July. Abbé Lévys hurries across the courtyard, a look of wonder on his face. Cécile is waiting on the steps. Too much moved to speak, she holds out both hands towards him. Then her eyes fill with tears.

The Abbé walks quickly up the stairs. Jean is stretched on his bed in the room that used to be his father's and in which his father died. His arms are outspread and his face is peaceful at last. He welcomes the priest with a happy smile.

JEAN: "Thank you for coming at once. I felt I couldn't wait."

A joy that passes understanding lights up his face; grace has touched his smiling lips, shines from his eyes.

The Abbé understands. His hands are trembling, his heart throbbing with emotion. All his doubts are dust before the wind, and in a moment, for a moment, he is once more the fervent priest of his young days.

THE ABBÉ: "Tell me . . . all!"

Jean's gaze lingers on the open window, then, coming back from very far away, settles on the priest's face.

JEAN: "You want to know what's happened?" He has to make an effort to piece together the dreamlike memories. "Let me begin at the beginning. Yesterday evening we met at the presbytery, you remember. But you didn't notice anything, and I found no words to say. Yet standing beside the body of poor Abbé Joziers, I had"— his eyes light up—"a decisive intimation of the soul's immortality." The Abbé gives him a questioning look. "I was sitting beside the body and kept my eyes fixed on those frozen features. I was trying to recapture the face I knew. But there was an essential difference —though I could not say exactly where it lay. Then I lit on an analogy. 'That corpse,' I told myself, 'is like an empty box.' Empty! That word was a revelation; the body was there, yet somehow it was itself no longer. Why? Because it had lost what gave it life. The tragic hour of dissociation had struck; the personality—that which had made it a man—had left it, and was somewhere else. In the past the notion of immortality seemed to me preposterous; now it is the contrary notion that seems to me untenable.

"Yes, the soul exists. A glance at that bed was enough to show me that it had left the body lying there; and this discovery was so obvious and yet so striking that it took my breath away!" The Abbé tightens his grip on Jean's hand.

"I was beginning to feel ill, but I mastered the discomfort I was feeling, so set was I on following up the train of thoughts which offered vistas of a life beyond the grave.

"Presently a servant came and helped me home. I was put to bed at once, and I had a most terrible night—choking fits, trouble with my heart, excruciating pain. Yes, I thought the end had come.

"Then I called on God with all my might; but I felt He was not listening to me. I wanted to be alone, but my wife insisted on staying with me, though I begged her to go. I tried again to pray, but could not. At last the pain began to die down, there was a respite.

But I was utterly exhausted, I felt half dead already, a mere shadow, on the borderland. Yes, I felt quite sure I was dying.

"Ah, it was a ghastly night! My head was like fire and my heart cold as ice—as if a mass of frozen darkness were constricting it. My brain was active, but to no purpose. I was caught between two conflicting currents, adrift. I tried to pray, I made frantic efforts to invoke God's attention, but after each effort I heard an inner voice telling me, 'No, no, no! No one will answer you. No one. You can see for yourself there's no one.'"

He is speaking calmly, without bitterness, his hand in the priest's, his eyes fixed on the blue effulgence framed in the window.

"I felt so weak I lost consciousness for a while. I suppose I slept. But even while I slept I was aware of a struggle going on above me, and I had a presentiment of its issue—that God's will would triumph in the end.

"And then I seemed to hear a voice and opened my eyes. Indeed, I heard my name called so distinctly that I thought my wife was there and asked, 'What is it?'

"Day was breaking; evidently I'd had a longish sleep. I could hear the breathing of our man-servant in the dressing-room. And though normally I sleep so heavily and feel so dull on waking, I suddenly was conscious of a wonderful lucidity. It was as if the fog had lifted miraculously from my mind.

"Then once again I tried to pray. The voice that had said 'No' was silent now. And that sense of impotence and nothingness had given place to one of confidence, vague as yet, but how comforting! I could feel brooding above me a friendly presence, a help in my time of need." With a smile of radiant happiness. "I don't know how to explain it. But I suddenly was conscious of having shaken off the lethargy that has weighed me down for years; of coming out of a tunnel into daylight; of, quite literally, starting a new life. A boundless joy within me and, above all, a peace so perfect that no words can describe it.

"So now I know my quest is ended, my will has fused, as it were, into the universal will, and I shall joyfully obey; yes, all now is clear, crystal-clear. At last everything has a meaning!"

He turns his head, sees the Abbé bending solicitously over him, and stretches forth his arms.

"So I sent for you, my friend, to hear my confession . . ."

4

Marc-Élie Luce is shown into the drawing-room, where Abbé Lévys is awaiting him.

THE ABBÉ, coming forward: "I've been asked by Madame Barois to let you know that your friend is only just recovering from his recent relapse. He needs all the rest he can get."

LUCE: "Oh, I only want to shake his hand and say a few friendly words. Still, if you think that even a short conversation . . ."

THE ABBÉ, somewhat embarrassed: "No, Monsieur Luce, I don't think a short conversation would do him any harm. Provided the subject was—well, you will understand, anything that might tire him should be avoided."

Luce smiles, but there is some bitterness in it.

LUCE: "Please tell Madame Barois she need have no anxiety. Barois has informed me of his conversion and I've no intention of trying to shake his faith." The Abbé reddens, his face is twitching nervously. Luce continues dryly: "In any case I have very little time; I intend to take the three o'clock train back."

THE ABBÉ, quickly: "The station's quite near and there's a short cut. If you like, I shall be glad to act as your guide."

Jean has insisted on getting up. He has had himself dressed and is seated at his desk, which has been moved up into his bedroom, for he no longer goes downstairs. His black coat, though buttoned, hangs loosely round him. Death's imminence is evident. A scanty beard masks the deep hollows of his cheeks, the skin seems welded to the bony structure of his head, his lips are drawn back over his teeth, his nails are the colour of old ivory, the collar gapes on his shrunken neck.

When Luce enters he tries to gauge by Luce's look the progress of his illness, but his friend's face is quite impassive as he comes forward, smiling.

JEAN, without waiting for Luce to speak: "You're wondering how it happened, aren't you?" Luce fails to grasp his meaning; he is above all startled by the faintness and hoarseness of Jean's voice. Jean picks up a crucifix lying beside his handkerchief on the otherwise empty surface of the desk. Both men are embarrassed. "How did it happen? I haven't an idea. But it's not the first *how* or the first *why* that you and I have failed to answer." He has a curious smile. *"Invocavi et venit in me spiritus sapientiae.* Anyhow, I'd long since ceased believing in—ideas."

LUCE, evasively: "Yes, it's from the heart that faith is born."

JEAN: "Ah, my dear Luce, it's wonderful! You feel that at last you're striking through the surface and seeing the universe from inside." He follows this up quickly, as though he fears being interrupted. "And don't forget—what one needs is a *practical* solution."

Luce nods assent with an affectionate smile. Jean has slipped back in his armchair; his eyes seem fixed on nothingness, like the glass eyes of a waxwork dummy. And Luce recalls the fighter who always stood his ground in wordy warfare, his legs planted well apart, his head cocked slightly to one side, his eyebrows bristling.

Jean gazes at Luce, then unexpectedly laughs softly to himself.

JEAN: "I'm sorry for you, old chap. You're still at the resisting stage. You're putting up a fight." Luce begins to murmur a protest, but, still smiling, Jean talks him down. "Just as I did. Yes, I can speak from bitter experience." He shrugs his shoulders. "But what's the good of struggling? You know quite well that in the end you too will come to this." Once again he holds up the little crucifix. "Only see for yourself how calmly I can face death, now I know I shall live again beside Him."

But there is a tremor of apprehension in Jean's voice, and Luce gazes at him compassionately. He himself has skirted the abyss near enough no longer to despise those who are dizzied by it. But he finds nothing to say and, after some silent minutes, rises.

Jean watches him prepare to go, almost without regret. Faith has intervened, and a whole new layer of impressions lies between his present self and his past. Luce's face is very pale.

JEAN: "You and I were sowers of doubts, my friend. May God forgive us."

Luce goes down the stairs, profoundly depressed. When entering the drawing-room, he seems to hear the rustle of a skirt, and has the impression that a woman has just left.

LUCE, to the priest: "Could I have a word with Madame Barois?"

THE ABBÉ: "I doubt if Madame Barois will be back in time. As we're going to the station on foot, we had better start at once."

Luce acquiesces. Outside, the air is cold and dry. Once they are in the street, the Abbé turns to Luce.

THE ABBÉ: "Well? How did you find him?"

Luce pauses almost imperceptibly, glances at the priest, then moves forward again. Now, anyhow, with the Abbé, he has not the motive for hiding his true feelings that he had with Jean.

LUCE: "He has changed beyond recognition. His intelligence has completely gone; all that keeps him alive is a tiny flicker of emotion."

THE ABBÉ: "You're mistaken there. I can assure you he applied his mind to the matter before he found the Way."

LUCE, bitterly: " 'Applied his mind'? But he'd already ceased to be capable of doing that when he left Paris!" Quietly. "No, our poor friend Barois is, like so many another, a victim of the age we live in. His life, like that of so many men of my generation, ran on tragic lines." For a moment he forgets that the man beside him is a priest. In his eyes shines that clear-visioned penetration and that zest for understanding which have been the poetry of his life. "One day his Catholic education foundered on the rock of science; almost all intelligent young men have that experience. But, unfortunately, the moral code which we have in the blood and of which we are so proud has been transmitted to us through many mystical-minded generations. How can we renounce so noble an inheritance? It's a painful process. Not every man succeeds in strengthening his intellect enough for it to ride out the storm, when all the winds of instinct and waves of memory bear down on it. Those sentimental yearnings of the human heart—how strong they are, for all their futility!

"Most men in their prime contrive, as Barois did, to break free of these nets. But when the later years bring disappointments and ill health, and above all when they feel the end approaching, they give way all along the line and you see them scurrying back to those consoling fairy-tales." The Abbé, his chin buried in his cape, quickens his steps. "You held out the hope of survival and he grasped at it desperately—as all men do who have ceased believing in themselves and are no longer satisfied with realities." The Abbé makes a gesture of protest. "Oh, I know that was your duty. And I recognize that the Church has a vast experience in handling such predicaments. Your life beyond the grave is a marvellous invention; it's a promise located so far away that the faculty of reason cannot forbid the heart's believing in it—if it's bent that way. For, by its very nature, the future life can neither be proved nor disproved.

"Yes, it's the great discovery your religion made—that there are ways of convincing a man that he must desist from trying to understand."

THE ABBÉ, raising his head: "That, Monsieur Luce, is how our Lord himself gave us his message. He does not prove or argue. He says quite simply, 'Believe in me.' And even more simply, 'If any man thirst, let him come unto me, and drink.' "

After a short silence Luce speaks, with a bitterness he cannot repress.

LUCE: "Well, you've made a sensational conversion. You may well be proud of it."

THE ABBÉ, stopping for a moment: "Yes, I *am* proud of it."

A sudden gust whipping round the street corner slaps his cape against his chest. His gaze is dark, impenetrable, as he faces Luce.

THE ABBÉ: "Were you capable of consoling him? No. Whereas I brought him peace, I opened to him fields of radiant light. All you had to offer were vistas without hope."

LUCE, quickly: "Why 'without hope'? My hope lies in the belief that my efforts for good are indestructible. And so strong is it—believe me or not!—that all the partial triumphs of evil in the world cannot shake it. This hope of mine does not, like yours, entail an abdication of my faculty of reason; on the contrary, my reason confirms it. It proves to me that a human life is not 'empty of concern,' it is neither a meaningless ordeal nor a quest for individual happiness. It proves to me that everything I do shares in the great forward movement of the universe, and it discloses, on every hand, new ground for hope. Everywhere I see life being born out of death, energy being born of pain, folly giving place to knowledge, disorder making way for harmony. And the same evolutions are daily taking place within me."

"Yes, I too had a faith to give him, and one as good as yours, sir."

THE ABBÉ: "But it did not satisfy his needs, that's evident." With a rush of passion. "And even though you think that what I gave him was a lie, you should rejoice that I was able, no matter how, to bring him the peace he desperately longed for."

LUCE: "I don't recognize two standards of morality. A man should attain happiness without being duped by any sort of mumbo-jumbo, through truth alone." He pauses. "Ah, we are living through a catastrophic phase in the evolution of science; at no other time, I imagine, has its conflict with religion been so violent."

THE ABBÉ, with a brusqueness that betrays his irritation: "Really, Monsieur Luce, you belong to another age. That age we have happily outlived, when all the bridges linking us with the past were rashly being destroyed. You believe in a man-made, automatic regeneration of society, and so you've been able to dispense with prayer and a belief in survival after death. But you're blind to what is going on around you. You've failed to see that everywhere the need for religion, for something far more vital than your arid theories, is gaining ground." With a harsh laugh. "But no, an atheist will never understand what happens in the soul of a man when he sinks to his knees and prays."

LUCE, smiling: "Such lapses are inevitable. But the rational belief to which we have won through—often at the cost of much mental suffering—cannot be wholly lost. Little by little it is making its imprint on the soul of the nation, and thus bringing freedom nearer for the generations to come."

THE ABBÉ, indignantly: "No. Men will never be able to dispense with God. Life is ruled by death, and religion alone can teach men to await death and submit to it—sometimes even to desire it."

LUCE, with a look of deep sadness: "Death is implicit in life, and I accept the idea of death as I accept that of birth."

THE ABBÉ, smiling bitterly: "Yes—for the moment! You're fit enough today to make light of death. But let me tell you, Monsieur Luce, a day will come when you feel death very near, when its cold breath fans your cheeks, and then you'll realize how little comfort can be got from your sterile negations!"

They are outside the station, people are hurrying up the steps, cabs rattling over the cobbles. Luce stops walking; pools of shadow have formed under his grey eyes.

LUCE, gravely: "At my age—in other words, upon the brink of death—one is bound to be sincere, don't you agree? It's no time for wasting one's breath on idle phrase-making. Well, I can assure you that I face death with all the equanimity that's possible to man— as calmly as you will face it." The priest averts his gaze. "What is it that will ease for you the agony of dying? The peace that comes of a quiet conscience. I am as well qualified as you to feel that peace."

THE ABBÉ, harshly, still without looking at Luce: "But what you, Monsieur Luce, will not have is a priest, God's messenger, to stand beside you in your last agony, and with a simple gesture of absolution blot out even the memory of your worst offences."

LUCE, gently: "I don't need one." He has suddenly gone pale. A

proud smile hovers on his lips as he holds out his hand to the Abbé.
"Good-bye. And let's part on good terms. Still, you've touched a
sore spot, let me tell you. I'd almost forgotten that I'm a dying man.
You've reminded me of it—and it hurts." The priest makes a contrite gesture. Luce is still smiling. "I know that within a month or
two I shall have to undergo an operation—a hopeless one. And one
of my reasons for coming to see Barois was that I know my number's up—even more certainly than his."

THE ABBÉ, greatly moved: "Oh, things mayn't be so bad as you
think."

LUCE, the smile fading from his lips: "Please don't suppose I have
no dread of death. I have. But I look it in the face." He shudders.
"I'm afraid, as all men are, because the flesh is weak. But it's a
purely physical fear. Mentally I have no qualms at all."

With a firm, decided step he walks towards the station entrance.
The priest watches the receding figure until it is out of sight.

5

My dear Barois: I have been meaning to write to you ever since
Luce died, but could not do so until now, as my right side has been
immobilized owing to a slight congestion.

His doctors had decided for an operation. Luce consented, but he
had no illusions about it. He asked me to help him to set his manu-
scripts in order during the fortnight preceding the operation, and
I was with him all the time.

One day when we were compiling his notes for the book which
he has left unfinished he noticed that I was weeping. He came up
to me, and what he then said sums up the man, I think. "You too,
Woldsmuth? But why? That's how life goes on its way. We mustn't
let ourselves be blinded by the individual."

The operation took place.

It was more successful than we had dared to hope. Even the
surgeon seemed to forget that it meant only a reprieve, and all of

us shared his optimism. By the eighteenth day Luce was on his feet and allowed to go home. "Now I'll get back to work," he said. "I have so much still to do."

But abruptly, from that day, the improvement ceased, one by one the symptoms reappeared. He was conscious of this setback, but kept on postponing the day of letting his children know of it, and they, though they saw what was happening, professed to believe he had been cured.

I visited him daily, and he was always talking to me about death. "I've been fortunate enough," he said, "to have been warned well in advance, and enabled to prepare to face death as it should be faced. It's the last act I've now to tackle, and thus round off the programme I set before myself. I have always tried to make my life conform to my ideas, so as to give them their maximum efficacy. Now it's up to me to die without deviating from them; to show I'm not afraid of death; that I can see it coming and welcome it, and die without breaking faith with myself.

"The moral effect produced by a tranquil end on our poor distraught fraternity of men condemned to death can be immense. Socrates understood this well. The more one studies the record of his last days, the clearer it becomes that Socrates had no wish to get himself acquitted. He was seventy, his life's work was done. He had the supreme wisdom of seeking to enforce his teachings, yet again, by the manner of his death—a death that was not passive, but an active demonstration of the truth that was in him. My dearest hope is for an end like his."

But then I saw a shadow fall on his face.

"And yet we're told that often men who have awaited death with perfect calmness are precisely those who, at the last moment, rebel most passionately against it." But he hastened to add, "It's merely a nervous reflex, of course."

Not a single day did I see him waver in his acceptance of life and death; and yet he suffered terribly. He was engaged in reviewing his past life, as a whole. One morning, after a sleepless night, he said to me, "It's a consolation to me to see how harmonious my existence will have proved to be. While one's involved in active life, the feeling of a lack of unity of purpose often makes one feel despondent. But now I see I've little to complain of on that score. I've come across so many unhappy people, people who are always being flung this side or that from their true centre of gravity, and this makes them restless, dissatisfied. My life had none of these commotions; it could be summed up in two or three quite simple axioms. And this enables me to 'depart in peace.'

"I was born with confidence in myself, in the daily tasks I shouldered, and in the future of mankind. The well-balanced life came easy to me. My lot was that of an apple tree planted in good soil that bears its fruit season after season."

The last week was particularly hard for him. But the day before he died he was in much less pain. His older grandchildren came to the bedroom for a few moments. But by now he had almost ceased speaking. When he saw them entering, he said, "Go away, my dears, good-bye. I don't want you to see—that."

Towards six the lamps were lit. He looked round the room, as if to make sure all his children were present. There was something extraordinary in his gaze, as though at last he could see to the heart of things, nothing was hidden from him now. It seemed that, had he still been able to speak, he could have spoken the final, liberating word about himself, his life, the lives of all men. But propping himself on a shoulder he merely said, in a far-away voice, as though awaking from a dream, "Ah, this time it's death."

His daughters, kneeling round the bed, could not restrain their tears. Then he placed his hand on their heads, one by one, and murmured as if talking to himself, "How fine they are, my children!" Then sank back upon the pillow.

Night had fallen. Next morning he died, without having opened his eyes.

This is what I have been meaning for many days to write to you, my dear Barois; for I know the manner of our friend's dying will do you good, as it did to me. It consoles us for the disappointments we have encountered on our path. After seeing Luce die, I am more convinced than ever that I have not been wrong in staking my faith on human reason.

Ever yours,
Ulric Woldsmuth

P.S. My sight is so bad now that I have had practically to give up working at the laboratory. I am engaged in writing an account of my research work on the origins of life. Thus, though I myself have not achieved my purpose, I can bequeath to others the results of my work. Time is a necessary factor of progress; it is more than probable that someone else will discover what I have been looking for—and that's a very cheering thought.

6

Since early morning Jean has been delirious. It is now eight in the evening. He awakes, feeling desperately tired. The room is full of shadows, and the movements of the living persons near his bed seem a continuation of his nightmare.

Suddenly he sees Cécile holding up a lamp. Abbé Lévys stands beside her, his clerical stole round his neck, and the vessel containing the holy oils in his hand.

A gust of panic sweeps him, his gaze shifts from one face to the other.

JEAN: "Am I going to die? Answer me, please. Am I dying?"

He does not hear their answer; a violent spasm of coughing tears at his lungs, half stifling him.

When he sees Cécile bending over the bed he clutches her to him in a desperate embrace. Gently she presses him back onto the pillows. He is too exhausted to resist, his eyes are shut, his breath comes in hissing gasps. The sheets are drenched in sweat.

Through the fever buzzing in his ears he hears the Latin phrases, while a cool film of oil is laid on his eyelids, ears, and palms.

JEAN: "Help, oh, help me! Don't let me suffer!" His hands beat the air and, meeting the priest's long sleeves, cling to them as to the arms of a divine judge. "Are you sure He has forgiven me? Or . . ." In a last desperate effort he draws himself up from the pillow. ". . . hell fire?"

His mouth gapes on a cry of horror, then a moist râle rasps his throat. The Abbé holds the crucifix out to him; in a blind revolt he thrusts it away. Then his eyes fall on the effigy of Christ and, grasping the crucifix, he sinks back upon the pillow and crushes it passionately to his lips.

Too heavy for his feeble grasp, the crucifix slips from his hands. His limbs have ceased to respond to his will and seem to be receding from him. His heart-beats are a weak flutter, but thoughts race through his mind in wild confusion. Suddenly every fibre of his being grows tense; arrows of fiery pain flash across his body, through every vital cell. He makes some last convulsive movements. Then, immobility.

A new day is breaking. Cécile and the Abbé are alone in the death chamber. Kneeling beside the bed, her head between her hands, Cécile is conjuring up her past life, year by year. It was in this same room, one morning in her early youth, that she partook of the Sacrament with Jean at his dying father's bedside.

Dawn is filtering through the shutters. A fire blazes in the fireplace, and its gleams dance on the wall behind the dead body, now growing rigid.

The priest, who is seated, gazes at the form of him who was Jean Barois. The face muscles have set, the sparse grey hair stands stiffly up, like bristles planted in the skull, the skin has grown gelatinous, and the head seems too heavy for the wasted neck. But on the face there broods an infinite peace.

Presently Cécile opens the drawers of the desk, one by one, to see if the dead man left any last instructions. She finds none. But in a file-case, under the files, there is a sealed envelope marked, "To be opened after my death."

She breaks the seal, runs her eyes over the first page, and suddenly turns pale. Going up to the priest, she hands him the manuscript. He moves to the window to read it. The writing is in a firm, bold hand.

This is my last Will and Testament. What I write today, in my early forties, in the full mental vigour of my prime, should obviously outweigh anything I may say or think or write at the close of my existence, when my intellect and judgment may well be impaired by the infirmities of age. I know nothing more harrowing than to see an old man, whose whole life has been devoted to the furtherance of some noble idea, go back in his declining years on the principles that inspired his life's work and play traitor to his past.

When I reflect that conceivably this may be my fate, and my life's work end with a betrayal of this nature, and when I picture the use to which those whose lies and malpractices I have combated with so much ardour will not fail to put this final, miserable lapse of mine, my whole being is up in arms, and I protest in advance, with all the energy of the man I now am, the living *man I shall have been, against the groundless repudiations—even, perhaps, the prayers in extremis!—of the dotard I may then have become.*

I deserve to die, combatant and defiant, as I have lived, without capitulating, without whoring after idle hopes, without fearing my return to the primal matter that nourishes the slow processes of evolution....

The priest shudders; he recognizes the tone—it is as if the dead Barois were speaking. He turns to the next page.

I do not believe in an immortal, independently existing soul....
...I know that my personality is but an agglomeration of particles of matter, whose disintegration will end it absolutely.
I believe in universal determinism....
Good and Evil are mere arbitrary distinctions....

He reads no further. Folding the sheets, he hands them to Cécile, shunning the question in her eyes.

Deliberately she moves towards the fireplace. The Abbé guesses what she has in mind and could prevent it. But his eyes stay fixed on the dead body; he makes no movement. He is reflecting that Barois had long ceased being able to defend his views, and he thinks, too, of the Church that has done so much to alleviate his passing, and to which this sacrifice is due—perhaps.

A sudden blaze lights up the room.

Le Verger d'Augy
April 1910–May 1913